About

For the last twenty-eight
ature and creative writing
He is the author of twelve
Body Language, *Rough Draft* and *Blackwater Sound*.

James Hall

'Hall writes splendidly plotted tales which, largely inhabited by comic but terrifying psychopaths, delight as they dismay . . . Do not miss.'
GERALD KAUFMAN

'Hall delivers oddball fun at a rip of a pace, without letting you forget that he is a literate, stylish writer. Like beer from the bottom of a bait well, Hall's books *psst* and bubble over as soon as you open them.
Los Angeles Times

'Think Walter Mosley and James Lee Burke. Hall's writing is terse like Mosley's, but he can also nail a vivid metaphor and turn your head with a violent twist as well as Burke does. Multicharactered, darkly comic . . . sharp laughs and heart-stopping thrills.'
Houston Chronicle

'Hall is the finest and most literate of thriller writers.'
San Francisco Chronicle

'Like top-drawer Leonard turned inside out – funnier, much more skewed, substantially more moving. Hall's psychopaths are so well drawn and amusing that they make you giddy.'
JAMES ELLROY

'The real pleasures in Jim Hall's books are the sensual ones of place and people. It's the honest feel of South Florida, with all its menacing rhythms and contagious lassitude, that Hall nails down so well.'
CARL HIAASEN

Off the Chart

'Reminiscent of Humphrey Bogart in *Key Largo* . . . wonderfully evocative of Florida, the oceans and the jungle. A page-turner that would make a great film.'   *Oxford Times*

'I love Hall's hard-nosed Florida thrillers, they ooze sunshine and sinister menace from every sweaty pore. The writing is wonderful, his enigmatic hero Thorn a guy you'd like to be on your side in a fight, and this story of piracy and kidnap takes the reader on a violent trip from Florida to the Caribbean.'   *Peterborough Evening Telegraph*

'In the talented pool of South Florida suspense writers, James Hall pretty much has the deep end to himself. Out of reach for most, it's a place of nameless primal fears and motivations, of twisted psyches and murky evil, from which Hall shapes compelling characters in riveting stories. *Off the Chart* is wonderfully disturbing . . . the plot spirals toward a nail-biting climax. It's about a lot of things: the loss of a way of life to big money; the corruption of power; the strength of love; and most of all, the permanence of evil. All of which make the carefully crafted, darkly resonant *Off the Chart* stay with you.'   *Miami Herald*

'Hall sweeps the sand, surf and swamps of Key Largo in a hyperdramatic mystery. His crisp writing, plus the ticking-clock suspense make this an exhilarating addition to the series.'
Publishers Weekly

Blackwater Sound

'James Hall has been one of my favourite crime writers for a long time. He's great. Hall has the same concern for the Florida wetlands as Carl Hiaasen but doesn't try to be so wacky. And I think he does it better. This is a bodacious novel: cool and violent, but with an energy that's hard to resist. Top of the class.'
MARK TIMLIN, *Independent on Sunday*

'James Hall really pulls it all together in *Blackwater Sound*: the stun-gun shocks and the delicately orchestrated mayhem; the monstrous villains and their elegantly evil schemes; the noble hero and his savage defence of Florida's fragile marine ecology. If violence can be poetic, Hall has the lyric voice for it. Truly haunting.'
New York Times Book Review

'Like James Lee Burke's, James Hall's novels are complicated but rewarding. A poetic sensibility is evident in his fiction.'
Daily Mail

'An enjoyably racy tale. The fallibility of his hero, Thorn, is part of his charm. With a pair of wonderfully over-the-top psychopathic siblings as villains, Hall has come up with another lively thriller.'
Sunday Telegraph

'In combining deep-sea lore with paranoid conspiracy, Hall creates something wholly his own.'
Guardian

'I believe no one has written more lyrically of the Gulf Stream since Ernest Hemingway. His fascinating characters and obvious love of the natural world make this a wonderful reading experience.'
JAMES LEE BURKE

By James Hall

JAMES HALL

OFF THE CHART

HarperCollins*Publishers*

HarperCollins*Publishers*
77–85 Fulham Palace Road,
Hammersmith, London W6 8JB

www.harpercollins.co.uk

This paperback edition 2004
1 3 5 7 9 8 6 4 2

First published in Great Britain by
HarperCollins*Publishers* 2003

First published in the USA by
St Martin's Press 2003

ISBN 0 00 711277 7

Typeset in Meridien by
Palimpsest Book Production Limited, Polmont, Stirlingshire

Printed and bound in Great Britain by
Clays Limited, St Ives plc

For Evelyn,
my rock, my love

Acknowledgments

Thanks to Stephen Bell and Garry Kravit, who kept me flying straight and true. To Arthur Lane, who untangled the high-tech aspects. To Richard and Charlie for their unfailing editorial support, clarity, and great ideas. Deepest thanks to Vaughn Morrison, a man who is truly at home in the natural world and whose knowledge of birds and beasts and the sky above is a constant inspiration.

We are wiser than we know.

—RALPH WALDO EMERSON

Prologue

Glittering with moonlight and sweat, Thorn and Anne Joy were lying naked in Thorn's bed when she launched into the story of her turbulent childhood in Kentucky. Her parents murdered. Lunacy and violence. Pirates, pirates, pirates.

Until that night, they'd shared nothing about their pasts. A breathless fever possessed them for their monthlong affair. An unquenchable horniness. Bruises from the clash of hipbones, flushed and tender tissue, their heat rekindled with the slightest rasp of skin on skin. For hours at a time they barely spoke, and when they did it was increasingly clear the chief thing they had in common was this agitated lust.

Then that night in a calm moment she told the

1

vivid story of her youth, details she claimed to have never shared with anyone before. Saying she had no idea why she was confessing this to him but blundering ahead anyway.

Struck by the oddity of this tight-lipped woman opening up in such detail, Thorn lay quiet, listening intently. At the time, of course, he had no inkling that lurking in that account of Anne's youth was a foretelling of the torture and torment of Thorn's own loved ones, the kidnapping of a child, the murders of many others. But even though there was no way in hell he could have known, no way he could have heard in her gaudy tale the dark rumbles of his own future, that didn't keep him from blaming himself forever after.

It was a raw afternoon in eastern Kentucky. The winter sky had turned the brittle gray of old ice, but Anne's outlaw father and her older brother, Vic, were shirtless in the cold, hammering together the rickety frame under her mother's watchful gaze. As Anne described it, the Joys' yard was treeless and mangy, their property perched on a bluff overlooking the grim, defeated town of Harlan.

Anne stood at her bedroom window watching her family work in the front yard. For an hour she'd ignored her mother's calls to join in. Only seven years old, Anne already knew she wanted nothing to do with this foolishness.

By dusk the structure was finished and her father and brother had strung Christmas lights along its edges and raised the Jolly Roger flag on its mast. Skull and crossbones flapping in the frigid breeze. When her father plugged in the cord, the flimsy creation burst to life in a phosphorescent flash. Twenty feet high, fifty feet long with red and green and blue lights twinkling in a perfect outline of the brawny hull and blooming sails of a pirate schooner.

For the next eight years the contraption stood in their front yard with those strands of colored bulbs flickering all through the gloomy winter nights of that Kentucky hill country and even into the first soft breaths of spring and the muggy, star-dazzled evenings, blinking in time with summer crickets and the whoop of owls, blazing incessantly into the fall when the sky above the sugar maples filled with the sweet perfume of rot and looming cold; those lights shimmered and winked and that pirate ship sailed endlessly through the rocky, mortified seas of Anne Joy's youth. Visible for any sane man in that region to see – a ludicrous beacon, a steady rainbow pulse of don't-give-a-damn lunacy.

Since her own childhood in the Florida Keys, Anne's mother, Antoinette, had been consumed with pirates, a juvenile hobby that over time turned into a full-blown obsession and finally was to become the compulsory enthusiasm of the entire Joy clan. Even Jack Joy succumbed. Anne's father was a raven-haired, extravagantly tattooed ex-navy man who drove a fuel-injected Nash Rambler to distribute a variety of unlawful drugs for the Woodson brothers to truck stops throughout eastern Kentucky, Tennessee, and West Virginia. Even such a rough-neck as Jack Joy yielded to his wife's fixation and became an authority on Long John Silver, Captain Kidd, and Blackbeard and eventually came to measure his own daring and lawlessness by their far-fetched standards.

Anne learned to endure the schoolyard catcalls, the relentless smirks, and those chilling midnights when carloads of boys parked out front and hooted and whistled and slung beer cans at Antoinette's pirate ship until she or Jack snatched the shotgun from the brackets on the back of the front door and stalked outside and fired a warning shot over the bow of that landlocked schooner.

Other than those visits from local hooligans, the Joy home was peaceful and Anne's parents' love affair was luminous and sweet-hearted. Although the townsfolk gave Jack Joy a wide berth whenever he went out in public, Anne never caught so much as a whiff of violence on him once he entered those four walls. There was even a boyish innocence about the way he adored his wife and indulged her every caprice.

Each evening when the meal was done, Jack Joy sat in hillbilly rapture while Antoinette read to the family from the book that provided that night's enter-tainment. Radios and televisions were banished from the Joys' home, and the only books allowed were those that transported them across the centuries to the days of swashbuckling sea raiders.

'There's other books, you know,' Anne said before the reading commenced one night. 'About other kinds of people.'

'But not one of those people measure up to buccaneers.'

'And how would we ever know that, Mama?' Anne said.

'Pirates are beyond compare. They made their own rules, roamed at will, survived by their wits. Even famous outlaws like Jesse James were trapped inside the straight and narrow of highways and city streets. They drove cars; they wore ordinary clothes. But pirates were untamed, free to wander. To move with the wind like the big hawks and eagles. High up on the heavenly currents.'

'And they had cool eye patches,' Vic said. 'And hooks for hands.'

'We're not one bit free,' Anne said. 'Look around us. This isn't free.'

'Pirates are in our blood, Anne. You should be as proud of your heritage as the rest of us are. Sooner or later you're going to have to accept it.'

'Even if your daddy did run liquor,' Anne said, 'that makes him a smuggler, not a pirate.'

'Same difference,' her father said. 'A seafaring outlaw.'

'A crook in a boat,' Vic said.

'The point is, darling,' said Antoinette, 'we're not common folk. Our bloodline sets us apart.'

'I don't want to be special,' Anne said. 'I want to be like everyone else.'

'Too late,' Vic said. 'You're weird to the bone.'

On Saturdays the four of them would sometimes drive a half-day to the closest movie house to catch a matinee of *Captain Blood* or *Morgan the Pirate*, and on the return voyage Antoinette would dote on the dozens of Hollywood atrocities that had been committed on the truth, grilling Vic and Anne, forcing them to chime out the movie blunders.

True pirates never sailed galleons, those sluggish warships that took a full hour to alter course. They used swift and nimble schooners like the one in the Joys' front yard or sloops or small frigates, sometimes brigantines and three-masted square-riggers. And no pirate under God's blue heaven ever relied on such a pansy-ass fencing foil as Errol Flynn waved about. Those real-life buccaneers swung heavy cutlasses that would slash a man in half in a single roundhouse blow.

'Shiver me timbers,' Jack Joy might say at such moments. 'Blow me down.' And he'd heavy-foot that full-race Rambler till the tires screamed against the asphalt and Anne and Vic were pinned giddy to their seats.

An unschooled man, Jack Joy was made sappy by love, swept away by what he considered his wife's refined tastes and higher education. Around his wife he played a courtly role, part Southern gentleman, part movie idol. And for her part, Antoinette regularly assured any who would listen that her Jack was double the man of any Errol Flynn or Tyrone Power. For almost two decades of married life she and Jack stayed tipsy on that fantasy.

But Anne Joy had been born with a disbeliever's eye, and when the sun poured into her bedroom each morning, she began her day by staring beyond the rickety maze of pine slats that formed the pirate schooner at the gashed hills below and the gray haze and acid stench of the underground fire that had plagued that town since before her birth. And she reminded herself of her own dream – an escape from those hills so complete that once she was out of Harlan she intended never to allow a stray memory of the place to flit through her head.

On this point Vic was her total opposite. Vic was his mother's sworn disciple, the first mate on her wacky voyage. Vic's favorite chore was to track down the burned-out bulbs that occasionally shut down the light show in their yard. He would spend entire dutiful afternoons unscrewing one bulb after another until he'd located the latest dud.

Whether her mother was insane or just fanatically determined to separate herself from the hard-faced local citizens was impossible for Anne to say. Such distinctions had little currency in that time and place, and it wasn't for a child to diagnose her parents but simply to endure. Though she was sorely humiliated by her mother's fixation, it had the positive effect of sending Anne on an inward journey in search of safer, more solid ground, starting a habit of introspection she might never have acquired had she lived in a less outlandish household.

In that town of coal hackers, dope and religion were the only release from the daily grind, and the Woodson brothers year by year grew fatter and more pig-eyed on the profits from their fields of marijuana and meth labs. Over time the entire Woodson clan, which populated the back roads of the countryside, took to driving flashy pickups and staggering drunk in public.

From time to time Big Al Woodson and his little brother, Sherman, made sudden appearances in the Joys' living room. With big whiskey grins, they dusted their hats against their trouser legs and shuffled and nodded at Antoinette, repeating her name aloud more than was necessary as if to feel its exotic taste on their tongue.

It was on just such a night in early April that the Woodson boys made their last call and Anne Joy's childhood was forever finished. Vic was seventeen, with sinewy muscles and his black hair swept back in an Elvis ducktail. Anne, two years his junior, already had been cursed with the lush swell of hips and breasts that was to lure men to her all the rest of her days.

Not quite summer, with green pine popping in the woodstove to chase the chill, the family had assembled in their usual fashion in the cramped living room. Anne sat on the ratty corduroy love seat while her father lay out on the blue-and-red rag rug in the center of the room. In the far corner, Antoinette was dabbing at the canvas she'd set up on a makeshift easel. An old hobby she'd recently resumed when Vic questioned her once too often about her child-hood days in the lawless Florida Keys.

'Don't have any photographs of those days,' she said. 'Painting will have to do.'

After two weeks of labor, a scrap of beach and two crooked palm trees were emerging from the canvas, and in the sand by the shoreline there was something resembling a treasure chest tipped on its side with its glorious contents spilling out. In the last few days as she worked at her canvas on lonely afternoons, Antoinette had let slip that on that very beach her courtship with their father had reached its first ecstatic peak. Perhaps, she whispered to her two children, that was even the very spot where Vic was conceived.

For as long as Anne could recall, her parents had talked of returning to that far-off land where they had met and fallen in love. Someday very soon, the story went, when their savings grew to ample size, the Joys would abandon those wretched hills and make the long pilgrimage back to paradise to reclaim their rightful place in that balmy land of sun and water and abundant fish and forever thaw the bitter chill from their joints.

'We'll never do it,' Anne said on one of those quiet afternoons.

'What's that?' Her mother continued to paint.

'We're never going to Florida. That's all a fairy tale.'

Antoinette set aside her brush and looked around at her daughter.

'Of course we're going. Soon as the nest egg's big enough.'

'We could go now,' Anne said. 'There's nothing keeping us here. You could work. We all could work.'

'And what would you have me do, Anne Bonny?'

'You could waitress,' she said. 'I could baby-sit. Vic could have a paper route. Daddy could do anything – drive a truck, deliver things. Or he could be a mailman. They have mailmen down there, don't they?'

'Waitress?' Her mother laughed and turned back to her painting. 'Lord, lord, you'll never catch me slopping food for a bunch of overfed idiots. No, sir. I'd rather die in these hills than waitress down there in Florida. And your daddy's way too fine a man to stoop to delivering people's bills and catalogs. When I go back home, I'm going in style.'

'You're just scared,' Anne said. 'You'd rather have us eat coal dust the rest of our lives. It's all a lie. Every bit of it. Just one big goddamn lie.'

Her mother dabbed at the canvas and slipped off into one of her deadly silences.

On that final evening, Anne was sprawled on the

love seat listening to Vic struggle with the archaic locutions of a pirate novel he'd plucked from the shelves of the school library. It was then she heard the rumble of Al Woodson's GTO coming up the dirt drive. Her brother halted the scene and closed the book around his finger. As was his habit, Al pulled up beside the front porch and gunned his engine three times before shutting it down.

Anne's mother put aside her brush and looked across at Jack.

'Tell the man it's too late for a social call. Kids got school.'

'He doesn't come but if it's important. Just be a minute.'

His words were neutral enough, but Anne saw the cocky edge had drained from her father's face. Her mother saw it, too, and stood up, and her hands knotted into fists and hung beside her hips.

'You didn't do anything you shouldn't have, Jack. Tell me.'

Her father hesitated a moment, then shrugged his admission and made a wave at her painting.

'Just to get us where we want to go a little quicker. Handful now and then, nothing serious.'

'Oh, Jack, no.'

'Risk worth taking,' her father said. 'Anyhow, there's no way those old boys sniffed me out.'

'Don't go out there, Jack. Just poke your head out and send them home. Tell them we're putting the kids to bed, saying our prayers. Settle it in daylight

11

if there's anything to settle. Give us time to think. Or else make a run for it.'

'All right,' her father said. But his words were as vacant as his eyes.

He opened the door, put his head out, then slowly opened it the rest of the way and stepped onto the porch. It was only a few seconds before the voices went wrong, turning high and croaky, then flaming up with curses and a sudden unnatural silence. Then Anne heard the moist thump of fist on bone and the scuffle of heavy boots on the planks of their front porch. The living room floor trembled and Al Woodson grunted a command to his little brother.

Frozen in the center of the room, Antoinette stared at the curtains. Just beyond that window Jack Joy groaned like a man lifting more than he could manage, and the whole house shuddered.

Antoinette flew across the room, whisked the shotgun from its bracket, and was out the door barrel-first. A second later the shotgun's blast got two quick pistol shots in reply and the front window exploded. Jack Joy hurtled into the room, tearing down the red-checkered curtains and coming to rest in a sprawl of blood and mangled parts.

Outside, the shotgun roared again, and Vic stepped out the door with Anne close behind him.

Through the smoky dark Anne saw Al Woodson blown backward against the blinking schooner, his arms and legs tangled in the nest of wires. The bulbs continued their beat, but the big man was unmoving.

On the floor at Anne's feet lay her mother. She'd taken a slug in her seamless forehead and lay with arms flung wide against the porch as if waiting for her darling man to lower himself onto her one last time. Her foolish eyes still open, catching the green lights and the blue ones and the red, the eternal blinking of that schooner.

In the yard Sherman Woodson knelt with his hands high. Vic held the shotgun his mother had dropped. In his right hand Woodson still gripped his chrome pistol, but his hands waved unsteady circles in the air.

'Your daddy done wrong, kid. Had his hand in the fucking cookie jar. We didn't have no choice but to pay a visit. But didn't nobody mean for this—'

Vic unloaded on the man and kicked him spread-eagled beside his brother into that web of lights that continued to twinkle across the dark valley below.

Anne stooped down and fingertipped her mother's throat, felt the cold silence of the woman's flesh, then raked the bloody hair off her face and closed the woman's eyes. Anne blinked away the itch of tears, then turned on her brother.

'Now what? There's a hundred Woodsons within earshot.'

Vic dropped the shotgun in the dirt and stalked into the house and came out with a flour sack under one arm and Antoinette's painting under the other.

'What's that?'

'Our nest egg,' Vic said.

Vic marched across the barren yard and stuffed the painting and the sack of money into the backseat and got in behind the wheel and cranked it up.

Full of the dreamy numbness that was to take up residence inside her head like a never-ending trance, Anne walked over to the car and got into the shotgun seat, and the two of them rolled silently down the hill, headlights off, and idled through the darkened town, then hit the highway south. For the next few hours bright lights raced up behind them, then slowly fell away as Vic held the pedal down and screamed through the black night.

Outrunning the Woodsons at last, they drove hard through Tennessee and Georgia, then entered the ceaseless gray monotony of north Florida, driving without rest or food, until the sky turned blue again and winter changed to summer in a single day and the birds grew stalky and white and America finally petered out and became no more than a dribble of rocky islands where the road ran narrow and low, seeming to plow a path right through the blue sea, as if Moses himself had gotten there just seconds before, leading the way to the promised land.

Beside her in the dark, Thorn listened to Anne Joy's impetuous purging come to a close. When she was done, he lay silent for a moment more, staggered by her tale, searching for something to say. But before he could find the words, Anne slid from the bed,

14

tramped to the bathroom, dressed quickly, and left his house without even a good-bye. Thorn hustled down the stairs after her, but she beat him to her car and was gone in a hail of pebbles.

She never returned to Thorn's house and would only smile brightly at him when he showed up at her apartment to talk, giving no reply to his questions and finally asking him to leave.

Over time Thorn came to believe that the bond he and Anne had forged in that month of ravenous lust was simply too flimsy to support the sudden, unwieldy bulk of her past. Maybe later on if the structure had grown more secure and their trust more solid it would've been fine. God knew, Thorn's own story could match hers death for death and shame for shame. But it was too early in the cycle for such a heavy dose of truth, and their fragile bond had crumbled to powder in that instant of confession.

Later, when Thorn returned to the memory of that evening, the seeds of what was to come were so obvious in Anne's story, the warnings so goddamn clear. If only somehow he'd managed to grasp the prophetic hints, he would have climbed out of bed that very night, loaded his pistol, and driven a few miles down the Overseas Highway to kill one particular man – an act that would have spared many from death and shielded a young girl from terrible harm, that blameless, intelligent kid who was as close to a daughter as Thorn had ever known.

1

On that warm Sunday afternoon, when Thorn got back from the john, the drinks were just arriving. He and Alexandra Collins were at a table for six on the outside deck at the Lorelei in Islamorada. The sheer February light had turned the spacious bay to a brilliant blue mica. Over at the rail Lawton and Sugarman and his twin girls were peering down at the resident school of tarpon that threaded between the pilings.

'Hey, stranger,' the waitress said as she set their beers down on the table and put the Cokes in front of the empty places.

Thorn stumbled for a half-second, fetching for her name.

'Oh, hey, Anne. How's it going?'

'Just another day in paradise,' she said. 'How about yourself?'

'Fine, fine.'

She bent forward and pressed her lips to his. Inhaling that familiar scent of her shampoo, lime and something herbal, Thorn had a quick cascade of memories, a blur of nights together, their bodies knotted, sheets kicked to the floor. The final story that broke their bond for good.

More than a year had passed since Thorn had last seen Anne Joy. In her early thirties, she still kept her auburn hair cropped short, and her dark eyes had the same electric shine. Thin-lipped, with soft cheekbones, a sleek and coppery complexion, and the coolly impassive smile of a runway model. But her body was far too lushly proportioned for that profession, and no matter what bulky and unflattering styles Anne wore, she couldn't conceal it.

She stepped back from the table and clutched her tray against her breasts.

Alexandra was looking up at Anne with a curious arch of eyebrow.

'I think we'll wait on the order,' Thorn said. 'Kids are feeding the fish.'

'Sure, okay,' she said. 'Be back in a few.'

She took a second look at Alexandra, then gave Thorn a quick, approving smile and turned and set off toward her other tables.

'I'm sorry,' Thorn said. 'I should've introduced you.'

'So this is another one?' Alex said.

'Another what?'

'Oh, come on, Thorn. Do you usually kiss your waitress? And this time don't tell me you two were just old high school friends. She's ten years too young.'

Alex shook her head, her smile wearing thin.

'Hey, it's a small town,' he said. 'Limited supply of single women.'

Alexandra tasted her Heineken. She watched Sugarman's girls fling bits of bread into the water. The Lorelei was packed, tourists lining up to be seated.

'Was it serious?'

'A month maybe. Not serious, no.'

'A month by my definition is fairly noteworthy.' Alex peered into his eyes, cocking her head slightly, as if searching for a flicker of deceit.

'We didn't click,' he said. 'Anne's a little intense, bottled-up.'

'Not laidback and gregarious like you.'

She shook her head and looked out at the hazy blue of the bay, a flats boat skimming past, the white rip of foam behind it.

'Oh, come on. You can't be jealous. You know how I feel about you.'

'It's just amazing,' she said. 'Everywhere we go there's another one.'

'I've lived here all my life,' Thorn said.

'Yeah, and it's a small town. But still.'

'Look, I'm no ladies' man,' Thorn said.

'What would you call it then?'

Thorn knew better than to field that one. He poured the rest of his Red Stripe into the stein and watched the foam rise exactly to the brim, not a single trickle running down the side – another of his highly refined, utterly useless motor skills. When he looked up, Alexandra was smiling at him, but her eyes still had a stern edge.

'You heard of Vic Joy?' he asked her.

'Name sounds familiar.'

'Owns half the upper Keys,' Thorn said. 'Not a big favorite with law enforcement. Runs that casino boat behind the Holiday Inn, owns a dozen marinas and waterfront joints from Islamorada to Key Largo. Doesn't pay a lot of attention to what's legal, what's not. Has a whole law firm working for him full-time to keep him out of jail. In the past fifteen, twenty years, there've been a half-dozen murders with Vic Joy's name floating around in the background. Then witnesses change their story, refuse to cooperate, or flat out disappear. That kind of guy. Anne never tells anyone she's Vic's sister, but people know.'

'Brother's a big-shot hoodlum, but she's still a waitress.'

'There's some tension between them. Plus Vic spies on her. Checks out her boyfriends, lets them know they're swimming in serious waters. First week we went out, he stopped by the house, asked me a lot of questions. Took a good look around. Started giving me a list of dos and don'ts.'

19

'I bet you were very polite.'

'Things started to go wrong when I grabbed him by the shirt and hauled him back to his car and threw him inside.'

'You're kidding.'

'I lost it,' he said. 'This crook lecturing me about good manners.'

'You were willing to risk the gangster's wrath to keep playing around with his sister.'

'Come on, Alex. Let it go.'

'You have a long and sordid past, Thorn. I'm continually surprised.'

'Point is,' he said, 'Anne and I didn't mesh. And you and I do.'

'Is that what you call it? We're meshing?'

'I think that's an accurate description. Yeah, I'll stand by that.'

He tried to smile his way past this mess, but Alex wasn't buying just yet.

Lawton ambled back to the table and sat down. Alex gave Thorn's shoulder a quiet stroke. Okay, interrogation over, all forgiven. Sort of.

Lawton had a sip of his Coke and the three of them gazed over at Sugarman and his daughters. He was Thorn's oldest and closest friend. Sugarman had stood by Thorn through some blinding shit-storms, even risked his life on more than one occasion when everyone else deserted. Ten years ago Sugar had been a sheriff's deputy; now he was struggling along as a private investigator.

This weekend was Sugarman's monthly visit with his twins. Lunch, a boat ride, a cookout later at Thorn's house, then Sugar and the girls would make the long trek back to Fort Lauderdale where his ex-wife, Jeannie, lived. The girls were eight. In May they'd turn nine.

Uncle Thorn, they called him.

More than likely those two girls were as close as he was ever going to come to having children of his own. Biologically he was probably okay, but he was too damn rigid for kids, too private, too rooted in habit. Still, he loved Sugar's girls, loved their raucous games, their delight in tiny discoveries – holding a magnifying glass up to a hibiscus bloom while their daddy recited the names of its parts, their functions, showing off his flawless recall of high school biology. Thorn didn't mind the girls' pouts, their tantrums that came and went like summer thunderstorms, so quickly replaced by sunshine, it seemed never to have rained at all.

Twins, but very different. Jackie was devoted to television and was usually clamped inside the head-set of her portable CD player, and she had her eye on a BMW convertible for her sixteenth birthday. Janey was fascinated by birds, bugs, frogs, and snakes. An amazing memory for the names of things. Tell her one time, it was there. Janey was constantly testing her dad's knowledge of natural history. Forcing Sugarman to expand his library, stock up on multiple field guides, which the two of them pored

21

over for hours at a time. Janey was a quiet kid, eyes always following Thorn like she might be working up a crush. She enjoyed watching him tie his bone-fish flies. The slow, intricate wrapping and twisting, the bright Mylar threads and gaudy puffs of fur and feathers. A month ago she'd taken a shot at tying one herself and when she was done she snipped the final threads and held up her mangled creation and said, 'Let's go catch a lunker.'

Alexandra and Lawton were fond of the girls, too. When they came over some weekends, Thorn could see Alex soften – squatting down to help them tie a shoe or soothe a scuffed knee. An easy, natural gift for girls that age. Lawton grumbled about their noise, their rambunctiousness, but when they left he grew solemn and introspective, and it was clear the old man felt their absence more strongly than he could admit.

Thorn might be too damn old for kids, but he wasn't too old for these.

Lawton had another deep sip of his Coke and set his glass down on the table and patted his mouth with the paper napkin.

'You two should go over and look at those tarpon. They're gigantic.'

'We looked at them already, Dad, when we came in.'

'You did?'

'Yeah. Just a minute ago, before we sat down. You were with us.'

22

Lawton raised his hands and raked his fingers through his mane of white hair, then laid his hands flat on the table and pressed down as if he meant to levitate it.

'Oh,' he said. 'That explains why I don't remember. Something happens a minute ago, why should I waste my mental faculties on that? Most likely it's not going to turn out to be worth remembering anyway. All the important stuff happened a long time ago.'

'I don't know about that,' Alex said, giving Thorn a brief look. 'I believe some of the important stuff may still be unfolding.'

She had a sip of her beer and patted her father's hand.

'Hey, did either of you see the tarpon?' Lawton said. 'Over by the pilings. They're huge. You should go look.'

Closing in on seventy-five, Lawton suffered from an evaporating memory and a growing confusion about things great and small. So far, no doctor had given his condition a name. Apparently he was headed down the steep and irreversible slope of dementia. There had been times lately when the old man's focus narrowed so severely, he seemed to be peering at the world through a pinprick hole. Staring mutely for a solid hour at a blade of grass, water dripping from a faucet, the hairs on the back of his knuckle.

For the last few months he'd been preoccupied

with returning to his boyhood home in Ohio. Packing his bag at any hour of the day and night, heading out toward the highway to catch a bus. Twice Thorn and Alex had woken in the night to find Lawton missing from his living room cot, and both times they'd finally located him sitting in the bus shelter a mile from Thorn's house, his valise on his lap, dead set on a journey back to Columbus.

When Alex asked him why in the world he'd want to abandon the paradise of the Florida Keys for Columbus, Ohio, Lawton puzzled on it for a moment, then told her that he wanted to go home so he could dig up a time capsule he and his younger brother Charlie buried sixty-five years before. A time capsule? Alexandra wanted to know what was so important about a time capsule. 'My past,' he said. 'It's buried in the dirt behind a white frame house at 215 Oak Street.' But what was in the capsule that required Lawton to depart on a journey in the middle of the night to retrieve it? 'What's in it?' he said. 'How the hell am I supposed to remember what I buried sixty-five years ago? That's why I've got to go dig the damn thing up.' He looked hard into her eyes and said, 'So maybe I can find out who the hell I used to be.'

Now each night before she put him to bed, Alexandra lectured Lawton sternly. If he wandered off from the house one more time, she would have to start padlocking the door. Lawton always listened with a deadly earnest look. Although the midnight

24

jaunts had ceased, neither Thorn nor Alexandra was sleeping easy.

During the day Thorn looked after the old guy while Alexandra labored as a crime scene photographer for the same Miami police department Lawton had once served as a homicide detective. For the last few months she'd been making the sixty-mile journey from Key Largo to the treacherous streets of Miami, then back each evening. A commute she claimed to find restful.

They'd met a few months back when Lawton showed up on Thorn's doorstep. The old detective was on a self-appointed mission to track a killer and Thorn had been just a quick stop on his erratic journey. Hours after Lawton disappeared, Alexandra showed up at Thorn's searching for him. And though things had started badly between them, the clash of his flint against her steel had sparked a smoldering connection that since then had been growing ever hotter.

While Alex dabbed her napkin at a spill of Coke on her father's lap, Thorn's gaze drifted over to Anne Joy, who was waiting on a nearby table. He'd nearly forgotten about the woman. So much intensity at the time, but the months had fleeted by and Anne had turned to smoke and drifted almost completely from his memory.

'Thorn?' Alex tapped him on the shoulder. He turned to her, but she'd already tracked down the source of his attention, and her smile was tart.

'Yeah?'

'Dad and I are going to take another look at the pet tarpon. You want to come, or stay here and ogle?'

'Those fish are huge,' Lawton said. 'Wish to hell I'd brought my pole.'

Thorn got up and took Alexandra's hand in his. She answered his squeeze with the slightest pressure, and they walked over to the rail to join Sugarman and his girls.

Like everyone else sitting outside at the Lorelei that sunny Sunday afternoon, Anne Bonny Joy noticed the sleek black Donzi sliding up to the restaurant dock – just another flashy Miami asshole down to the Keys for brunch – and she wouldn't have given him a second look except for the name printed in gold script on the stern of the big rumbling speedboat, the *Black Swan*, which happened to be the name of her mother's all-time-favorite pirate flick.

The boat's captain and two top-heavy blondes barely out of their teens took one of Anne's tables, and while the girls sat reading their menus, the guy tilted his head back and closed his eyes to bask in the sun. Anne Bonny came over, placed their water glasses in front of them, and stood next to the table until the man rocked his head forward and revealed his dark blue eyes. Longer and thicker lashes than her own.

'Take your order?' she said.

26

Standing there in the Lorelei uniform, green shorts and a tight white T-shirt. The girls in bikini tops and snug shorts, the guy bare-chested, with a caramel tan. His dark hair was long and swept back like a teen idol from forty years earlier. A man too handsome for his own good, and for anyone else's.

'How it's usually done,' he said, giving her a lazy grin, 'you're supposed to say, "Hi, I'm Mandy; I'll be your server."'

The girls were both platinum blondes. They might've been twins. Anne looked at them as they giggled at the man's wit; then she looked back at the man.

'Take your order.'

'What's good here?' one of the girls said. 'Let's have what's good.'

'Cheeseburger,' the other girl said. 'You have cheeseburgers, don't you?'

'It's a fish joint, Angie,' her double said. 'You should order fish.'

'I hate fish. It smells funny.'

'Your name?' The man was in his mid-thirties, about Anne's age, and had a coarse black beard he hadn't bothered with that morning, bristles glinting in the harsh sunlight.

'It's there on her shirt, the little tag,' one of the girls said. 'Anne Bonny.'

The man turned his head to the blonde.

'I see the tag,' he said. 'I'd like to hear her say her name out loud.'

The blonde's lips wrinkled into a practiced pout.

'My name is Anne Bonny Joy. Can I take your order?'

'That's a weird name,' the other girl said.

'It's an illustrious name,' said the man. 'Legendary.'

'Never heard of it,' the pouting girl said. 'I think it's stupid.'

'Three hundred years ago,' the man said, 'Anne Bonny was the most famous woman in the world. Bigger than a movie star.'

'There weren't any movies three hundred years ago,' the blonde said. 'Were there?'

He was watching Anne's face. His voice was dark and liquid and his blue eyes were fastened to hers, stealing past her usually impenetrable shield. She held her ground, her pencil poised above her pad. It was all she could manage. Seagulls squealed overhead. On the other side of the patio the reggae band started their version of 'I Shot the Sheriff.' The bell in the kitchen rang, another order up. Garlic and shrimp and coconut suntan oil floating on the breeze.

'Anne Bonny was the greatest pirate of the Caribbean, ruthless and daring, the equal of any man.'

'Big deal,' the sulky one said.

'My mother named me,' Anne said. 'It's just a name.'

'Whatever you say.'

The man touched a fingertip to the lip of his water glass, smiling down.

'And your boat?' Anne said. Irritated now, wanting to push back.

'My boat?'

'The *Black Swan*.'

'Oh.' He glanced out toward the docks, then let his eyes drift back to her. 'It's the name of an old movie with Tyrone Power.'

'And Maureen O'Hara,' said Anne.

'Yes, of course,' he said, giving her a more careful look. 'Who could forget Maureen O'Hara?'

'Hey,' said the sulky blonde. 'Are we having lunch or what?'

In the Lorelei kitchen, Vic Joy made an offer. Seven million dollars.

And Milton Stammer, who owned the joint, said sure, sure, he'd think about it and get back to Vic real soon. Blowing Vic off.

'What's to think about?' Vic said. 'It's two million more than the goddamn place is worth.'

Milton Stammer was a short balding man with a formidable paunch. He kept smoothing his hands across his bloated belly like a pregnant woman trying to get used to how big she'd grown.

'Okay, so I sell you the restaurant, what am I going to do then, Vic? Move to Boca, sit in a golf cart all day, cocktails at four, early bird at five, sit around, talk about how everybody did on the back nine? I'm a blue-collar guy; I'm too freaking old to pick up golf.'

Vic glanced out the serving window and watched Thorn and his group sitting in the sun, waiting for their lunch. In his free time for the last few months, Vic had made Thorn his project. Shadowing him, asking around about the guy, trying to get a feel for what would motivate the asshole.

Today Vic had tagged along two cars back and wound up at the Lorelei, where his own sister worked. His estranged sister. Two of them hadn't spoken in years.

When Thorn and his gang pulled into the Lorelei, Vic parked a few spaces away facing the sprawling restaurant and bar. He sat there for a moment watching Thorn and his friends walk into the place. Vic must've driven by the Lorelei a million times, but he'd never given it any serious real estate scrutiny. It had a nice ramshackle feel. A laidback, outdoorsy vibe. A nice fit with the rest of his holdings. Five minutes after pulling into the parking lot, he was inside the noisy kitchen, waving seven million bucks in front of the owner's face. That's how Vic Joy worked, relying on his creative juices. Weaving and bobbing as events took shape. He'd built a damn nice empire that way.

'Place like this,' Vic said, staring up at the ceiling, 'all this wood. Must be a bitch to insure.'

Milton closed his eyes and shook his head solemnly.

'A grease fire,' Vic said. 'Or maybe a smoker flicking his butt in the bathroom waste can, or bad wiring, overloaded circuits. Shit, it could start a hundred different ways. All this old timber, about twenty minutes all you got is ash and rubble. Then you'd be sorry as hell you didn't take the six million.'

'What happened to seven?'

'Did I say seven? Well, I meant six.' Vic watched the hubbub of the kitchen. Steam rising from the dishwashing machine. A darker steam coming from the deep-fat fryers. The Lorelei was a busy place, and prickly hot. Kitchen staff hustling back and forth, sending uneasy looks their way. Everyone knew Vic Joy, how he worked. 'Actually, Milton, now that I take a careful look around, I'm going to have to back down to five mil. All this wood. This place is a fucking fire trap. I don't know how it's lasted as long as it has.'

Milton's stubby arms hung at his sides. The man's eyes were grayish and bulgy. A large man's large eyes. Pry them out of their sockets, they'd fill your palm. For a second Vic flashed on an image of a couple of gray eyeballs floating inside a glass jar, suspended in formaldehyde. Make a nice addition to his collection.

He smiled at the big man, but Milton wasn't in the smiling frame of mind.

'I'll tell you what I'm doing, Vic. I'm taking all that fire shit as a threat. I don't know if that's how you meant it, but that's how I'm taking it. Now I

31

want you to get the hell out of here. If I ever see your sorry ass around my restaurant again, I'll call the cops. You got that? Tell them you been threatening me.'

'The cops?' Vic shivered and wobbled his hands in the air. 'Be still my heart. Not the cops.'

Milton gave Vic a bitter glare, then about-faced and tramped across the buzzing kitchen to his office and shoved the door closed behind him.

Vic stepped over to the fry cook, a tall thin man with a hook nose. Guy'd been eavesdropping, sneaking looks.

'You know who I am, kid?'

'Vic Joy,' the hook nose said.

'Bingo.'

With a wide spatula the cook slid a burger onto a plate, then settled a fish sandwich onto another. Lettuce, tomato, pickle on the side.

'Let me see that ticket.' Vic reached out and snapped the order slip from the clip. A few minutes earlier he'd watched Anne Bonny hang it there. When she'd appeared, Vic swung around and kept his back to her. Didn't want to give his little sister a cardiac right there at work, bumping into her long-lost brother after all these years. Vic studied the order slip. In his sister's scrawl, *Thorn* was written out next to the guy's order.

'Which one's the grouper with Swiss?'

Vic nodded at the six plates lined up in the window.

The hook nose took a careful look at Vic.

'Which one?' Vic said again.

The fry cook reached out his spatula and tapped one of the sandwiches.

Thorn's lunch. Fried fish with a layer of melted cheese. Guy was going to choke on cholesterol if he wasn't careful. Which suited Vic fine, as long as the jerkhole waited till after Vic was completely done with him.

'Guy's a friend of mine,' Vic said. 'We do this, me and him. Little pranks back and forth.'

'Whatever.' The fry cook got busy with the dressing on a cheese-burger.

Vic peeled back the bun on the grouper sandwich and laid it on the plate. He reached into his pocket and drew out his penknife and flicked open the blade. Out on the sunny patio Anne Bonny was taking the order at another table. Two blondes and a dark-haired guy. Vic craned forward and squinted into the sunlight.

Dark-haired Romeo smiling up at Vic's little sister. Batting his eyes and Anne batting back.

Vic laid the blade against the palm of his left hand. He looked over at the fry cook, but the guy was focused on his work.

Vic gritted his teeth and sliced the blade across his palm, an inch, another inch, just deep enough to get a trickle of blood rising from the seam, spilling into the web of creases.

He reached out to Thorn's open sandwich and

made a fist and watched the dark fluid dribble out. Six, seven drops spattering against the melted Swiss.

He milked out a few more drips, then closed up the sandwich and set it back under the warming lights just as the fry cook smacked the signal bell.

A few seconds later Anne headed back toward the window to pick up her order. There was a tiny smile on her lips. Probably nobody else would've noticed, but Vic was her brother and he'd spent years studying the looks that came and went on Anne Bonny's face. He'd never seen that exact smile before. Not once.

Vic ducked away from the window. He rubbed his bloody hand on the leg of his jeans and tried to shape his lips into a replay of Anne's smile, but it felt slippery and uncertain on his face.

When he looked back, Anne was at Thorn's table dealing out the plates. Vic stayed in the shadows to the side of the window and watched until finally Thorn picked up his sandwich and held it for a moment near his mouth while he laughed at something one of the little girls said. Then he took a bite and munched on the fried grouper seasoned with Vic Joy's blood.

Vic grinned, watched Thorn swallow, watched him take another bite. Swallow that one, too. The lumps of food snaking down Thorn's throat and into his esophagus, heading toward his belly. Wouldn't be long until Vic Joy was slipping inside the fucker's bloodstream, mingling, festering. Taking root.

'That's some weird prank,' the fry cook said.

Vic turned to the cook, then fixed his eyes on the hand holding the spatula.

'Think you could still flip burgers with a metal hook on the end of your arm?'

The guy stared down at his right hand, then back at Vic. His Adam's apple jiggled.

'Hell, Mr Joy, I wouldn't say anything. Not a goddamn word. Really.'

Vic winked at the kid and headed for the parking lot.

2

Three weeks after their meeting at the Lorelei, Daniel Salbone and Anne were having breakfast on the outside patio of the Cheeca Lodge.

Overnight a late-season cold front had muscled in and the sky was hanging low – as heavy and ominous as a slab of slate. A few yards away from their table the Atlantic thrashed and foamed against the resort's white beach. While they sipped their coffee Daniel's gaze kept drifting out toward the end of the long dock where a white sport-fishing yacht was moored. For the last half hour several men had been rolling dollies down the dock, then heaving the supplies aboard.

Anne's mind was whirling, her body inflamed from the three-week frenzy of sex and extravagant food and full-throttle cruises on the *Black Swan*, both of them naked, racing the moonlight. Except for the boat rides, they'd not left their room at the Cheeca Lodge. DO NOT DISTURB on the doorknob. Room service trays piling up in the corner, their sheets growing funkier by the hour. They'd switched off the air conditioner because they wanted to marinate in their own juices, breathe the other's true scent. They opened the windows to hear the ocean and the gulls, inhale the marshy breeze. Lying in the black night or at noon, feet tangled in the sheets, skin glistening, she trailed her fingertips across his long stretches of muscled flesh.

A few nights ago in the dark, Daniel said, 'Is this love?'

'Hell, no,' she said. 'This is sex, plain and simple.'

He laughed and she laughed with him.

A moment later he said, 'You don't want it to be love.'

'What does that mean?'

'You want something flimsy, something you can control, something you can walk away from when you're ready.'

'This isn't real,' Anne said. 'It's heat lightning on a summer evening.'

'You're worried, aren't you? You're scared.'

'Of what?'

'That it's real. That it's solid.'

She was silent. Staring up at the darkness.

'I don't scare easy,' she said.

'Then you're a rare woman.'

'You're just noticing?'

The ghostly curtains stirred with a warm breeze.

'So who was that guy at the restaurant?'

'Restaurant? What guy?'

'The Lorelei, that day we met. I saw you kiss some guy. Your boyfriend?'

'Oh,' she said. 'He's nobody. A local I went out with for a while. It was finished centuries ago.'

'What's his name?'

She hesitated a half-second and said, 'Thorn.'

'First or last?'

'That's what he goes by. I don't know which it is.'

'So it's over, is it? He won't be wondering where you've gone off to these last three weeks?'

'Stone-cold over.'

'You kissed him. I saw that. You still have feelings.'

His body stiff, Daniel stared up into the dark.

'Hey, what is this? You store away a meaningless kiss from weeks ago. Are you some kind of green-eyed control freak? Tell me now. I don't want any big surprises later on.'

Her words hung in the darkness. When he answered, his voice was solemn, almost apologetic.

'All right,' he said. 'I won't lie to you. I suppose I can be fiercely protective of what I care about. Is that a crime?'

'Well, there's nobody to be jealous of, Daniel. Nobody at all.'

He took her hand and shifted beside her. As he fit his length more snugly against hers, the tension seemed to drain from his body.

'So you've been saving yourself for me,' he said. 'For this.'

'No,' she said. 'You're not at all what I had in mind.'

'What about now? Do you have me in mind?'

He touched her in the dark and she made an uncertain groan.

'You're not happy? This doesn't make you happy, Anne Bonny?'

'Two inches lower and it will.'

Anne called in sick one day too many and the Lorelei let her go. Three weeks together, she and Daniel had talked easily, focused on the moment, but without sharing history on either side. Now it was over.

This morning while Anne lay in bed, Daniel's cell phone rang for the first time since they'd met and he stepped out on their balcony and spoke quietly for a moment, then came back inside and told her that he was going to have to leave.

'For the day?' she said.

He shook his head.

'And do what? Go where?'

'I can't talk about it.'

'Oh, you can't talk about it. I see.'

Anne rose from the bed and went to the closet and yanked her clothes off the hangers: Large structures were collapsing in her chest. Her vision muddy.

'Not right now.' Daniel waved at her, then motioned her to the far wall.

Naked, she hesitated at the closet door, then stalked across the room. Daniel tipped the table lamp to the side and tilted its golden shade. He pointed at the white plastic disk mounted there. Hardly larger than a bottle cap, with a tiny aerial sprouting from its edge. Anne stared at it and was about to speak, but Daniel pressed a finger to her lips.

He pointed to his ear, then pointed to the lamp.

'Oh,' she said. 'Oh.'

'Breakfast?' he said in a normal voice, settling the lamp back into place.

Now, outside on the patio of the Cheeca Lodge, their waitress brought the coffeepot and topped up their cups.

When she was gone, Anne said, 'Is anyone eavesdropping out here?'

'Not likely,' he said.

'So you're dirty?'

'Dirty?'

'Crime,' she said. 'A bad dude.'

Daniel smiled.

'You are, aren't you?'

He looked out at the yacht. One of the men was standing by a piling watching the others heave boxes aboard.

'For years I worked for my father,' he said. 'Vincent Salbone. Have you heard that name?'

It took her a moment to place it, then another moment to absorb the fact.

'On TV,' she said. 'Always surrounded by lawyers, always gets off.'

'Yes,' Daniel said. 'He always has.'

'So you grew up in the Mafia. A little prince.'

His smile faded.

'Hardly a prince,' he said. 'I've always been a disappointment to my father. Especially these last few years.'

Daniel scanned the patio. A family chattering two tables away, another young couple with a noisy toddler. The other tables were empty.

He reached out and took her hand and cradled it in both of his. His voice was quiet and resolved. But his words came haltingly, with awkward edges, as if he'd never pronounced these exact phrases before.

'The family business, I struggled to make it work for a few years, but I was restless, impatient. Doing things the same way they've always been done, I felt trapped. Not a good match. Drugs, gambling. I was confused. I felt tainted and unnatural. So I cast around for a while until I found something different, more stimulating. Cleaner. An old-fashioned form of commerce that died out a while back but is making a return. Something that suits me better. More adventurous.'

Anne fixed her eyes on him.

'What're you saying, Daniel?'

'My father was from the streets. Philly, a city guy. But I was born here. I'm South Florida through and through. Boats, water. I'm more at home when I'm out of sight of land.'

'You don't look like a fisherman to me.'

'I think you know what I am. I think you've known since the first time we spoke. Tyrone Power, Maureen O'Hara. All that.'

The toddler screamed and threw a handful of silverware onto the patio.

Anne leaned forward and drew her hand out of Daniel's grasp.

'You're telling me you're a pirate?'

'I've always preferred the sound of *buccaneer*,' he said.

She leaned back in her chair. The air was pinched in her throat. She brushed a hand through her hair, felt her face warming.

'Well, this is just perfect. My mother would've fainted away.'

'Those are my men out on the dock. That's one of my vessels.'

Anne stared out at the yacht. The work had finished, the men standing around smoking.

'So how does it work?' she said. 'You commandeer a ship at sea, repaint its name, hoist a new flag, sail it away like it's yours?'

'That's one way,' Daniel said.

'Kill everybody, throw them overboard?'

'We sometimes have to defend ourselves. But no,

we're not killers. Five years, no casualties yet. On either side.'

'But you would if you had to. You're armed.'

'If we had to protect ourselves. Yes.'

Daniel met her eyes, a defenseless gaze she hadn't seen from him before. Every spark of cockiness vanished, his debonair smile gone. This was who he was, no hedging, no juking and jiving. Her lover, a goddamn pirate.

Anne touched a fingertip to her forehead, combed a stray hair back into place. She hadn't been waiting for this man. She hadn't been waiting for any man. She was still young; other guys would come along, or no guys. She'd always told herself that either way suited her fine. She could grow old in Islamorada. A weathered waitress with sun-brittle hair, her voice coarsened from secondhand smoke. Take your order, sir? She knew a lot of those. Living in their silver Air-stream with their overfed cat and their quart of rum. Carpenters or boat captains sharing their bed for a week or two. It wasn't so bad.

She closed her eyes and listened to her body, felt the alien quiver spreading through her gut. All these years with little more than a tingle. Now this. This man who was way too handsome, way too dangerous. For all these years she'd stayed well inside the lines, a good citizen, invisible. Ten-hour shifts, then back to her apartment. At night in bed she'd read thick biographies from the library, getting lost in other people's lives, their quirks, the moments of triumph and despair. On her hours off she puttered through the mangroves in her aluminum boat, watched the endless reshaping of the clouds. There were a couple of waitresses she talked to, not friends exactly. Over the years she'd allowed a couple of dozen men to lead her to their beds, but no one who stirred her blood. Except maybe Thorn, and even with him she'd managed to cut it off on the brink of something more. She refused to let them charm her. Always disciplined, drawing back at the first warm shiver. She wasn't going to sacrifice everything. Hand her life over to a dark-eyed dreamboat. Be a martyr for love like some sappy heroine in a pirate movie.

'Who put that bug in our room?'

'I don't know,' he said. 'It could've been a number of people.'

'How long have you known it was there?'

'Since yesterday.'

The waitress came back. An older woman with thinning blond hair.

'More coffee?'

He turned to Anne and she shook her head.

'Just the check, please,' Daniel said.

The waitress gave Anne a look, then turned and headed for the register.

'I want you to come with me, Anne. Try it out. If it doesn't work, if there's anything at all you don't like, I'll bring you back here immediately. No questions, no hesitations.'

44

'You can't be serious, Daniel. Three weeks together, and you expect me to become a pirate? A criminal?'

'I'm very serious. I've never been more serious.'

One of Daniel's crew had come down the dock and was standing near the patio railing. Daniel looked over and the man touched a finger to his watch.

Anne watched the family at the nearby table. The mother was feeding the toddler from a jar, the father reading a newspaper.

Anne Bonny Joy had never needed any man. She'd worked hard to assemble her world, her routine, every austere second under her control. That feeling in her gut was real, yes, this new hum resonating in her bones, but if she waited long enough, the rumble would pass. She knew it would.

'It's okay,' Daniel said. 'I can understand your caution.'

Anne Bonny swung back to him. Her pulse was roaring.

'You're not going to say you love me, fall on your knees, plead?'

'Would it make any difference?'

'Hell, no,' she said.

'You already know I love you.'

Anne knew it all right. For whatever it was worth.

'If it doesn't work for you, I'll give up the life,' Daniel said. 'Take a job.'

'Oh, yeah. Go straight. Sure, Daniel.'

'If that's what it takes for us to be together,' he said. 'I wouldn't hesitate for a second.'

'You should've warned me, prepared me a little. You throw me into this cold. Men waiting out on the dock. The boat running. What did you expect?'

'I had hoped we would have more time. I could tell you in a more relaxed way.'

'And why didn't you?'

'The device in our room.'

'What? The law's closing in. We're about to be arrested?'

'Possibly,' he said. 'I don't believe we have the luxury of time.'

'But you bring your boat right here. You're not worried?'

'The boat's clean. If they had enough to arrest me, it would've happened by now.'

'You couldn't work nine to five, Daniel. You'd hate it. And before long you'd start resenting the hell out of me for forcing you into it, and oh boy, what fun we'd have then.'

'People change,' Daniel said. 'I know I could do it, Anne. If that's what you truly want.'

Daniel's eyes were quiet and exposed, nothing shifty, no attempt to turn up the volume, radiate charm. Glossy blue with those calm depths. At ease in his skin. In their weeks together he had shown her nothing but a steadfast courtesy, a gentility approaching shyness. Just that one flare-up of jealousy about Thorn. Even when both of them were dizzy with lust, Daniel was still reserved, dignified. An honorable man, an outlaw.

Then again, she had little trust in her judgment. Bad training, corrupted genes, a flawed vision. Long ago she'd banished herself to solitary confinement, lived out the sentence she believed was her due.

She watched the waitress returning to the table carrying the check in a padded leather folder. The woman was in her sixties. She wore no rings, and the creases in her face hadn't come from smiling. She padded toward them carefully, as if walking a tightwire of exhaustion.

At the nearby table the toddler flung his plastic drinking cup in the air, and it rolled across the patio. Daniel pushed back his chair and went over and retrieved the cup and took it back to the young family. The father set the newspaper aside and nodded his thanks. Daniel said a few words to the couple, and they laughed, then he returned to the table.

'I'll take that when you're ready,' the waitress said.

'We're ready now.' Daniel counted out the bills, leaving her a tip that would have been sufficient for a dinner of twelve. The waitress stared at the cash and Daniel said, 'Thank you for taking such good care of us.'

The woman gave Anne another look, then left.

'I barely know you,' Anne said.

'You know more about me than anyone has ever known. This isn't easy for me, either, Anne. But it's right. I know that much. It's real.'

'And I'm supposed to step aboard that ship and just go riding off? Leave everything behind.'

Anne watched the waitress refilling saltshakers.

'If you don't feel the same way I'm feeling, Anne, you should stay here. I'll respect your decision either way.'

The man from Daniel's crew came onto the patio and walked over to the table. He had a narrow face and an olive complexion and was wearing a white shirt and khakis and his sunglasses hung from a leather strap around his neck. He carried what looked like a small radio. He nodded at Anne.

'Weather's deteriorating in the straits,' he said. 'We got maybe till tonight before things kick up out there. It'll be rough after that.'

'Thanks, Sal. I'll be there in a second.'

Sal nodded again at Anne and left.

'This has been wonderful,' Daniel said. He took her hand again. 'Like nothing I've ever known.'

'Stop it,' she said. 'Don't give me some goddamn good-bye.'

She turned her eyes from his and watched the waves shatter against the beach. A musky, sexual scent rode the briny mist that drifted to the patio. Seaweed, crabs, barnacles exposed to the sun – as if the surface of the ocean had been peeled back to divulge all the sensory richness below.

The truth was, Anne had felt an axis shift inside her. It happened days ago. Maybe it had even begun to tilt that first moment she'd seen Daniel at the

Lorelei. She'd been denying it. Pretending he was simply another man she'd admitted to her bed. But that was a lie. He'd changed her, awakened appetites and aspirations she'd stifled until now. A dangerous man. A pirate.

'All right, goddamn it.' Anne Bonny heard the words rise from her throat unbidden. A voice more certain than her own. 'But let's get one thing absolutely straight, Mr Buccaneer.'

'Yes?' Daniel said.

She reached out for his hand and gripped it hard.

'I won't be some goddamn scullery maid for a bunch of scurvy dogs.'

Daniel's mouth relaxed into a smile. And the sun was never brighter.

'Marbled godwit,' Janey said.

'Where?' Sugarman lifted his binoculars.

'Eleven o'clock, two hundred yards.'

Sugar swung to the left and caught only a flash of the bird. The godwit made a wide arc to the west to avoid some tourist strapped into a parasail.

'Yeah, yeah. Good eyes, Janey. Good eyes. Or was that a curlew?'

'It's a godwit, Daddy. The bill's too straight for a curlew.'

Janey trained her binoculars on a platoon of pelicans skimming a foot above the leaden surface of Blackwater Sound. It was the first weekend in March, another blast of cold air pushing through, chopping up the water, tossing the palms, a spritz of chilly rain now and then from the blue-black clouds sailing past. Thorn was upstairs with Alexandra making lunch while Lawton snoozed in the hammock that was strung up between two coconut palms.

At the picnic table on the upstairs porch, Jackie had her chin propped on her fists. She was fuming again. She'd wanted to go back to the Lorelei to hear that reggae band they'd listened to three weeks ago. Sugarman said no. Uncle Thorn had invited them to lunch and he'd gone to a lot of trouble. Just yesterday he'd traded a few dozen of his custom bonefish flies with one of his regular customers for ten pounds of stone crabs and a bucket of fresh shrimp.

Jackie said she hated stone crabs and she was pretty sure she hated shrimp, too. Before it escalated further, Alexandra said she'd run down to the Upper Crust for a double cheese and pepperoni twelve-incher. But nothing would appease Jackie. She had inherited a heavy dose of her mother's pissy tendencies. Me first and last and always. Sugarman tried to treat the twins evenhandedly, but at times like this it was rough. Jackie was just so damn frustrating, coasting along fine one minute, in a full-blown snit the next.

Beside Sugarman at the end of Thorn's dock, Janey sat with binoculars pressed to her eyes. For the last half hour she and Sugar had been scanning the overcast sky, the rocky shoreline, and the snarl of woods that edged both sides of Thorn's property, spotting birds, racing to see who could ID them first.

As usual, Janey was way ahead. On the drive down the eighteen-mile stretch from the mainland into the Keys, she'd already collected five roseate spoonbills, a dozen white pelicans, uncountable egrets and herons, and five kingfishers on the telephone wires. Since they'd been at Thorn's she'd spotted another kingfisher, two warblers, a red-shouldered hawk, and an osprey. Suspended about a half-mile overhead, there was a single frigate bird holding its place in the currents with small tips of its wings. So far Janey had missed the frigate bird, but Sugarman was confident she'd notice it soon enough.

While she combed the darkening sky, Sugar set aside his binoculars and began to thumb through *The Sibley Guide to Birds*. He wanted to have the Latin name ready when she finally noticed the frigate bird. A juicy factoid would be nice, too. Lately, Janey had been sponging up the names of birds and bugs and reptiles so fast, Sugar had started to worry he was slipping in his parental duties. Each week before their visitation, he'd been doing homework – an hour or two poring over *Sibley* or one of the Audubon field guides he'd been collecting. From a lifetime in the Keys he already had a pretty good command of shorebirds and waders, and he was good on the diurnal raptors. The anhinga, boobies, cormorants, and the rest of the pelecaniformes he knew. He was weak on small sandpipers, but the tourist birds were what really threw him. The Keys were a north-south highway for a variety of the migratory species, some pretty exotic specimens flittering past all through the winter and spring. Purple martins, swallow-tailed kites, parrots, shrikes and vireos, wrens and finches and sparrows. It'd take him two more lifetimes to keep all those sparrows straight.

'Over there by those ferns,' Sugar said. 'What's that bobbing its tail?'

She swung her binoculars around and found the bird.

'Oh, you know what that is, Daddy. It's a palm warbler. They're always in the dirt, hardly ever in tree branches.' She panned the binoculars slowly back and forth across the dense foliage. 'Did I tell you about the tufted titmouse?'

'The one in Orlando?' Sugar said.

'At Disney World. It was sitting in a bush shaped like a brontosaurus. Its call is real loud. *Peter-peter-peter*. Tufted titmouses are rare down here in the Keys, huh?'

'Yeah, you hardly ever see them this far south,' Sugar said. 'But I think the plural is *titmice*.'

'Look at that, Daddy. Up there.' Janey had her binoculars tilted up.

Sugarman was ready for her.

'*Fregata magnificens*,' he said. 'The frigate has the longest wings relative to its weight of any bird there is. Steals food from other birds, a pirate.'

'Not the frigate bird,' Janey said. 'That man in the kite.'

'Is that damn flasher back again?' Thorn had come out on the dock behind them with a plate of crackers and smoked fish spread. 'Close your eyes, Janey. This guy is gross.'

'He's taking pictures of us,' Janey said. 'Look.'

She raised her binoculars and handed them to Thorn.

It took him a few seconds to locate the big blue parasail against that dark sky and then tilt down to see the guy strapped into the sling below it. He wore a black tank top and white shorts and a red bandanna on his head. He was holding a camera, clicking away.

'Well, I'll be damned,' said Thorn. 'That who I think it is?'

Sugarman tightened his focus.

'Maybe he thinks I'm still dating his sister.'

'I'd heard about this,' Sugarman said. 'The guy's been working up and down the coast taking pictures. Three or four people told me about it, but I didn't believe it.'

'Who is it?' Janey said.

'A bad man,' said Thorn. 'A crook.'

Sugarman said, 'His name is Vic Joy, honey.'

The boat that was hauling the parasail made a slow turn away from shore, circling out to deeper waters.

'What makes him so bad?'

'Probably his past,' Thorn said. 'Things that happened to him when he was a kid.'

53

'No,' Janey said. 'What does he do that's so bad?'

'He takes advantage of people, sweetheart,' Sugar said. 'He doesn't play fair. He tries to get what he wants no matter who it hurts.'

Janey stared out at the bay for a moment, filing away this new fact. The water was glazed with silver like cooling lava. The shifting scent of the cold front rode the breeze, mingling its rough blend of fall leaves, wood smoke, and the sweet burn of fresh-cut pine with the sulfur and saffron of the resident tropical air mass.

Janey lifted her binoculars and swung them to the right. So much for bad men – now back to work.

'Yellow-crowned night heron, Daddy. Look, three o'clock.'

3

It was Monday morning after another raucous weekend with Sugar's kids. A day of bird-watching and
hide-and-go-seek. Lawton was pretty funny, doing
a stiff-legged Frankenstein walk, arms outstretched,
eyes squinty, as he searched for the squealing girls,
who hid behind bushes and in closets. At dinner
Jackie nibbled at her pizza while the rest of them
scarfed stone crabs and shrimp.

After Alexandra left for work and Lawton climbed
into his hammock with a stack of fishing magazines,
Thorn tied on his carpenter's apron, filled the pockets with nails, and dug into his latest project. He'd
been working on it for the last month and had almost
finished the framing, raiding the tall stack of milled
hardwood planks that had been lying on the gravel

beneath his stilt house for years. They were leftovers from the time when he'd had to rebuild the place entirely, and now he'd decided those old boards would work perfectly for enclosing the downstairs area – the open space between the eight telephone poles that held his house fifteen feet above the ground.

It was to be a room for Lawton, granting all of them a measure of privacy they hadn't known since Alex and her dad moved in. For the last few months Lawton had been sleeping on a cot in Thorn's living room, a mere ten feet away from where he and Alexandra shared a bed. Thorn had told the two of them that he was building a workshop, wanting to keep the real intention secret until the room had actually taken decent shape.

At Thorn's current rate, he figured Lawton's room would take another month to finish. By then he was fairly certain he'd know if it was safe to tell Alexandra the true purpose of the space. The reason he'd shied away from confessing it already was that he didn't want to scare her off. It seemed so permanent, such a pivotal step. A room for Lawton. An unmistakable display of the growing bond he felt toward the old man and his beautiful daughter.

At noon he'd finally finished the framing. To celebrate he decided to take Lawton on the skiff, go out past Crocodile Dragover to McCormick Creek, check some snook holes he knew. Do some damage to the fish population.

So he showered, put on fresh shorts and a white

T-shirt, and carried his spinning rods and tackle box down to the skiff. Out at the end of his dock, he heard the grinding roar, a noise he'd become all too familiar with lately. Two properties to the north a bulldozer was leveling the Island House. For fifty years the small motel with a half-dozen quaint bungalows had been at that location. He'd heard Doug and Debbie Johnson had sold out but assumed the new owner would keep it intact as all the previous owners had for half a century.

Thorn stood at the end of his dock and watched the big machine uproot an old gumbo-limbo, then flatten a stand of wispy Australian pines, mowing down those shallow-rooted trees that took decades to reach those heights. That rocky shore and the rickety motel had been in his peripheral vision for so many hours and so many years that now, with the coastline so suddenly altered, he was feeling a whirl of vertigo.

When the land clearing was done, Thorn's neighborhood was probably going to be getting another of those ten-thousand-square-foot get-away-for-the-weekend mansions. A million-dollar party house owned by a Miami heart surgeon or a pitcher for the Florida Marlins – with a half-dozen Jet Skis and a flashy red speedboat at the dock. Progress.

Back on the shoreline Lawton was standing in water to his ankles with fishing line tangled around both arms. In the stiff breeze, his casting practice had been going badly.

In a couple of hours Alexandra would be home and they'd open a bottle of wine and hold hands while they watched the last trickle of the daylight drain from the sky. If she was in the mood, she'd tell him about one of her cases that day. Keeping it light but still managing to give him a glimpse of the brutalities that were commonplace in her daytime world. He'd recount his time with Lawton, things the old man had said or done. And she would listen without comment, her eyes on the distance. After these few months, their routine felt solid and reliable. Thorn, his lover, and his lover's father, an odd little family but a family nonetheless. For someone who'd spent most of his life working hard to stay isolated, it was startling to discover how much satisfaction he found in the constant presence of that old man and his strong-willed, beautiful daughter.

Thorn smiled at Lawton's struggle with the fly line and headed over to give him a hand – glad to have some reason to pull away from the bulldozer's dismal work. He was halfway down the dock when the car pulled off the Overseas Highway and began to inch down Thorn's gravel drive. A dark blue Crown Victoria.

The car parked in the shade near his house and the man who got out from behind the wheel was squat and square-faced, with a paunch stressing the buttons on his blue madras shirt. Despite his stumpy legs, the man advanced on Thorn with a cocky stride. His head was shaved and gleaming and his beard ran in a narrow, precise band along the outlines of his jaws and chin. He had on jeans and boat shoes, but both looked as if they'd been purchased an hour earlier and hadn't yet been broken in. This seemed to be a man for whom casual dress did not come easy.

'Thorn,' he said as he came across the yard.

Lawton was swiping at the wispy fishing line as if trying to pluck a spiderweb from his skin.

'You okay, Lawton?'

'Fine, fine,' the old man said. 'I've caught a monster this time. Me.'

The stranger held out his hand, and after a moment's reluctance Thorn shook it.

'Do I know you?'

'You should,' the man said. 'Mind if we stand in the shade?'

Thorn followed the man over to the shadows of the tamarind tree.

'Jimmy Lee Webster,' the man said.

'Listen,' Thorn said. 'I don't mean to be impolite, but—'

'Yeah, yeah,' Webster said. 'You're busy tying flies, or whatever it is you do with your free time.' He flashed Thorn a one-second smile, then said, 'Which seems to be most of your day. And a lot of your night.'

The man produced that miserable smile again, like something he'd acquired from a second-rate drama coach.

'You might've seen me on TV,' Webster said.

'If I had one.'

'Or in the newspaper.'

Thorn shook his head.

'Jimmy Lee Webster.'

'I heard you the first time.'

'Really? Not even the faint tinkle of a little bell?'

'What're you, a TV star?'

'Secretary Webster.'

'Oh, okay. You're the guy that answers the phone, takes dictation.'

'Yeah, I was warned,' Webster said, 'what a smart-ass you are.'

'Fair enough,' Thorn said. 'But I still don't know you, Webster.'

'I was Secretary of the Navy, last administration.' Lawton had dropped down in the grass and was peeling the knotted strands of line off his legs and sandals. He noticed Thorn looking at him and showed him his palms. Didn't need any help, doing just fine.

'I know,' Webster said. 'Looking at me, it's hard to believe. Don't exactly have a military bearing. Not the tall, top-gun prototype. But fortunately, advancement in the armed services isn't based on appearance.'

'Well, congratulations,' Thorn said. 'Your parents must be very proud.'

'Reason I was on TV is because I was controversial,' Webster said. 'I butted heads with the big boys, but I held my own. Damn well got some things accomplished in those four years.'

A shift in the breeze sent Webster's aftershave Thorn's way. An abrasive blend of wood smoke and motor oil.

'Look,' Webster said. 'You don't know me, but I know a little about you. You're a loner. You don't like strangers wandering up to your house. Hey, who does? I can appreciate that. And the fact that I was Secretary of the Navy doesn't cut any ice with you, okay, that's fine, too.'

Jimmy Lee Webster drew a white handkerchief from his jeans pocket and dabbed the sweat off his face, then did a quick swipe across his dome.

'I don't know how you folks put up with this heat.'

'There's not a lot to do about it.'

'Okay, here it is,' Webster said. He spread his legs apart and reset his feet as if he were about to snatch Thorn by the lapels and body-slam him. He produced his fake smile again and said, 'My style is to go for the throat. That way we don't waste any more of your valuable fly-tying time. So here's what's going on. Your name came up in an investigation I'm running. And I decided I should come have a chat.'

'Whoa,' Thorn said. 'Stop right there.'

'Look, I can explain the whole enchilada to you out here in the sun. Or we can go upstairs, have a beer, discuss it in detail in the air-conditioning.'

'Only air-conditioning I have is what you feel right now.'

Lawton had extricated himself from the fishing

line, and it lay in a nasty tangle near the dock. He dusted off his hands as if he'd just knocked a bully flat, and marched over to join them in the shade of the tamarind.

'Okay, then,' Webster said. 'I understand you had a hot and heavy fling with Anne Bonny Joy.'

Lawton settled in between Jimmy Webster and Thorn. Leaning forward, giving Webster a good going-over.

'You're that navy guy,' Lawton said. 'From TV. You sunk that ship.'

Webster smiled at Thorn. See, somebody recognized him.

'That particular fling you're referring to,' Thorn said, 'was over a long time ago.'

'That's not how I heard it. I heard there was still considerable heat there. Some sparks.'

Thorn took a calming breath, glanced out at the water, then turned his eyes back to Webster.

'Look, Mr Secretary—'

'Not anymore,' Webster said. 'I'm out of the cabinet these days. Still got one foot in government, but I'm in other areas. A bit more low-profile.'

'Clandestine,' Lawton said. 'Covert operations.'

Jimmy Lee looked at Lawton.

'This your father?' Webster said.

'Practically.'

'You came to the right place, Webster,' Lawton said, 'because it just so happens I did a bit of under-cover work myself at one time. Miami PD. Several high-profile sting operations. Stolen merchandise, cocaine. So I know how it's done. We took down some pretty rotten apples.'

Jimmy Lee nodded uncertainly at the old man.

'Forget about Thorn,' Lawton said. 'He's the shy, retiring type. The guy you want to talk to is standing right here.'

Thorn rested a hand on Webster's shoulder and eased him firmly toward his car.

'I just want to pick your brain about Anne Joy.'

'You already picked it clean, partner. Time you hit the highway.'

'You didn't even ask him what he wanted?' Alex said. Lawton was stretched out in his cot, the full moon had risen above the trees, and Blackwater Sound was frosted with gold.

'I ushered him to his car and sent him on his way.'

'Jeez, Thorn. Jimmy Lee Webster.'

'Big shot, huh?'

'Was for a while.'

'He claimed he was controversial.'

'Oh, yeah,' Alex said. 'He's the guy who gave the go-ahead for a navy destroyer to fire on some commercial ship in Malaysia, somewhere over there.'

'Why?'

'Something about pirates. Problem was, he got the wrong boat. Bad intelligence. I forget the details.

Bunch of civilians got killed, ship sank. That's how I remember it. Major international incident. A lot of saber rattling afterward. There was a Senate hearing on TV for a week or two. Haven't heard much about him lately.'

'Pirates?'

'I think what it was, navy intelligence thought an American oil tanker had been taken over by thugs and they were sailing off somewhere after murdering the crew. They had that part right. There was an oil tanker that got pirated; our folks just got the wrong ship. A US destroyer tried to get this other tanker to stop; when they didn't respond, our guys opened fire. A dozen men killed, that's what I recall. Maybe more. Big oil spill.'

'Well, he's doing something else now. CIA maybe. Who knows?'

Alex leaned against his shoulder. They were standing at the rail looking out at the darkness.

'Your name came up?'

'That's what he said.'

Thorn considered for a half-second telling her about the Anne Joy connection but decided to pass. No need to stir that up again.

'It might've been interesting just to hear his pitch.'

'No way. I'm on vacation.'

'Oh, yeah? For how long?'

'Rest of my natural life.'

'Well, that's fine. But me, I'd want to know what the deal was.'

'Whatever it was, I've got my hands full already,' Thorn said, nudging her hip with his. 'My cup is overflowing.'

'Hey, I know what it was,' Alexandra said. 'Your name came up in an investigation of international Lotharios.'

'Funny,' he said. 'Hilarious.'

He poked his elbow lightly in her ribs.

'They wanted to know what makes you so irresistible to women. Start distilling it. Put it in bottles, lob it at the enemy. A weapon of mass seduction.'

Thorn laughed. He lifted his glass and clinked it to hers and had another sip of wine. She gave his cheek a peck, then drew away and looked back at the dark view.

'Irresistible?' he said. 'How irresistible?'

'Mesmerizing.' Alexandra finished the last swallow of her cabernet and set the glass on the table behind them. 'An overpowering magnetism.'

In the thick mangroves that bordered his land, a bird keened. A warning screech or maybe a late-night mating call. He wasn't sure what kind of bird it was. Didn't sound like an osprey or the red-shouldered hawk, not the screech owl, either. Sugarman or Janey would know.

'Well, it's nice to know,' Thorn said, 'I'm such hot shit.'

'Yes,' she said. 'You are. You most certainly are.'

She laced her fingers in his and drew him away from the water a quarter-turn and into her strong arms. And there he stayed until they were breath-less and dizzy with their mutual heat. Then she stepped out of his embrace, took his hand, and led him quietly past Lawton's cot into the bedroom they shared.

4

For the next few weeks, Anne Bonny lived the life she'd been named for. They didn't roam the open seas with a lookout clinging high to the mast, peering through a spyglass, searching for a ship to take. Daniel's operation used a simple scheme that relied on the shipping industry's antipirate tracking system, FROM. Fleet Remote Monitoring units were installed aboard security-conscious transport ships and relayed an automated signal six times a day that informed corporate headquarters of their ships' exact position, speed, and direction. A seagoing LoJack. The system was designed to give the owners an early warning if one of their ships made a drastic change in course and allowed them to track it once it left its charted route and send assistance.

Sal Gardino, Daniel's young computer guy, had penetrated the system's security firewall – a worm, a backdoor; Anne Bonny could never keep the hacker jargon straight. But now with a few minutes of work on his laptop, Daniel could enter the site and prowl through the code to determine the exact positions of thousands of different vessels at sea. Freighters, tankers, container ships. Maersk, Hanjin, TransAsia, Global Transport, the entire fleets of dozens of shipping companies were open books to him. Daniel relished the irony of it, using their system against them.

They stayed at sea for four weeks straight. Two boats. The sleek forty-five-foot Hatteras sportfishing yacht that had picked them up from the Cheeca Lodge. High-performance diesels below its decks. Anne and Daniel, Sal and Marty lived aboard that one. And the Nicaraguans and the rest of the crew manned a second vessel, a shrimp trawler that had been outfitted with enough horsepower to stay up with the Hatteras. Both boats were equipped with seven-man inflatables powered by four-stroke Yamahas. These they used as boarding craft. While they were under way, they kept a two- or three-mile cushion between the two boats, moving from location to location through the West Indies, off the South American coast, and through the islands. The Hatteras carried a cache of automatic weapons, the satellite communications system, and the computer that Sal used to crack the FROM site.

With all that shipping data arrayed before them, selecting a new target was a little like going to the track. You studied the program, checked the stats, figured the odds, one ship against another based on what else was racing that day, considered the value of the cargo, the difficulty of disposing of it, and above all you didn't bet more than you could afford to lose.

Early in April, after hitting four ships in as many weeks, they bivouacked at the Gray Ghost Lodge, a fishing camp Daniel owned. Thirty acres in the Barra de Colorado, on the Costa Rican–Nicaraguan border.

Ten primitive wood cabins, a small dining hall, a marina big enough for half a dozen open fishing boats. Daniel stored his Donzi there, the *Black Swan*, that playboy speedboat he'd used so successfully to court Anne Bonny.

The fishing camp was bordered on the west and south by dense rain forest, a roadless nature preserve that was well off the tourist track. To the north and east were a labyrinth of estuaries and lagoons and a system of shallow, nearly impenetrable bays that led to the Caribbean Sea.

Partly for appearances, partly for his own amusement, Daniel kept the fishing lodge open during the winter season, hiring guides, cooks, and service help, operating it as a legit business. From November to February, rich anglers paid five hundred dollars a day to stay in the shacks and fish with guides for the giant bonefish and tarpon that streaked across the sand flats.

But in the sweltering spring and summer months, when the rains began and most of the bonefish and silver kings migrated away, Daniel shut down the business and used the lodge off and on for regrouping, making repairs to vessels and weapons, for a little rum and relaxation by the tropical lagoon.

Not far from the Gray Ghost Lodge, hundreds of ships a day passed within striking distance of the coastline. Even with all those easy targets near at hand, it had been Daniel's custom to lie low when they were based at the lodge. No reason to draw attention to that particular region when there were countless square miles of unpatrolled ocean available. They tried, when possible, to work in international waters. Between the never-ending hunt for terrorists and dope smugglers, the US Coast Guard was spread impossibly thin throughout their own territorial waters, which left much of the rest of the hemisphere relatively free of naval law enforcement.

With his satellite phone and laptop computer Daniel could turn virtually any location into a command and control station – staying in constant contact with his people in Taipei and Rio, Montevideo and Jakarta, Singapore, Hong Kong, and Anchorage. The same network he'd constructed years before when he worked for his father, trafficking in hash and cocaine, now helped Daniel dispose of even the most exotic cargo.

In those few weeks Anne had adjusted to the routine, the guns, the constant movement, the controlled thrill of boarding ships. Whatever daytime doubts Anne developed were wiped away by the long nights with Daniel. His measured calm, his certainty. Not the dashing, risk-taking swashbuckler her mother had dreamed of, but a man on a simple mission – to pile up as much cash as quickly as he could with the smallest possible risk.

'Some pirates we are,' she said one night at the fishing lodge. 'A whole month and we've not slit a single throat.'

'I like to think of myself as an entrepreneur. An adventure capitalist.'

'That's a good one.'

'We're simply skimming a little of the obscene corporate profits and letting the insurance conglomerates cover the shipping company losses. The daisy chain of high finance kicks in. The big boys passing around the big bucks.'

'You've got it all rationalized.'

'I have my morals,' Daniel said.

'Most entrepreneurs don't use automatic weapons.'

'They're just props,' Daniel said. 'Have we fired one shot?'

'But they're loaded,' Anne said. 'Guns have a way of going off.'

'Are you having trouble with this, Anne? You want to go home, back to a safe routine? Say the word, I'll take you back.'

'It's just the guns,' she said. 'I told you about my

parents. I've seen it with my own eyes, what can happen.'

'I know,' he said. 'But this is different. Your dad was skimming from redneck dopers. This is the other end of the spectrum.'

'The sophisticated end,' Anne said.

'The safe end,' said Daniel. 'The smart end.'

When Daniel hit a target, they usually outnumbered the crew, storming the ship in the dark, half from port, half from starboard, taking the bridge first, subduing the captain. Screaming, threatening, bashing defiant crew members with the butts of the Mac-10s, the AK-47s. In those four weeks they'd clubbed a few to their knees, left some heroes bleeding and broken, but nothing worse. Since she'd joined Daniel and his men, they'd taken everything from eighty thousand gallons of flaxseed oil to fourteen hundred new Toyota ATVs and a container ship full of refrigerators and microwaves, and in all that time they'd not fired a shot. The ships were never armed; the men were sailors, not fighters. Not a single chase at sea, not even a close call.

Once they disabled the FROM, they handed off the ship, then one of Daniel's Latin American accomplices piloted the vessel to a friendly port in Colombia or Venezuela, where the goods were unloaded. What happened to the vessel after that was up to his business partners. Sometimes they simply walked away from the unloaded vessel after pocketing their profit. Other times they turned the stolen craft into a phantom ship. Repainted and reflagged it, picked up another load from a legitimate shipping company, sailed away, and promptly docked at a nearby port where they unloaded the goods. Two loads with one ship.

But Daniel wanted no stake in all that. Hit and run, that was his game. Skim the cream, leave the awkward problem of disposing of the cargo and the ships to others. Even with the camouflage of new papers and new paint, phantom ships were relatively easy targets for the Coast Guard or foreign navy patrols. For Daniel it simply wasn't worth the risk of being caught aboard a stolen transport ship just to pilfer one bonus load of olive oil.

It was during the first week in April while their group relaxed at the Gray Ghost Lodge that one afternoon Daniel handed Anne Bonny the latest stack of FROM printouts. In the next two weeks there were fifty-seven ships on their way toward the Caribbean Sea, most of them passing within a hundred miles of their location.

'It's time you chose,' he said. 'You know what we're looking for.'

'I thought we didn't hit ships in this part of the Gulf?'

'Just this once,' he said. 'It couldn't hurt.'

'Well, I'm not ready to pick the ship.'

'Oh, you're ready.'

Daniel had already shown her the access codes to break into the FROM site, made her practice the steps till she could slip inside in less than ten minutes. Treating her with respect, a business partner on equal footing with him, not simply his lover. So Anne took the stack of papers and went out to the tiki hut beside the lagoon and for an hour she studied the printouts.

'The *Rainmaker*,' she told Daniel later in their cabin.

'And why that one?'

'I liked the name.'

Sal Gardino and Marty Messina looked on in silence.

'You like the name. Oh, come on, Anne. Be serious.'

'Four or five of these meet our conditions,' she said. 'Cargo's roughly equivalent in value, all headed through the Yucatán Channel to New Orleans or Galveston, an easy shot from here, all with about the same number of crew, so everything being equal, I picked a name I liked. The *Rainmaker*, like some old Indian chief chanting for the skies to open up. The end of a long drought.'

Sal Gardino smiled, but Marty Messina, who'd been standing in the doorway with his arms crossed over his chest, grimaced and stalked away.

Marty was a beefy man in his late thirties who only a few months before had been released from prison after serving a six-year term for running drugs for Daniel. Before Marty went to trial, the DEA

offered him full immunity, witness protection, a lifetime pension, if he'd inform on the Salbones. But
he hung tough, served his time, and came home to
Miami expecting, by God, to be Daniel's chief lieutenant, a role Anne was already filling.

From their first meeting, when he realized the
situation, Marty was bitterly polite, all smiles, 'yes,
ma'am, no, ma'am,' but he was a lousy actor. He
damn well wanted to claim his rightful place. To
appease Marty, Daniel had assigned Messina the role
of maintaining their foreign contacts and cultivating
new ones. Though it was a crucial part of the operation, Marty didn't seem particularly satisfied.

Daniel studied the data on the *Rainmaker*,
humming to himself.

'She's a quick study,' said Sal.

'Crude oil,' Daniel said. 'We'll have to find a buyer
right away.'

'Guy in Buenos Aires,' said Sal. 'With the new
refinery. Or the Texan.'

'You want to make the call, Anne? Negotiate the
numbers?'

'That's Marty's job.'

'All right,' he said. 'I'll tell Marty, have him look
around, see who's thirsty. We'll have to off-load at
sea.'

'Still, it should be easier to get rid of than that
damn flaxseed oil.'

He paged through the printouts a moment more,
then smiled at her.

'Okay,' he said. 'That's the one. Excellent choice, Anne. The *Rainmaker*. Now, you know how it's done. If something ever happens to me.'

Daniel smiled, but there was a shadow lurking in the depths of his blue eyes as if he'd sensed already what no one else had, the gleaming missile on its downward arc.

'Oh, come on,' Anne said. 'This is safer than waitressing. Restaurant work, there's a truly perilous career. Never know what dangerous characters you're going to run across.'

Sal Gardino stood up, nodded his approval, and left.

'One more year,' Daniel said when Sal was gone. 'Six months if we're lucky. Then we call it a day.'

'You're worried about something?'

'Not worried, no. It's just that my perspective on risk and danger has changed lately. Having someone I care about.'

'If you're really worried, we could stop now.'

'Do you want that, Anne?'

'What do *you* want?'

He looked at her for a moment, then turned back to the stack of papers.

'Six more months, we'll never have to dirty our hands again.'

'And then?'

'And then we can retire to this lovely spot.'

'Live in the jungle.'

'Build your dream house, a tropical bungalow,

whatever you want. It's perfect here. Wild parrots, fantastic fishing. Like the Keys, only more pristine. Not to mention excellent tax advantages.'

'Live here and do what?'

'You know what.'

'I want to hear you say it.'

'All right,' Daniel said. 'Raise our children in the Garden of Eden, start over, get it right.'

'Keep them isolated? No cartoons, no computer games.'

'We'd be great parents,' he said.

'What makes you think that?'

'Because we love each other.'

'That's all it takes?'

'It's a damn good start,' he said.

For the next ten days, they followed the ship's progress on the laptop.

After taking on 840,000 barrels of North Slope crude, the *Rainmaker* departed from Berth 5 of the Alyeska Marine Terminal across the bay from Valdez, Alaska, on a blustery afternoon. All eleven of the *Rainmaker*'s tanks were full and she rode low and slow in the heavy seas of the northern Pacific. The ship was owned by TransOcean Shipping Lines, an American corporation based in San Francisco, although for tax purposes the *Rainmaker* was registered in Panama and flew the Panamanian flag of convenience. For the first few hundred miles the ship was battered by gales. She took eight days to steam down the coast of California and around the Baja Peninsula and across the eastern Pacific to the Panama Canal. For their purposes, the canal was an ideal choke point, funneling a huge percentage of the hemisphere's traffic through a narrow band of sea.

When the tanker passed through the Miraflores Lock on the Pacific side at four-thirty in the afternoon, the ship's image was captured by a Web camera and a few seconds later the image was broadcast on the Internet Web site operated by the Panama Canal Authority. The Web camera was updated every few seconds and showed the constant stream of ships through the first Pacific lock. Sal monitored the Web site to double-check the data coming from the FROM system.

'Headed our way,' Sal said. 'Right on schedule.'

With Anne looking over his shoulder, Sal sat at their tiny desk and tapped out the code to slip into the FROM. From this point on, they'd camp inside the Web site for the moment-by-moment updates on the ship's position.

'Shit,' Sal said. 'Shit, shit, shit.'

Daniel set aside the Mac-10 he was cleaning and came over.

'What?'

'There's a lag,' Sal said. 'Look.'

Anne and Daniel leaned close to the computer. The stream of data that had always flowed smoothly across the screen, updated every two or three seconds, had slowed to a crawl.

'What is that?'

'I don't know,' Sal said. 'But it's not right.'

'Have they fingered us? They know we're inside?'

'Could be the satellite. Some kind of weather interference. But it's never been this slow.'

As they watched, the screen blinked as if the laptop were losing power; then the stream of numbers and coded letters resumed its normal flow.

Daniel stepped back.

'A hiccup in the transmission,' Daniel said. 'Nothing to worry about. A thunderstorm over the Pacific. Lightning in Guam. No big deal.'

'Yeah,' Sal said. 'Could be.'

Anne said, 'They could do that, know we're watching? Figure our location?'

'If they had reason to be suspicious, yeah, top security people might be able to discover we've hacked the site,' Sal said. 'But track us back here? Not unless they've got the Pentagon in on it, a supercomputer doing the work. Not some piddling corporate security system. Or it could be the mercs.'

Daniel shook his head at Sal, but Anne said, 'Mercs? What's that?'

Turning away from her, Daniel said, 'Mercenaries. Hired guns.'

'First I've heard of that,' she said.

'There've been a couple of cases,' said Daniel. 'Both times in the China Sea. A gang of ex-soldiers hired by the shipping companies.'

'And what? They arrested some pirates?'

'Took them out is more like it,' Sal said.

'Took them out? Murdered them?'

Daniel flashed a look at Sal and said to Anne, 'The details are sketchy.'

'But they're out there,' Anne said. 'And that's who this is?'

'It's the weather,' Sal said. 'Just some damn lightning storm.'

They watched for a while longer as the data scrolled at a steady pace.

Daniel tapped Sal on the shoulder and asked him to step outside. Sal rose, took another look at the screen, then shrugged and left. Daniel shut the door behind him.

'Anne,' he said. 'I think you should stay ashore for this one.'

His eyes showed her nothing. A depthless smile.

'What? You're having a premonition? This computer thing?'

'Just do me this favor, one time. Okay?'

'We don't need to hit it at all,' she said. 'There's nothing special about this one. Something doesn't feel right, let's bail.'

Daniel came over to her and put his hands on her shoulders.

'You won't do this for me? Just this once. Stay home.'

'What's going on? You're phasing me out? I'm supposed to start training to be the happy home-maker?'

He drew his hands away as if they'd been stung. She hadn't meant to lash out like that. But she couldn't bring herself to apologize. He had a different look. Unsure, lost. It unnerved her, seeing him like that. The ground beneath her growing unsteady.

He swept both hands back through his glossy hair and turned his eyes to a window in the cabin.

'If I died,' he said, 'or we got separated, what would you do, Anne?'

'You're not going to die.'

He turned to her then, his eyes as harsh as she'd ever seen them.

'I asked you what you'd do.'

'Okay,' she said. 'I'd probably go home.'

'Back to Key Largo.'

'Yes.'

'Back to your brother and your boyfriend?'

His blue eyes were full of twisting light.

'You asked me a question, Daniel, I'm trying to be honest. I'd go home, try to resume my life. There is no boyfriend. And I have no desire to see Vic.'

'Key Largo,' he said. 'Okay, that's good. Something ever happens, I'll find you there. That's where I'll come.'

'Daniel? What's wrong? What's going on?'

He stared at her for several moments, then said, 'I'm sorry, Anne. I'm tensed up, that's all. I'm sorry I bullied you. Forgive me.'

'Of course,' she said. 'Of course.'

But when he came to her and held her, for the

first time since they'd met, the fusion of their bodies, that disappearance of their separate selves she'd come to expect and depend on, did not occur.

On that steamy April afternoon, the *Rainmaker* passed through the Pedro Miguel Locks, Gatun Lake, and finally the Gatun Locks, then out of the Panama Canal and into the Caribbean Sea, where she went north on her last leg, following the busiest of several shipping lanes that would take her through the Yucatán Straits, up into the Gulf, then into the Mississippi, headed to the Marathon Oil refinery in Garyville, Louisiana, which was midway between New Orleans and Baton Rouge. She carried a crew of fourteen.

Using two of the fishing boats from the Gray Ghost Lodge, Daniel and Anne and their crew shoved off three hours after the *Rainmaker* passed through the last lock of the Panama Canal. Earlier in the day, Marty Messina had set up the rendezvous with two small tankers based in Barranquilla, providing them a GPS location out in the Colombian Basin where they would converge near dawn tomorrow to off-load the crude before scuttling the ship.

Their crew was a mixed lot. Five former Sandinista guerrillas, well-armed, quiet men who doubled as Gray Ghost fishing guides in the winter. And there were Pedro and Manuel Cruz, two Cuban brothers from Miami who'd assisted Daniel with various rip-offs at the Port of Miami before he strayed from the family business. Two others had peeled off from Vincent Salbone's Miami crew: Sal Gardino, the young computer guy, and Marty Messina.

Two hours after departing the Gray Ghost, they spotted the oil tanker a mile to the east, and for the next hour Daniel in the lead boat and Anne Bonny following with Sal Gardino and three of the Nicaraguans shadowed the *Rainmaker* as it moved north a hundred miles off the Central American coast. At that distance in their high-powered craft, they could seize the ship, tie up the crew, take her to the designated meeting spot, off-load the crude, and still be back in the maze of estuaries of the Barra de Colorado by the day after tomorrow. Long enough for a watchful owner to become alarmed at losing touch with one of his vessels, but too quick to send help.

When the sea was clear in every direction, Daniel signaled, and the boats came along opposite sides of the *Rainmaker*. Hull to hull with the tanker, the men readied the grappling hooks. That part hadn't changed in hundreds of years, same four-pronged steel hooks. Only difference was that theirs were coated with a rubberized layer to soften the *clang* when they caught the rail.

In recent years, as piracy had boomed, shipping companies had begun to install laser devices that sensed boarders climbing over the side. Alarms sounded, decks were flooded with light, and usually the pirates fled. If they didn't, the tanker's crew was usually ready with powered-up fire hoses to blow them back over the side.

But Sal Gardino had researched the *Rainmaker*'s specs and her recent maintenance history and was certain she wasn't equipped with alarms. Once aboard, Sal would only have to locate and disable the FROM system and the ship would simply vanish from computer screens.

At Daniel's signal, the hooks were heaved and they caught to the rails of the big ship and the rope ladders uncoiled beneath them. The *Rainmaker* was a midsize tanker, just under a thousand feet long and 166 feet wide. At that hour of night, with most sailors customarily spending their free time in quarters and only a skeleton crew working the bridge, it was highly unlikely a boarder would encounter one of the tanker's crewmen when coming over the side.

But this night was different from any before.

Anne Bonny was halfway up the ladder, Pedro, one of the Nicaraguans, and Sal Gardino ahead of her, when she heard the first sharp pops. Her breath seized in her lungs and her hands fumbled for a grip.

She'd practiced with the Mac-10 at the Gray Ghost Lodge target range and recognized the quick burst. And those first few shots were answered by a duller noise, the suppressed puffs of what surely were silenced weapons.

At the railing, Pedro hesitated, gripping the rope with one hand while he struggled to unsling the

AK-40 from his back. Then there was another round of firing, this one longer. Panicked shouts from the deck, and the metallic chime of slugs flattening against the ship's iron sides. She heard Daniel's voice, strangely calm, commanding Marty Messina to take cover.

'Move!' Anne shouted. 'They're in trouble. Move, goddamn it!'

Raising up, Pedro lifted one foot to the lowest rail, and a half-second later the small man was kicked backward by a burst of fire. He shrieked and somersaulted, the heel of his boot clipping Anne Bonny on the shoulder as he pitched into the sea. For a half-second she lost her grip, burned her hand on the rope as she fought to regain her hold, and scrambled up the rope ladder and wrestled past Sal Gardino, who was paralyzed and gibbering to himself. A techno geek, rendered useless by the first sounds of a gunfight.

On the top rung of the rope ladder, Anne Bonny paused and found her breath. Head down, crouched below the gunwale, she gripped her Mac-10, formed a quick image of her next move, then sprang up and tumbled over the rail, ducking a shoulder, slamming into the rough pebbled deck, and rolling once, twice, a third time until she came to rest against an iron wall.

She was dizzy and nauseous and for a moment thought she'd been hit by one of the slugs strafing the deck. She closed her eyes and scanned her body but sensed no numbness, no hot prickling. Just a throb in her shoulder where she'd slammed the steel deck.

She sat up, pressed her back flat against the wall, and was fumbling with the Mac-10, trying to find the right grip, when she made out the shadow of a man moving to the rail. Then saw the bright flashes as he unleashed on Sal and the rest of her crew following her up the ladder.

The man got off a dozen rounds before Anne Bonny could raise her weapon. Sal screamed and one of the Nicaraguans cursed in Spanish and went silent. Anne Bonny aimed at the center of the body armor sheathing the man's back and curled her finger against the cool metal and the tall man bucked forward and tumbled over the side.

She blew out a breath, but before she could move again, dozens of spotlights bathed the deck in staggering brightness and in the same instant the *whup* and blare of a helicopter sounded from the north.

'Stay down, Anne. Stay down!'

All around her, automatic weapons erupted, the raw thuds and clangs of bullets slamming the ship's tough hide.

Daniel's voice had come from her right, roughly fifty feet away. She rose from her crouch and craned around the edge of the wall, which she could see in the blue-white glare was not a wall at all but a yellow cargo container emblazoned with the logo of the Maersk shipping line.

'Anne, flat on the deck! Stay down.'

A staccato chain of blasts cut him off. Louder ones answered back and a dozen more of the muffled shots replied. Then it was silent. To the north she saw the helicopter searchlight prowling the dark waters on the starboard side of the ship. Again and again, a large-caliber machine gun unloaded on men in the water. One of their speedboats exploded, the fireball blooming against the black sky.

Facedown, she wormed to the edge of the yellow container and peered toward the spot where she'd last heard Daniel's voice.

Two men in camouflage pants and black T-shirts were standing over Daniel's body. They gripped silenced weapons. The taller of the two men said something to the other and the man unloaded his weapon at Daniel's body. She thought she saw Daniel twist aside in time to avoid the gunfire; then both men scrambled out of view.

A wail broke from Anne's throat, but before she could rise to fire, she was staring at a pair of black boots not more than a yard from her nose.

'Fuckin' move and you're dead.' His growl was all New York, the nasal bray of a street punk. 'Shove it out slow, that fucking gun. You hear me, cunt? Twitch and you're dead.'

A year before, she would have obeyed instantly, raising her hands in relief that this long and terrifying dream was done. But that was before Daniel. Before he led her to the edge of the precipice, took her hand in his, and looked past the surface of her eyes into regions of her self she had barely sensed were there and the two of them leaped over the brink, dropping and dropping in one long ecstatic rush, only to land in the black heart of this moment.

Anne Bonny Joy nudged the Mac-10 forward along the deck, inch by inch until it was fully exposed; then without a flicker of hesitation she slid her hand down the stock and squeezed off a half-dozen rounds at the toes of the black boots and watched them jerk and dance for a half-second; then she spun to the right, came to her feet and sprinted to the rail, and dived into the bottomless dark.

In the choppy sea she stripped a life jacket from one of the Nicaraguans. She ducked away from the spotlights, stroking slowly and steadily beyond the perimeter of their search zone. Through the night, she paddled and drifted in a swoon of dehydration, rage, and despair. She was carried by the current mile after mile northward until an hour after sunrise she was spotted by a Panamanian fishing boat and plucked from the sea.

They put her ashore on a beach at Puerto Cabezas, Nicaragua, and she used some of the American dollars she was carrying to work her way south by bus down the Mosquito Coast. Campesinos on the bus turned to stare at her. As Anne slumped in her seat, an old woman nudged her shoulder, checking for life. At Punta Castillo Anne chartered a skiff to the Barra de Colorado. In a deadened haze, she left the boat behind and trekked through fifteen miles of rain forest and made it to the lodge late in the afternoon four full days after the disaster on the *Rainmaker*.

Taking cover in a gully on the outskirts of the camp, she spent an hour listening to the shrieks of parrots and howler monkeys. She sniffed the air but detected neither foreign aromas nor the charred ruin of the camp. Until dusk she waited; then finally she rose and entered the camp.

In the gathering darkness she inched along the shadowy edges of the buildings, a pocketknife her only weapon. The sour stench of the staff latrine, a can of garbage overturned and raided by jungle creatures. The cigarette reek of the bunkhouse where the Sandinistas slept, and at every step there were the vaporous echoes of voices.

She slipped into the main cabin that she and Daniel had shared the last weeks. Their bed was neatly made. She stared at his comb lying on the dresser and her brush, which lay beside it. She wiped her eyes clear and stepped over to the bathroom mirror and took it down from its hook. She calmed the jitter in her fingers and dialed the numbers and swung open the steel door. For a moment in the gloom she thought all was well, then she reached out and ran her hands across the

89

bare shelves and a low groan rose from her chest. Someone had beaten her back to the camp and looted the reserves.

The journey back to Florida took two weeks. Riding Greyhounds through the long nights, exiting at dawn, eyes down, speaking to no one. Staying in cheap motels along the coast, Texas, Louisiana, and Florida. Blinds shut tight against the daylight, drinking herself to oblivion while she spent the impossibly long days staring at the pitted walls and the blank screens of televisions. Paranoid, grieving, so twitchy she couldn't sleep. Not even in those desperate weeks after her parents' deaths had she felt so hopeless.

Somewhere east of Pensacola she woke from a drowse, jerked upright in her bus seat, and startled the teenage kid in a cowboy hat beside her.

'You okay, ma'am?' The kid had taken his Stetson off and set it in his lap. 'Bad dream?'

Anne looked at the boy for a moment, then turned her eyes to her window, at the palm trees and scrub brush flashing past.

'I wish it were,' she said. 'I wish to hell it were.'

5

Oh, come on, Thorn. Even a guy like you could find a use for two million bucks.'

'Not really, Marty.'

Marty Messina shook his head and groaned. He was a big man with a blocky head and coarse black hair that he wore in a military flattop. An inch of hair across the front was greased into a small curl like a perfect wave rolling off the black ocean of his skull. He was several inches above six feet. In the years since Thorn had seen him last, Marty had chunked up, and now dangerous muscles flared in his shoulders and arms. His neck was so thick, he probably had to custom-order his flowered shirts. He wore white high-top tennis shoes with a complicated lacing system, and skintight blue jeans and a black rayon shirt printed with yellow hibiscus blooms. The shirt was opened to the sternum, showing off a pad of black hair that rose to his throat. Five, six years ago when he'd been sent away to prison, Marty had been fond of heavy gold jewelry, but they must've had a fashion class up there, because now he wore only a single diamond stud pinned to the top of his right ear.

Marty shook his head and made a show of sighing and marching over to the wood stairway of Thorn's stilt house and planting his butt on the fourth step with such resolve, it appeared he meant to stay as long as it took for Thorn to cave in.

Resetting his grip on the pine slat, Thorn pressed it against the sawhorse, then drew the handsaw back and forth through the last inch of softwood. When the excess piece dropped in the grass, he smoothed away a couple of brittle ends on the slat and stepped over to the shade of a tamarind tree and set it on the bench that was three-quarters complete. He brushed the sawdust from his hands and wrists and looked out at Lawton Collins, who was napping in a hammock strung between two coconut palms a few yards from the rocky shore of Blackwater Sound.

It was about four o'clock on that May afternoon, and Blackwater Sound shivered with sharp blue light. A brown pelican coasted a few feet above the still water, carried along by a warm draft from the west. An Everglades breeze full of mold spores and mosquitoes and the first ozone whiffs of a spring thunderstorm. It had been a brutally dry year. During the winter only a couple of cold fronts had plowed all the way down the state, and those brought no rain. And so far, the summer monsoon season still hadn't kicked in.

His grass was charred and crispy underfoot, but the bougainvillea seemed ecstatic about the drought, and their great clouds of purple and pink and white cascaded over trees and lesser shrubs all around the perimeter of his five acres. The wild lantana and the penta were doing fine as well. For generations those indigenous plants had thrived in the inch of sandy soil dusting the limestone rubble that passed for land in the Florida Keys. Regularly flooded by the salty sea or scraped back to nubs by hurricanes, those native plants seemed to bloom with even greater flourish after each new trial.

The year of relentless heat had been nearly ruinous for Thorn's fly-tying business. Out on the flats the bonefish and reds were lethargic in the overheated water. A warmer-than-average winter in the Northeast and a series of airline crashes had cut the tourist flow by half, so the fishing guides who worked the flats hadn't snapped up Thorn's custom flies in the numbers they had in the years before. And though Thorn had almost exhausted his savings and was starting to make uneasy calculations whenever he looked into the pantry, he wasn't about to confess any of that to Marty Messina.

Back when Marty Messina had been a bush-league

dope peddler around the upper Keys, word was Marty was connected to a Miami crime family. Whether it was true or not Thorn didn't know, but the guy certainly had acted the part. As a sideline, he'd laundered some of his profits through Tarpon's, a waterfront restaurant he operated in nearby Rock Harbor. Probably through dumb luck, Marty signed on a young chef who'd discovered some creative uses for cinnamon and bananas and exotic Caribbean fruits in his fish dishes. Nobody had ever cooked that way in Key Largo before, and the restaurant became a trendy hit with locals. Even Thorn had gone there once or twice for special occasions.

Marty kept the prices low, routinely buying rounds of drinks for the whole bar to celebrate his great good fortune. But then a trawler Marty was piloting was boarded by the DEA just off Islamorada. Nearly a ton of Mexican grass was aboard at the time. Within a few weeks Marty was sent away to perfect his croquet skills in a minimum-security prison somewhere in north Florida, a place that housed corrupt politicos, white-collar embezzlers, and other well-lawyered crooks. In his absence, the restaurant changed hands, the chef moved on, and finally the place became just another tourist joint, pumping out fish sandwiches and limp fries.

A couple of weeks ago Marty Messina had materialized again in Key Largo. Thorn had heard from one of his fishing guide buddies that Messina had been planting his butt on a stool at the bar of his old restaurant, running the place down to anyone who'd listen. Reminding everyone what a cutting-edge hot spot it had once been.

'So you a Realtor now, Marty? Get your license in prison?'

'Fuck you, Thorn.'

'Seems reasonable,' Thorn said. 'Real estate's the logical next career choice after apprenticing in crime.'

'Hey, Thorn, come on, man, I don't have all fucking day. Just say yes, and I'll go back and draw up the papers and get your money bundled up.'

Marty gave him a cheerless grin.

'My buyer will pay all cash,' he said. 'Two and a half mil.'

'A minute ago you said two.'

'I'm negotiating.'

'Oh, is that how it's done?'

'Okay, three,' Marty said. 'Three million dollars, Thorn.'

Marty stood up and lumbered back over to the sawhorse.

'You're negotiating in a vacuum. I'm not selling.'

'Yeah, that's what I told him. You were a first-class knucklehead.'

Thorn glanced up, but Marty was looking out at the glassy bay.

'Tell him to drop by. I'll refuse him to his face.'

'This guy doesn't drop by, Thorn. He pays people to drop by.'

Marty turned and looked Thorn in the eyes and

a smile spread slowly across his face as if he'd surprised himself with his own ominous wit.

'What's his name, Marty? The guy who wants this place so bad.'

'Look, Thorn. If you fuck with me, you fuck with him. And believe me, buddy, you don't want to fuck with him.'

'Oh, really?'

'Yeah, really.'

Marty's dark eyes held to Thorn's and he clamped his lips together as if to keep from blurting out the name. The buyer could've been any of a hundred of Marty's old associates, dope runners of an earlier era who'd stashed away enough to buy their way into legit businesses around the Keys. Thorn had nothing against their kind. He'd smoked his share of funny stuff back in his younger days before grass got all inbred and so full of hallucinogenic juice that one toke would give you the munchies for a month. He knew a ton of plumbers and electricians and roofers around the island who'd bought their first tools and panel trucks with the proceeds of one successful dope run. Most of them were upstanding citizens now. Churchgoers with a mortgage, kids in high school, a small fishing boat they took out week-end yellowtailing. But there were other guys he'd run into back in the good old dope days who'd gaffed and gutted one too many of their competitors, waded a little too deep into the dark sea of deadened senses. They were still around the island, but you didn't see them out and about. They sent their lackeys, guys like Marty Messina, to do their bidding.

'Okay,' Thorn said. 'So what exactly does he want to do with my land?'

'Improve it,' Marty said.

'Ah, yes.' Thorn lined up another slat of pine on the sawhorse and drew out the aluminum tape. 'This land's long overdue for improving.'

'Don't get funny with me, Thorn. I'm running low on patience.'

'Hey, Marty. I have a tip. Tell your guy to swoop in and buy the tract where the Island House motel used to be. Back in March somebody knocked all the trees down, scraped the land bare, then left it sitting there. Guy must've run out of money. That'd be a nice spot to improve.'

'He wants *this* land,' Marty said.

'You hit town one week, you're out throwing around millions of dollars the next. How do I know you're even legit? You know what I'm saying?'

'This is for real, Thorn. A bona fide offer. Far as just getting into town, yeah, that's true. But some people around here remember me, respect my abilities. I got excellent credentials.'

'A stretch in jail being near the top of the list.'

'I been out for a while, jerkhole. I been into some other things; now I'm into this. Not that it's any of your fucking business.'

'You're standing here trying to buy my land. That sort of makes it my business, doesn't it?'

Thorn took the pencil from behind his ear and marked the slat, then set the blade of the saw against the mark, drew it back an inch to score the spot. But before he could begin to saw, Marty stepped close to the horse, blocking his stroke.

'Look, Thorn. You got a piece-of-shit car; it's rusting through. Same fucking car you had before I went off to the joint.'

Thorn looked up at Marty. He held the saw in place.

'You got this falling-down house, one good storm comes along, a puff of wind, trust me, Thorn, that shack's gonna wash right into the bay.'

Marty made his eyes go droopy like he was bored with this, bored trying to reason with a knucklehead, but still trying real hard to be decent.

'Three million, you could buy any car you want. Buy ten cars. A house on the water anyplace in Florida. Put the rest in mutual funds, live off the interest. See what it feels like to be an adult for once in your life.'

Thorn looked over at Lawton stretching his arms, yawning, then rearranging himself in the hammock and easing back for the rest of his nap. Lately the old man had taken to dressing in Thorn's clothes. Today he was wearing a baggy white T-shirt and khaki fishing shorts with flap pockets in the front, the exact same outfit Thorn had on. The official uniform for Camp Thorn.

'I've already got a house on the water, Marty. I

have the piece-of-shit car I want. So why don't you go on back to Mr Hotshot's office and tell him to find another plantation to sack and plunder.'

Marty peered into Thorn's eyes for several seconds, then shook his head sadly as if about to deliver a fatal diagnosis.

'I told my guy how you were. But he said to come anyway, 'cause he believed I could talk you into selling. Man has that kind of confidence in me. Now I got to go back and tell him you blew me off. You're going to make me look bad, Thorn. I don't like looking bad.'

Thorn held the saw steady against the notch.

'Seems like you'd be used to it by now, Marty.'

Overhead a warm breeze crackled through the brittle fronds. Marty's eyes grew even droopier. He'd heard it all. Been there, pissed on that. He was too jaded to get riled by some amateur smart-ass. But all the same, Thorn could see the flush inching up his neck like the mercury on an August afternoon.

Marty held his stare, then shifted his gaze to the saw in Thorn's hand. His dark eyes going flat.

'You're a crazy motherfucker, aren't you, Thorn?'

'So I've been told.'

'I believe you'd use that, wouldn't you? That saw. Take a swipe at me, try to saw my fucking head off if you could.'

'You could stick around about two more minutes and find out.'

Thorn gave him an innocent smile.

99

'Assholes like you, Thorn, they're a dime a dozen in the joint. Thing is, they don't last long with that hard-ass attitude. Sooner or later they smart off one too many times and wind up getting their fucking tongue cut out and handed to them on a clean white plate.'

Thorn looked down at the wood slat and nudged the saw back and forth across it, the blade missing Marty's leg by half an inch. He spoke without looking up.

'You might want to go home, Marty, stand in front of the mirror, work some more on that sales technique. 'Cause it's not working worth a damn.'

Marty took a few steps toward his car, then stopped and swung around.

'He's coming after you, Thorn. This guy doesn't take no for an answer. He's going to have this land one way or the other. That's just fair warning.'

'Bring him on,' Thorn said. 'Bring the fucker on.'

Just inside the front door of Tarpon's, Marty snagged the portable phone off the podium and headed into the bar to use it. Tying up their only line right at early bird time. The old lady hostess came over and tapped on his shoulder and held out her hand, but Marty turned his back to her until she went away. What he needed was a damn cell phone, but he hadn't put away enough cash yet.

He checked in with his boss, broke the bad news

about Thorn, and his boss was pissed at the pigheaded asshole, but he wasn't surprised.

Marty's boss thought about it for a minute, humming to himself the whole time like he might be shaving or some damn thing; then he came back on and told Marty he could redeem himself by doing another job for him, one he could probably manage on the telephone. Marty got the details and hung up and about then the hostess came back, tapped on his shoulder again, but Marty ignored her and dialed the next number, hoping he'd catch the guy before he knocked off for the day, then had to wait another five minutes while the secretary who answered carried the phone outside to the guy on his forklift.

Marty didn't even have to bully the forklift guy. Just used his boss's name and offered him a foreman's job at another marina, double what he was making, and the guy said hell, yes, he'd do fucking backflips for that kind of money. And after two more minutes on hold, listening to the background music at Morada Bay Marina, with the Tarpon's hostess coming and going, pecking him on the shoulder to get the phone back, the forklift guy came back and said he had it. Five pages, the complete May calendar, the float plans for every boat in the marina. Marty gave him his boss's fax number and the guy said he'd send it right over.

'Fine,' Marty said. 'Come by on Monday morning, Paradise Boatyard, there'll be a job with your name on it.'

'Hey, thanks,' the guy said.

Marty said, 'Go fax the thing. And don't go telling anybody what the fuck you're doing, either, or your ass is chum.'

Two minutes later he called his boss again and the guy right away said, 'Finally you did something right, Marty, I was beginning to wonder.'

'You see anything there you can use?' Marty ignored the put-down. He'd had enough of those for one day from Thorn.

'Thursday night coming up. It's perfect. Two birds, one stone. Thorn's ass is mine.'

'The guy's a hardhead. I don't know.'

'I know all about this guy, Marty. I been making a little study of the asshole. And what I've decided, once I take this guy's land, I'm going to cut off his balls and pickle them.'

'I want to see that.'

His boss said, 'The guy's got a friend, Sugarman.'

'Yeah,' Marty said. 'Used to be a cop, now he's some kind of half-assed private eye.'

'Way I hear it, these two guys are joined at the hip. Tickle Sugarman's nose, Thorn sneezes.'

'That's about right.'

'Well, I got a way to tickle the ever-loving shit out of Sugarman's nose.'

'So Thorn sneezes.'

'That's right, Marty. So Thorn sneezes his fucking brains out.'

A minute later when they were done Marty hung

up and took the phone back over to the podium and set it down.

'I believe this is yours.'

The old lady hostess blasted him with a glare, then turned and smiled at her next party and led them to their table.

6

By late afternoon Thorn was almost finished with the bench. Out in the western sky a few wispy cirrus clouds sprang from the horizon like the fine sprigs of hair curling off the neck of an elegant woman. The sun was brassy red and poised only minutes from another fiery crash into the Gulf. Already the western clouds were rimmed with gold and a gloss of crimson spread across the bay as if somewhere deep below the water's surface the Earth had opened a vein.

While he rested his eyes on the showy sky, out of the dense woods that bordered his land a yellow Labrador puppy stumbled into the open lawn and halted beside the trunk of a giant sea grape tree. A mockingbird in the sea grape shrieked at the pup, then fluttered down and dive-bombed his head, but the Lab seemed oblivious.

After scanning the yard, the puppy spotted Lawton sleeping with one leg looped over the edge of the hammock. He ambled over and stopped below Lawton's bare foot, cocked his head up, eyed the pale flesh, then washed his tongue across the old man's sole. With a whoop, Lawton jerked awake.

Thorn smiled and picked up the handsaw and finished cutting the final slat of pine. While Lawton spoke to the puppy, Thorn carried the slat over to the bench and lined it up. When he was satisfied it was parallel, he screwed it into place and ran his eye along each of the slats to check its spacing. Then he turned and settled his rump on it and leaned back. Solid and secure. Maybe not the most comfortable bench, but good enough for what he had in mind.

Across the yard, Lawton rolled out of the hammock and tumbled into the tall grass and giggled like a child. The puppy staggered out of his way, then charged in to lap at the white grizzle on Lawton's cheeks.

Thorn called over to see if Lawton was okay, and the old man gave a just-fine wave while the dog snuffled in close.

Thorn brushed some sawdust off the bench, then walked over for a better view of the wrestling match. He squatted in the grass as the puppy drew out of Lawton's grasp, shook himself hard, then marched over to one of the old man's leather sandals that lay in the grass. He plopped down and began to gnaw on his tail. His fur was matted and there were dark greasy streaks across his golden back. His ribs were showing through his scruffy coat.

'Kind of mangy,' said Thorn. 'Looks like he's been sleeping in a tar pit.'

'He's a survivor,' Lawton said. 'Been living off the fat of the land.'

'And how do you know that?'

'He just told me.'

Lawton wriggled his finger in a patch of grass and the dog paused midmunch and peered at this new quarry. Lawton wagged his finger again and the puppy dropped his tail, rose to a crouch, lowered his head an inch, focusing like a well-schooled bird dog. Lawton wiggled his finger again and the puppy leaped a few inches in the air and pounced on Lawton's hand.

The old man laughed, turning his gray eyes on Thorn.

'Goddamn it, I want this dog, and I'm going to have it, so don't fuck with me, mister.'

Thorn drew a breath. In the last few months Lawton's condition had suffered a series of small and quirky downturns. For one thing, there were these new flashes of irritability. Curses flared to the old man's lips without warning or cause.

'This puppy and me,' Lawton said, 'we've bonded. It'd be a goddamn criminal travesty to separate us.'

'We'll talk to Alex when she gets home. See what she says.'

'I don't give a shit what she says. If I want a dog, by God, I'll have a dog. I'm too goddamn old to take orders anymore.'

The puppy fastened his teeth onto the tip of Lawton's finger. But as Lawton stroked the Lab's throat, the spiky puppy's eyes closed and with a quiet groan he began to nurse on the old man's crinkled fingertip.

'I need a dog, goddamn it,' Lawton said. 'I need somebody to talk to.'

'You can talk to me,' said Thorn. 'Anytime you want.'

'You know what I mean,' Lawton said. 'Somebody on my own level.'

Thorn smiled.

'How old am I anyway?' Lawton said.

'Not all that old.'

'Am I still a boy?'

Thorn shook his head.

'Older than a boy.'

'Well, damn it, I feel like a boy,' Lawton said. 'I feel twelve. That's all right, isn't it? Feeling twelve? I mean, it's not sick, is it, feeling that way?'

'I'd say that's fine. Twelve is a damn good age.'

'Well, good, then I'm a boy,' Lawton said. 'And every boy needs a goddamn dog. So this one's mine.'

As Lawton stroked the pup, Thorn leaned back, propped his elbows in the brittle grass. The sky had gone pink with honeyed whisks and spatters of color as bright and unnameable as the garish shades of reef fish. A school of cherry clouds cruised in formation a hundred miles aloft, and the entire bay had turned the hazy pink of brick dust.

As the final glint of sun disappeared, he heard the foghorn blare of a conch shell blown from a neighbor's rooftop. A venerable Keys tradition still hanging on, a long single-noted salute to the dying day performed with the shell of the nearly extinct gastropod. The queen conch, official symbol of the Florida Keys, had almost vanished from her waters. Too many roadside stands, too many tourists looking for a cheap memento of their week in paradise, too many conch fritters and bowls of conch chowder. These days the roadside stands had to air-freight their conch shells from distant oceans where the locals still believed they were the keepers of a limitless supply.

While Lawton tussled with the puppy, Thorn got back up and went over to the shade of the gumbo-limbo. He opened a can of yellow paint, stirred it till it was oily thick, then began to spread it on the new bench.

As the first coat of paint dried, Thorn lit the charcoal in the grill and went back upstairs to marinate the fillet of a dolphin that he and Lawton had caught the day before out on the edge of the Gulf Stream. He set a pan of brown rice to boil on the stove and sliced up a fresh avocado, a portobello mushroom, and a meaty tomato, fresh produce Alexandra had selected last weekend at the farmer's stall in the Key Largo flea market.

Thorn drew the cork on a bottle of wine she'd brought down from Miami and poured himself an inch in a squat highball glass. It was her favorite wine, a lush cabernet from Oregon. They'd been indulging themselves these last few months. Good wines, fresh fish, chocolates for dessert. A diet far richer than either of them was used to. He supposed it was the flush of love that gave them such indulgent appetites, as if their senses had become so inflamed from the constant sight and touch and smell of each other's flesh that only the most luscious foods could compete.

When he was finished with the preparations he walked onto the porch. The sky was a dreary gray. Only a seam of red still burned along the horizon. Lawton was out by the dock, trying to teach the dog to sit. The puppy had no attention span and barked in protest each time Lawton set his rump back down in the grass and commanded him to stay put.

As Thorn was settling the mahimahi steaks and portobello onto the grill, Alex pulled in the gravel drive and parked her glossy blue Honda behind his rusty VW. Thorn pushed the steaks to the edge away from the fire. He walked over and met her at the car.

'He's got a dog,' Thorn said.

Alexandra looked past him into the yard. 'I see that.'

'It just came wandering out of the woods and he adopted it.'

'And you said he could keep it?'

'I said we'd wait till you got home and talk about it then.'

'So I get to be the bad guy.'

'I'll do it. If that's what you decide.'

Thorn leaned in and gave her a kiss on the lips, which after a couple of seconds warmed to something more than a hello.

The tart scent of her long day's work in Miami clung to her clothes and flesh. She averaged a half-dozen crime scenes on a typical shift, shooting several rolls of film on each one, using her video camera on the larger scenes. From what Thorn gathered, it was hardly glamorous, rarely more than routine. Women beaten to death by boyfriends, teenage boys shot down in their first drug deal, geriatric suicides, babies fatally shaken by mothers trying to keep the little brats quiet. Mainly Alexandra moved through small dismal rooms with peeling paint and furniture abandoned by long-departed occupants, one sprawling body after another, usually discarded hypodermics, baggies of crack somewhere nearby. In the years she'd been doing it, Alexandra had cataloged so much death and misery, made such a study of cruelty's stark poses, it was a wonder the heavy shadows of her work didn't mute her laughter or dim her nearly ceaseless smile.

Finally she drew out of the embrace and pressed a

hand to his chest to hold him at bay, a not-now-but-definitely-later smile in her eyes.

'So about this dog.'

'Well, I tried to stay neutral because I thought it was your call.'

'Because he's my dad.'

'I didn't think it was my place to decide.'

'Meanwhile, look at him.'

Lawton was lying in the grass near the dock, flat on his back, hands laced behind his head, with the Lab's snout propped on Lawton's chest.

'A dog is a long-term commitment,' she said. 'You ready for that?'

She turned her head slowly and fixed her eyes on Thorn's.

'Never been readier.'

A ghost of skepticism hovered just below the surface of her smile.

'So it just came walking out of the woods?'

'*Poof*, like that.'

She lifted her hands and raked her fingers through her thick black hair as if unsnarling the thousand invisible knots from her long day. He heard what sounded like a quiet groan of pleasure escape from her throat. Then she tipped her head back and shook her hair so it rustled along the back of her white sleeveless blouse. Thorn looked at her neck, at her delicate ears, at the dusting of dark hair that formed her sideburns.

'A boy and his dog,' she said. 'Oh, hell, why not?'

She put an arm around his waist and they walked down to the shoreline.

'I've named him,' Lawton said. 'I've named the dog.'

'Hello, Dad,' she said.

'I'm calling him Lawton.'

'But that's your name.'

The dog was staring up at Lawton as if waiting for the next command.

'I know it's my name. What do you think, I'm so far gone I don't know my own name?'

'You think that's a good idea?' Thorn said. 'Two Lawtons, that might be one too many.'

'Why not? It's a good name,' Lawton said. 'It's served me well.'

'We might get you two confused. Lawton the dog, Lawton the dad.'

'Get us confused? Now who's losing their mind? I'm a man, this is a dog. How're you going to get us confused?'

'He's got a point,' Thorn said.

She looked at him and closed her eyes briefly.

'Okay, okay,' she said. 'But you're going to have to take care of him, Dad. That's a big job. Are you ready for that? Bathing him, taking him to the vet. He'll need shots.'

'Watch,' he said. 'I've taught him to sit already. He's a smart little fur ball.'

With an open hand Lawton motioned the dog down, and the puppy jumped up and tried to nip his fingers.

'Down, Lawton. Sit.'

With a single bark of complaint, the puppy planted his rear on a sandy patch and stared up at Lawton, his tail brushing back and forth across the bare earth.

'See,' the old man said. 'He's a fast learner.'

'That's good, Dad. And you're obviously a good teacher.'

'He'd better be fast,' Lawton said. 'Because I don't have much time left to teach him much.'

'Oh, come on. Don't say that.'

'Where'd that guy Webster go? He offered me a job working undercover. I need to talk to him about when I'm going to start.'

'That was months ago, Dad. That was March; this is May. He went away and he's not coming back.'

'Went away?'

'Anyway, you've got this dog. You don't need any more jobs.'

'But Webster was counting on me. It was a national emergency. I could be putting us all in peril. This woman Anne Joy is at the root of it.'

'Anne Joy?'

Alexandra stooped down beside the dog and scratched him beneath the throat. The puppy grew limp at her touch.

'Her name came up,' Thorn said.

'First I've heard of that.'

'Webster mentioned her. That's when I shut him up and kicked him out.'

'Oh, yeah, I feel it coming,' Lawton said. 'The end

is definitely near. It won't be long. This dog is going to have to be my legacy.'

'Dad,' Alex said. 'Please stop.'

'It doesn't matter,' Lawton said. 'I'm ready. Now that you're finally in good hands and there's someone to carry on my name, it's time for me to exit.'

Alexandra stood up, her mouth clamped tight.

'It's okay,' Thorn said. 'It's just words.'

'I know. I know. But still.'

'You ready for a glass of red?'

'Thorn, what did Webster want with Anne Joy?'

'He thought I knew something about her. I assured him I didn't.'

'You should've told me that.'

'I know,' he said. 'But I didn't want you to get the wrong idea.'

'The kind I have right now, you mean.'

'Yeah, that kind.'

'We shouldn't conceal things.'

'I'm sorry. You're right. Really, I'm sorry.'

She looked into his eyes, and he could see her letting it go. Most of it.

'So I had another visitor,' he said as they strolled back toward the house.

'What, they sent the vice president this time?'

'When'd you get so funny?'

She stopped next to the bench.

'And what in the world is this?'

'A bench. A yellow bench.'

'What is it, Thorn?'

'I was thinking Lawton might like it. You know, for his midnight rambles. Might keep him off the highway if we can convince him the Greyhound stops here.'

She stared at the bench, then looked up at Thorn, a smile warming her lips.

'Worth a try,' he said. 'I was thinking of putting it over there, next to the gumbo-limbo. Kind of like the bus shelter.'

'You're something, Thorn.'

'Well, I'm not much of a furniture maker, that's for sure.'

She leaned in and gave him a kiss on the mouth so deep and long, it closed his eyes and kept them closed a second or two after she'd drawn away.

'So who was your visitor this time?'

He took her hand in his and waved his free hand at the open yard and the darkening bay.

'Would you trade all this for three million dollars?'

'All this?'

'The house, the land, my car. All of it.'

'Three million for that heap of rust you call a car?'

'I'm serious. The house, land, all of it. Would you?'

She held his eyes.

'It's not mine to sell.'

'But let's say it were. You could take the three mil, go someplace else, invest some of the money in mutual funds, live off the interest. Never have to work again, do whatever you wanted.'

'Mutual funds?' She reached out and pressed her palm against his forehead. 'You been outside all day without a hat?'

'Answer the question,' he said, startled by the impatience in his own voice.

She took her hand from his forehead. Her smile drifted away.

'Would I swap all this for a truckload of cash?' she said. 'Not in a million years, Thorn. Not in three million.'

Thorn let go of the air that had been building in his lungs.

'Yeah, that's what I thought.'

'Was that some kind of test, Thorn?'

'What do you mean?'

'Because I thought we were a little past the testing phase.'

'We are,' he said. 'It's just that sometimes, your job, all the shit you put up with every day, I wonder if you wouldn't be happier retired.'

'You'd sell all this so I could retire?'

'It'd be nice to have you around.'

'And what? Hang out all day, weave palm frond hats and carve faces into dried coconuts?'

She watched Lawton tickling the pup's nose with a blade of grass.

'Man,' he said. 'You play rough.'

She shifted her gaze from her father and settled it on him. The wistful fog that seemed to fill her eyes whenever she looked at Lawton burned away in an instant and they were clear again. A cautious smile rose in slow stages to her wide mouth.

'I'm a city girl, Thorn. The stink of baking asphalt, screech of tires, sirens wailing. I've got to have my daily dose. It's who I am. Even taking the photos of the victims, working the crime scenes. It keeps me sharp, alert. At the end of the workday I love coming back down here. This is a glorious place. It makes me want to sip tequila, take off my clothes, and crawl in bed beside you. But I need the other, Thorn. I just do.'

'I know.'

'Yeah,' she said. 'I know you know. You just forget sometimes.'

She kissed him on the edge of his mouth, then stepped away. Her smile full of naked light.

'Okay,' he said. 'So let's get the wine and I'll tell you all about Marty Messina. You'll enjoy this.'

7

Thursday morning, May second, when Anne stepped out of the taxi, her landlady was stooped over her white gravel yard pulling weeds. Anne's rusty Corolla was still parked where she'd left it when she ran off to play pirate. Her efficiency apartment was downstairs below the widow lady's concrete stilt house on the edge of a canal in Stillwright Point. Room for a single bed, a tiny stove, and a couple of bonsai plants. The fridge was so small, a six-pack of Bud Lite and a stalk of celery strained it.

'It's rented.' The landlady had bright white hair and a leathery tan. She approached Anne, gripping a three-pronged tool for prying up weeds. 'A nice young man with the Park Service is in there now.'

'You rented my apartment,' Anne said.

'You disappeared; I didn't hear from you.'

'And my stuff?'

'Salvation Army,' the woman said.

'I'm surprised you didn't tow my car.'

The woman came a step closer to Anne.

'Your brother came by.'

'What?'

'Vic Joy stopped by last week. He said he was your brother. That true?'

'And what did he want?'

'He said when you showed up again for me to tell you to come see him.'

'He did, did he?'

The landlady's calico cat sat primly in the gravel nearby and watched.

'He said it's about your boyfriend, what happened to him out on the boat. He said you'd understand.'

Vic Joy worked out of the Paradise Funeral Home in north Key Largo.

Anne had tried, but you couldn't work in a Keys restaurant, a bar, a hotel, without hearing about Vic Joy once or twice a week. His latest conquest, his most recent outrageous offense. Another resort or marina on his ledger, another casino boat added to his fleet, his latest run-in with county officials over illegal dredging or flushing one of his casino boat's bilges in a local waterway, all that crankcase oil, all those tourist turds, floating in the canals behind million-dollar homes, courtesy of Vic Joy. His people had been caught a dozen times bulldozing acres of protected mangroves, engaged in bribery and shake-downs to cover their tracks. Vic never bothered with the rules. His policy was simple. If an endangered tree is buzz-sawed in the forest and no one's around to hear it fall, did it ever happen? On the other hand, if somebody made a fuss, that's what lawyers were for. And Vic had an army of Miami's sleaziest for that.

Anne Bonny had passed the Paradise Funeral Home a hundred times on her way up and down the islands, but she never allowed herself to look. Eyes straight ahead until she was well past. But today she roared into the gravel lot and slid to a stop next to a white Cadillac. A half-dozen Harley-Davidsons slouched around the parking lots, their potbellied riders in full dress black clustered in the shade of a poinciana tree drinking long-neck Buds.

The funeral home was a low, sprawling stucco building with a life-size angel perched on the roof. A view of Tarpon Basin out the mortuary windows.

As she marched to the door, a couple of the rough-necks leered her way, but when she stopped and looked back at them, they got busy with their beers.

Behind the reception desk was a woman in her seventies, frail, with a mass of white curls as deli-cate as ice shavings.

'He's in a meeting. Without an appointment, there's nothing I can do.'

Organ music seeped from the sanctuary, someone

practicing 'Sympathy for the Devil.' Starting over, mangling the first few chords, starting again.

'Buzz him,' Anne said. 'Tell him it's his long-lost sister.'

The old woman drew a quick breath, then, with her eyes still fixed on Anne, fumbled with the phone, mashed in a number, and whispered into the receiver, and a second later she set it down.

'I didn't realize,' she said, and motioned down the gloomy hallway. 'Mr Joy has been expecting you.'

When Anne opened the door, Vic stood up from behind his desk and came around to greet her, his arms sweeping open for an embrace. She backed off, held up her hand, and he halted, but his grin didn't fade a fraction.

He wore a plain white T-shirt and gray jeans and boat shoes. His shoulder-length hair had turned silver since she'd seen him last. Ten years, fifteen? She wasn't sure and hadn't bothered to add it up. His arms were sinewy and blued with ancient tattoos. He was still slim, shoulders unstooped, just an inch over six feet. His flesh was sallow, a shade lighter than the creamy yellow of calfskin. Even after decades in the tropical sun it was all the tan he could muster. Vic had their father's pallid bloodline, descended from a long string of Kentucky hillbillies who'd spent their years in lightless pits hacking out lumps of anthracite.

The knotty pine walls of Vic's office were decorated with plaques and photographs. She glanced around at the history of Vic's civic bullshit. All the commissioners and sheriffs who'd succumbed to his charm or pocketed his payoffs.

'Annie, Annie. After all this time you're not going to give me a hug?'

Before she could answer, she caught a flash behind the open door.

'Oh, yeah,' Vic said, waving in that direction. 'I believe you already know Marty Messina.'

Anne slashed a look at Marty.

'What the hell?'

'Marty's working for me now. My new right-hand man.'

'You bastard. How'd you get away?'

'Went overboard, like you. I'm a good swimmer.'

'Bullshit.' Anne stepped toward Vic's desk. 'Now it all makes sense.'

'Cool down, honey,' Vic said. 'Marty's cool.'

'Marty's a goddamn informant. He's feeding the feds. He brought down Daniel, now he's going after you.'

'That's funny,' Vic said. 'Marty said the same thing about you.'

'It was him,' Anne said. 'He was the only one made it out alive.'

'Except for you,' Marty said.

'Okay, kiddies,' Vic said. 'So nobody trusts each other. Fine, so now we're all on equal footing.'

A second later there was a gold letter opener in Anne's right hand. It must've been on Vic's desk, must have already caught her attention before Marty Messina rose from his chair behind the door, wearing a cocky grin, his mouth opening, about to say something cute, then his face changed as Anne snatched the dagger, whirled, and Marty's hand came up, a big paw, hairy arms, and his fingers knotted to her wrist.

The letter opener was poised an inch from his throat, where the dark curly hair stopped in a precise line just below his Adam's apple. She'd seen him at the Gray Ghost Lodge, meticulously hacking away the pelt that otherwise would've overgrown his entire body in a day or two, drowned him in hair.

The point trembled closer to his white flesh. She was out-of-body, feeling no rage, no exertion, watching from beyond the ceiling as the dagger altered course, turning back toward her, taking aim at her own throat.

Marty's breath blew in her face, chili peppers, onions, a peppermint mouthwash that had curdled to some putrid gas. Her hand had numbed from his grip on her wrist, her arm bending backward against the joint, then Vic was there shouting, prying them apart, but Anne Bonny was lost in the rush of blood and she drove a knee into the big man's groin, felt his hold loosen, and in that half-second she tore free and plunged the narrow blade into the meat of Marty's chest, a slab of muscle over his heart, jammed it hard against all that gristle.

Marty howled and fell away, and Vic got some

leverage on Anne's arm and slung her at the opposite wall. She lost her footing, spun once, thumped
headfirst, and saw a dazzling splash of water, then
felt her body go limp, her back press flat against the
wall, then slide down. At the office door, the old
woman with the fragile white hair covered her
mouth while Anne sank below the surface of a warm
ocean, drifting down into a breathless dark.

'You got him in the armpit, honey,' Vic said when
Anne opened her eyes.

She was propped up in a leather chair across from
his desk. In the far corner, Marty Messina sprawled
in another chair. Shirtless, with a yard of gauze
wrapped around his left shoulder, a blotch of blood
spreading. Organ music vibrated the photos, their
frames clicking against the wall. The voices of the
mourners were out-of-key and trailing several notes
behind the organist.

'Another inch you would've had his aorta. And I
would've had to lay a new carpet in here.'

Anne tried to rise, make another run at the son
of a bitch, but the room turned pale, started to drain
away, and she fell back into the chair.

'You took a bump, darling. Sit still, relax. You can
knife Marty again later if you want. I think he's up
for another round, aren't you, Marty?'

The man looked across at Vic, then steered his
hatred back to her.

Vic leaned back in his chair, laced his fingers behind his head.

'I mean it's not like you have anywhere important to go, sweetheart. And no offense, you look like ever-loving shit. Like somebody backed over you with a dump truck.'

She shifted in the seat. It was useless, her body shut down. She fixed her gaze on Marty Messina – no matter what he said, how good his story was, she wasn't buying it.

'And hey, look. You lay off Marty. He and I go way back to the bad old days. We're buds. Right, Marty?'

Marty said nothing, just continued to glare at Anne.

Vic said, 'Ten, fifteen years back, Marty was running grass for your boyfriend, Salbone. Didn't matter he was working for the competition, I still liked Marty, liked his outlook on life. Not unlike my own. Aspiring to better things. Willing to get in there, get his hands dirty. Truth is, I tried like hell to recruit him away from Salbone, but he wouldn't come.'

'Pay wasn't right,' Marty said.

'But if you'd come with me, you'd have saved yourself a six-year stretch. None of my people ever been convicted. Not even a freaking speeding ticket. You made a strategic error, my friend. Took a short-sighted view. But hey, Marty comes back to town, I hear about it, go down to his old haunt, that seafood joint he ran, and bam, Marty's my man. My heavy lifter, my first lieutenant.'

'You deserve each other,' she said.

'Man, you got a lot of anger, Annie. Stored-up shit like that, it'll give you tumors. You need to let go of some of that poison. Find a positive outlet for it.'

'Mental health advice from Vic Joy? Give me a break.'

Vic chuckled.

'So, Annie, Marty tells me you been pirating big boats. Tankers, cargo ships, big fucking vessels. Is that right? He wasn't making that up, trying to impress me?'

'That's one thing he isn't lying about,' she said.

'Well, I'm proud of you, Annie. I'm very proud. Mom would be, too.' He looked over at Marty. 'Like I said, our mama was a pirate nut. Took us to all those old movies, got us reading the books. Loved that shit. Errol Flynn, Charles Laughton, Douglas Fairbanks. The woman was crazy for buccaneers. Wrote fan letters to Hollywood, criticized these big studio guys for getting their historical facts wrong. I mean hell, look at us, here we are, doing our Oedipal thing, stuck in the endless cycle. With that kind of early training, we didn't have a chance to be anything else but crooks.'

'Sure we did,' Anne said. 'We could've been anything.'

Vic leaned forward, laid his arms on his desk,

starting fiddling with a big fountain pen, taking off the cap, putting it back on. Through the wall, the organist was playing another oldie, a shaky contralto doing the lyrics. 'I saw her today at the reception.'

Vic nodded at the wall.

'Another biker busted his melon-head on US 1. Last few months I've been specializing in these idiots. No-helmet law is great for business. Morons get all weepy, play their stupid road warrior music; after the ceremony, they jump on their hogs, ride a half-mile down the strip to the Caribbean Club, get shit-faced, and break up the furniture. One of them wrecks on the way home, and we do the whole goddamn thing over again next week.

'But dumb as they are, you still gotta love 'em. For fifty bucks, they'll tear open a guy's chest; a hundred, they'll bring back his heart on a paper plate. Cheapest muscle I ever had.'

Anne Bonny stared at the door five feet away, measuring her exit. But her head was still whirling, a pulse of light stabbing behind her eyes at every chord of the organ music.

'What do you know about Daniel?'

'We'll get to that, honey. In good time.'

'Don't screw with me, Vic. If you know something, tell me.'

'I got my own order for doing things, Annie,' Vic said. *'Tranquilo.'*

'Yeah, *tranquilo*, bitch,' Marty said.

'Okay, so here's how it is,' Vic said. 'As heredity

would have it, since last we spoke I've had a few pirating experiences myself. Kind of following a parallel path to yours, though nothing as awe-inspiring as oil tankers. Like I told Marty, I've been specializing in pleasure craft. Yachts, sailboats. More like a recreational thing really, a little side business with a high thrill factor. A way to stay limber, keep my hands dirty. So far I've done maybe a dozen, thirteen. Just getting started, really. All the business enterprises I got going, I get crimps in my cash flow now and then. It's good to have something that nets some extra loot.

'And I work it different than how Marty says you guys handled it. I line up a buyer first, then I locate the boat they have in mind. Hell, sometimes I pick it right from one of my own marinas, vast fucking selection. You know I own eleven boatyards, Annie, all up and down the Keys, a couple over in Naples, Fort Myers, one in Tampa. I've been doing fine since I saw you last, adding jewels to my crown.'

Vic scooped up the pen and pitched it at her under-handed. It came whirling right at her face. Anne flinched, then shot a hand out and snatched it from the air and in the same motion slung it back at him. Vic caught it two-handed and smiled at her.

'Nice,' he said. 'Hey, Marty, I think her reflexes might be a little quicker than yours. You might want to keep a close watch on this lady.'

'Yeah, like I'm fucking worried,' he said.

Vic pointed the pen at her.

'But it's true, Annie. I'm in awe of what you and Marty accomplished. Fucking oil tankers. That's a business I'd like to know more about.'

'Marty didn't have much do with it. He was just along for the ride.'

'I heard different,' Vic said. 'I heard he handled the foreign contacts. Working the phones. Sounds to me like that might be a pretty important part of the business.'

'Sure,' Anne said. 'Whatever you say, Vic.'

'I mean, yeah, I understand it was Danny Salbone running the show. Oh, and too bad about him. I hear he got his head blown off. Sorry about that. I always liked the guy. Played fair. Respected my territory. We had a few encounters over the years, but it was always businesslike. I liked him. Guy was pretty cool for a wop guinea fuck-head goomba bastard.'

Marty chuckled.

Since he was a kid, Vic had been a big-time bullshitter. Words streaming from him constantly, coming out too fast to mean anything. Just white noise, like he was swinging a watch in front of your eyes, trying to put you into a trance before he stole your wallet.

'Thing is,' Vic said. 'Top of my hit parade at this moment, I'm trying to acquire a parcel of land down the road. It's like the cornerstone for a major project. Part of my legacy. That's one thing I'm working on these days: my legacy. Way I'm remembered.'

'Like anybody cares,' she said.

'What I decided I want,' Vic said, 'I want the

biggest goddamn tombstone in the graveyard, if you know what I'm saying. Big monster headstone celebrating my larger-than-life stay on earth.'

Anne shifted her gaze to the photos on the far wall, the pack of elected thieves shaking Vic's hand. If you looked close enough, you'd probably see the hundred-dollar bills they were palming.

'So anyway, Marty had no luck with the owner of the land, though he made the guy a hugely generous offer and silver-tongued the hell out of him. All to no avail. So I was telling him just now when you showed up that I'm coming at this from an oblique angel. You know that word, Annie, *oblique*? It means sideways. Catty-corner.'

He drummed the pen against his desktop and smiled at her.

'So what I'm doing,' Vic said, 'it's like the way you cut a diamond. Something hard, you locate its flaw, the little invisible crack, then all you need is a light tap, just one bump, and the thing's in a million pieces. That's what we're going to do with this guy Thorn. You following me, Annie? We're going to break this fucker into a million pieces.'

'Thorn?' she said.

Vic smiled.

'Yeah, your old boyfriend. Mr Laidback Shithead himself.'

'What kind of bullshit is this, Vic?'

'Truth is, Annie, I owe you a serious debt of gratitude. You hadn't been banging this guy Thorn, I would've never known he existed. Fucker keeps such a low profile. Last year when you two started going at it, I made it my business to look him up, go over, have a talk, see if he was up to the challenge of being a full-fledged member of the Joy family, and that's when I see this prime piece of real estate the dumbshit's squatting on.'

Anne sat forward in her chair.

'I don't believe this. You fucked around in my personal life?'

'Just making sure my little sister isn't climbing in the sack with some loser. It's like a surrogate father thing. Anyway, this Thorn guy, I was thankful when it fell apart. No way I would've had that pain in the ass for a brother-in-law. Fucking smart-ass do-nothing. I took an instant dislike to the fucker.'

'And how many times did you do that, talk to my boyfriends?'

'I don't know. How many men you sleep with over the years? Twelve, thirteen? That's my count.'

'You asshole.'

'Just watching out for my little sister. Same as Dad would've done.'

In the sanctuary, the organist was mangling 'Yesterday.' Some hoarse voices trying to join in, 'All my troubles seemed so far away.'

'So anyway,' Vic said, 'this Thorn asshole, he's got this hard-core lack-of-motivation thing going on. Doesn't respond to normal business stimuli. But that's all about to change because me and Marty are going

131

to put him in the nutcracker and turn the crank. Right, Marty?'

Marty grinned.

'Vic,' Anne said. 'What the hell does this have to do with me?'

'Well, I know it's short notice, but I was hoping maybe you'd come along on a boarding party I got planned for tonight. You might be a help, given your vast expertise with piracy and all. Plus it'd give you a chance to prove you're for real.'

'I don't need to prove anything to you.'

She shot Marty another look. The same smug grin on his face.

'Okay. You don't want to go along, fine. So then let's come at this from a different direction. What would you say to a half-million dollars for about ten minutes of your time? You could use some spending money, couldn't you?'

'A half-million.' Anne tried for ironic, unimpressed, but she heard a wisp of eagerness get through.

Vic said, 'A few minutes, that's all it'd take. Teach me how to crack into this FROM thing Marty told me about, so I could see where all the tankers and cargo ships are. Now that's something we could use.'

'So that's what this is all about. The code to break into FROM.'

'Hell, make it a million,' Vic said. 'A couple of oil tankers, I'll recoup it.'

'You don't know anything about Daniel, do you?'

Vic's simpleton smile surfaced again.

'A million bucks, Annie. One million.'

Anne looked at the walls of Vic's office. Scattered among the photos of mayors and commissioners were a few pirate trinkets from their mother's collection, some old gold coins, a black Jolly Roger flag, a flint-lock pistol.

'I'll give it some thought,' she said.

Vic stood up. Dropped his pen on the ink blotter.

'Okay, little sister, you do that,' Vic said. 'You give it some thought.'

He cast a slow look across her face, as if searching for some sign of deception. Anne kept her mouth bland, muscles relaxed.

Vic said, 'I understand you need a place to stay. Fact is, I got lots of room at my place. Plus there's a couple of things there I'd like to show you.'

From the weeks of travel Anne was exhausted, a heaviness in her bones. Wondering how Daniel would find her if she was no longer working at the Lorelei or living in her apartment. Like it or not, Vic's was the next best bet.

'Why not?' she said. 'Sure, Vic. Why the hell not?'

'And maybe you'll change your mind about coming along tonight on our little boarding party.'

'No, Vic. My pirate days are over.'

'Don't be so sure about that, Annie girl. It's in our blood. That shit's in our freaking blood.'

8

Closing in on nine o'clock that same night, Vic and Marty were twenty miles offshore, the Atlantic Ocean an oily black slick in every direction. Marty was at the wheel and Vic stood beside him staring out through the windscreen, standing there feeling the itch grow in his bloodstream. A mile ahead was the yacht they were tracking, glowing from the big-ass full moon.

'Pretty night,' Vic said. 'Too bad Annie couldn't come. She'd enjoy this.'

Marty turned his head and peered at Vic like maybe he was losing it.

'Hey,' Vic said. 'Just because we're about to commit mayhem doesn't mean we can't enjoy the moon and stars above.'

Vic gazed out at the empty expanse of ocean and

told Marty to speed up a notch. The big man tapped the throttle forward, gaining slightly on the monster yacht. The big pleasure craft had all its deck lights illuminated, making about twenty knots across the calm seas, leaving a white foamy path. Hell of a lot harder for anyone on the yacht to see into the darkness with all those lights blaring. Which was just fine, just fine and dandy.

Vic picked up the binoculars and fixed them on the lighted fly-bridge, found the focus. Still the one skinny man in a white shirt and white trousers at the wheel. Gold buttons glimmered. A uniformed captain, all alone, been like that for the last hour since they pulled out of the channel at Morada Bay Marina.

Vic wasn't sure, but he guessed there were a couple more crew down below serving cocktails, young guys probably, suntanned studs plumping pillows, chilling the mousse pâté. Back at the marina, he'd counted five getting aboard. Didn't see the crew, who were probably already down below. Two, three, it didn't matter. Only person that counted was the one at the controls, the guy who could grab the radio, make the Mayday call.

But he wouldn't have time. He wouldn't know what hit him till he was on his butt. Vic had mounted two superquiet four-cycle engines on the twenty-five-foot Interceptor, three hundred horses no louder than a snoring kitten. And anyway, the fifteen-mile-an-hour breeze was in their face, carrying away any sound. They were tucked directly inside the big boat's

135

wake. Their running lights off. The captain would have to have night-vision goggles to see him. Vic only had to close the half-mile gap, slide up alongside, then the fun could begin.

'You guys use knives when you stormed your ships?'

'Knives?' Marty said.

'You heard me.'

'We didn't need knives, Vic. We had Uzis, Mac-10s, that's what we used, heavy firepower.'

'Knife-between-the-teeth, that's my approach. You got both hands free to pull yourself over the side, then you got the knife ready when you need it, slice a throat. Plus a sharp blade has a high impact factor. They see me coming at them like that, they shit their shorts.'

Marty pulled back on the throttle and they fell off-plane.

'You telling me you didn't bring any guns, Vic? I'm not doing this without a gun.'

'I brought guns, sure I brought guns. Whatta you think, I'm crazy? I just got a soft spot for knives is all. Part of the pirate tradition. And for good reason. Wait'll you see their reaction, they get a look at the knife in my mouth.'

Marty revved them back up to speed and Vic turned his eyes back to the dark water. Not even a gleam out there on the glassy tabletop.

'You weren't lying? You did this before, Vic? Small boats like this.'

'If you call a seventy-five-foot Davis small, yeah, I've done my share. Like I said, I'm up to maybe a dozen. Enough to know it's profitable. More money out here tonight than I turn in a month on that cheap-ass casino boat. And my restaurants, motels? Hell, don't get me started. This is the kind of business makes sense, Marty. Simple, neat, and clean. Plus this time out, I get two for the price of one. That's my philosophy of life. Two birds, one rock.'

Vic took the binoculars and sighted on the bridge. There was a blond woman talking to the captain, pretty lady in a low-cut white dress fluttering in the night air. One of the guests hobnobbing with the help, but the captain was still looking back in their direction, raising the binoculars again.

With the yacht so close, the itch in Vic's blood was turning into a serious jingle. He drew the red scarf from the back pocket of his jeans, shook it out, folded it, and fit it over his hair so it rode an inch down his forehead. He knotted it in the back, then dug in his hip pocket and got the eye patches and offered one to Marty.

The big man looked at Vic and shook his head.

Vic stretched the elastic band over his head and snugged the patch into place. The yacht was coming into clear view. Three hundred yards, at most a minute more, they'd be over the side.

'You don't want an eye patch, fine,' said Vic. 'But I'm a known quantity around these parts. I can't go out doing havoc and anarchy without some kind of fucking disguise.'

Vic bent down behind the leaning post and opened the lid on the chest and drew out a couple of hand-guns. He tapped Marty on the shoulder and handed one of them over.

Marty held it up to the moonlight, twisted it around in his big paw.

'Jesus, Vic. These are .22s. Goddamn plinkers.'

'Those are Rugers. Special Forces uses them. There's two for each of us. One for each hand. It's a nice effect.'

'Shit, these aren't but half a step up from a BB gun.'

Vic dabbed at the eye patch to keep it planted.

'Yeah, okay, so if this was an oil tanker maybe we'd pull out the heavy stuff. You're the acknowledged expert on that. But a boat like that Davis, believe me, .22s are best. We have to shoot somebody, the slug goes in, it doesn't come out. On these posh yachts, you spray a bunch of high-caliber shit around, you're in there patching teak for a month before you can deliver the boat to your buyer. Not to mention the goddamn bloodstains. It's not cost-effective.'

Marty came up to the stern, keeping pace with the big boat, riding its bumpy wake, then eased in beside its starboard hull. Vic reached out for the cleat on the dive platform, lashed a line to it, and gave Marty a grin, then hoisted himself up the side.

Vic was wrong about the crew. There was only

one, the captain, tall, fiftyish guy with a long, skinny face and big ears. Jughead would've been his nickname back in Harlan. Bony man, like a tangle of oak branches stuffed inside that white admiral's uniform. See him on the street, you'd say he was a harmless scrawny guy, but as Vic came over the side with his knife between his teeth, that man stood only a foot away with one mean-ass, throat-ripping look in his eyes.

A second after Vic glimpsed the captain, he caught the blur of something dark flashing at the side of his head. Pool cue, something like that.

Vic ducked back below the gunwale, but the stick clipped him on the shoulder. And for a half-second he lost his grip, slipped backward, the rope burning his palm. Inside the pain, Vic felt a wild thrill. He sucked down a breath and surged back up the line, directly into the next thump of the club, feeling reckless, growling.

Vic took the second blow on his other shoulder. With a yowl, he heaved his body over the transom, flopped on the deck, rolled once, got to his feet. He dipped and sidestepped, and blocked the next blow with his numb arm. He spit the knife into his right hand while the next strike hurtled in. The captain was swinging the goddamn pool cue as methodically as a carpenter hammering home a tenpenny nail.

Vic bobbed once and waded in, took another thump to his neck, nearly slipped away into blackness, tasting blood this time, so close to the guy he inhaled the captain's lime aftershave, then thrust the knife into soft meat somewhere in all that starched white, Cloroxed white, gold-buttoned cloth.

And twisted. And heard the meat tear, felt the give of flesh, the softening of the man's stance, sticky lather coating his right hand. Looking up then into the man's eyes as they changed, as they fell away into nowhere.

He lifted his head and turned and saw Marty standing a yard away with his hand clamped over the mouth of the woman in the white dress. Thin, with her hair woven into a braid coming undone. She squirmed against Marty's hold and stared down at the captain's body.

'You're just standing there,' he said, 'watching.'

'You were doing fine.'

Vic massaged his left shoulder, a throbbing lump.

'Am I going to have to keep looking over my shoulder, see if you've split?'

Marty hardened his grip on the woman and she stopped struggling.

Vic let his eyes linger on Marty a moment, then turned and climbed up to the bridge and backed down the engines. He drew a pair of wire clippers from his holster and snipped off the microphone and hurled it over the side.

Vic climbed back to the deck and drank down a huge breath of that fine salt air, held it as long as he could, then blew it out.

'I'll take her,' Vic said.

Marty let the woman go and Vic took hold of her shoulder and shoved her toward the salon door. He clamped the bloody knife between his teeth, drew one of his Rugers from his belt, threw open the glass door, jostled the woman ahead of him into the cabin, and followed her inside.

Lounging around a big circular table were three adults. A four-tier birthday cake sat in the center of the table. An old white-haired woman in a cocktail dress and the two guys wearing yachting clothes. White loafers, sporty white pants, shirts with epaulets, shirttails out. The younger man was the jerkwad who owned the seventy-footer. Dr Andy Markham. The woman gasped and Markham puffed out his narrow chest, took a step toward Vic, then halted.

Markham was in his forties, with pale blue eyes and heavy lips. His sandy hair was styled to look shaggy. One of those haircuts you had to touch up every other day to keep it looking right. Boyish face, good tan and sandy hair, prep school, Princeton. All the advantages.

'What's the meaning of this?'

Vic took the knife from his mouth and holstered it beneath his belt. He drew out the other Ruger and aimed his right pistol at Markham and swung the other one at the two men behind the table.

'Meaning?' Vic looked at Marty. The big man was sweating heavily, starting to give off a sour gas. 'We're fresh out of meaning. All we got left is chaos and random disorder.'

'Is this a joke? What the hell do you want?'

'More than you got,' Vic said.

Then the yellow-haired woman who'd been talking to the captain edged up behind Markham and touched his back with her fingertips, prodding him.

'That man killed the captain,' she said. 'He stabbed him in the stomach. I think he's dead, Andy. I think he's dead.'

The shrink looked at her, then turned back to Vic, squinting. He took a wary step his way.

'Okay, let's all lie down, why don't we?' Vic said. 'Doc and the rest of you old-timers. Make yourself comfortable. Choose a spot, spread out.'

The old folks moved to obey, but Markham shouted no.

'Stay where you are. No one's ordering my guests around.'

The white-haired woman swung her gaze back and forth across Vic and Marty, her lips quivering until finally she broke into a long belly laugh.

Vic moved a step closer to her and her laughter sputtered to a stop, but her smile stayed wide. Big red lips trembling like she was holding back another guffaw. The woman wore a black low-cut gown with thin straps, a pound of diamonds around her neck, and strapless gold sandals. She had white fleshy arms, and sun freckles scattered over the tops of her deflated breasts. Her eyes wouldn't hold still, moving from Vic to Andy Markham, back to Vic.

'What's so funny?' Vic said.

'Oh, really, Andy, these aren't nearly as good as the last ones. Those harem slaves, now they had me going, yes, they did. All those muscles and shaved chests and baby oil. But these are so scruffy. A little on the clichéd side.'

'Clichéd?' Vic said.

'Scarf, eye patches, knife in the teeth. Come now, that's bad Errol Flynn.'

Vic swung his pistols back to Markham.

'But it's true,' the blond one said. 'I saw it. That man stabbed Captain Johnson in the belly. He's dead. It's true. I saw it happen.'

'They're actors, Charlotte,' the old lady said. 'Andy does this now and then. It's one of his little dramas to spice things up, get us in the proper mood. Only this time it's all a little cartoonish.'

'Cartoonish, huh?'

Vic snorted at the old woman and aimed his pistol at the shrink.

'So, Markham. I take it we interrupted one of your séances?'

'Who are you?' The doctor stared at Vic, tipping his head to the side as if to find a better angle.

'That's what you do, isn't it? You hypnotize these nimrods, take them on a magical mystery ride. That's how you bought this boat? Scamming weak-minded idiots?'

'It's no swindle,' the old man said. He had a mane of dignified white hair and a red face and a blue ascot at his throat. A British banker dressed for dinner after a long day on safari. 'Dr Markham is world-renowned. He's a marvelous guide into the world of past lives.'

The shrink took another uncertain step forward.

'Take them outside, Marty,' Vic said. 'Start with the laughing lady.'

'And do what?'

Vic ripped off his eye patch and stuffed it in his pants pocket.

'Buy her a ticket to her next life.'

'Oh, this is ridiculous,' the old woman said. 'This isn't the least bit amusing, Andy. Do something. Stop this at once.'

'Take her, Marty. Take her outside where she can laugh her head off. Show her what kind of cartoon this is.'

Marty hesitated, so Vic went over to the old woman and pressed the muzzle of his Ruger to the side of her neck and jabbed. The woman stumbled forward and Vic jabbed again, harder this time, and she whimpered as she moved toward the cabin door. Markham shifted in her direction, but Vic waved his pistols at him and the air went out of him.

'Andy? Andy? This isn't right, Andy. This isn't right at all.'

The doctor licked his lips.

'You want to see how it's done, Marty? This is how it's done.'

Vic shoved the woman out the cabin door, pushed her onto the deck and over to the port side.

'Watch, Marty. Maybe you'll learn something.'

Marty looked out of the cabin window and Vic pressed the pistol to the old lady's head and fired. She slumped against the gunwale and Vic had to lift her up by her flabby waist to heave her over.

He walked back inside.

'Get the picture, Marty? What'd they fucking teach you in that country club prison, anyway? Ballroom dancing?'

Marty stared silently at Vic.

Vic swung around and aimed his pistol at the shrink.

'Now where's the girl?'

The shrink blinked twice and tried a smile, which turned sickly on his lips. The other two looked at each other.

'You won't get away with this. You'll be caught.'

'Take another one, Marty,' Vic said. 'Your turn.'

'Who?'

'Take Henry Wadsworth Longfellow.' Vic nodded at the guy in the ascot.

Marty went over, grabbed the man's right biceps, and yanked him around the table and out onto the deck. The old man tried to twist from Marty's grip, but it was useless.

Vic waited until out on the deck there was a sharp pop. No one said anything; they just stood there trying to breathe. Then Marty reappeared at the cabin door looking a little green.

'I'll say it one more time, Markham.' Vic jiggled the pistol at him. 'Where's the fucking girl?'

9

In his back bedroom, with his legs wedged beneath his ex-wife's antique dressing table, Sugarman stared at the screen of his second-rate laptop computer while out in the Atlantic Ocean Janey held up a pair of binoculars to her Web camera. Showing the present she'd received from her soon-to-be stepfather, Andrew Prescott Markham.

Janey wasn't letting Sugarman say a word as she demonstrated all the cool stuff the binoculars could do.

The antique table where he'd set up the computer was one of only three things Jeannie left behind when she departed after their marriage. That and a mirror whose frame she'd decorated with seashells she'd harvested from beaches around Florida early in their marriage, and an unwieldy mobile she'd constructed with tiny dried alligators attached to strands of yellow yarn.

'It's a "Zeiss Victor, eight by fifty-six S,"' Janey recited from the manual. '"Waterproofed for submersion and dry-nitrogen purged to prevent fogging."'

'Wow,' Sugarman said. 'That's a mouthful.'

Janey positioned the binoculars squarely in the camera's eye. Sugarman glanced across the room at the hundred-dollar pair of binoculars he'd bought Janey for her birthday lying on the bed next to Jackie's new MP3 player. Wrapping paper and Scotch tape lay beside them.

With *The Sibley Guide to Birds* open beside him, it'd taken Sugar a couple of hours to draw fifteen different birds on Janey's birthday card. Marbled godwit, frigate bird, roseate spoonbill, the palm warbler. A damn good job, if he did say so.

'Cool present, huh? Lot better than that old pair I've been using.'

'Yeah, they look very nice, sweetie. Nitrogen-purged is a good feature with all the humidity.'

But he wasn't sure his voice made it across the black gulf between them. Janey was celebrating her ninth birthday aboard Markham's yacht. The laptop computer she was using had a satellite phone built into its base. Markham always had the latest high-tech gadgets so he could commune at any time and from any location with his addlebrained clients. Sugar and Janey were dialed into Markham's server that hosted a warren of private chat rooms available twenty-four/seven for just such video chats. Clients talking to clients, or one of Markham's flunkies spreading the gospel one-on-one with some rich chump.

But tonight there must have been solar storms, because the image of Janey's face was choppy, freezing, then jumping ahead a few seconds, and dense snow came and went, once or twice almost whiting out the image entirely. And the audio wasn't cooperating, either. For the last half hour Janey's voice kept dropping into a lower register as if she were being possessed by evil spirits.

Her sister, Jackie, had caught the flu the day before, and she and her mother had stayed home in Fort Lauderdale. But given the choice, Janey went along on the boat ride anyway. She liked boats a lot more than her twin did, and more than Jeannie, for that matter. Another area where Janey had inherited considerably more of Sugarman's disposition than her mother's.

These computer chats were still uncomfortable for him. Sugar would much rather use an old-fashioned telephone, but the girls seemed energized by the Web cameras, and with only two weekend visits a month allowed by the divorce agreement, this way Sugar at least got a chance to *see* his daughters more often, even if it was on these flattened and grainy screens. Last fall when Jeannie floated the computer-visitation idea, Sugarman balked. He didn't own a computer, and with his private security and investigation business floundering on the brink of bankruptcy, he certainly didn't have the cash to buy one. Anyway, it all seemed wrong, too impersonal, too technical.

But when Jeannie said, okay, forget it, if you don't care enough about your own flesh and blood to learn how to use a simple computer, Sugarman caved. He had to max out his one credit card to buy the cheapest laptop he could find. Took lessons from a teenage geek in his neighborhood to get up and running, which set him back another hundred bucks he didn't have. Not to mention what he had to pay for the DSL hookup, the monthly service fee. But after a dozen or so video chats he was getting used to the idea and was grateful to have the increased contact with his girls, even if it meant he'd be eating peanut butter sandwiches three times a day for the rest of his natural life.

When Janey paused in the demonstration of the binoculars, Sugarman said, 'So, sweetheart, you feeling okay? No sign of the flu?'

'Dr Andy said I'm too tough for the flu.'

Some doctor, Sugar wanted to say. Doctor of hocuspocus. Dr Flimflam Man. Physician to affluent suckers. Just so happened that every single one of his rich clients used to be Cleopatra or Julius Caesar or Shakespeare. Not a single galley slave or field hand in the bunch. Markham wrote books, had a weekly cable TV show, took a few rich idiots on these cruises once a month so they could reincarnate his bank account. Jeannie had been cohabiting with Markham for over a year and still denied he was a charlatan.

'So where are you all going tonight, sweetie?'

'Into the ocean, Daddy. We're on the yacht.'

'Just out and back, or you headed up to Lauderdale?'

Markham kept his yacht in a classy marina down in Islamorada. A long and inconvenient drive from his home in Lauderdale, which made Sugar wonder if it was Jeannie's idea to store the boat there, a way to rub her ex-husband's nose in her greatly improved status. Almost every weekend Markham and Jeannie were showboating around Sugarman's backyard, the flashy couple with the pretty blond twins. Their pictures showing up regularly in the local paper's social scene section.

'Janey, can you hear me?'

Janey's reply was lost in the three seconds of static that blasted from the speaker. The screen went white, then came back.

'You're out kind of late,' Sugar said. 'Thursday, a school night.'

'It's only nine o'clock, Daddy. And anyway, I'm skipping tomorrow. Mother said it was okay.'

'She did, huh?'

'Oh, I forgot to tell you,' Janey said. 'Dr Andy is going to take us around the world. I get to miss school for a whole month.'

That was news. Sugarman was fairly sure Jeannie

had to get permission from him for something like that, but then again he hadn't actually studied the divorce agreement like he should have, gotten out a magnifying glass and pored over the tiny print. Once or twice he'd tried, but his eyes always burned and clouded before he'd gotten more than a sentence or two.

'Around the world? When is that supposed to happen?'

She pressed the binoculars up to her eyes and peered into the Web camera.

'I don't know, sometime,' she said. 'Around the whole world. Africa and Paris and all the nice places.'

'Well, I don't think you can get to Paris on that boat, sweetie.'

'I know that, Daddy. Dr Andy says we'll take a private jet to Paris.'

Sugarman sighed.

She was toying with the binocular's focus and didn't seem to hear.

'Janey, will you be back tonight? Because Daddy's supposed to pick you up Saturday morning, day after tomorrow.'

She lowered the binoculars and looked into the camera's eye and smiled.

'What're we going to do? Can we go to the beach?'

Jeannie refused to take the girls to the beach. She claimed to be worried that their skin would coarsen and permanent damage would be done. Sugarman knew it was more than that, but he'd never called her on it. It was too tender a subject. But the truth was, Jeannie was afraid if her daughters' precious milky complexions turned a shade or two darker, people might notice they were of mixed race.

Their grandfather, Sugarman's old man, had been a hard-core Rastafarian from Kingston, Jamaica, complete with giant ganja cigars, dreadlocks and all. Lead singer for a reggae band in an Islamorada bar till the place was shut down by drug agents. Sugar's mother, an ardent groupie of the band, was a statuesque Norwegian ice queen. They married a month after they met and divorced a month after Sugar was born. It was a weird and unsustainable marriage. And Sugar, their only child, tilted hard toward his mother's looks, his skin the faintest mahogany, his facial features chiseled with her severe Nordic angles. It was ironic, really. His father had been so fiercely proud of his African heritage, flaunting it in nearly every way he could imagine, yet that blood he considered so noble had been thinned to pale froth in his only son.

For her part, Jeannie was doggedly and proudly all-American, a Scotch-Irish princess who desperately wanted her daughters to pass for the same. Though she'd never said it straight out, Sugarman knew that even so much as a light tan on the two young girls terrified her. What lengths she was willing to go to keep them out of the Florida sun for the rest of their days were frightening to consider. Once during the divorce when Sugarman asked

Jeannie why in the hell she married him in the first place, she said, 'Because you were a football hero, honey. I was eighteen years old, in a swoon over the star running back.'

On the computer screen Janey was paging through the binocular manual.

'We can't go to the beach, honey. We're invited to Thorn's house, remember? We're going to catch some fish and grill them.'

'Oh, yeah. I forgot. Thorn's house is better than the beach. A lot better.'

'What kind of cake are you having for your party tonight?'

'Chocolate,' Janey said. 'You know these binoculars cost eleven hundred dollars, Daddy?'

'Eleven hundred?'

'Yeah. Dr Andy showed me the receipt. Eleven hundred's a lot, huh?'

'Showed you the receipt,' Sugarman said quietly.

Janey asked him to say again.

'It's the thought that counts,' Sugarman said. 'Money isn't the only way to measure things.'

Then Janey jerked away from the camera and swung her gaze upward.

'Janey?'

She continued to stare up at the ceiling.

'What is it, Janey?'

With her face turned away, her words came to him as electronic garble.

'Is something wrong?'

She half-turned to the microphone.

'Fireworks, I think.'

Sugarman heard a faint pop of static, followed by another buzzing pulse as if the connection were flickering and about to break.

'Daddy's shooting firecrackers,' she said.

'Daddy?' The word escaped Sugarman in an airless croak. It was the first time either of his girls had referred to Markham that way, and Sugarman felt his heart lurch and a thick fog of gloom rise inside his chest.

Janey was still peering upward, leaning away from the Web cam, giving Sugar her right cheek in hazy profile. His computer had terrible depth of field. On the expensive models he could've counted the freckles on her nose and read an eye chart on the wall behind her. But with the piece-of-shit version he'd bought, if one of the girls moved two inches too close to the camera, his screen became a fluttery funhouse mirror. Put that together with all the garble from the satellite connection, it was a wonder he could see Janey at all.

'Janey?'

'They didn't wait for me. They didn't tell me they were starting.'

'Well, maybe you should go,' Sugar said. 'You don't want to miss your own party.'

But she didn't reply. She swung around, putting her back to the camera, and her blond curls fluttered hard as if she were refusing some command.

Sugarman leaned close to the screen, peering at the bright mist of electrons. He spoke her name.

Then he heard her say a single word, 'Daddy.'

Sugarman was bent forward, inches from the screen, when Janey came briefly into view, her mouth drawn back into what might have been either a large smile or a grimace of alarm. A sphincter shut hard in Sugarman's throat.

In the next second another face pressed close beside his daughter's and bent toward the video camera. The man's features hovered on the edge of focus. Too blurry to determine much beyond the oblong shape of his face. All Sugar could make out for sure was a red bandanna tied over the man's head and the glint of what looked like a large blade gripped in his teeth.

He was cheek to cheek with Janey, with the point of the blade dangerously close to her flesh. Then through the fuzzy speaker came his daughter's voice, a single girlish squeal that might have been either delight or terror. And then the two of them were gone.

10

'I'm still not used to it,' Alexandra said. 'How quiet it gets. Nine o'clock, half the island's in bed.'

They were sitting outside on the upstairs porch looking out at the glossy black water. All the shoreline houses in either direction were dark, only a few dock lights burning. Lawton was asleep on his cot in the living room. On the floor beneath him, the puppy was stretched out, legs trembling, making small yips at some rival in his dream.

'My neighbors,' Thorn said. 'Crashing after another long day of leisure.'

'It's unreal,' she said. 'Up in Miami, people haven't eaten dinner yet.'

She had a taste of her wine and leaned back in the low-slung chair, tipping her head back to look up at the heavens. The stars were all there. Showing off a little in the clear sky.

Thorn had a sip of wine and set the glass back on the deck. He saw the flitter of dark wings above the tamarind tree. Bats or mosquito hawks clearing swaths of air.

'You miss it, don't you? Living in the city, the twenty-four-hour hum.'

'I'm there all day. I don't miss it. I'm still in it.'

'I don't know if I could do it. Adjust to the pace up there,' Thorn said. 'When it gets dark here, it gets dark. Up there, the lights don't ever shut off. The sky's orange.'

'No one's asking you to adjust. We're here. This is what we're doing.'

'For now,' he said.

'What're you saying? You thinking about taking that offer for your land, living in a big house with lots of light switches and bathrooms, going out to dinner at ten o'clock?'

'I don't know what I'm saying.'

'You're worried about me, that's what. That city girl speech I gave the other day. That's bothering you.'

Thorn watched a slow boat passing across the sound, headed for Adam's Cut and the oceanside. A catamaran, its small engine nudging it along at less than ten knots. Only a single light burning at the wheelhouse.

'I'm not worried about you,' Thorn said.

'But it's on your mind. You think I feel the tug of Miami. You think this is just temporary. A fling. My heart's not really in it, living down here.'

Thorn watched the sailboat disappear. The bay was empty. Thursday night, second day of May, already entering the long sluggish summer, when only the mosquitoes seemed to have any motivation.

'Key Largo's a tough place,' Thorn said. 'It's beautiful, but it's not easy. I know how it works. Eventually the beauty part wears off, then it just feels isolated. Some people start getting antsy after a while.'

'They miss the hum,' she said.

'Yeah, they miss the hum.'

'Well, I get a good healthy dose of hum every day,' she said. 'Don't worry about me.'

Her hand found his and she squeezed and he gave an answering grasp.

'I like spending time with Lawton,' Thorn said. 'I like that a lot.'

'The dog or the dad?'

Thorn smiled at her in the dark.

'Even like he is, he's funny and smart,' Thorn said. 'I can't believe the stuff he comes up with. He must've been one hell of a guy when he was young.'

Alexandra said nothing for a moment. Thorn could feel her grip soften as if the blood were seeping from her veins.

'He was,' she said at last. 'You would've liked him then, too, and he would've liked you. A lot.'

'He seems to like me now.'

'He does,' she said. 'But that's not Dad. That's a wonderful, sweet, brave old man who's short-circuiting.'

Thorn held her hand and watched the shimmer of dark water, a warm gust flooding in from the Atlantic side, keeping the mosquitoes at bay.

'It's awfully quiet,' he said.

'Quiet is good,' she said. 'Quiet is wonderful.'

'You ready to go inside, be quiet in there?'

'I'm ready,' she said. 'But I don't know how quiet I can be.'

'We'll hum,' he said. 'We'll make our own hum.'

She stood up and bent over to kiss Thorn on the top of his head. He could feel the heat of her lips through his hair, feel her whisper against his scalp. Her wordless breath calling out his secret name.

Thorn woke with a gasp and pushed himself upright against the pillow, his heart floundering. The dream of snapping jaws had evaporated so quickly, he had no memory of it beyond the flash of two rows of sharpened teeth. Maybe a crocodile, or a great white, or maybe only a plastic set of chattering dentures wound up by the practical joker who roamed his psyche. He sat there staring out at the darkness, feeling silly. Just a dream, unhooked from any reasonable fear, only a random image bubbling up from the cauldron of his general anxiety. Nothing to analyze, not even a story to share with Alex over morning coffee. Just those disembodied teeth snapping the air inches from his nose.

Across the room a chalky dust seemed to coat the dresser and the rough-hewn walls. A haze hung in the room like electrified fog. He blinked his eyes and worked to fill his lungs. It took another moment before his head cleared and he saw the pearly glow was simply the full moon leaking through a thousand microscopic chinks in his plank house.

Beside him Alexandra was sleeping on her right side, one arm tucked beneath her pillow, the other hidden by the quilted bedspread. Her long black hair was coiled into a glossy rope lying across the pale blue sheets. As he crawled out of the bed, she snuffled twice as if flirting with wakefulness, then dug deeper into the same pose as before, a sleeper descending with firm resolve back down into the shadowy nowhere.

Naked, Thorn padded across the room and opened the door and stepped into the living area. With the shades open, the room was as bright as noon. Their dishes from dinner sparkled in the drying rack, and the mirror on the far wall was full of golden tree branches and gleaming bay water.

It was a small open kitchen with a tiled counter, an ancient Frigidaire that chugged on into a new century, and a two-seater breakfast nook. That nook and every beam and plank and joist in the rest of the house had been fashioned out of rain-forest hardwoods that Thorn had salvaged from the Miami dump. Used to ship VCRs and color TVs and fax machines from Asia and South America to the hungry shores of the US, those once-used crates were often made from two-hundred-year-old cinnamon teak and rosewood and mangium, ebony, and purpleheart. In Miami the crates were crowbarred open, the shabby contents removed, then those scraps of noble wood were burned and pulverized at the city landfill. With Sugarman's help he'd rescued a few tons of the treasure and milled the wood into planks to rebuild his house, every day for a year making the long trip to Miami to pick through piles of abandoned timber.

Forever after, his house gave off a welter of pungent aromas. Dark roasted coffee mingled with peppermint and citrus and leather and tangy spices so exotic they had not yet been named. With every breeze the wood house flexed. Each barometric shift made the boards creak and groan like dry hinges on an old gate. But the structure was tough beyond steel, curing each year into something ever harder as the sap turned inward. A wood so dense it would not yield to fire or rot or termites. And Thorn was certain the house would be the last building to go down to the inevitable hurricane that would someday sandblast these coral islands smooth. For years it had been his bunker against change, his hideaway from the ceaseless onslaught of human folly. Inside those four walls, perched on stilts fifteen feet above mean high tide, he sometimes felt himself disappearing into all that wood, as if those old trees still grew around him, ring by ring, spreading their girth, rising heavenward with Thorn trapped happily inside.

As he stood in the center of the living room, with the last ghostly tatters of dream departing, Thorn's eyes fell on the empty cot. Across the room beneath the west window the moon brightened against Lawton's disheveled sheets. The old man was gone and so was the pup.

Thorn marched out to the porch and leaned over the rail and peered into the snarl of shadows. On the yellow bench beneath the gumbo-limbo in a halo of moonlight Lawton sat primly, knees together, feet flat on the ground. He was wearing a white short-sleeved shirt and a string tie, and his valise sat at his feet. Beside him on the bench, Lawton, the dog, was sprawled on his side with the edge of his snout resting on Lawton's thigh. The old man's eyes were open and he was looking to his right, back toward the highway as if he heard the heavy *whoosh* of air brakes, his Greyhound bus come at last.

Thorn went inside the house and stepped into a pair of baggy gym shorts, then went back outside and walked down the stairs. Lawton was speaking, and the pup had stirred awake.

Sugarman stood at the edge of the bench.

Thorn walked over and even in that half-light he could see in Sugar's hunched shoulders and his bowed head that all was not well.

'That bus late again?' Thorn said.

'Hell, yes,' said Lawton. 'I'm a half-second from walking out to the highway and hitching a ride with the next passing stranger.'

'This time of night most of the idiots out there are tanked up on margaritas,' Thorn said. 'Probably best to wait till daylight.'

Thorn sat down beside the old man. He reached over and scratched the pup's throat.

'That's true,' Lawton said. 'About the only enjoyable thing to do on this godforsaken rock is get plastered. That's another reason I'm heading out.'

'Aren't you sleepy, Lawton? Need a little shut-eye?'

'Old people don't need sleep,' he said. 'You'll see someday.'

Lawton, the pup, sighed and snuggled against Lawton's thigh.

'And you, Sugar. What're you doing out here, middle of the night?'

'I needed to talk, but I didn't want to wake you.'

'You were going to sit out here till sunup?'

'I been running around for the last couple of hours, trying to figure this thing out and getting nowhere. I didn't know where else to go.'

'What is it?'

'I don't know,' he said. 'Probably nothing.'

'Okay,' Thorn said. 'So now that you're here, you going to share it with us or do we have to arm-wrestle it out of you?'

'I'm sorry, man. I shouldn't bother you with this.' He looked at Lawton, then back at Thorn. 'You got your hands full and everything.'

'Goddamn it, Sugar.'

Thorn waved a mosquito away from his ear.

'Okay, okay. It's Janey.'

'What about her?'

'I was doing a virtual visitation with her tonight. On the computer, you know, that laptop I bought. Talking to her on-line.'

'Yeah.'

'Well, we were talking, and she was showing me this pair of binoculars she got for her birthday, then all of a sudden there's this guy next to her. Never saw him before. He's dressed like a goddamn pirate, of all things. Knife in the teeth, bandanna over his head, maybe even an eye patch, I don't know. The image was fuzzy.'

'A pirate.'

'Janey was on Markham's yacht, out in the Atlantic. One of those bullshit cruises where he takes out a bunch of true believers, puts them in a trance, and they go back a few thousand years, find out all the people they've been. Reincarnation, channeling, whatever it's called.'

Lawton turned his head and peered through the darkness at Sugarman.

'Don't tell me you believe in that horseshit?'

Sugarman shook his head at Lawton, then turned back to Thorn.

'I was talking to Janey, then out of nowhere there were fireworks or some kind of noise up on deck, then this guy dressed like a pirate sticks his face in the screen and Janey makes a little squeal and the two of them disappear.'

Thorn looked out at Blackwater Sound, acres of shimmering moonlight framed by the dark mangrove islands. The constant blink of a channel marker off to the south.

'Some kind of entertainment maybe,' Thorn said. 'It's her birthday.'

'Yeah, yeah,' said Sugar. 'I know it's probably that. A while back on one of these cruises Markham hired a bunch of bodybuilders and dressed them up like harem slaves and gave all the old ladies a thrill. Another time he did gladiators. Trying to get them in the mood for a little time travel.'

'So it was probably that, goofy entertainment.'

'Yeah,' Sugarman said.

'But you don't really think so.'

Sugarman looked out at the water. Something was splashing about a hundred yards out. Barracuda after pinfish, or maybe a mullet trying to launch itself at the giant moon.

'I should go,' he said. 'It's the middle of the goddamn night. I'm being an idiot.'

'It's allowed,' Thorn said. 'Around here it's even encouraged.'

'Well, there's my bus,' Lawton said. He stooped over and nabbed his suitcase, then hitched the dog under his arm and stood. 'I've got to hit the high-way, boys. It's been fun.'

'Where you going, Lawton?'

'Columbus, Ohio. My birthplace.'

'But this is the midnight bus,' Thorn said.

'So?'

'So this one doesn't go to Ohio. That one's tomorrow.'

'Tomorrow?'

'That's right.'

'First I heard of that.'

'It's been that way for years, Lawton. Ohio is in the morning.'

'You wouldn't be trying to trick an old man, would you?'

'Still some good sleeping hours left before daybreak,' said Thorn. 'Soon as Sugar and I are finished, I plan to crawl back into bed myself.'

'All right, goddamn it,' Lawton said. 'But tomorrow there's no stopping me. You hear?'

'Yes, sir.'

Lawton walked over to the foot of the stairs and halted. He swung his head from side to side, staring at the trees and the bay and all those familiar sights with a puzzled look as if he might be waking from a session of sleepwalking.

Then he hitched the dog under his arm and started up the stairway.

'He's getting worse,' Sugarman said.

'I don't know about worse, but he's not any better.'

'At least he's stopped with the Houdini stuff. Breaking out of handcuffs, the escape artist routine.'

'Yeah, this month it's Zen.'

'Zen?'

'Few weeks ago he found a calendar at the flea market. Twenty-five cents. It's five years out-of-date, but that doesn't matter to him. Every page has another Zen saying on it. He's decided he's a Buddhist.'

Sugarman sighed and sat down on the bench.

'Tell me I'm crazy, Thorn. Tell me I'm imagining things.'

'You try Jeannie?'

'Nonstop busy signal,' he said. 'I called the phone company; they said the phone's off the hook. Jackie has the flu, so Jeannie probably shut everything down. So then I called Bill Stokey at the Coast Guard station, see if there was anything they could do. If Markham filed a float plan, we have to wait till the marina opens in the morning to see what it was. He didn't send a Mayday, so according to Stokey, till we know when he planned to return, there's no way to know he's overdue, no cause for alarm. I mean they got their official manual, some kind of damn checklist they run down, and this didn't fit their red alert profile.'

'You could call a neighbor of Jeannie's. Have them knock on her door.'

'I don't know her neighbors.'

'It's only a couple of hours up there by car. I'll go with you.'

'She and Markham moved last week,' Sugar said.

'You don't have their new address?'

'Somewhere on Las Olas,' Sugarman said. 'Fancy-ass high-rise, that's all I know. I got the phone number but no address. She was going to give it to me tomorrow so I could pick the girls up.'

'The phone company must have it.'

'Number's unlisted. I asked the operator, talked to her supervisor. They won't give it to me.'

'Not even in an emergency?'

'I don't know it's an emergency,' Sugar said. 'I couldn't tell them that.'

'You could've lied.'

Sugarman looked up at Thorn, then looked back out at the watery gleam.

'That's what you would've done,' Sugarman said. 'You would've lied. And you'd have the address and we'd be driving up there right now.'

'Probably,' Thorn said.

'That's the difference between us,' Sugar said. 'One of them.'

'Scruples,' said Thorn. 'I've got none.'

'I can't do it, Thorn. I can't pretend it's an emergency when I don't know if it is or not. My own daughter, and I'm paralyzed by goddamn scruples.'

'I'll do it then. Give me the phone.'

Thorn took Sugarman's cell and dialed the operator and walked out to the edge of the sound. Out of earshot, so Sugar wouldn't have to listen to a lie. Thorn went through the whole thing, skipping the pirate part, getting a good dose of anxiety into his voice, but the operator was bored and running her protocol and wouldn't hand out the address. Thorn asked for the supervisor and got put on hold for a few minutes. When the supervisor finally came on, the guy was even more unyielding than the operator. Unless the police instructed them to release that information, it was strictly confidential. Thorn asked the guy if he had a daughter and the guy hesitated, then after a moment said no, he had no children.

'Well, that explains it then,' Thorn said. 'Why you're such an asshole.'

Sugarman was on the bench when Thorn came back from the shoreline.

'No go.' Thorn handed Sugar his cell phone. 'Maybe it's time to call the sheriff's office.'

'Did that already,' Sugar said. 'I'm supposed to call back at eight o'clock if the boat hasn't returned; *then* they'll do something.'

'Christ,' Thorn said. 'Nobody can be bothered.'

'Hell,' Sugar said. 'Even if I had Jeannie's address and showed up at her door, waking her up in the middle of the night, with Jackie sick and everything, she'd look at me and get that sarcastic thing in her voice and tell me it was just guys dressed up like pirates. And then she'd make fun of me in front of Jackie.'

'She does that.'

'Yeah, you've seen her. That's how she is.' Sugar

was quiet for a moment, then said, 'I forget why I married her. What the love was based on.'

'You were both young,' Thorn said.

'That's no excuse,' Sugarman said.

'Something good came out of it,' said Thorn. 'The girls.'

Sugarman was silent. Eyes closed, worry creasing his forehead.

Thorn watched a shadow stealing along the shoreline. Raccoon probably, or maybe a possum. There'd been an outbreak of rabies lately and the health department was trying to catch all the varmints they could. Last week Thorn put out his one cage baited with peanut butter, but so far, nobody had dropped by. They were probably holding out for extra-crunchy.

'A guy dressed like a pirate?' Thorn said.

Sugar opened his eyes and nodded solemnly.

'Bandanna on his head, knife between the teeth, yeah.'

'Had to be a joke,' said Thorn. 'Too goddamn goofy to be real.'

'Yeah,' Sugarman said. 'A birthday party thing.'

'Had to be,' Thorn said.

11

'"If I own a cow,"' Lawton said, '"the cow owns me."'

They were having breakfast at the long picnic table on the upstairs porch overlooking Blackwater Sound. The water was iron gray and kicking up. Thorn noticed in the stiller water close to shore the V of ripples spreading out behind the fin of a bonnet head shark.

'And who said that, Dad?'

Alexandra sat beside the old man. She had on a white polo shirt and blue jeans and tennis shoes. Her long hair was tied back in a ponytail and her dark eyes sparkled quietly in the rising light. She didn't look like a woman who'd seen a thousand corpses. A woman who'd probably see twice that many more before she retired.

'Ralph Waldo Emerson said it. The famous American Buddhist.'

Lawton brushed a crumb off the chest of his white T-shirt and reset the blue baseball cap, tightening it down on his thick white hair.

Through the open bedroom door Thorn could see Sugarman perched on the edge of the bed with his cell phone pressed to his ear. Sugar wore the same faded black jeans and blue work shirt he'd had on yesterday. Wrinkled and saturated with the harsh essence of his fatigue and anxiety.

A minute earlier he'd finally gotten through to his ex-wife, Jeannie, and now he was hunched forward, listening to her voice. Even from twenty feet away Thorn could hear her metallic screech. Sugarman looked up with a pained squint, then stooped back down to endure more of the chewing out.

'I think Emerson was a poet, Dad. And a New England minister.'

'Jesus, girl. You're always looking for something to argue about. Just like your mother. So goddamned contrary. I don't know how I endured it all those years. All that negativity. Nag, nag, nag.'

'You loved Mother, Dad. You two never fought.'

'If you want to believe that, go ahead. Live in a goddamn dream-world.'

Alex flinched, her right hand drifting up from her lap, moving to her face. With her palm she smoothed away the bruised clench in her mouth. Thorn could see in her eyes that she was struggling to locate the reservoir of patience. 'Only words, only words.' That was the mantra she and Thorn had been using lately, but with limited success.

She watched her father pour more syrup on his stack, then use a forkful of pancakes to sop up some of the bacon grease that glittered on the edge of his plate. He wedged the flapjacks into his mouth, then spoke around the unchewed lump.

'A man can be a Buddhist and not even know it,' Lawton said. 'Take me. I thought I was a Catholic, now I come to find out I been a Buddhist all along.'

'More flapjacks?' Thorn offered the plate around, and when no one accepted he speared another.

'"If I own a cow, the cow owns me,"' Lawton said to Thorn. 'That's a line from Ralph Emerson, the famous New England Buddhist.'

Lawton looked sternly at Alexandra, daring her to contradict him.

'I knew about your dog,' Thorn said. 'But I didn't realize you owned a cow, too.'

Lawton used his knife and fork to straighten up the remaining stack on his plate, then he sliced them into ten neatly identical pie wedges.

'I don't own a cow,' Lawton said. 'I don't own anything.'

'What about the dog?' said Thorn.

'I don't *own* Lawton. Hell, I didn't pay anything for him. He was free. So it doesn't apply.'

'But you have to keep him up, food, vet bills. That costs something.'

'You asking me to let that pup starve to death? That what you want?'

Alexandra sighed and pushed her plate away. They'd been trying, whenever they could, to use logic on the old man, force him to stay on the steel rails of reason. And though it seemed to work okay some of the time, more and more lately Lawton would veer off into absurdity.

Beneath the table Thorn felt the puppy sit up and lean against his leg. The scent of bacon stirring him awake. Lawton had bathed and brushed him and his coat was gleaming and smelled like lilacs.

'You'll have to excuse me, gentlemen,' Alex said. 'Miami calls. Thanks for the carbs, Thorn. You're a masterful chef.'

'Wait'll you taste my toasted cheese sandwich.'

'It's a date.'

'I loved your mother, goddamn it.' Lawton's eyes glossed and there was a small tremble in his jaw. 'I loved her bones. Her lips and eyes, the smell of her hair. We never raised our voices to each other. Not in forty years. And don't say we did, Alexandra. Because it's not true.'

'I know,' she said. 'I know.'

Alexandra looked at her father for a moment more, then took her plate inside, rinsed it, and went into the bathroom to touch up her minimal makeup.

A minute or two later Lawton lost interest in his breakfast and he stood up and wandered down to the yard. The puppy followed, cantering along beside him as unsteady as a child in outsize galoshes. The Lab nipped at the old man's bare ankles, inviting him to play. The two of them came to a halt in the tall grass that grew in the shade of the tamarind tree and Lawton lay back in the grass and the puppy settled in beside him and the two of them fell into an almost immediate doze.

Thorn was washing the dishes when Sugarman came striding out of the bedroom. His face was pale and the skin was as pinched as a man rocketing out of the pull of the Earth's gravity. He snapped his cell phone shut and jammed it into the front pocket of his jeans.

'She never misses an opportunity to slam you.' Thorn rinsed the soap off a plate and set it in the drying rack.

'There weren't any pirates scheduled for the birthday party,' Sugar said.

Thorn ran some water over his hands and toweled them off and followed Sugarman out onto the porch.

'She's sure of that?'

'No pirates, no harem slaves, nothing like that. Markham left out of Morada Bay Marina down in Islamorada and was supposed to be back by ten-thirty last night. The whole gang had reservations at Cheeca and everyone was going to hang out on the beach this morning, then drive back to Lauderdale later today.'

'She hasn't heard from him?'

Sugarman shook his head.

'Never checked into the motel. Doesn't answer his cell.'

'We have to call the Coast Guard.'

'Jeannie's doing it. She says I blew it once already. I can't be trusted. According to her, I should've stamped my feet last night, made a big fuss, got them going. I'm a worthless wimp. She says I didn't have enough gumption to protect my own daughter. And I think maybe she's right.'

Thorn moved up beside Sugar and put a hand on his shoulder.

'Bullshit. You did what you could with the information you had. You were trying to get the facts. You were staying calm, thinking it through.'

'I should've done something right then. At least we could've taken out the *Heart Pounder*, gone looking for her.' Sugarman waved out at Thorn's ancient cabin cruiser moored at the coral dock. 'But hell, no, I'm dillydallying around here in the middle of the night, digging my toe in the dirt, acting like some gutless civilian without a clue.'

'We'll take the *Heart Pounder*,' Thorn said. 'It's gassed up.'

'What about Lawton? You're supposed to watch him.'

'He's always up for a boat ride. I'll get the keys; we'll go out to the shipping lanes, get on the radio, see if anybody's seen anything.'

'Goddamn guy dressed like a pirate,' Sugarman said. 'It's too weird.'

'You know better,' said Thorn. 'This is the Keys. Nothing's too weird.'

Narrow pressure gradients were squeezing a thirty-knot wind out of the east, kicking up five-foot swells even at the mouth of North Creek on the way out of Largo Sound. A clear sky, no sign of rain, but as blustery as the leading edge of a hurricane. And though the bulky *Heart Pounder* plowed smoothly enough through the waves, the rhythmic rise and fall of the deck was more than the puppy could endure. About a mile offshore, Lawton, the dog, stumbled toward the transom and began to dry heave. He chose a spot near the transom, strained his neck forward, and unloaded his breakfast in a strangled rush.

'Oh, well,' Lawton said. 'Little guy has to get his sea legs sooner or later.'

While Lawton used buckets of seawater to wash down the deck, Sugarman stayed on the VHF radio, talking to the Coast Guard station operator. It was half past nine, a standard-issue May morning, already easing toward ninety degrees, eighty percent humidity, a few downy cumulus bloomed along the horizon. Overhead, riding the mile-high currents, a single frigate bird shadowed them like a dark angel.

Hunched down out of the rush of wind, Sugarman thumbed the mike of the scratchy VHF, spoke in rapid sentences, then leaned his ear close to the speaker. A long burst of something closer to static than language crackled back. Thorn watched as Sugarman shook his head and the microphone dropped from his hand and bounced at the end of its spiral cord.

Backing off the throttle, Thorn waited for Sugar to join him at the wheel.

'What is it? You hear something?'

'Not good. Not good at all.'

Back by the transom, Lawton was on his knees scrub-brushing the last of the mess. The puppy nipped at the bristles while the old man worked.

'They found bodies,' Sugarman said.

'Aw, shit.'

'Coast Guard and Marine Patrol are working the scene. They said we could come on out, but we have to stay out of the search zone. Bodies are snagged on the anchor buoys at Carysfort Reef.'

Thorn rammed the throttle forward, cut the wheel so they swung around into the stiff, quartering sea. The *Heart Pounder* battered the swells and the rear deck was drenched in spray. The pup shook water from his coat and went sliding into the starboard hull.

'No sign of Janey,' Sugarman said. 'That's the good news. No sign of the boat, either.'

'And the bodies?'

'One female, late sixties, early seventies, wearing a ball gown. One old male in white pants, a red ascot. Shot in the head. Execution style.'

'Ball gown, ascot?' Thorn said. 'Does that sound like Markham?'

Sugarman's eyes searched the middle distance.

'The idiots in his inner circle take this past lives bullshit seriously. A date with Markham is prom night for these people. Get out the patent-leather shoes and the tuxes. Yeah, that's them.'

'Christ, Sugar.'

'It's okay,' he said. 'It's going to be okay.'

Sugar patted Thorn on the back. Comforting *him*. The way he always did when the shit rained down, bucking up his buddies – more concerned about them than the steel shaft buried in his own heart.

It was probably some syndrome with a fancy name, some blood disorder that could be cured with long-term therapy. Chronic altruism, post-traumatic selflessness. It was how Sugar had been since child-hood. Some inborn alchemy transformed his anger or grief into serenity, as if the grimmest moments triggered some spurt of psychic morphine. More than once Thorn had tried to use Sugar as his model. Tried to smooth his own ragged breath, flatten the spike in his blood. But it was no use. Thorn's emotional fulcrum tilted hard in the other direc-tion. A tinderbox forever on the verge of conflagra-tion.

A head-on slam into the face of a wave sent Lawton lurching into Thorn's back, their arms briefly tangling like bedmates waking from conflicting dreams.

'You want me to put the trolling lines out?' Lawton said.

'We're not fishing, Lawton.'

'Good sailfish weather.'

'Not today, Lawton.'

'Not fishing?'

'No, we're just taking a boat ride. That's all. A little fresh air.'

'Well, you picked a damn shitty day for pleasure boating.'

'Maybe you should go down below. Stay dry.'

'I'm all right,' the old man said. 'But little Lawton's a bit on the queasy side. Then again, if he's going to be a boat dog, he'll damn well have to get used to rough seas. That's what we Buddhists say: "It's not the same to talk of bulls as to be in the bull-ring."'

Sugarman peered at the horizon, face into the spray, the bow hammering wave after wave. As they worked into deeper water, the wind stiffened and the swells rose to seven and eight feet. Not dangerous yet, but banging that old wood hull pretty good. In the troughs, they lost touch with the horizon. Just the foamy crests blocking the sky, then they wallowed back up the cliff for a quick view and slid down the other side. The deck was slick, and seawater piled up at the scuppers. Behind him, Lawton swayed and stumbled, gripping hard to the handrail and chattering to himself – more wisdom from the East.

Thorn fought the wheel until his hands were crabbed and nearly useless, his arms on the verge of cramping. By the time they sighted the lighthouse tower at Carysfort he was ready to give up boating, move to Kansas, plant his feet forever in the firm soil of the heartland.

On the eastern edge of the reef they spotted the Coast Guard cutter and a couple of Marine Patrol cruisers working. Sugarman got on the radio and asked one more time if they could assist with the search. When he got the response, he settled the microphone back in its slot.

'Stay where we are.' His gaze drifted to the cutter. 'This is a crime scene.'

Laying up behind the reef, Thorn found a patch of smoother water and was about to drop anchor on a patch of sand when the dog began a frantic barking. Stretching up on his hind legs, he stuck his nose over the gunwale and clawed at the side until he found a hold and began to lever himself over.

Just in time Thorn scooped him up, ready to stow the Lab in the cabin, but he was wild and slimy with sea spray and he squirmed and bucked and with a yelp he tore free from Thorn's grasp and pitched over the side.

'Aw, Christ.'

A gray wave snatched the dog away, and a moment later he was surfing on the leading edge of the swell, headed toward the rim of the reef.

'Don't do it, Thorn.' Sugar put a hand on his

shoulder and drew him back from the side. 'Way too choppy for a swim.'

Lawton was standing at the port rail, two fingers poked in his mouth, whistling and shouting the dog's name. His yellow head bobbed into view, then disappeared as he pawed forward toward the reef. Since boyhood Thorn had snorkeled across that acre of elkhorn coral, and he was very aware that lurking only a foot or two below the surface was a solid mass of bony, unforgiving razor teeth. Beautiful but treacherous, that coral could shred the flesh to pulp with a glancing brush.

Thorn didn't take off his boat shoes. He climbed on the gunwale and was stretched out into a flat racer's dive before Sugarman had a chance to grab him.

Two strokes, then ducking into the curl of a rolling wave, then two more strokes and he was beside the puppy. He grabbed Lawton by the scruff and yanked him to a stop and was turning to haul him back to the boat when the dog yipped and squealed and tore from his grasp and pointed his nose to the white drifting mass a few inches below the surface of the sea. Thorn let the puppy loose and he promptly turned and paddled back toward the boat, leaving him with the waterlogged body.

It was as if the dog had heard the undetectable pierce of a whistle, a subsonic death song rising from the sea, and he had been unable to withstand its allure.

Staring up at Thorn through inches of salt water was a man's face, his white teeth showing. The blue cloud of iridescent damselfish that had been pecking at his lips scattered like some gorgeous last belch.

Thorn grabbed a handful of the man's white shirt and dragged the body to the surface, broke the corpse loose from the elkhorn coral's grasp, and then behind him, in a rush of white bubbles, came another body. In a blur he saw her blond hair, her flesh as white and luminescent as a newly minted pearl. Her eyes were stretched wide open, a sharp blue, bluer than the sky or the ocean, those blue eyes and white skin flooding up, bumping the man's corpse aside and ramming into Thorn's chest, into his arms, her cold flesh and bony limbs clutching like some lost lover come to reclaim him, drag him down with her into the seabed, the cold depths of longing and loss.

The middle-aged woman who surged into Thorn's arms wore a white cocktail dress that clung to her waifish frame. She'd been shot through the temple – one small hole, and a much larger hole exiting her opposite cheek. As he dragged their bodies toward the boat, Thorn recognized the man as Dr Andrew Markham, psychic Sherpa.

One after the other, Thorn heaved the bodies up to Sugarman's waiting hands, then he climbed aboard.

Silently they laid the bodies out in the cabin, stripped the sheets from the bunk, and covered their faces.

'Bad day at Black Rock,' Lawton said.

Sugarman looked at the old man for a long moment but said nothing.

After delivering the bodies to the Coast Guard cutter, Thorn and Sugar were granted permission to work alongside the Marine Patrol and the other Coast Guard ships. They took their place in the strict search pattern, spreading out in concentric circles, farther and farther from the reef. Just after noon they were joined by two helicopters that crossed and recrossed the search area.

By late afternoon the wind laid down and the body count had reached five. One man, apparently the captain of the yacht, had been knifed in the stomach, while Markham and another man and two women all had been put to death by small-caliber pistols. Dr Andy and his spiritual day-trippers had journeyed on to the next incarnation full of high hopes.

Patched in to the VHF, Jeannie Sugarman confirmed that the five bodies they'd found accounted for all the adults on board. Only Janey and the yacht itself were missing.

They worked till dark and for an hour afterward, using high-power searchlights to sweep the black sea, until finally the commander of operations called off the exercise till daylight. On the ride in, Sugarman went below and used the VHF to hail any of his fishing captain friends who might be listening, sending out the alert that his daughter was lost at sea. Thorn caught snatches of his talk. Calm, restrained, even apologetic about bothering them.

On the final leg of their journey home, as they came out of Adam's Cut, heading into Blackwater Sound, the blue strobe of a police car pulsed across the dark water. Thorn tracked the light along the shoreline, north beyond Sundowners restaurant and the Caribbean Club, both brightly lit; a short distance farther north was the dark zone where his stilt house stood and where the flashing blue light originated. Thorn throttled up and made it across the sound in less than two minutes.

'Monroe County,' Sugar said as they idled up to the dock. 'Taft himself.'

Thorn drew the *Heart Pounder* alongside the pilings and Sugarman jumped ashore with the bowline.

Upstairs on his porch there was a bright yellow flare and then another.

'What the hell!'

Lawton dropped to his knees, ducked his head.

'Muzzle flash!' he called out. 'Take cover!'

Up on the porch there were two more explosions of light and this time Thorn caught Alexandra's profile, her camera poised before her eye.

Thorn helped the old man to his feet.

'It's just Alex. She's taking pictures.'

'Oh, lord,' Lawton said. 'When that woman takes pictures, it's never good.'

Sugarman made the *Heart Pounder* fast to the dock cleats, then trotted off toward the cop car. Taft stood beside the cruiser talking on his radio.

Thorn helped Lawton climb over the side. The old man settled the puppy down on the grass, and he wandered off into the shadows.

While Sugar spoke with the sheriff in the blue throb of light, Thorn hustled over to the house and up the stairs.

'What's going on?'

Alexandra stepped into a wedge of light coming from the house. She dug a MagLite out of her trouser pocket and handed it to him and pointed at the French doors. Thorn flicked it on and swung the beam.

At eye level a black-handled fillet knife was stuck deep in the door's wood frame. Fluttering in a light breeze was a yellow Post-it note pinned in place by the point of the blade. Thorn leaned close and read the words scrawled in what looked like purple crayon:

THREE MILLION DOLLARS FOR THE
GIRL. OR ITEMS OF EQUAL VALUE.
GO AHEAD CALL THE POLICE IF YOU
CAN'T HELP YOURSELF, BUT IT WON'T
DO YOU ANY GOOD.

Thorn leaned closer to the sheet of paper. Focused the light on the blade, sniffed the air but couldn't pick up the scent.

'That what I think it is?'

'Looks a lot like blood to me. But you know not to touch anything.'

'Son of a bitch.'

'Stay calm, Thorn. Don't freak on me.'

'This is about my land,' he said. 'That fucking bastard, Marty Messina. "Three million dollars or items of equal value."'

'Marty or the man he's working for.'

Lawton carried his puppy past them into the house.

'Going to take a shower,' he said. 'Not that it makes any goddamn difference.'

'What're you talking about, Dad?'

'"Everything we do is futile, but we must do it anyway." That's Gandhi, the guy in the loincloth. Futile, like taking showers. Do it one day, you gotta do it again tomorrow. Roll the rock up the hill, it comes rolling back down.'

Sugarman and Sheriff Taft moved out of the halo of the blue strobe and headed toward the house. Sugarman's head was bowed. Taft had his hand on Sugar's shoulder.

'You have to tell Taft about Marty,' Alex said.

'Do I?'

'Yes, you do.'

'And then what? Stand back and watch the police once again efficiently and swiftly nab the suspects? Bring Janey to safety?'

'The FBI will come in on this,' Alex said. 'This'll get serious heat.'

'Yeah, like they're so much better.'

'I'm a sworn police officer, Thorn. I can't let you withhold evidence.'

He looked at the dark glitter of her eyes.

'Even though it's your natural tendency and you've had so much practice at it over the years.'

'You're right, you're right.'

'So you agree you'll stay out of it. Let the officials take over.'

'It's too obvious,' Thorn said. 'One week a guy tries to buy my place for three million dollars and I send him packing; the next week, Janey's ransomed for the same amount. Or items of equal value. Too goddamn easy.'

'Crooks aren't usually high-wattage intellects.'

'I know, I know. But this is way too dumb.'

'Thorn, the police can handle it. It's what they're trained for. They've got the tools, the manpower. It's their goddamn job, not yours.'

'Okay, okay. Point taken.'

The sheriff and Sugar were coming up the stairs. Thorn bent forward and gave her a quick kiss on the cheek.

'Don't patronize me, Thorn.'

'I kissed you.'

'Patting me on the head and dismissing me. That's what it felt like.'

'Jesus, you're tough.' Thorn reached out and touched her arm. 'I'm sorry. I'm not dismissing you. It's just that I've never developed much confidence

188

in our esteemed law enforcement establishment.'

'Which includes me.'

He apologized again, but her jaw was still hard when Taft stepped onto the porch, Sugarman right behind him.

The sheriff was a compact man in his mid-fifties. He'd been putting in some serious gym time, and his gray uniform shirt was cut tight across his tapered waist to prove it. He wore his black hair in a carefully shaggy John Kennedy style, a look he'd maintained for the two decades he'd been in office. He moved with the mildly bowlegged strut of a lifelong jock who'd just that morning done more work on some obscure muscle group than Thorn had managed in his entire existence. Though he'd had some hostile run-ins with the sheriff and his people over the years, Thorn never considered Taft a bad man. Neither incompetent nor corrupt. Maybe just a fraction over-impressed with his position in the world.

'Thorn,' Taft said.

'Hey, Rick. You're looking good.'

He nodded his agreement.

'Forensics are on the way,' he said to Alex. 'But thanks for the assist.'

She said he was quite welcome.

'You're coming up in the world, Thorn.' Taft shined his billy-club flashlight on the door and leaned in to inspect the knife. 'An ID tech from Miami PD. That's a major advance for a guy like you.'

Sugarman kept his distance. Bent forward just enough to read the note.

When he was finished he stared over Taft's shoulder at Thorn. His eyes shadowed with something as close to rage as Thorn had ever seen there.

'This strike anyone as odd?' Taft was still peering at the ransom note.

'*Odd* wouldn't be my word of choice,' Thorn said.

'Odd how?' Alex said.

'The whole deal. A girl kidnapped off a boat right before her own daddy's eyes. It was what, seven, eight o'clock.'

'Nine,' Sugarman said.

'And the point?' Thorn said.

'All right, it goes down at nine o'clock. Apparently about the same time as she's being taken captive, the rest of the passengers are murdered and the boat's stolen. A major crime. Going to make headlines, no two ways about it, be a big deal, lead stories for days, even around here, might even go national. But still, the guy who's doing this has the balls to waltz right up to Thorn's house, not Sugarman's, mind you, and stick a knife, possibly even a murder weapon, in the front door demanding a quantity of money that I'm fairly sure Thorn and Sugarman together haven't earned in their entire lives.'

'Whoever stuck that note in my door knew we weren't here,' Thorn said. 'That we'd gone out on the *Heart Pounder*.'

Taft looked out at the dark water, swiveling for a view north, then south along the shore.

'Well, yeah. It wouldn't be hard for somebody to keep a watch on your comings and goings from a hundred different locations along the shoreline, even anchored out on a boat. When they saw you leave, they came in, left the message, and got the hell away. Still, I'd call that fairly brazen.'

'Brazen,' Thorn said. 'Or crazy.'

Taft straightened up and switched off his flashlight.

'And why your house, not Sugarman's? And how about the outrageous figure, three million bucks?'

'Marty Messina,' Thorn said.

He heard Alexandra's sigh. All this time waiting for him to do the right thing. She set her camera on the picnic table and took a seat on the bench.

Taft turned and stared at Thorn.

'Marty Messina? What're you talking about?'

'This is about me, Rick,' Thorn said.

Taft flicked on the flashlight and brought the blinding beam onto Thorn's face and held it there. Thorn squinted but kept staring into the brightness.

'Christ almighty,' Taft said. 'It never stops with you, does it? It never fucking stops.'

12

They waited at Thorn's till the crime scene people arrived. Thorn gave the sheriff a quick summary of Messina's offer on his land. Taft looking dubious until Thorn told him the amount. Three million dollars.

'Steal a child to get some land?' Taft shook his head. 'Never heard of that.'

'How's it supposed to work?' Alex said. 'I don't get it.'

'Maybe we're supposed to wait for further details,' Thorn said. 'Then again maybe this is the one shot we get.'

'We need to find Messina,' Sugar said. 'We're wasting time.'

'And do what?' Taft said. 'We've got no evidence tying him to this.'

'Enough evidence for me,' Sugarman said.

After staring out at the dark for a moment, Taft let go of a lungful of air and agreed they could come along. Just this once, though. Don't get any ideas he was bringing them in on the investigation.

Fifteen minutes later at Tarpon's, Taft questioned the bartender, and yeah, the young guy thought he remembered seeing Messina hanging out at the bar a few times lately but told the sheriff that the dishwasher might know Marty a little better, giving them a slimy wink. In the steamy kitchen the Mexican kid running the big silver machine shut off his spray hose, eyed the sheriff anxiously, brushing a glop of food off his chin with a soapy hand.

'Big guy, black hair, thick fucking neck?'

'That's the description we have,' said Taft.

'I think Mary knows the guy,' he said. 'Seen her with him once or twice.'

'Which Mary?' Sugarman said.

The sheriff turned a stony look on Sugar but said nothing.

'Mary Miller?' Thorn said.

The dishwasher said yeah, that Mary.

'Never heard of her.' Taft looked at Thorn.

'She's a lady of the evening,' Thorn said. 'Works out of the Marriott bar. A nice young lady with green hair and a scorpion tattoo on her belly.'

'What? You got an inventory of all the local tattoos, Thorn?'

'Everyone knows Mary's scorpion,' Sugar said. 'Even I know about it.'

'I guess I been staying in the office too much,' Taft said.

'This time of night, where would we find Mary?' Sugarman asked the dishwasher. His voice was dead. The sheriff clenched his teeth but kept silent. Caught between his normal alpha dog tendencies and grudging deference for Sugar's grief.

The dishwasher gave them an address in Tavernier.

'Oceanside, down by Harry Harris Park. Weird round fucking house.'

'This what you do, amigo?' Taft said. 'You Mary's pimp?'

'No, man, it's not like that,' the Mexican said. 'I just know a lot of people, that's all. Put 'em together if I can.'

'So you're a matchmaker.'

'Yeah, yeah, whatever. But I ain't no pimp. No way, man.'

'We're wasting time, Taft,' Sugar said.

The sheriff swallowed a lump of anger, gave the Mexican kid a last vicious look, then led the way out of the restaurant.

Everyone was silent in the car. Taft steaming, handling the cruiser with brutish disregard. It took ten minutes to get to Mary's round house a block from Harry Harris Park. In the driveway, Taft slammed the shifter into park and turned on Sugar, then shot Thorn a look as well.

'Now look, you shit dicks. I'll handle this. As a token of respect for Sugarman's history in law enforcement, I'm letting you come along, but I have my own way of doing things. Sugarman, you're not on the force anymore. Let's not forget that, all right?'

'So handle it,' Sugar said quietly.

After the second round of knocking, Mary Miller threw open the door. She had on a pair of green bikini panties that matched her hair and wore nothing on top. She was as flat-chested as a ten-year-old boy, her ribs shining in the streetlight. The scorpion was red and yellow and smoldered against her white flesh. Its spiked tail was curled around her navel, its spidery legs disappearing into the brim of her panties.

'What're you looking at?' she said to the bunch of them. 'You never seen titties before?'

'Marty Messina,' Sugar said. 'You know where he lives?'

'Jesus Christ, Sugarman,' Taft said. 'Go sit in the goddamn car.'

The sheriff stepped between Sugar and Mary.

'That goon Messina,' Mary said, talking past the sheriff to Sugarman. 'Hell, yes, I know where he lives. That street across from Rowell's Marina. The one with the dive shop out front.'

'Largo Lane?' Sugarman said.

'That's it, yeah, Largo Lane.'

From the shadows behind her a tall black man

with dreadlocks appeared. He was naked and seemed to shine with a coating of oil. The joint he was smoking was as big as a ballyhoo. He gave the sheriff a lingering appraisal but didn't seem impressed enough to hide his dope.

'Anything wrong, Miss Mary?'

She said no, there wasn't, and without turning around she reached behind her and patted him twice on the chest. Good dog.

'Second house on the right, when you come off the highway. Downstairs rental apartment.'

'Thanks, Mary,' Sugar said, and turned to go.

'Kick him in the nuts when you see him. Scumsucking pig had his fun and stiffed me. Fucker needs to go back to jail, learn some manners.'

It was nearly midnight when they pulled off the highway onto Largo Lane. Thorn's neighborhood. Taft had said nothing since leaving Mary's, and Thorn sure as hell wasn't up for small talk. Sugar sat in the front seat and stared out the side window and rubbed a fingertip back and forth across his forehead as if trying to smooth away a blinding migraine.

The house was concrete block, painted gray. It rose up to the usual fifteen feet on cement pilings. The downstairs apartment was wedged between the pilings. The windows in the apartment were louvered, most of them either cracked or missing. Anyone living in that dump would hear every eighteen-wheeler, every shift of gear and burp of exhaust, from thirty yards away on the Overseas Highway.

Below the croton bushes planted by the front door a white cat was prowling, but otherwise there was no sign of activity.

No one answered the sheriff's knock on the door of the downstairs apartment. No cars in the drive. Above them the windows of the main house were shuttered tight – owners gone for hurricane season, already back in Chicago, Toronto, or Trenton. Sugarman stepped past the sheriff and turned the knob and swung open the door and stepped inside.

'You can't fucking do that, Sugarman. Get back out here.'

'He doesn't need a warrant,' Thorn said. 'He's a friend of Marty's. So am I. We're just stopping by for a beer.'

'You guys go sit in the goddamn car or I'll put cuffs on the both of you.'

Thorn edged past the sheriff and followed Sugarman into the dark apartment. Behind him Thorn heard what sounded like the sheriff unholstering his gun, but he continued into the apartment anyway. Even though Taft had his black belt in machismo, Thorn was pretty sure the sheriff wasn't about to shoot a couple of locals in the back over a failure to obey.

Marty's room was bare. From the glow of the highway lights and the flares of passing cars Thorn could see there was nothing but a refrigerator and a single bed stripped to the mattress. No dresser, no knickknacks or family portraits. A cheap plastic phone lay on the floor. Even for a crash pad it was spartan – unless you'd been living in a prison cell for the last ten years.

'Okay, come on, you two,' the sheriff said. 'There's nothing here. If he was here at all, he's long gone. I'll send some people over tomorrow, check for prints, do a shakedown.'

Sugarman opened the refrigerator. Nothing but a box of baking soda, a jar of pickles, and a moldering pork chop.

'Goddamn it,' Taft said. 'That's it! Now you're disturbing evidence. Fucking with a criminal investigation.'

Sugarman swung around and Thorn stepped out of his way. Sugar marched outside and headed back to the car and opened the passenger door and stood waiting until Taft and Thorn followed. When Taft was behind the wheel clipping on his seat belt and Thorn settled in the back, Sugar turned back and with long strides was inside the apartment before Taft even noticed.

Taft looked across at the open passenger door, then swung around to peer out the back window.

'Where the hell did he go?'

A moment later Sugarman came out the apartment door again but walked right past the cruiser and headed out to the highway.

'What the fuck is he doing?'

'Oh, he gets like this,' Thorn said. 'Whenever one of his daughters is kidnapped.'

Thorn hopped out of the back and trotted to catch up with Sugar. He was walking south down the shoulder of the highway. Not fast, not slow, just his usual methodical gait.

'What is it, man? What'd you find?'

'I pressed redial on his phone.'

'And?'

'Got the message machine for Paradise Funeral Home.'

'Jesus Christ,' Thorn said.

'Yeah,' said Sugar. 'My thought exactly.'

'Should've seen that coming. Marty and Vic. Match made in heaven.'

'Vic Joy,' Sugar said. 'Everybody's favorite lawbreaker.'

'Is that where we're going? The funeral home, this time of night?'

'That's where *I'm* going.'

'Mind if I tag along?'

'Suit yourself.'

'Nobody'll be there, Sugar. It's after midnight.'

'Won't know till we get there, will we?'

'Vic lives down in Islamorada, oceanside, one of those estates on millionaire row. I'm not sure which.'

'We'll find out,' Sugarman said. 'If he's not at the funeral home, his address will be.'

They found a break in the traffic and sprinted

across the four-lane to the bay side of the highway. A moment later Taft pulled alongside them, his blue strobe going. He lowered the passenger window and leaned across the seat.

'Where you boys headed?'

'Cactus Jack's,' Thorn said. 'A couple shots before bed.'

Taft looked dubious, idling along, keeping pace with them as the traffic hurtled by in the outside lane. Sugarman's eyes were focused down the highway.

'All right then,' Taft said. 'But I'm going to be watching you two. You hear that? I don't want any of your bullshit, Thorn. Taking the law into your hands. We got that loud and clear?'

Sugarman halted and came over to the window of the car.

He leaned down, gripped the door, and stared at Taft.

'And we're going to be watching you, too, Sheriff. Believe it.'

They looked at each other for a few seconds. Then Sugar straightened up and Taft raised the window, stepped on the gas, and sped away into the night, his blue light still whirling.

'Hey, listen,' Thorn said. 'Maybe we should wait till morning, take a break, think this through.'

Sugarman was walking again; Thorn had to work to stay even. He'd never seen Sugar eat up so much distance with such ease.

'Think what through?' Sugar said.

'What we're going to do. Our approach. Even if he's there this time of night, we can't just go crashing into Vic Joy's home, slam him up against the wall, and torture him till he tells us what's going on.'

'Why not?'

'That's not you, Sugar. You play by the book.'

'And look where it's gotten me.'

'Just slow down. Let's talk this over, come up with a plan of action.'

'You're saying that, Thorn? You of all people?'

Sugar halted near the gate of Rowell's Marina, a long, sloping, grassy meadow that ran down to the gleam of the bay. For a moment he looked out at the traffic that rushed by a couple of yards away. Even at that late hour the four-lane was busy. Bleary tourists heading north to Miami International for the red-eye home. Big trucks blasting south loaded down with supplies for Marathon and Big Pine, Sugarloaf and the outlandish and insatiable appetites of Key West.

Buffeted by the tailwinds of the passing cars, Thorn had to reset his feet to hold his ground.

'Don't commit a crime to solve a crime, that's always been your motto. Revenge poisons the avenger.'

A stream of headlights blazed in his eyes, but Sugar didn't flinch.

Sugar turned his back on the traffic and looked

out past Rowell's at the dark water where the two of them had spent so many contented hours.

'This is my daughter, Thorn.'

'Yeah, it is.'

'It's only fair I should warn you,' Sugar said, 'because I know you've been using me over the years as your safety line. You go berserk, get yourself knee-deep in shit, and count on me to drag you back to high ground. Well, this time you need to look for another safety line. Because there isn't a goddamn thing under the sun I won't do to get Janey back.'

An eighteen-wheeler flew past and kicked up a tornado of road dust. When Thorn had rubbed his eyes clear, Sugar was already twenty yards down the shoulder. Thorn broke into a trot and caught up. He patted Sugar on the shoulder, then settled in and tried to match his stride.

A few hundred yards south, they passed Thorn's driveway. They could've ducked in there and gotten the VW, made it to the funeral home ten minutes quicker, but then again, he'd have to explain everything to Alexandra and get caught up in evasions or outright lies, hiding from her that he was doing exactly what he'd promised he wouldn't.

As they passed the drive, he felt a spasm of guilt, but the black heat rising off Sugarman was irresistible. For a quick moment Janey's face floated into his vision and his flesh prickled. And damn it all, if he was honest about it, he had to admit that after months of domestication and quiet, the hot rush of emotions felt good, a virtuous fury sweeping through him, permission to surrender all prudence and good sense to these base animal instincts. He'd have to consider that later, how good it felt to be this angry. But for now, he was rolling with it, caught in Sugar's wake, ready to go deep into the heart of the fire if that's where this led.

Twenty minutes later, huffing and damp with sweat, they stood outside the darkened building. Paradise Funeral Home. The front door was locked, no cars in the lot, no lights anywhere.

'What's your pleasure?' Thorn said. 'Windows or doors?'

Sugarman stood for a moment in silence, blinking at the shadowy structure, his face unsettled as though waking from some rabid nightmare and gradually coming to the terrible understanding that it had been no dream at all.

'Maybe we should take a look around first,' Thorn said. 'Place could be alarmed. We don't want to get thrown in jail before we even get started.'

A fleeting melancholy came to Sugar's eyes and seemed to weigh down his shoulders. Then he shook himself hard, lifted his head, shrugged it away, and turned to the door, and with a suddenness that made Thorn stumble backward, Sugar broke into a three-step charge, heaved his shoulder against the double doors, bounced off the heavy wood, then drew back and slammed again. The doors were damn solid, but

Sugar's second blow seemed to loosen the hardware and an inch or two of play was appearing.

Maybe it was the buzz in Thorn's blood, a jangle in the synapses that had temporarily deafened him to the natural world, but Thorn didn't hear it coming. Didn't have even a tickle of warning.

All he saw was a blur of something large and dark in his peripheral vision; then he felt a stunning thump on the back of his neck. His vision shrank to a pinhole, and a bitter reflux rose into his throat. He hovered in the dizzy twilight for a moment, feeling his legs give.

Then as the white moonlit gravel spun upward toward him, Thorn caught a peep of Sugarman turning a half-second too late as a large man hurtled out of the darkness with uncanny speed, arm upraised, blackjack already falling against Sugar's flesh.

13

'Pirates,' the man said. 'What you're looking at is the gruesome and heartless work of modern maritime pirates. A new breed of seafaring bandit. Men as bloodthirsty and wild as any criminal element the world has ever known.'

A wave of nausea rose from Thorn's gut and swelled through his chest. The room was dark and he was sitting. That much he knew. On a screen in front of him was a color slide of half a dozen bodies littering a dark pebbled beach. The men were small and dark, wearing mostly white T-shirts and baggy shorts. Throats cut, stab wounds in their chests or stomachs. Thorn's vision blurred. He might have slipped off into a doze for a few seconds.

'These men are not Americans. But they have

children and wives just like we do. They were young, hardworking. Indonesians, Filipinos, Straits Chinese. Other cultures, other ways of doing things, but by God, they're humans. They count. That's one of the problems we're dealing with, lack of public outrage. These people live on the other side of the globe, so it's not our problem. Plus, everybody is so focused on terrorists, nothing further down the food chain matters anymore.'

The man was standing somewhere behind them, out of sight.

'But here's the facts, Mr Thorn. In the last ten years, maritime pirates accounted for thousands of civilian casualties. But does anybody know that? And more important, does anybody care? No, because it happens out on the high seas. A few million dollars in lost cargo here and few million there, no one's ringing it up. Newspapers won't cover it. Same amount of cash gets stolen from a bank, or gold from a depository, it's big news. 'Cause it happens on land, in somebody's neighborhood. But you lose fifteen million dollars' worth of motor-cycles or electric generators or plumbing pipes, because it happens out at sea, it might as well be Mars.

'If somebody hijacked the equivalent amount of cargo from eighteen-wheelers off our highways, our economy would shut down. We'd think we were under attack. And consider this: It'd take a few hundred transfer trucks to equal the value in freight of just one of these cargo ships. Happens out in the ocean, big deal. A bunch of Filipino crew members killed, how's that our business? Well, it *is* our business. It damn well is. It's costing the world economy billions. That's with a *b*, Thorn. And it's just about to get a whole hell of a lot worse.'

On Thorn's cheek, a strip of flesh began to itch. But when he tried to lift his arm to rub the spot, he found his wrists were bound to the arms of the chair. His ankles and calves were strapped tightly to the chair's legs.

'Private yachts, sailboats, even superstars like Sir Peter Greene, shot down on a trip up the Amazon where he was doing environmental research. Guy wins every sailboat race there is, the America's Cup, all that, he's an international celebrity. You can't be any more high-profile. And he's off doing good for the world and gets murdered for his Rolex and a couple of handguns he had onboard.'

A tall, craggy red-haired man filled the screen. He gripped the wheel of a racing craft, his hair wind-blown and his yellow foul-weather gear glistening with rain. The next shot showed his naked body stretched out on what looked like a kitchen table. A sheet over his waist. A crude morgue set up in the jungle.

After sucking down a breath, Thorn yanked all four limbs against the restraints, but the only result was a wrenching stab in his ribs. Must've bruised something in his fall, which would also explain the tenpenny nail that had been spiking into his liver every time he filled his lungs. He groaned and slumped back.

'Where's Sugarman? What'd you do with him?'

Thorn lifted his head and turned to the right.

'He's next door,' the man said. 'With my associate. This information is strictly for you, Thorn, not for Mr Sugarman. He's safe and sound, and when we're done here you two will be reunited. Now pay attention. We don't have a lot of time for banter.'

Thorn recognized the voice but couldn't place it. Something distasteful in the way he spoke. A smacking sound between his words as if his lips were gluey with excess spit. Then the vision trickled into focus, the face first, the gleaming bald head, that precise ribbon of beard running along his jawline. It took a few more seconds of poking around in Thorn's stunned memory banks before he had the name.

'Webster?' Thorn said. 'Jimmy Lee.'

'Well, I'm pleased you remember me.' Webster stood somewhere close behind them. 'Now pay attention. You need to get up to speed before you're going to do anyone any good.'

'Where's the girl?'

'She's fine,' Webster said. 'Don't sweat it.'

Thorn thrashed against his bindings, got nowhere, then surged upward, tried to stand, break the chair with a straining grunt, but a man in black slacks and a black jersey slammed a hand on his shoulder and forced him down again.

'What the hell have you done with her!'

'We haven't done anything with her,' Webster said. 'Now, are you going to sit still and listen or will Zashie exhibit his rabbit punch again?'

Webster flashed another slide. It appeared to be a publicity file photo of yet another tanker. Thorn wasn't any expert on commercial ships, but this was one of the big ones. Supertanker, megatanker, whatever they called it.

'The *Global Mars*,' Webster said. 'Crew of twenty. Ship loaded with palm oil. Disappeared from the Strait of Malacca last autumn. Ship plus the cargo was worth close to forty million dollars. Twenty souls missing, presumed dead. The pirates take the ship, toss the crew overboard, sell the cargo, then repaint and reflag the ship and sail into port in southern China and sell the tanker itself. Chinese officials are in on it. They know it's stolen. But is anybody putting pressure on them? Hell, no.

'These people are taking a huge bite out of international commerce. In the realm of criminal activity, drugs are a solid number one, but maritime piracy is closing fast. And lately these bastards are getting more bold. Last month one group we've been tracking for years targeted a French freighter carrying military hardware. Did you hear that? We're talking serious armaments. Missiles, shoulder-fired antiaircraft rocket launchers. Some bad explosive stuff. Hasn't made the news because it's in no one's interest that it should, some serious information suppression going on, government to government, people covering their asses.

'And what did our friends the pirates do with the arms? Well, we're not sure. They may have diverted them to a country we'd rather not have those particular weapons. Or an even more disturbing possibility is they stole these weapons for their own use. Do I have your attention?'

Webster fast-flicked through a dozen more slides. Ships plundered, crew slaughtered. A couple of flashy sailboats, the bodies of their handsome young crew members slung about the decks. Too fast for most of it to register.

'These people have penetrated shipping companies, port authorities, national customs services. These aren't our great-granddaddies' pirates. Some of these are college grads, they've acquired high-end communications systems, they're heavily armed, and they're greedy as hell. They'll sell anything to anyone, steal whatever they find floating on the seven seas, kill crews without a second thought. Private sailboats disappearing somewhere in the world at the rate of five a week, yachts, Christ, even fishing trawlers. If you're out of sight of land, you're a target. And they're depending on public apathy. And every day these thugs are getting more audacious. We've been shifting massive resources away from conventional targets to terrorist concerns, and they know it. Nobody gave a shit about pirates before; now they're even farther off the radar screen.'

Thorn drew a breath and said, 'But not off yours.'

'It's my calling,' he said. 'I work the gray zone. International Maritime Bureau, which monitors criminal acts at sea, they cover some of my expenses and pass on a good deal of information from the shipping companies, but I'm still punching the clock at the Pentagon.'

'You're connected,' Thorn said. 'And I'm not.'

'The fact is,' Webster said, 'you're about as unconnected as any asshole I've ever run across.'

Zashie snorted.

Webster came around into the light and stood directly in the projected image of a dozen corpses strewn across the deck of an oil tanker.

'What does this have to do with Janey?'

'Who's Janey?'

'Sugarman's daughter,' Thorn said. 'You idiot.'

'Oh, it's Janey, is it? I didn't know her name. Well, you can rev down your engines. She's fine. Like I said. We're looking after her welfare.'

'What does that mean? Where is she?'

'In a safe location.'

'Where, goddamn it?'

Projected on Webster's slick white forehead was a young man with a half-dozen bullet holes perforating his blue work shirt.

'You're going to stay calm, Mr Thorn, or you won't do her or yourself any good. And listen, I deeply regret having to use force with you and your friend. But the way you were acting, trying to batter

211

down Vic Joy's front door, it looked to me like we didn't have any choice. I can release your restraints if you promise to be a gentleman.'

Thorn rattled his chair again. Not having any of it.

The runt paced back and forth in front of the screen a moment more. Then he went over to the far wall and flicked on a desk lamp. They were in a hotel room, generic furniture, a watercolor of sandpipers strutting along a beach. The beds pushed aside to make room for the screen.

Webster's henchman, Zashie, was a rawboned man with a long, horsy face. His head was shaved, but he'd let his sideburns grow in, strips of hair running from nowhere to nowhere. Some half-assed attempt at novelty. His eyes were dark and seemed permanently unimpressed with what passed before them, as if he'd long ago rid himself of the emotions that stirred other men. He studied Thorn with the indifference of an entomologist who is merely trying to detect the variation between this doomed insect and all the others.

'Vincent Salbone, is that a name you've heard?'

Thorn wrenched his arms again, but the Velcro didn't give. A bullet of pain seared across his rib cage.

The little man stepped beside Thorn and squatted down.

'Daniel Salbone, how about that name?'

'Never heard of him.'

'Daniel was Vincent Salbone's only son.'

'Why the hell should I care?'

Webster said, 'The father, Vincent Salbone, orchestrates a good portion of the organized crime south of Fort Lauderdale. Trucking, sports books, an escort service, beer distribution. Not to mention cocaine and heroin on the side. Daniel is his son. Mid-thirties. Tall kid. Very suave. You sure you don't know him?'

Thorn stared into Webster's eyes but said nothing.

'Okay, so you don't know him. That's fine. I believe that. It doesn't matter really.'

Webster rose and stepped out of Thorn's line of vision and aimed the remote at the slide projector.

With the desk lamp on, the new image was slightly washed out but clear enough for Thorn to see an overhead shot of the deck of another large ship. Some kind of tanker with more bodies strewn across its deck. The photo apparently taken from a helicopter hovering a few hundred feet above.

'Look closely, Thorn,' Webster said. 'This is the *Rainmaker*, an oil tanker that was making its regular run from Alaska to a refinery up the Mississippi River.'

On the bright screen the dead bodies strewn across the deck were different from the ones in the previous shots. These men were dressed in solid black clothing and they were taller, heavier – Americans or Europeans. Automatic weapons were scattered about near their bodies.

Webster advanced the slide and said, 'Notice the men at the rear.'

It took Thorn a second to spot them. A half-dozen crew members hog-tied in sitting positions, their backs against a bright yellow container. A couple were slumped forward, maybe dead, maybe passed out.

'Six of the thirteen crew members survived. The other seven died of dehydration.'

'I'm sorry to hear it.'

'Last month the *Rainmaker* was found adrift several hundred miles off the Nicaraguan coast. From the reports the surviving crew members gave, a squad of well-trained men boarded their ship early in the afternoon on April sixteenth, tied them up, and lay in wait until approximately two in the morning of the seventeenth, when the *Rainmaker* was boarded by two boatloads of pirates. The mercenaries or soldiers or whatever they were then proceeded to ambush the pirates, slaughtering most of them. As far as we know for sure, two of the pirate gang managed to escape. Then the mercenaries left the ship without releasing the crew. Two days later the ship was sighted by a passing freighter and the surviving crew members rescued.'

Thorn said, 'I must be dense, Jimmy Lee. None of this seems to have one fucking thing to do with me or Sugarman or Janey's kidnapping.'

Webster seemed not to have heard, his tone unaltered as he continued.

214

'We know for certain those mercenaries weren't with my organization, although we've mounted several similar operations in the past year. So that part remains a mystery. But from identifying the corpses, and from other physical evidence gathered at the scene, we're certain the pirates who attacked the *Rainmaker* were led by Daniel Salbone.'

'The son of the Mafia guy.'

'Yes.'

Webster strutted in front of the screen, back straight, head tilted upward like some haughty professor choosing his phraseology with fussy care.

'I'm sure you remember the afternoon when I came to you, asking for your help, Thorn, that day you dismissed me so rudely.'

'How could I forget?'

'Did you tell Mr Sugarman about our encounter that afternoon?'

He shook his head no.

'I thought that might be the case. So my friend in the other room is letting Mr Sugarman know the details of that meeting. I thought he might find it noteworthy that you'd refused to help. And that this refusal is part of the reason why we're here.'

'I don't get it. What's the connection with that and all this pirate crap?'

'Anne Bonny Joy is the connection.'

'Anne?'

'Yes, Anne,' said Webster. 'Last February, shortly after she served you at the Lorelei restaurant, Anne

Bonny Joy waited on Daniel Salbone, who was lunching at the same restaurant and at the same time as you and your group. Subsequently, Ms Joy and Mr Salbone spent three weeks together in seclusion at the Cheeca Lodge. From what we could determine on our audio pickups, they had a highly charged sexual encounter. You see, we've been working on this case for some time, trying to harden our evidence on Salbone. And when I came to you asking for your help with any information you might have about Anne Joy, it was because your name had just emerged in the pillow talk at the Cheeca Lodge.'

Thorn stared down at the floor and shook his head.

'What kind of bullshit is this, Webster? You think I'm involved with these goddamn pirates?'

'Hardly,' Webster said, making it sound like he would've found Thorn more admirable if he had been. 'I came to you asking for your help that day because you seemed to have intimate knowledge of this young woman, and had you been more forthcoming on that occasion, we might not be standing in this room in the predicament we find ourselves.'

'Wait a goddamn minute.' Thorn bulled his chair forward. Zashie made a move, but Webster waved him back. 'You're not blaming this on me.'

The small man let a bit of smugness creep into his smile.

'No, no,' Webster said. 'Just because you blew me off that day, it doesn't mean you could've prevented any of this from happening. But then again, we'll never know what quality of intelligence you might have provided, something you didn't even know the relevance of. Something we could have used to move on Salbone and stop him dead that very afternoon.'

'And why the fuck haven't you moved on him? You know he's a pirate. You bugged his hotel room. What the hell's keeping you from arresting the son of a bitch?'

'There's more to it, Thorn. Trust me, when we have the information we need, we'll move.'

'And now?'

Jimmy Lee Webster's lips twisted again into that miserable smile.

'Now you're going to help us, Mr Thorn, whether you want to or not. The safe return of Mr Sugarman's daughter absolutely depends on it.'

14

'Is she all right?' Thorn said. 'Tell me, goddamn it. Tell me the truth. Is Janey all right?'

Webster said she was fine, just fine, she was doing quite well, given the circumstances. A smart, resilient young lady, she was handling the difficult situation extremely well. But Thorn read something in his eyes that was lagging behind the words, a disconnect, either outright dishonesty or some tricky evasion of semantics that amounted to the same thing.

'Where is she, goddamn it?'

'How many times do I have to say it, Thorn? We have that situation contained. The girl is under our control. No harm will come to her.'

'The United States government is aiding and

abetting the kidnapping of a child? Tell me you're not serious.'

'Listen to me, sir. From this point forward the fate of that girl is inextricably linked with your own actions. Is that clear?'

'Where is she?' Thorn repeated the words with a level of menace that brought a smile to Zashie's lips. Another bone-crushing opportunity.

'There's one way and one way only that girl is coming home,' Webster said. 'It's very simple.'

'You don't have her,' Thorn said. 'You don't know where she is.'

'You're going to perform the one task you manage so well.'

'I am, am I? And what would that be?'

'You're going to rekindle your romance with Miss Joy.'

'The hell I am.'

As Webster's lips came apart in a grin there was another gluey pop.

'Oh, yes. Yes, indeed, you are.'

'And what would that accomplish?' Thorn glanced at the screen, at those huddled crewmen, hog-tied and dying of thirst.

'It might interest you to know that one of the people who escaped that night from the *Rainmaker* was your old friend, Anne Joy. We know with a high degree of certainty that for over a month she played a leading role in Salbone's crew and was involved in several acts of piracy before the final incident.'

'Anne Joy, a pirate?'

'That's correct, Mr Thorn.'

'I don't believe it.'

'You're free to believe what you want,' Webster said. 'But it's true.'

Thorn stared at the screen, the corpses of ordinary seamen, those ghostly crews.

'The other person who escaped that night,' Webster continued, 'was a man we believe was acting as Salbone's chief lieutenant. His name is Marty Messina.'

Thorn watched the screen. The haunted look in those seamen's eyes.

'As you already surmised,' Webster said, 'Marty Messina has recently joined forces with Vic Joy.'

'Yeah, I surmised it all right.'

'That Messina should turn up in Key Largo only a week after his escape from the ship and successfully worm into Vic Joy's inner circle, I have to say, this caught us off guard. But finally, the more I considered it, the more it made sense, and the more it became clear that what we were witnessing was a carefully orchestrated plan. A little sleight of hand that almost threw us off the hunt.'

Webster snapped the remote and the screen filled with the face of a man in his thirties, darkly tanned, with swept-back hair that was a thick, glossy black. His milky blue eyes were a dazzling contrast to his hair and his sun-darkened skin. Sensuous lips, almost girlish lashes. He had a finely molded jaw and a nose

220

that hinted of Roman nobility. It was a magazine face, no doubt considered exquisitely handsome by a certain type of woman. Equal parts rugged and debonair, but with a lurking tinge of insincerity somewhere in the curl of his lips and the sharp spark in his eyes.

It was tough to find its exact location, but Thorn saw in that mix of features a man he knew all too well. This guy was a fixture at certain local bars and nightclubs. A charmer so used to trading on his looks, he'd lost a measure of respect for those who surrendered to the spell. Over time, Thorn had seen that lack of respect toward the very women who found him irresistible could turn into quiet disdain. It was a lot to base on a snapshot. First impressions, of course, could be wildly off the mark. But Thorn had run into plenty of these dreamboats, many of them rich kids with flashy cars and boats, heavy gold on their wrists, diamond studs in their earlobes. Blessed by bone structure and dreamy eyes, more than a few of these playboys wound up forever doubting the authenticity of affection that was lavished on them. And what was once pride and genuine relish in their own good genetic fortune soured over time into spite and sometimes even a streak of hatefulness that could be dangerous to all involved.

Webster advanced the projector. The same young man was piloting a long, sleek speedboat with the *Black Swan* inscribed in gold script on its stern. The young playboy was sandwiched between two over-blown blondes in matching blue thongs.

'Daniel Salbone?' Thorn said.

'The man of the hour,' Webster said. 'The rogue who has brought us together tonight.'

At last Thorn thought he was untangling the snarl of Webster's narrative. A knot or two left, but most of it starting to clarify.

'You believe Salbone also escaped the *Rainmaker*,' he said.

Webster smiled indulgently as if his slow child had finally spoken his first word.

'All we know for sure is that after the events on the *Rainmaker* Salbone's body was not recovered, and he's dropped out of sight. It's possible he was killed that night and his body lost at sea. Or as you say, he might have escaped, which could mean that right now he could be out searching for the people that attacked him. Or simply plotting his next move.'

'Does Anne know this?' said Thorn. 'Or does she believe he's dead?'

'What's your guess, Thorn?'

'If the guy's still alive, maybe he left her in the dark to protect her while he's off seeking revenge. Or maybe for other reasons. Maybe he's not sure how he feels about her and he's making up his mind, or else he's dumped her. Who the hell knows?'

'Good, good. You're very intuitive. I like that.'

'And then there's Marty Messina,' Thorn said.

'Yes?'

'Marty's still working for Salbone,' Thorn said. 'He came back to Key Largo to be Anne's guardian angel on Salbone's behalf.'

Webster punched the air in an ironic salute to Thorn's intellect.

'What a surprise. Zashie. Our insouciant young man who pretends to be so dense and full of disregard for world affairs isn't at all what he appears to be.'

But Zashie was finding none of this amusing. He was fondling his blackjack as if it had nerve endings linked to his own brain.

'Where does Janey fit in?'

'I think the more relevant question, my friend,' Webster said, 'is where do you fit in?'

'All right, where?'

'The pillow talk I referred to earlier, you remember?'

'When my name came up.'

'Yes, you came up because, as I said, Daniel Salbone happened to be at the Lorelei restaurant the same afternoon you were. Apparently he witnessed Anne Joy kissing you in public. A fluky bit of good fortune for us.'

Thorn remembered the moment vividly. Alexandra's cool reaction. Her qualms about Thorn's disreputable past.

'Well, it seems that during the first weeks of their romance, Salbone questioned Anne extensively about you and that kiss. She claimed to have no feelings for you, but Salbone wasn't buying it. It appears the man has quite a jealous streak.'

Webster clicked the remote and a wide-angle shot appeared. A two-story creamy yellow house with a wraparound porch and gingerbread trim along the eaves. The ocean spread blue and ancient before it. Off to the southern edge of the property was a small red-brick house, squat and ugly. Along the sandy shoreline, two men stood looking out to sea.

'Marty Messina and Vic Joy,' Webster said. 'Savoring the gentle trade winds wafting off the Atlantic.'

'Okay.'

'So this is Vic Joy's estate in Islamorada. Marty's living there with Vic and now Anne has moved in as well. If Marty's job is to spy on Anne, then this arrangement makes it quite simple for him to carry that out.'

'But you don't know any of this for sure. You don't even know if Salbone is alive, so maybe this is all wishful thinking, Marty spying on Anne.'

'That's correct. We don't know for certain. Thus we're forced to make certain assumptions. And certainly there is some wishfulness involved. I won't deny that. But our operating theory at the moment is that Salbone staged the ambush on the *Rainmaker* and left the crew behind as witnesses to the event.'

'So he could drop out of sight,' Thorn said.

'That's right. We believe this charade was executed to throw us off his trail. He sensed we were closing in.'

'He hired a second crew to kill his original one?'

'Exactly,' Webster said. 'Several of these men who died on the *Rainmaker* had been loyal to Salbone for years, taken great risks on his behalf. And he slaughtered them as casually as one might dismiss an employee. This is the kind of man we're dealing with here, Thorn.'

'Okay,' Thorn said, taking a moment to absorb this. 'Either way, you don't need me. If Salbone is alive and Marty's communicating with the guy, use some of your high-tech shit and intercept the transmissions and go get him.'

'That's just the point, Thorn. So far Marty has not attempted any kind of communication.'

'So maybe Salbone's dead and your theory's full of shit.'

'Maybe he is,' Webster said. 'Then again, maybe he's alive and Marty Messina simply hasn't seen anything worth reporting.'

'So why am I here?'

'Because,' Webster said, 'we are going to give Marty something to report. He's going to see Anne Joy and that well-known Casanova Mr Thorn together, their old affair heating up again.'

'I seduce Anne and just like that, Salbone pops out of hiding?'

'Maybe,' Webster said. 'Or maybe, as you say, we'll get lucky and get an intercept between Messina and Salbone and capture the man before he has a chance to make his move.'

'And Vic is going to let me waltz into his compound?'

'Vic wants your land. You'll go to him, dicker over the price, string him along, and while you're there, you and Anne will puff on the embers of your old romance.'

'And Vic's going to let me woo his little sister right in front of him?'

'Yes, he will. He most certainly will. I can assure you Vic Joy will be most cooperative.'

Webster clicked the remote and the projector began to flash the remaining slides one after the other, holding for a half-second and moving on. Like some macabre disco, a light show from hell, the screen filled with image after image of shipboard slaughter, men sprawled on decks, decomposed bodies snagged against rocks, ghost ships adrift in empty seas, a half-naked woman, her body spread-eagled on the bow of a gleaming white yacht, apparently raped, murdered.

'Vic's working with you. He's on your payroll.'

'That would be an imprecise description of our relationship with Mr Joy,' Webster said. 'Let me put it this way. My esteemed colleagues in the Justice Department were kind enough to suspend their prosecution of certain of Mr Joy's unlawful business dealings in exchange for his cooperation in our project. A project my colleagues in Justice were forced to admit was a far more serious matter than Vic Joy's minor offenses.'

'Minor offenses like murdering five people.'

'That was an unfortunate circumstance,' said Jimmy Lee.

'Unfortunate?' Thorn looked away from the screen and regarded Webster with quiet loathing. 'My friend's daughter was on that boat and was a witness to what happened out there. Wherever she is, she's terrified. She's been traumatized and because those assholes know she can identify them, she's probably also in extreme danger. And this is the guy you're making deals with, a minor offender? This fucker is a killer, a mass murderer. A kidnapper of children.'

'We're aware of the incident on Dr Markham's boat.'

'Aware of it?' Thorn said. 'That's it?'

'At this moment there's no proof Vic Joy was involved in the murders of those unfortunate people.'

'Bullshit.'

'What you've got to understand, Thorn, is that everything's a trade-off. Lives lost versus lives saved. We make bargains with the devil every day of the week. In this business we have to work with some despicable people. Naturally we regret the suffering of any innocent civilians. When deaths occur as they did aboard Dr Markham's yacht, it is a tragedy, no question, and our hearts go out. But believe me, if Salbone is still alive and we're able to bring him to justice, to my way of thinking that will more than offset the loss of life you're referring to.'

'I can't believe what I'm hearing.'

'And furthermore,' Webster said, 'the good people in Justice are fully prepared to go forward with their investigations of the murders of those five poor souls as soon as our goals are met. If Vic Joy is the culprit, he'll be duly prosecuted. We don't make the kinds of deals that let mass killers walk. We're simply suspending that part of things for the moment.'

Thorn said, 'How does capturing Salbone get Janey back?'

'Don't worry about that,' Webster said. 'You don't need to know every facet of our arrangement.'

'This is all about you getting a feather in your cap, isn't it, Webster? You could care less about the people involved, this little kid.'

'Capturing Salbone would be a feather, yes,' said Webster. 'But there's more to it than that. A lot more.'

'Such as?'

Webster paced in front of the screen for a moment, then halted and faced Thorn.

'You've probably never heard of Ching Shih.' Webster gave him a second, then said, 'A female pirate in the early nineteenth century. She was brilliant, a master strategist, daring, creative, a cutthroat. For a decade she terrorized the China Sea. In her prime she controlled eighteen hundred ships and about eighty thousand pirates.'

Zashie stroked his sap like an outfielder keeping his glove warm.

'We have strong evidence that there's an individual now attempting to do something very similar:

228

bring together dozens of loosely affiliated groups scattered through the Far East and South America and the Caribbean into a confederation of pirates.

'Our intelligence suggests this individual has managed to arrange for a sit-down where these men are to devise a master plan, divide up territory. They are apparently in the process of creating an alliance of seafaring criminals that would surpass anything we've ever seen. And let's say those armaments that I mentioned earlier were indeed stolen for their own use; that would mean that there would be only a few navies on earth that would be as well equipped. In short, what this looks like to some of us, Thorn, is that we're on the verge of a new golden age of piracy.'

Thorn glanced at the screen, then back at Jimmy Lee Webster. The pompous shrimp had perched his butt on the edge of the long chest of drawers. His black leather shoes dangling inches above the floor. A Napoléon in blue jeans and white button-down. America's secret admiral. A man who had learned to swagger before most kids could crawl. If the future of the free world depended on the likes of Jimmy Lee Webster, then freedom had a short half-life.

'The individual who is organizing these groups of pirates may or may not be Daniel Salbone. We don't know that he's alive, but this project has all his earmarks. We know Salbone to be highly intelligent and ambitious. He's a charismatic young man

and can be quite persuasive. There aren't many
people who could bring together such disparate
bands of outlaws, warring factions in some cases,
but Daniel Salbone is one of the few who could
manage it. And this theory would certainly explain
why Salbone felt he had to resort to killing his own
crew. It was done so he might convince his new
associates he'd outwitted his pursuers and therefore
they might be more willing to join with him in this
new enterprise.'

'Count me out,' Thorn said. 'Unless I hear how
any of this gets Janey back, the whole goddamn
world could fill up with pirates for all I care.'

Webster grimaced and shook his head like some
dismayed math teacher whose student has made the
most basic error in addition.

'But you see, you *are* going to do it, Thorn. You
have no choice.'

'Look, Jimmy Lee, even if I agreed, Anne Joy has
no interest in me. When we parted, it was final. She
left no doubt about that.'

'You'll simply employ your much-vaunted
magnetism.'

'Why not use one of your agents? Some tall dashing type like Zashie here. He can hit on Anne Joy
just as easily as I can. You don't need me.'

'Daniel Salbone has already taken a special interest in you, Thorn. He knows your name. He knows
you have an intimate history with Anne.'

'Forget it, Webster. It isn't happening.'

'All you have to do is make an effort, Thorn. Make it appear things are heating up between you and Anne. I'm not saying you have to take this woman to bed and give her the mother of all orgasms. You simply have to create the illusion of intimacy. If it works, fine. If we're wrong about Salbone being alive and Marty's reason for being back in Key Largo, then we've lost nothing from our attempt.'

'Except the life of a little girl.'

'I told you, Thorn, she's safe. She's under our protection.'

'So I'm supposed to bring Anne flowers and bonbons, write her poems. That's going to fool Marty?'

'All right, look,' Webster said. 'For reasons that elude me, Vic Joy wants your parcel of land. Apparently the man believed he needed to do something extreme to motivate you into selling it to him, so he's holding your friend's daughter hostage. While the plan might seem idiotic and doomed to failure, when I became aware of it I realized how effectively it might dovetail with our own needs. Because by then I'd discovered what apparently Vic Joy had already realized: that you, Thorn, would require an extra motivational boost.

'Think about it, my friend. If you had been even a little less hard-headed and determined to ridicule me at every turn, if you'd been even close to a normal patriotic American, then less persuasive measures would have been fine. If you'd shown any willingness to help, then when Vic began to execute his outrageous plan with Sugarman's daughter we would have stepped in, plucked the girl from Vic's grasp, and gone ahead with our scheme to use you to lure Salbone out of hiding. But you're not that person, Thorn. You're a defiant asshole. And that's why your friend's daughter is suffering. As repugnant as the idea is to all of us, you've forced us, Thorn, to piggyback our plan onto Vic Joy's.'

'What the fuck are you talking about?'

'Here's how it's going to be, Thorn. When I get what I want, then and only then do you get what you want. You go through the motions with Anne Bonny Joy, and in no time little Janey is back in her father's arms. All is well.'

Thorn watched Webster trace a fingertip down the neat edge of his beard.

'And one more thing,' the little man said. 'Just so we're perfectly clear. You'll find no assistance in securing the girl's release from any law enforcement body in the United States, not here in the Florida Keys, not in Miami, nowhere. I may not be Secretary of the Navy any longer, but even those who were once my fiercest critics now realize I was right all along. Oceans cover three-quarters of the Earth's surface, and unless we quash these thugs and do it quick, they're going to gain control of the biggest piece of real estate there is. And that's not good for business, any business. We're not talking about a

232

threat to civilization as we know it, or anything like that. These guys have been a nuisance for a long time and a certain number of them are going to be out there no matter what we do. But there's a place, a certain tipping point, when things go from shit-you-can-put-up-with to something else entirely. And we're at that point, Thorn.'

Thorn looked down at the Velcro bands holding his arms to the chair. All those nylon eyelets and hooks clutching at each other – somebody's clever invention. Hooks and eyelets, opposites gripping tight.

'All right, goddamn it,' he said. 'But only because of Janey.'

Webster shot a smirk at Zashie as if he'd won their private bet, gotten Thorn to cave in without even spilling blood. With a sour look, Zashie tucked the blackjack into his back pocket.

'How're we going to communicate?' Thorn said. 'If I need to talk to you, tell you something. Ask for help.'

'When you leave this room tonight,' Webster said, 'we won't be in contact anymore until this is concluded.'

The projector continued to flash images of death onto the screen. A war going on that Thorn had never heard about. Hundreds and hundreds of perfect, sunny days at sea turning ghastly.

'And how am I supposed to know when that is, when I'm done?'

Webster's lips snapped apart in a wan smile.

'Oh, you'll know, Thorn. Believe me, we'll make sure you know.'

Outside, Thorn found himself in the parking lot of the Holiday Inn, in the center of the quiet downtown of Key Largo. A little dizzy and lost after that worldwide tour of the brutal and unforgiving oceans. Across the lot he saw Sugarman marching out to the highway, and trotted over.

'You okay, Sugar?'

'Oh, sure. I'm great, Thorn. Fantastic. Never better.'

Sugar wouldn't meet Thorn's gaze. He stalked out to the bike path that ran along the edge of the highway.

'What's going on with you, man? What'd I do?'

Sugarman halted and swung around to face him. Eyes stewing with rage.

'What did you do? Nothing. You didn't do anything. You're a saint, Thorn. A perfect saint.'

'What did they tell you? Some kind of bullshit to turn you against me?'

'Didn't sound like bullshit to me. Sounded like you, Thorn. Fit you to a T.'

'What?'

Behind them a white Cadillac squealed into the Holiday Inn parking lot. Windows dark. It roared down the motel wing and swung into a space near the room where Thorn had been held. Two large men got out. Long hair, dark clothing. The two walked to the motel room and pounded on the door.

'Something's happening,' Thorn said. 'We should go back.'

Webster's door opened and the two men went inside.

Sugarman shook his head sadly, looking at Thorn.

'Janey's kidnapped,' he said. 'My daughter's gone. And you're playing games, Thorn.'

Thorn swung back to him.

'Hey, Sugar, what'd they tell you?'

'They didn't have to tell me anything, Thorn. I've seen it too many times already. You got a black cloud over your head, Thorn. Sooner or later, anybody hangs around you gets struck down by lightning. It's been this way forever, Thorn. And I've had enough.'

Sugar's eyes were avoiding Thorn's.

'What'd I do, Sugar?'

'It's what you didn't do, Thorn. You had a chance to help this guy catch the goddamn pirate, all you had to do was tell him something about Anne Joy, take five minutes of your precious time, but no, you gave him the heave-ho.'

'Yeah, that's true. But, Sugar, that's not what started this thing.'

'At this point I don't care what your goddamn rationalization is, Thorn. I've heard it before. And before that. I'm just sick of this shit. It's one thing after another with you. It never ever stops. And now it's Janey. I'm sick of it, Thorn. Sick sick sick.'

Sugarman had turned and was heading north on the bike path.

Thorn caught up with him, matched his stride, but Sugar wouldn't look his way.

'Listen, man, we can work together on this. We'll get Janey back. We can do it, I know we can.'

Sugar was striding fast, not even looking at Thorn.

'This guy, Webster, he's got to be a rogue agent. That's not how these guys operate. Christ, they don't get involved with kidnapping children. They're straight arrows, they have rules, oversight. It's outrageous. Impossible. We'll call the FBI field office in Miami, talk to that guy you know, Sheffield, whatever the hell his name is.'

Sugarman kept walking, shooting Thorn a quick look and shaking his head.

'Yeah, Thorn, whatever you say. A rogue agent. Like all of a sudden you're an expert on international intrigue. What'd you do, read a spy novel, now you're an authority? Like the feebs are going to come to attention for you and me? No way, Thorn, we're out in the cold, man. We're out in the goddamn Arctic Circle.'

'Look, we need to stick together on this, Sugar.'

'Leave me alone, goddamn it. Janey's gone. I don't need your help and I don't want your help. You'd just suck us deeper into this bullshit. This is my daughter. I'll handle it my own way.'

'Why'd they take us in separate rooms, Sugar? Show you one thing, me another? Because they want to break us up, isolate me, control me better. Convince you I caused this whole thing.'

'So long, Thorn,' Sugarman called back. 'Good luck.'

Thorn tagged along for a half-mile, then stopped and watched Sugarman plowing ahead at a furious clip. He stood there as his friend disappeared into the darkness up ahead.

15

Backing off the throttle to a near stall, Vic circled once over his Islamorada property, tipped the Mallard's wings, and caught a quick glimpse of Anne lying on a chaise lounge next to the pool, one of the servants in her white uniform standing at attention near the pool house.

'Feature films are the logical next step, Marty. These days, you want to tell a story, you got to do it on the silver screen.'

Marty looked out of the windscreen and didn't reply. Still queasy from the trip. After all those hours in the plane, any normal person would be over it by now. But Marty still looked like he was about to dump his breakfast on the instrument panel. Or maybe it was all the blood from Thursday night still floating around in his head. He'd puked then, too, over the side of Markham's boat. Disappointing Vic, tarnishing the luster of the night's work.

'You've seen one or two movies, right, Marty?'

Marty nodded.

'Well, the minute I'm finished with this land deal, what I'm doing next is, I'm going to put together a Hollywood film. I know people on the Coast, thrown some business their way over the years. Soon as we get a story line together, I'll make the calls. Mom would love that, a movie all her own. Hell, I could even dedicate the fucker to her, get her name on the screen, first words you see when the lights go down, even before the actors or the title. "*In loving memory of Antoinette Joy, the greatest mom a boy could have*." She'd fucking love it. A pirate movie that got it right for once.'

Vic came down easy and set the Mallard on the flat blue water, a buttery landing, though Marty tightened his harness and tightened it again as they were touching down, never relaxing his grip on the overhead handle till Vic slowed to an idle and headed for the ramp.

Back on land, he and Marty walking up the easy slope toward the pool, Vic said, 'You know what that airplane cost me, Marty?'

Marty swallowed and said, no, no, he had no idea.

'A million five for the turboprop. I could've gone with the recip engine, but hell, I wanted the extra muscle. That's something I got from my daddy: love of horsepower.'

Marty followed him over to the pool, Vic stretching his arms, taking off his yellow baseball cap, tossing it on the patio, then stretching out in the chaise next to Anne. She was wearing khaki shorts and a sleeveless flowered shirt, both of which looked new. A shopping bag from Island Silver and Spice lay on the umbrella table. Anne was reading the *Miami Herald*, no hello, nothing, didn't even look up. So Vic made like she wasn't there, either. Motioning at Jewel, the Jamaican on duty. Pointing at Anne's glass of OJ and holding up two fingers. Jewel turned and disappeared into the pool house.

Marty kept stretching his neck, opening and closing his hands. Sore from clenching so long. All those hours in the air, never relaxed his fists for a second.

'Okay, here's how I see our story line,' Vic said. 'Right from the get-go, no farting around, little boat sneaking up on a big one. A yacht like Markham's. Two people or three on the fancy boat. Crank up the suspense, lots of close-ups of the people's throats and bare flesh. Creepy music. The audience squirming because they know what's coming, these badass bloody pirates closing in.'

'Truth is, I don't watch movies, Vic. I got no experience in this area.'

Vic watched his dock guys cranking the Mallard up the ramp. Twin radial engines on a high-mounted wing with underwing floats, retractable undercarriage, and an upswept tail unit. He loved that damn airplane. Wished his mom could've known he was a pilot now. A pilot among about a hundred other amazing damn things. He'd transcended the hell out of his roots. But somehow it didn't mean as much, his mom not there to see it happen. Vic had thought maybe Anne Bonny would change that. Give him some strokes, a compliment or two on his rise to power and glory. But no, his sister, his only living flesh and blood, was just sitting there, newspaper spread open in front of her, no appreciation for the lavish layout or the view or anything.

Jewel brought the two OJs. Put one on Marty's table, one on Vic's, asked if there'd be anything else.

'Not for me,' Vic said. 'You, Marty? Eggs, bacon, pancakes. Blow job, maybe.' Smiling up at Jewel, who didn't smile back.

The big man shook his head and Jewel slipped back to her post in the shade by the pool house. Anne turned the page, shook the paper out straight, doing a first-class job of ignoring the two of them.

'Okay, so you're inexperienced with the film world. That can be a plus, Marty. Give you a fresh perspective. Anyway, we're just brainstorming, coming up with some ideas. I throw in a few, then you throw in a few from your vast experience.'

'I only did it for a month,' Marty said. 'It's not like I'm some expert. Far as I could see, it wasn't anything special. Like knocking over a fucking warehouse, that's all, except it's out on the water. Most times the sailors, they drop down on their faces, give up without a fight. It's not very exciting.'

'Yeah, except that last time when they were waiting for you.'

Marty nodded. 'Yeah, that time was different. Real different.'

Vic could tell Anne was listening. Paper still in front of her face, but eyes not moving anymore.

'But look, Marty, you're missing the point about movies. There's a long tradition here. An illustrious history of swashbuckling cinema. A wider frame of reference we have to pay homage to. So how I see it is, the first few seconds of our movie, like when the credits are rolling, we show the audience what they're in for. Make it pop from the first frame, snap and crackle. Pirates boiling out of their little boat, crawling over the side of the big ship, *bippity-bop*, *bippity-boom*. Don't hold a fucking thing back. All our cards on the table. Then later on, five, ten minutes into it, we find a way to top that scene, explosions, lasers, nukes, whatever. That's creativity: You start with everything you got, then you dig down and you find more and after that you find more, and more after that.'

Vic Joy gave Marty Messina a quick look to see if he was absorbing this.

'Snap, crackle, and pop,' Marty said. 'Like the cereal.'

Vic smiled, but he could feel a spurt of bile stinging the back of his throat. He wasn't a fan of sarcasm, irony, whatever the fuck you called it. Words were for saying things straight out. You put your words up against the other guy's to see which ones were stronger. No tricks. You didn't say one thing, then mock what you'd said with a grin or your tone of voice.

'Okay, Marty. So then the other thing to remember is, we can't shy away from something that's already been done. I don't know how you guys did it, but as you already witnessed firsthand, when I storm a yacht, I like a knife in my mouth like the pirates of old. Blackbeard, Captain Blood. Gripping it between the teeth, blade out. That's an important detail. Blade out.'

Vic slugged down his OJ in one swallow, wiped his mouth, and said, 'It's time I took some of this shit I been doing and put it up on the silver screen. Hell, my run-of-the-mill ordinary day is ten times as exciting as most of the shit people buy tickets to see.'

'These last couple of days,' Marty said, 'I'd rather not see them again.'

'What's wrong, Butch? What happened to our prison-tough hombre?'

Marty sipped his juice and flexed his free hand, working the blood back.

'You know, maybe I made a mistake with you, Marty. Hell, I already let you see more of my operation than I've ever shown anyone. That's something new for me. I'm not the kind to delegate anything. Shit, I don't even let the right lawyer know what the left lawyer's doing.'

Marty looked at him, his big moon face showing a trace of worry.

'Maybe it was a moment of weakness, bringing you aboard. I thought you had more piss in your blood than you've shown me so far.'

Marty sipped his juice. In his black jeans and dark socks and ankle-high white tennis shoes. His yellow T-shirt was from Snook's Bayside, one of the two or three good local waterfront restaurants Vic didn't own. But give him time, he'd be adding Snook's to the list.

'Look, Marty. You got an opportunity here, kind of chance doesn't come around that often. Hell, look at me and Anne, we didn't have two turds to rub together when we started out. A couple of kids with a drug runner's car and a couple hundred dollars. All I had going for me was some hick-from-the-sticks anger stewing in my veins, a crazy spunk. Now look around you, boy. Take a minute and absorb the scene. Whatta you think a place like this costs anyway?'

Marty said, 'I'm grateful, Vic. I am.'

'Eleven million and change, that's what. After I built the main house, I had that brick house carted down here from Harlan. That's our childhood home, Marty; ask Anne Bonny. Same furniture, rugs, even the damn washing machine. You think that wasn't expensive to do, think again. And where'd all that

244

money come from, boy? Did I inherit any from my old man? Shit, no. I worked my bony ass off for this place and all the other goodies I got. I took chances; I went so far out on the limb there wasn't any limb left. Then I went a little farther. I used the old creative right brain and I used it again. I out-smarted the boys in the suits with their Harvard MBAs and their bullshit lawyers.'

Vic got up and stripped off his clothes and left them in a pile by his chaise, and buck naked he dived into his own goddamn blue-water swimming pool. Most expensive water in the world, piped down all the way from the well fields in Miami. He did a couple laps, up and back again, and one more time to clean off the kerosene stink of the jet fuel and the sweat and grime and blood from the night before. And climbed out. He stood on the apron and shook the water off his arms and gave his penis a little whip jiggle for everybody's amusement. But no one was watching. Marty looking off at the ocean, Anne staring into her newspaper, Jewel, the maid, shielding her view with the white terry-cloth robe she was holding open for him.

Vic put it on, didn't belt it, and walked back to the chaise with everything hanging out and lay down, exposing himself to the elements, getting a little midmorning sun on his tan lines.

'Cover yourself, Vic.' Saying it like his mother used to give commands. A schoolteacher's voice. 'No one wants to see your cock.'

'Hey, we're all family here,' Vic said. 'You and me, we used to take our baths together.'

'Cover yourself,' she said. And again he heard that echo of his mother's voice. Pissed off, barely under control, *don't make me swat you, boy*.

He closed his robe and belted it.

Anne folded her newspaper and set it on the ground and cranked her chaise lower to catch the midmorning rays on her face. His little sister. What was left of the family back together again. Vic felt a flush of satisfaction for accomplishing that. Another thing his mother would love to see. What was left of the Joy clan, together in paradise.

'Anybody want to hear a joke?' Vic said.

Marty looked over at him but didn't reply.

'Ever hear the one about the two pirates?'

Anne kept her eyes closed, but he could see she was listening.

'Okay, so one pirate says to the other, "Hey, matey, how'd you get that wooden leg?" And the second pirate says, "Arrr, it done got bit off by a goddamn shark." The first pirate is impressed: "Aye, you're one tough son of a bitch. And how'd ya get that metal hook?" The other one says, "Well, I lost her in a sword fight. Bastard cut off me bloody hand." "Aw, shit, that must've hurt like hell," says the first pirate. "And so how'd you get that patch on your eye?" "Well now," says the second pirate. "I was up in the crow's nest, and I looked up just as a seagull flew over the mast, and the damn thing shit right in me eye."

246

'The second pirate, he's staring at the first one. "And how the hell did seagull shit make you blind?" The first pirate gets a funny look and says, "Arrr, it was the first day I had me hook."'

Vic laughed, kept on laughing for half a minute. He wiped the tears from his eyes when he was done.

Marty cleared his throat, took a deliberate breath, and said, 'You okay, Vic?'

'Okay? What the fuck are you talking about *okay?*'

'I mean, this joke, all right, it's kind of funny, yeah. But I'm sitting here, I'm wondering, Who the hell is this guy? This big joker or the guy out on the boat, the shit you pulled out there, which guy is it I'm working for?'

Vic turned his head carefully and looked at Marty.

'You want to know who I am?' Vic said.

Marty shrugged, like he wasn't so sure anymore, hearing Vic's voice bubble with acid.

Marty said, 'I'm talking about the knife-in-the-teeth thing and all that movie talk. I just want to know if I'm on solid ground here, throwing in with you like I'm doing.'

'You mean, am I crazy?'

'I never said *crazy*.'

Vic looked over at Anne. She was still soaking up the beneficial rays of the sun, eyes closed like she might be asleep. Though Vic could see her listening.

'Fuck yes, I'm crazy. Name me anybody worth a shit that isn't crazy. Go on, Marty, name me one person in the whole fucking history of mankind that made a major mark on the world that wasn't an over-the-top lunatic one way or the other. It's the nature of genius to be crazy. Napoléon, Julius Caesar, Marco Polo, Christopher fucking Columbus. You think any of those guys were sane? Sailing off into the blue, without a goddamn map. Is that sane? Where would the world be without those guys, the crazy fucks that took risks, made things happen?'

'Marco Polo?'

'Hey, Marty. Listen to me. You want to work for some sane fucking boss, go sell life insurance. Flip burgers.'

Marty nodded like he was trying to buy Vic's argument but not quite there yet.

'Okay, then,' Marty said, 'take this movie thing, for instance.'

'Making a movie is crazy, Marty?'

'What I think,' Marty said, 'nobody's going to want to see that shit.'

Vic wiped his lips and craned in Marty's direction.

'Screw that,' Vic said. 'Pirate movies have a long and celebrated history.'

'Okay, Vic. So tell me. Whose story is it?'

'What do you mean? It's my story.'

'I mean who's the audience supposed to root for?'

'Root for? What kind of crap is that?'

'I might be full of shit,' Marty said. 'But what I think is, that's why people go to movies, Vic. To cheer when the good guy creams the bad guy. That's why they stand in line, spend their bread. That's what I think.'

'Well, they can root for the fucking pirate this time,' Vic said.

'Yeah, but why would they? I mean, you and me, okay, we'd root for him, 'cause we're the way we are. Fucked up. But a normal working Joe. Why would he give a rat's ass about a pirate? Think about it, Vic. A guy sneaks aboard somebody's boat and slits their throats and shoots old ladies in the head, kidnaps little girls. Why would anyone care about a shithead like that?'

'Hey, watch it.'

Anne propped herself up on her elbows and looked over and asked Marty what the hell he was talking about.

He shook his head and took another prissy sip of juice. Vic reached over and snatched the glass out of Marty's hand and slung it into the pool and watched it sink.

'You're wrong, Marty. People love pirates. Always have, always will.'

Marty was looking at the pool, the little ripples the glass made.

'All I'm saying, Vic, I can't see anybody paying to watch shit like that.'

'You kidnapped a little girl, Vic?'

'Don't worry about it,' he said. 'I invited you along, but you didn't want to go. So that makes it officially none of your business.'

'This is about Thorn, isn't it?'

'Hey, you hear what I just said? It's none of your freaking business. Marty's just passing gas out his blowhole. Aren't you, kid?'

'Me and Anne and the others, we knocked over freighters,' Marty said. 'We got away with millions in TV sets and dirt bikes and all kinds of shit and we never fired a shot. Not that whole time.'

'What little girl, Marty?' she said, looking past Vic at the big man.

Marty shook his head, not about to get into this brother-sister thing.

'Okay, okay,' Vic said. 'You want to know so bad, it was Sugarman's daughter, that's who. Sugarman, you know, Thorn's asshole buddy.'

'I met that girl,' Anne said. 'I served her lunch once. Little blond girl.'

'Served her lunch. Well, hell, then you're practically related.'

'Where is she? What'd you do with her?'

'What do you care?'

Darien, the pool boy, slid out of the shade and whisked over to the edge of the water with his long-poled scoop and started going after the orange juice glass. When he had it, he turned around and grabbed up the yellow baseball cap, too, and carried them both away. Best help money could buy. Always hire illegals, that was Vic's policy. Deportation hanging over their heads kept them focused.

'What'd you do with Sugarman's little girl, Vic?'

'She's safe and sound off in a secluded location. That's all you need to know and that's all I'm telling you.'

Vic looked over at his sister as Anne was standing up. She picked up her shopping bag and came over and stood at the foot of Vic's chaise lounge.

'Forget the FROM code, Vic, I'm out of here.'

'What? What'd I do?'

'The little girl.'

'Hell,' Marty said. 'The little girl's the least of it.'

'Aw, shit, settle down, Anne Bonny. The girl's fine. Isn't she, Marty?'

'Last we saw.'

'Hell, she's got a ton of food, she's got shelter, a bathroom. I even let her take along binoculars she'd gotten for her freaking birthday. Little thing was whimpering about them so much. Isn't that right, Marty?'

'And her laptop,' he said.

'Yeah, the kid might get bored and want to play some video games. Shit, I was as nice as pie to the girl. I may be a pirate, but I got a heart of gold.'

Anne glared at Vic, then shifted her eyes to Marty.

'Is that true, Marty?'

'It is,' he said. 'Computer, binoculars, food. She should be okay for a day or two.'

'See?' Vic said. 'You're worried over nothing, Anne. The girl's going to be just fine. We didn't muss a hair on her pretty little noggin. What do you think, I'm some kind of monster?'

16

'You can't tell me, Thorn? Why can't you tell me?'

Thorn sat on a stool at the breakfast counter and blew on his coffee. Alexandra was on her fourth mug. Already wired, but cranking herself higher.

'I'm not going to lie to you, Alex.'

'I'm not asking you to lie, I'm asking where the hell you were all night and where you got those cuts and bruises. That seems like a reasonable request of the man I'm living with.'

Thorn got off the stool and came over to her, but Alexandra turned away. She'd sent Lawton outside, told him to wait for her on the lawn, and even the old man could hear the iron in her voice and for once didn't question instructions. She had on a pair of loose-fitting black shorts and a peasant blouse with a flowery trim. Her hair clenched back in a ponytail and her skin scrubbed clean of the work-day makeup. Alex swallowed the rest of her coffee and angled past Thorn and set the mug in the sink.

'I owe you an explanation,' he said. 'I don't blame you for being angry.'

'Okay then, where were you?'

'I can't talk about it right now, Alex. I'm sorry, I wish I could, but I can't.'

Tiny muscles flinched in her face. He could see in her eyes that he was now dangerously close to joining that whirling collection of asshole men who'd abandoned or deeply disappointed her in the past, shitheads who'd tried to suffocate her spirit, even one who'd tried to take her life. He was on the verge of becoming just one more in a string of appalling mistakes.

'I'm working on this thing with Janey,' Thorn blurted. 'I was recruited to help. But I can't talk about it.'

'Recruited?'

Thorn reached out and took her hand, tried to draw off some of the heat of her anger with his touch, but after a second she jerked it from his grasp.

'That's all I can tell you. None of the details.'

'Top secret, huh? Agent Thorn called into battle to save the Earth.'

'I know,' he said. 'It sounds absurd.'

'Thorn, I thought we were getting somewhere. I'd been feeling pretty solid lately about us, about the way Dad is holding his own. Then this. You're gone all night. I don't know what to do. Call the sheriff, go driving around, see if I can find you. I'm lying in there worrying. Dad's out in the living room mumbling to himself. Of course, he's picked up on it, the tension. He kicked the goddamn dog, Thorn.'

'What?'

'This morning. No reason. Just drew back and punted the little thing across the room.'

'That's not fair about the dog.'

'Okay,' she said. 'But it's important you realize what you do has an impact. You stay out all night, don't explain where you were, it's not like we can just go sailing merrily along with that hanging there.'

'A few days,' he said. 'Two or three at the most, it'll be over and I can explain the whole thing.'

'Is this about Anne Joy?'

'What?!'

'It is, isn't it? This is about Anne Joy.'

'What the hell makes you say that?'

'You lie like a little kid, Thorn. You get that squinty, dodgy thing in your eyes. You're really bad at it. At least that's something in your favor.'

He took a breath and went back to the stool and sat down, then got back up and came over and took her hand in his, and this time she left it there.

'I love you.'

'And that's supposed to stop me in my tracks?'

'It's true.'

'You know what you should do? You should get

out a legal pad, a couple of pens, make a list, Thorn. It might be illuminating. All the women you've said that to.'

Thorn looked down at the floor. She was right, of course. He'd used those words a few times too often in just such cases. But still. He looked back at her.

'This is different, Alex. You and me, and Lawton. This is special. It's what I've been looking for. I can't lose this. I'll do whatever I can to keep you.'

'Except tell me the truth.'

Alexandra searched his face, tilting away from him an inch or two as if to bring him into better focus. Whatever she was looking for, she didn't find enough of it, for her weary eyes grew dim and distant and she looked away, drew an exhausted breath, then blew it out.

She went to the sink, busied herself with her coffee mug, rinsing it clean, then doing the same with his. Putting them upside down on the drain board.

With her back to him, she said, 'You said you were *recruited*. That's what Webster was trying to do, right? That time when you left out Anne Joy's name as you were telling me about his visit. He was trying to recruit you. Did he try again?'

'Goddamn it.' Thorn turned and walked out to the porch and let the screen door slam. Down on the lawn, Lawton was playing fetch with the puppy. The dog sprinted after the stick and brought it part-way back, then hesitated a few feet away from the old man. Sitting in the grass with the stick in his mouth, watching Lawton warily. Everything different from the night before. That was how fast it could disappear. A line crossed, a word spoken or withheld. That quick, and the puppy shied away and no matter what happened later on, in some hidden realm of his being, he would be mistrustful forever after.

For five minutes Alexandra was inside the house, and when she came out her black duffel was slung over her shoulder.

'Don't,' he said.

'I need to check on my house,' she said. 'Mail's piling up. Telephone messages. Vines and weeds are probably taking over. You can't just walk away from an old place like that.'

'Now who's lying, Alex?'

'You want to talk, you know my number.'

'Maybe I've lived alone too much. I don't know how it's done. The compromise thing.'

'Maybe you have.'

He didn't try to stop her. He watched as she went out into the yard and collected her father and scooped up the Lab. Lawton glanced up at him as they were walking to the car and shook his head.

In a voice ripe with regret, Lawton called up to Thorn.

'We're heading off to Ohio. Gonna dig up that damn time capsule once and for all. See ya, kid. And don't forget Seung Sahn's celebrated words: "If you don't enter the lion's den, you will never capture the lion."'

Alex took him by the shoulder and steered him ahead toward the car. The puppy barked and wriggled in her grasp, but she quieted him with a touch beneath his throat. No backward look, no hesitation, as she got into her Honda, shut the door, and started the engine and backed out of her place and headed out the drive. No sign that she was leaving for good. No sign that she was ever coming back.

Thorn lowered himself to the bench of the picnic table and watched the birds flow from their roosts miles away out beyond the mangroves that rimmed Blackwater Sound, heading across the island to the fishing grounds on the Atlantic side.

The throb in his ribs had eased. Nothing but a deep bruise – the spot would be tender for a week, make sneezing an unpleasant prospect, but nothing seemed to be broken. Though he couldn't say the same for his bond with Alexandra Collins. If there'd been a way to tell her the truth without having to explain the finer points of what he'd agreed to do, he would have done it. But as soon as Alex mentioned Anne Joy's name, it was clear that trying to describe the difference between a sham seduction and a real one might prove more destructive than remaining silent. Now he wasn't so sure. He could have tried at least. Looked for words that told her just enough. But Alex had been on such high alert about Anne Joy, so touchy, he'd simply backed away.

Over the years Thorn had lost so many friends and lovers and blood relations, he feared some crucial part of him had grown hard and impervious to that sort of grief. But this time, with Alexandra's departure, it came as some bitter relief to discover that even that part of him could still ache beyond all endurance.

And then there was Sugarman. Another ache. Different, but just as deep, just as final. And as Thorn looked out at the choppy bay, at the herons and gulls and egrets floating along the air currents with an ease that mocked all human enterprise, he wanted to believe his friendship with Sugarman had weathered worse than this, but as hard as he tried, he could remember nothing in their four decades that came even close to Janey's abduction and Thorn's guilty connection to the matter.

Webster had struck a nerve.

If Thorn had simply heard him out that day when he'd first appeared, none of this might have unfolded as it had. Something he revealed could have been the key to moving in on Salbone and thus prevented Janey's abduction. Or maybe not. Maybe that was all a ploy of Webster's, a recruiter's trick – hook him with guilt. It was impossible to know how complicit Thorn actually was. But Sugarman wasn't ignoring those possibilities. All he needed to hear was that this woman who was on Thorn's list of recent sexual partners was also in league with the people who'd taken his daughter. Blame stained them all.

And as Thorn watched the first guide boat of the day heading out to the remote fishing grounds, he began to recall the long-ago story Anne Bonny Joy had told him about the rickety pirate schooner draped with gaudy Christmas lights. Anne and Vic's early saturation training in pirate lore, their childhood abruptly ended by gunfire. At seventeen Vic Joy already an unrepentant murderer. And his sister, a willing accomplice. It was all of a piece. An inevitable series of spreading ripples that now washed ashore at Thorn's feet.

A moment later, he rose from the picnic table and went into the bedroom and pawed through his closet until he found a fresh blue shirt and a pair of clean shorts and laid them out on the bed, then he turned on the shower as hot as it would go and stripped off his rumpled clothes and threw them in the hamper. He stepped into the steaming spray and aimed the nozzle into his face and let it blast away what grime and exhaustion it could.

With a sliver of scented soap Alex left behind, he scrubbed his skin till it smoldered, then shut off the water, stepped out, and toweled off in front of the mirror. With a new blade in his ancient Schick he shaved carefully, and afterward he smoothed his hand across his cheeks and neck, tracking down the stray bristles he missed. Then, in the back corner of his medicine cabinet, he located an unopened bottle of cologne in a sleek black bottle. A gift from some lady whose name he could no longer recall. He sprinkled some into his hands, rubbed it into his palms, and slapped his cheeks until he radiated an odor something like a flaming gardenia bush extinguished with a vat of limeade.

He stalked back to the shower, climbed inside, and scrubbed away the stink as best he could. After he was done, he took Alexandra's remaining shard of scented soap and set it on the edge of the sink where her toothbrush had stood only an hour earlier. From the soap rose just a hint of her aroma. It wasn't much, but for now it would have to do.

17

'Daddy, Daddy.'

Sugarman finished loading the Glock nine and laid it on the bed next to the Remington shotgun. He'd been hearing the voice off and on for twenty minutes, a faint, ghostly call that seemed to rise from the black fog swirling in his chest. When he'd first heard it, he'd raced through the house in a stumbling frenzy, searched every closet and beneath all the furniture, even torn open the refrigerator door. But it had been an illusion. Her voice disembodied, floating up from the vaporous black pit of hope and despair that coiled inside him.

Now he was locked in a blind, methodical rage. Ignoring this phantom voice that mimicked Janey so well, determined not to be distracted again from his task. The charlatan was trying damn hard, insinuating and shrewd, but it wasn't throwing him again. By God, he was not going to surrender to some soft-headed fantasizing in which he swooped down heroically from the clouds and grabbed his little girl and sailed back up into the heavens with her joyful laugh and her cool breath bubbling against his throat. He was keeping himself hard. Staying tough and aloof. There was work to do. A plan to execute, no time to dawdle.

A while back he'd heard talk that Vic Joy had built a brick house on his estate. Though Sugarman didn't have Vic's address, he was nearly certain he'd recognize the place from offshore. It had to be the only property anywhere in the Keys with a brick structure. If he didn't see it on the first pass, he'd pull into one of Vic's marinas and ask a gas pump jockey.

When Sugarman completed his preparations, he'd ready his Boston Whaler, make sure the fishing poles were visible in the rod holders, and then cruise down to Islamorada, twenty miles south. First thing he'd do was a slow pass to evaluate security and possible cover – trees, shrubs, any vegetation along the shoreline. Then at twilight he'd work his way back up the coast, anchor the boat, and wade ashore, carrying the arsenal he was assembling on the blue quilt.

He'd strap the dive knife to his ankle. Take the two other handguns, the Beretta and the Smith, that were on the top shelf of his closet. Extra ammo in the pockets of his black jeans, an extra clip for the nine, pistols in each pocket of his black windbreaker. He'd already cut a coil of dock line into three-foot sections, just the right length to bind up any of Vic's security people he came across. He had a lead-weighted fish-stunning bat out with his tackle box. He'd carry that in his right hand, the nine-millimeter in his left. He'd have to rig a sling for the shotgun so he could wear it on his back.

'Daddy, Daddy?'

The voice was tired and frayed and seemed to echo across the cavernous expanse inside his gut, a void that was widening and deepening with every breath he took. But he wasn't going to make another ridiculous tour of the house. Yield to the frantic impulse. He wasn't going to go spinning off into the stratosphere. That wouldn't do Janey any good. And he wasn't going to let Jimmy Lee Webster throw him off, either. So what if there was no help from law enforcement? And so what if this time, he wouldn't even have Thorn at his side? He'd manage alone. This was his daughter, by God. No assistance required.

Last night on the walk home from the Holiday Inn he'd raged and muttered at Thorn for that first mile, but he couldn't keep the flames of fury going. Now, after weighing it a few hours more, the darkest emotion Sugar could summon was a deep sadness.

Sugar took the box of .38 shells out of the underwear drawer and dumped them in a heavy, clinking pile on the quilt.

Thorn was just being Thorn. He couldn't help himself. The guy was simply a product of a violent and unlucky past and the ingrown, rebellious disposition that came from living such a reclusive life.

Sugarman wasn't actually mad at Thorn, just deeply, terminally disappointed. And on this occasion, he'd decided to take a serious break from the guy. Maybe even use the time to rethink the whole friendship. Though Sugarman was pretty sure whatever Thorn's part had been in bringing on this catastrophe, it was innocent, an unintended consequence of his mulish nature, the bottom line was simple. Innocent or not, Thorn had somehow managed to put Janey in danger. So screw him. Screw him, screw him, screw him.

When Sugarman finished tucking all the pistols into his Nike duffel, he lugged the bag to the front door and set it down and went into the kitchen to throw together lunch. There was a whole day of sunlight to kill before he could mount his assault on Vic Joy's compound. He had to keep his mind busy, his focus sharp. He knew he could use a nap – an hour or two of shut-eye would probably do wonders, though he probably couldn't sleep and was, when he thought about it, concerned that if he did lie down and relax his vigilance, Janey's voice would seep into him again, her fright and confusion and horror resounding in his head until all his momentum and certainty were lost.

He tugged the cooler from the shelf above the

refrigerator and broke some ice cubes free from their trays and dumped them in. He crammed plastic bottles of water into the ice. As he was zipping the cooler shut, once again Janey's voice registered in some murky region of his head. But this time her voice was different. Not the mournful tone the phantom had used before. Now her words came as a whisper, hoarse and far away, and then there was another sound. It took him a moment to identify it. Something like the pop and sputter of static.

Sugarman lifted his head, tensed, listened a moment more to what was clearly the fizz and crackle of electronic interference, then he whirled from the counter and sprinted to the back bedroom.

He halted at the antique desk, dropped into the chair. Tilted up the screen of the laptop, which he'd folded down two nights before after seeing the man dressed as a pirate holding his daughter in his arms. He ran his finger across the touch pad and the dark screen fluttered and buzzed, then came to life, and Janey was there. The picture fuzzy with the white sputter of a badly strained reception. But it was her. His daughter, her face taut, blond hair messy.

'Janey, my God. Where are you?'

'Where were *you*, Daddy? I've been calling you all morning.'

'Oh, God,' he said. 'Well, it's okay. I'm here now. Are you all right?'

He bent closer to the screen, touched a finger to the black plastic frame.

'I think the battery is running down, Daddy. There's no electricity. Nowhere to plug it in and recharge. I don't know how long is left.'

'Don't worry about the battery, sweetheart. Where are you? I'll come get you right now. Where?'

'He brought me in an airplane. The man we saw in the kite thing flying over Thorn's house that day. Remember that man?'

'Yes, I know,' Sugarman said. 'Vic Joy.'

'It's raining here, Daddy.'

'Are you all right, Janey? Are you hurt? Did he do anything to you?'

'I'm all right. They didn't do anything to me.'

She turned her head and looked to the right. All he could see of the background was dark planks. Some kind of cabin or hut or paneled room.

'There's a bathroom, but it's dirty. And there's no toilet paper. And the water smells funny. I drank some of it, but then I realized it stunk and I spit it out and didn't drink any more.'

'That's good, Janey. Now where are you? Do you have any idea?'

'There's noises outside. Birds I've never heard, and shrieks and other noises, too. I'm really tired. But I'm afraid to close my eyes.'

Sugarman rubbed his hands together, his thoughts scattered wildly, something flapping in his chest like a caged raptor.

'How long were you in the airplane, Janey?'

'What? I can't hear you, Daddy.'

The picture was breaking up, freezing, then moving ahead in choppy spurts. Her voice a half-second out of sync with her lips.

Sugarman repeated his question and Janey said, 'I don't know. All night, I guess.'

'All night!'

'I fell asleep,' she said. 'When I woke up we were landing. We landed on the water, Daddy. I thought we were crashing.'

'On the water. Okay.'

'There were two men. Mr Joy, and the other one was big, with hairy arms. Both of them used the *f* word a lot.'

'And what did you see when you landed, Janey? Was it light?'

'The sun was just coming up. But I had my eyes closed. I was scared we were going to crash. I didn't know the plane could land on water. It was bumpy, that's all.'

'Listen, Janey. We're both going to have to be calm. We're going to figure this out together. Okay?'

'I'm tired,' she said. 'I want to go to sleep, but I'm afraid.'

'Is the man who took you there still close by, Janey?'

'He left. They put gas in the airplane and left.'

'You're alone? There's no one there?'

'They nailed boards over my windows so I can't get out. But I can see pretty good. It's a jungle, I think. I can see palm trees and vines and mangroves, I think. They let me keep my binoculars.'

'Do you have food, water?'

'Subs,' she said. 'Turkey and cheese with cucumbers and lettuce and mayonnaise.'

'Freshwater?'

'They left a cooler. Some ice, but it's mostly melted. Cokes and the sandwiches. Five sandwiches, all just alike. The foot-long ones.'

'There's no one else around? No one who could help you?'

'After the airplane left, I yelled till my throat hurt. Nobody came.'

Sugar rocked back in his chair and rubbed his hand across his mouth to smooth the crazy pain from his face.

'Okay,' he said. 'Okay, listen, Janey.'

But he had no idea what to ask or say. His chest felt like it was about to crack open, the giant hawk clawing its way out.

'I saw a kingfisher, Daddy. But it was different from any I've seen.'

Sugarman looked at her face on the screen. Tired but smiling with the memory of the bird sighting.

'Are you wearing your watch, Janey?'

She'd moved away from the screen and he saw only her ghostly outline, what appeared to be her back.

And then her face was there and the binoculars were in her hands.

'There's a sign, Daddy.'

'A sign?'

'On a post by the gravel road.'

'Great, great. What does it say?'

'I don't know. It's behind a palm frond. Maybe if the wind blows I'll be able to see it. I think there's a *G*, but I don't know for sure.'

'Okay, that's all right, no problem.' Sugarman's pulse was reeling. 'Look, Janey, are you wearing your wristwatch?'

'Yes.'

'Is it working?'

'I think so.'

'My watch says eleven forty-five. What does yours say?'

He could see her peering at her wrist.

'There's something screeching out there, Daddy. It's running around right outside the window.'

She got up and turned her back on the camera. She was gone for a long moment, then her face was close again. 'Wow, I couldn't see what was making the noise, but I saw a big blue butterfly right outside the window. It's shiny like tinfoil.'

'Iridescent,' he said.

'Big and blue and shiny. With a black edge along its wings.'

Sugarman was silent for a moment, thoughts scrambled, heart in disarray.

'Your watch, Janey, what time does it say?'

'Same as yours, Daddy. Fifteen minutes until twelve o'clock. It's very hot here. It's been raining and it's very hot.'

'Listen, sweetie. Listen carefully. Thursday night when the men first put you in the airplane, do you know what time that was?'

'They shot Dr Andy. They shot all the other people, too, his clients.'

'I know,' he said. 'That was terrible. But we need to put that behind us. We have to work on this, Janey. We need to concentrate, okay? It's important. You need to try to remember. It was nine o'clock on Thursday night when I saw the man dressed like a pirate on your Web camera. How long after that did you get on the airplane?'

'I don't know,' she said. 'I didn't notice my watch.'

'Did they take the boat back to shore before you got on the airplane?'

'Yeah, after they shot the people, they put me down in Dr Andy's cabin and locked the door and then drove the boat somewhere. I watched television and we drove for a long time and that's when they came and took me out of the cabin and put me on the airplane.'

'Okay,' Sugarman said. 'Okay.' Trying to stay sharp, but everything was tangled in his head, wave after wave of emotion, going from trough to peak and back again in a half-second.

'What were you watching? What was on the TV, Janey, when they came and got you?'

'News and stuff. Mostly news, the weather, boring stuff. Dr Andy can only get three channels on his boat. Is he dead?'

She was looking over her shoulder as if hearing something.

'There's lots of wildlife here, Daddy. Lots of birds.'

'And when you landed, the sun was just coming up? Is that right?'

'Yes.'

'And you flew all that time in between? From when you got onto the airplane till they landed, there weren't any other stops?'

'No stops, just a long trip.'

'And the airplane, can you describe it?'

'It was little. Just the place where the pilot sits. Two seats up there, and a few where I was.'

'How many seats in the back, Janey? Where you were.'

'A few. I'm not sure.'

Sugarman said, 'Sweetheart, does your computer have a little picture of a battery at the bottom of the screen?'

'Yeah,' she said. 'It's half-full. But I don't know how long it goes when it gets like that. This is Dr Andy's computer.'

'Will you be all right if we sign off now?'

'You've got to go, Daddy?'

'I need to think about this, sweetie, study a few things to help find where you are. You understand, don't you? We don't want your machine to die. We want to be able to talk as long as possible. Okay? Will you be all right?'

'Trace the phone call, Daddy. That's what they do

on TV. Call the police and they'll tell you where I am.'

'It might be more difficult than that.'

'Why?'

'You're on a satellite phone, for one thing.'

'I bet the police can do it. I've seen that show, the one on Thursday night. They do all kinds of stuff.'

'Okay,' Sugarman said. 'I'll call somebody. I'll look into it.'

'I've got windows,' she said. 'Four windows. They nailed boards over them and they locked the door, but I can see out around the boards. I'm going to look for birds, Daddy. I'll do that.'

'That's good, Janey. Birds, yes, anything else you can see. Keep looking at that sign. Maybe the wind will move the palm frond out of the way.'

'Yeah, okay.'

Sugar looked across the room at a mirror reflecting his backyard, squirrels chasing each other across the limbs of a mahogany tree. He was terrified of breaking this connection, losing this fragile contact maybe permanently, but it was the only way. He did a quick calculation in his head, the minimum time he'd need for the few things he'd thought of so far.

Sugarman spoke her name and Janey answered. She was staring directly into his eyes. He wasn't sure but thought he saw the glint of tears on her cheeks. He drew a breath and gripped the laptop screen with both hands, then eased his hands away. Staying strong for her. Showing her the way to act in this crisis. Don't lose it, don't lose it.

'Janey, I want you to dial back in to Dr Andy's site at six o'clock tonight, okay? That'll give me time to think about all this and make a plan. I'm going to come get you. Everything's going to be fine.'

'How can you get me if you don't know where I am?'

'We'll figure that out, Janey. Between the two of us, we'll figure it out. I promise. I just need to think about this a little while. But it shouldn't be too hard. We're pretty smart, you and me, right?'

'Okay,' she said. 'I'll look for birds and stuff.'

'Is there water, Janey?'

'I told you, Daddy. I got Cokes.'

'No, I mean, is there water anywhere outside your windows?'

She got up and left the chair.

The screen went fuzzy and he heard what sounded like the tapping of Morse code for a few seconds. Then a dial tone and someone else's voice speaking a few words in another language. Stray transmissions wandering in from the crowded heavens. He bent close to the screen and spoke her name. Trying not to sound frantic, trying to stay calm, though he felt anything but.

When her face came back, he let go of the air bunched in his lungs.

'There's water,' she said. 'It looks like a little lake. I don't know, there's trees in the way. But I see water and it smells like the ocean is somewhere close.'

'It does? You can smell that?'

'The ocean smells a certain way, Daddy. Haven't you ever noticed that?'

'Yes,' he said. 'I've noticed. I didn't realize you had.'

She tipped her head up, listening to something that came across the tiny speakers in Sugarman's laptop as a shrill piping, like a single key held down on a screechy church organ.

'Look, Janey, we need to save your battery. You reconnect to the site at six o'clock, okay?'

'We'll figure this out,' she said. 'The two of us will. And Thorn, too. Is he there?'

'Not right now, sweetie. But we'll do it together. You and me, we'll solve this thing, and I'll come get you. Okay?'

'Okay, Daddy. Six o'clock I'll call you.'

'And listen, Janey, don't drink those Cokes too fast, okay?'

'What?'

'Go slow with the Cokes. You don't want to drink them all at once and then have nothing left.'

'But you're coming right away.'

'I'm coming as soon as we can figure this out. But we don't know how long that's going to take, Janey. So go slow with the Cokes.'

He could see her face change, the smile drain away.

'I'll go slow then,' she said.

He had to work hard to summon the breath, and even then the words almost choked him as he said, 'I love you, sweetheart. Be strong, okay?'

'I love you, too, Daddy.'

And a second later his screen went dark.

18

'I'm not going in there, Vic. I told you, damn it.'

'Oh, come on, Annie. You're the only one who can really appreciate it. I show it to my friends, they smile and all, but it doesn't have the impact.'

'No, Vic.'

Anne and Vic were still poolside, Vic working on her to take a tour of the brick house. Off behind the main house there was a long low wood building that looked like a garage or work shop. All morning a couple of long-haired men had been coming and going. Shooting her looks as they passed in the distance. From the wood shop she'd been seeing the bright flutter of sparks and heard a shrill scream like a grinding wheel.

For hours she'd been reminding herself that this

was what she'd told Daniel she would do if something terrible ever split them up. She'd come to Key Largo, wait for him. Wait and wait, however long it took. And when Vic had made his offer of lodging she'd accepted impulsively. Out of weakness, her core gone soft and uncertain. She was waiting for Daniel. Even though she'd seen the men firing at him at close range, her instincts told her Daniel was still alive. A man so strong, so vital. She'd seen him roll away into the shadows. Maybe he'd gone over the side as she had done. She kept saying it to herself. It kept her sane, kept her moving forward. This was her new job, to wait for her lover to reappear.

'Isn't it pretty?' Vic said. 'No replica, either. That's the exact house, our family heritage. Brick for brick, board for board. Furniture, light fixtures, window treatments, rugs, the whole deal. Even the pots and pans. Those asshole Woodsons trashed it some, but I had all that fixed up. Good as new. Isn't it pretty?'

'It was ugly then, it's still ugly.'

'Jesus, why do you have to be so contrary, Annie? I haven't done anything to piss you off. I've given you a place to stay. A roof and servants. You got a big payday coming up soon, a half-million bucks. Why so angry?'

'We agreed on a million, Vic.'

'Okay, a million. I just misspoke.'

'Sure you did,' she said. 'And I'm not going into that goddamn house.'

'Where'd you sleep last night?'

'Upstairs,' she said. 'In the main house.'

'Christ, Anne, you could've slept in your old room, same mattress, everything. It's not like the place is haunted or anything. Come on, just take a quick look, humor me, for godsakes. Think of it as a museum. The Smithsonian of Joy.'

A short Hispanic man in a white jacket and dark trousers, another of Vic's servants, was striding across the patio with a phone in his hand. Anne had counted seven household staff, plus two more young men who'd arrived a few minutes earlier and were kneeling in the flower gardens weeding. Maybe full-time help, gardeners or goons, it was hard to tell about any of them. And then there were a couple of motorcycle guys posted out by the front gate. They smoked cigarettes and drank beers and tinkered with their bikes. Not exactly zealous sentries. Certainly nothing like the squad of sharks stationed around the grounds of the Salbone estate.

Vic took the phone and listened for a while, then stood up and ambled out to the edge of the pool. From a couple of his curt questions, Anne gathered it was a business call, one of his accountants or lawyers. A man named Ramon was getting cold feet about something, trying to back out. Vic bullying the guy, his voice rising and his vocabulary inflating to more syllables than was his habit. Telling Ramon if he didn't show up, he was going to lose his spot in the deal. It'd be his funeral. Glancing over to see if Anne was awed by his business prowess. Then speaking a few words in Spanish and hanging up.

Anne looked around again at the servants she could see. Five visible at that moment. Now that she was here, she wasn't sure how free she was to come and go with all these hired hands around. As if she might be more of a prisoner than she'd imagined.

Over at the workshop, Marty stood in the open doorway watching the flash and flicker inside.

Vic tossed the phone to the servant who stood twenty feet away, waiting. The young man fumbled the catch and the phone fell into the grass.

'Jesus, look at that, will you? Jorge, the klutz. Man, I go and hire the one Cuban in the whole world that isn't a professional baseball player.'

Vic came over and looked down at Anne, trying for something he probably meant as an affectionate smile.

'Hey, look, Annie, I'm not some uncaring asshole. I can appreciate why you wouldn't want to go into the old homestead again. The shit that happened that last night, all that mayhem at such an early age. You probably got a touch of the post-traumatic syndrome thing. I'm not insensitive to that. But I'm telling you, Annie, it did wonders for me buying the place, having it hauled down here. I probably saved a hundred grand in shrink bills. I walk through that old house every now and then, and man, it's like whatever's been bothering me, it just flies out of my chest.'

'I didn't realize you were bilingual, Vic.'

'Hell, these days you want to do business, you can't speak too many languages.'

'Look,' she said. 'You want me to go in that house, then you do something for me.'

Vic smiled. He lifted his hands and raked his fingers back through his long hair, stretching his arms out straight, untangling the gray snarls.

'You really got that bargaining thing going on, Anne. That Joy desire to strike a deal.'

'I need some cash. Some walking-around money.'

Vic laughed.

'Man, oh, man, Annie, you've been pirating for months and you got nothing to show for it?'

'To hell with you.'

'Okay, okay. What do you need money for? You got everything you could ask for right here. Food, servants . . .'

'I need clothes, toiletries,' she said.

'You been shopping at the Island Silver and Spice, got a nice new outfit.'

'I know one of the clerks. She let me charge it.'

'Well, I don't know.'

'Fuck you, Vic. Never mind. Just fuck you.'

He laughed again. Then he dug a finger in the corner of his eye, dug out the crumb, and flicked it away.

'Okay,' Vic said. 'I'll advance you some of the cash you got coming. How's that? A thousand, two? You can do a lot of walking around with two thousand.'

'Okay,' Anne said. 'Two thousand.'

'So come on, take a peek. I preserved it just like it was. You won't believe this, Annie.'

'All right, all right.'

She stood up, followed him over to the building, lagging a little.

'You're going to love this, Annie. The Woodsons ransacked it like they were looking for money, but all in all, when I got back there finally, it was still in pretty good shape. Personally, I'm surprised they didn't get a goddamn wrecking ball and level the place. That's what I would've done in their shoes. You know, I'm thinking of trying to resurrect that old schooner in the front yard. You want to help with that? I made some drawings.'

She'd stopped on the top step and was staring at the wood planks of the porch.

'Yeah, that's the bloodstains,' Vic said. 'I considered replacing the wood, but hell, that wouldn't be right. That's Mom and Dad, what's left of them. Like having them in an urn. Not any different from that.'

Anne stepped around the stains and pulled open the screen door and stepped across the threshold.

Vic didn't follow her inside, stayed out on the porch, maybe out of respect for her privacy. Anne stepped slowly across the living room, looking at the brown corduroy love seat where she'd reclined that final night, the same blue-and-red oval rag rug in the center of the tiny living room. That very book Vic had been reading lay open on the rug where

281

he'd left it. The kitchen was unchanged. A box of Martha White self-rising flour sitting out on the counter, ready for biscuit making. Dishes in the sink. Probably direct descendants of the Kentucky roaches scurried across the counter.

She felt the swoon of déjà vu, only far more intense than that. This house was more than some well-preserved museum, some replica of her past; this was the very thing. The same stale odors of human sweat and oily cooking and moldy boards, the same particles of lifeless dust swirling in the light.

She glanced back to see Vic standing on the porch, gazing out at his oceanfront property. Anne had a quick vision of the view off the Harlan porch, the grim landscape below, the acid stench of the mines. She walked down the narrow hallway, looked at the three photographs on the wall. One grainy black-and-white of her mother and father smiling broadly and leaning against the hood of that old Rambler, young lovers, with a palm tree in the background. The two other photos were class pictures of Vic and Anne from high school. Anne with long straight hair and a grim smile, performing for the photographer, but showing not a trace of real pleasure. Her eyes with a rabbity fear, a darting readiness to flee.

She was back there then, in Harlan, among the ghosts, among the awful, oppressive fantasy her mother had imposed. Realizing in that aching moment that her mother was undoubtedly mad.

More fixed and determined in her lunacy than Anne had ever supposed. Not merely eccentric, as she'd so long believed, but dangerously, chemically insane. A woman who had invented a dreamworld for herself and was committed to luring her husband and her children into that same hypnotic creation. There'd been no way to know it then. Anne had managed to resist only out of some blind instinct, but now she saw it, looking into her parents' bedroom, at the collection of pirate junk and Hollywood publicity photos of pirate actors on her wall. Three-cornered hats, daggers, a red sash that might have belted the waist of Errol Flynn.

Anne had had enough. She turned and was gathering herself to march from the house. But the cramped bedroom she'd shared with her brother all through their childhood and teenage years was one step away. She couldn't help herself and entered the room.

Bunk beds. Vic on top, Anne below. Vic's same portable radio on the narrow shelf he'd hammered into place. Her shabby green comforter still draped across her bunk. The desk where she'd done her homework, Vic's initials carved into the upper right corner. Even a shelf on one wall crammed with glass jars. The pickled remains of the dozens of frogs and snakes and field mice he'd tracked down in the nearby woods and killed. The floating heads of chickens, coiled intestines he'd pulled from possums and rabbits, the ear of a butchered hog.

She couldn't summon coherent thought, just looked at those marinated creatures and scraps of flesh. Standing in the cramped room she thought she'd left behind long ago. All that torment and sadness and confusion she'd known as a kid came welling back. This room, this house, the voices in the walls. A place she'd imagined had sunk into the bottomless sea of years. Lost down in the lightless depths.

'See what I been doing? My little hobby.'

Vic stood in the doorway.

'What?'

'The jars. The ones you're looking at.'

Anne looked back at the frogs and mice. Scattered among them were four or five other jars that contained what looked like pickled eggs. Floating in a clear broth, the white orbs were coated with a pinkish film.

'Every summer I been going back up there to Kentucky. I bag a Woodson. Been at it for six, seven years now. One's my limit, though. Don't want to deplete the supply. I fly up, take a week, hunt one down. These days they know it's coming, try to get ready, hunker down, defend themselves. But they don't know exactly when I'll be there, so they can't be prepared every second of every day. It's my way of paying homage to Mom, keeping her memory alive in those godforsaken hills. They think it's Mother's ghost coming for them. That's what I hear.'

'Woodsons?' Anne tried to focus on the jars, the pickled eggs.

'Their nuts, Annie. Those are Woodson *cojones*.'

Suspended in the gelatinous fluid, the white orbs stared out at her like sightless eyes.

After a while she heard Vic leaving the room, but Anne couldn't pull herself away. The light-headedness she'd been feeling had spun into full vertigo. Trying to breathe, trying to keep her balance in that room with its ancient dust, the stifling density of its air, its dark swirl of memories and terrors she thought she had long ago escaped. And those blind, white eyes.

'You got an appointment?' the motorcycle guy asked Thorn. Black T-shirts, torn jeans, heavy belts, and black boots, the standard uniform, except for the insignia on their shirts. A queen conch sprouting handlebars, and two spinning wheels. Maybe it was supposed to be funny and Thorn just wasn't in the mood. Hell's Conchs.

The runty one said, 'Charlie asked you a fucking question.' The man had long, ratty red hair and a crooked nose that looked like it might be handy for opening beer bottles. There was a heavy cast on his right foot that someone had spray-painted black.

'What happened to you? Been punting cement blocks again?'

'Is this guy funny, Charlie? 'Cause I'm not finding him humorous.'

For a half-second Thorn toyed with the idea of

taking these two on. Sucker-punch one, kick the other backward into his bike. But Thorn had come courting, playing a delicate game, and he had to remind himself to downshift his rage, keep Janey's face out of his head. And Alexandra's, too.

'My name's Thorn. Is himself around?'

'Himself?' the little one said.

'He means Vic. He's being a wiseass.'

'Mr Joy wants to see me,' Thorn said. 'He's gone to a lot of trouble to get me here and I don't think he'd want you two gentlemen to slow that process down.'

The big one reached into his jeans pocket and drew out a silver cell phone, flipped it open, hit a button. The small biker hobbled near Thorn and tipped his head a few inches closer like he was trying to draw in Thorn's scent so he could track him down later.

The large man put his phone away and reached around the cement column and pressed a button and the iron gates rolled apart.

'See you later, wiseass,' the little one said.

'Can't wait,' Thorn said.

A snowy egret stood frozen on the shoreline of Joy's property, its neck cocked as it peered into the shallows at its feet, ready to spear lunch. Holding so still it could have been an ornament.

Vic seemed to be watching the bird as he stood

out on the sunlit lawn between a large oval swimming pool and a redbrick house with asphalt shingles. Thorn had seen uglier houses, but not many. That brick structure was a jarring contrast to the graceful yellow-and-white conch mansion that stood on the north end of the property. The big house had a white tin roof and finely filigreed rails and balustrades, an abundance of French doors and lazy outdoor ceiling fans and white wicker furniture, that graceful, airy Keys style that the nineteenth-century shipbuilders had stolen from the Bahamas by way of New Orleans and Cape Cod. This was a copy of some of those dignified Victorian structures that filled the backstreets of Key West, and from a distance the house was pleasing enough to the eye for a blatant forgery.

In a way, the dingy brick house seemed the more authentic of the two structures. It didn't belong anywhere near a subtropical island, but it wasn't a copy of anything, either, wasn't intended to seduce. It was a crude and uncomplicated building, and if it wasn't pretty, at least it was honest.

Vic turned from his opulent view. He was wearing black trousers and a tight black T-shirt that showed off the sharp V of his torso.

'Well, if it isn't my favorite bowel obstruction come calling. We meet again, Mr Thorn.'

Vic Joy was an inch or two taller than he was, maybe twenty pounds lighter. A rangy man with crinkly iron-tinted hair that hung loose down his back and small, overactive eyes that struck Thorn as totally independent from the rest of his face. At that moment his gaze was trained on Thorn's face, judging, probing, while his mouth curled into a vacant smile.

'I got your note,' Thorn said.

'And which note would that be?'

'The one stuck to my door, suggesting you'd like to make a swap for my property. "Items of equal value."'

'So tell me,' Vic said. 'You here to start trouble or is there some commerce you'd like to transact? You should figure that out, Thorn, before we go forward, don't you think?'

'You know why I'm here. Because you kidnapped a little girl.'

For a few seconds Vic's eyes lost their hold on the moment and seemed to swim down into the lightless realms inside him as though he were drawing strength from the cesspool of his past. When he refocused on Thorn, some of that frigid darkness was still in his eyes.

'I don't like you,' Vic said. 'You should know that up front.'

'I'm crushed,' he said.

'I've made a little study of you, Thorn. Talked to people who know you, know where you came from, what you do with your time. It's the way I do business. I like to know my enemy.'

'And?'

'You're everything I despise, Thorn. A backward, shiftless do-nothing. A man who mocks the hard work and aspirations of others. A scoffer who believes in nothing but the bullshit orbiting his own navel.'

'You've done your homework.'

Vic reached out and poked a stiff finger into Thorn's arm.

'Don't think I'm just some run-of-the-mill businessman,' Vic said. 'Oh, I buy, I sell, I develop land. But the bottom line for me is fun. And that's exactly what this deal is going to be. Fucking you over, Thorn, that's going to be a major pleasure. And don't think you're going to walk in here and negotiate or bargain or play games. Because you're in my world now. And once you've stepped into my gravitational field, you don't get away, son. There's no escape from Vic Joy.'

Thorn watched as Anne Bonny came out the front door of the brick house. She glanced in their direction, but her gaze wandered across the two of them as if they were invisible. With an uncertain grip on the handrail, she leaned heavily against it as though her legs were about to fail.

'I'm here to get the girl back, that's all.'

'Yes, yes, the girl,' Vic said. 'I love it. A guy like you who prides himself on being such a fucking individualist. This rebel free spirit. Well, that's bullshit. You're typecast, Thorn. As predictable as Pavlov's dog. Stimulus, response. All I have to do is put a poor child in danger, and you salivate all over your shoes.'

Anne's legs gave way and she slumped sideways against the rail and half-slid, half-stumbled down the last two steps and went sprawling into the grass.

Thorn sprinted over and got to her as she was struggling to lift her head.

'Stay down,' Thorn said. 'You fainted.'

Her gaze roamed his face, but she seemed to see nothing there she comprehended. Her eyes were hazy and vague and her breath came in hurried heaves. She turned her head and glanced back at the brick building and a burst of dark panic flared in her face as if the phantom she'd been fleeing was stalking down the stairway after her.

Vic squatted beside them and laid a hand across her forehead.

'Poor thing's gotten feverish.' He nodded at the house. 'Memory lane can be one steep-ass road to climb.'

'That's the place where it happened?' Thorn said. 'The Harlan house?'

Vic gave Thorn a look of naked surprise.

'She told you about that?'

'You brought that piece of shit down here?'

'Damn right,' Vic said. 'Brick by brick, board by board. Man's got to preserve every scrap of his history he can. That goddamn house is the foundation of everything I am today.'

'And just as ugly,' Thorn said.

He scooped Anne Joy into his arms and hoisted her up.

'Where do you think you're going?'

'She needs to cool off,' he said. 'Lie down for a while.'

Vic tagged along, appraising Thorn's physique with the precision of a tailor sizing a customer.

'I don't like this,' Vic said. 'My sister sharing family history with some shit heel she picks up in a bar.'

Thorn carried her up the front stairs and a young man in a white jacket and dark trousers held the white door ajar.

'Which way's the bedroom?'

'Upstairs,' Vic said. 'First door on the left.'

Anne's eyes were closed and her features had turned soft and blurry as though she were suspended a couple of inches below the surface of a pool of clear water.

Cradling her, Thorn registered the familiar heft of her body, the well-muscled but limber frame. A sudden unwelcome tingle fired through him, this flesh that once had stimulated his flesh to such incessant heat.

He was halfway up when Marty Messina rounded the second-floor corner and halted abruptly.

'Well, fuck me,' he said. 'What do we have here?'

At the top of the stairs, breathing hard from the climb and his pulse rattled by that unsettling ghost of desire, Thorn nudged past the man. Messina was freshly scrubbed and wore tight white jeans and an orange tank top that exposed the mats of dark hair growing on his shoulders. A square patch of gauze was taped to the edge of his armpit, a dot of blood showing through.

'Orange isn't your color, Marty. Clashes with your shit-brown eyes.'

Thorn managed to turn the doorknob and knee open the door. He carried Anne across the Oriental carpet to the four-poster and laid her out, tucked the pillow under her head. He went to the windows and lowered the blinds.

'Get her some cold water,' Thorn told Marty. Vic was standing behind him in the doorway.

'Fuck you, Cheese Whiz.'

'Go ahead, do it, Marty,' Vic said. 'Some Perrier with ice and lime. A damp washcloth, too.'

Messina pouted for a moment, then wheeled and huffed away.

'Think that ought to do it?' Thorn said.

'Do what?' said Vic.

'Get Marty using his cell phone. The thing I'm here to accomplish.'

Anne moaned and dug her head deeper into the pillow.

'Like I said.' Vic chuckled from the doorway. 'Pavlov's idiot dog.'

19

'She's a beauty,' Kirk Graham said.

'You know what it is?' said Sugarman. Just past Vic Joy's estate, he made a wide U-turn, heading back north, farther off the coast, for the return trip to Key Largo.

'Been a while since I saw one, but hell, yeah, I know that plane. I even flew one for a while, down in Saint Croix, doing a little barefoot island-hopping for one of the hotels down there. Sight-seeing trips for the tourists. Lasted a few months, back in my wild and crazy youth.'

'I want to know how far it can fly in seven hours or maybe eight.'

Key Largo was full of pilots, but Kirk Graham was the only one he knew who was a full-blown aviation fanatic. Built model planes, flew the radio-controlled ones. He was a senior pilot for United Airlines, took weekend runs to Rio. Down one night, back two days later. Gave him the rest of the week to work on his tennis game. Sugarman knew him from the courts where Kirk spent most of his off-hours, giving lessons to the pretty ladies and hustling guys half his age who'd never seen an old guy like Kirk in such greyhound shape.

'That's Vic Joy's place, isn't it?'

Sugarman nodded.

'You working a case?'

He nodded again.

'I don't know,' Kirk said. 'If Joy's mixed up in it, you'd better call your life insurance agent, double your policy.'

'What do you know about that plane?'

Kirk tugged the bill of his baseball cap lower against the wind.

'I could go on the Net when we get back, pull up all the stats, give you the whole deal. But off the top of my head, I recall a few things.'

Sugarman passed along the eastern edge of Rodriquez Key, took a heading on the distant markers at South Creek that led to Largo Sound.

'It's a Grumman G-73 Mallard. Came after the Goose and the Widgeon. The Grumman people wanted an amphibian for commercial use with the regional airlines that work the islands. It seated ten or eleven besides the two pilots. But it never caught on and you don't see many these days. Chalk's Airlines, up in Miami, they still use them, the turbo-props, but otherwise they've pretty much disappeared.'

'What about fuel capacity, speed? What's its range?'

'Range and speed depend on a lot of factors, the number aboard for one.'

'Two adults and a child,' Sugarman said.

Graham peered at him.

'Child?'

'Young kid, less than a hundred pounds. The adults were big. Probably pushing two hundred.'

'Is this personal, Sugarman? About what happened on that yacht?'

'You don't want to get involved, Kirk. I just need the data.'

Kirk nodded, getting enough of the picture to let it go.

'Okay, well, I believe the Mallard has a maximum cruising speed of somewhere around one-sixty, one-seventy, that's knots. Pretty typical for a plane that size and weight. The floats slow it down, or it'd be up near two hundred.'

'So in seven hours?'

'Thousand nautical miles, maybe eleven hundred.'

'It carry enough fuel to do that in one hop?'

'A person who could afford the Mallard G-73 could afford to outfit it with an extra tank or two. But even without the added capacity, it could probably make eleven hundred easy enough if it wasn't flying into a gale.'

'Eleven hundred miles,' Sugarman said. 'Jesus God.'

'Bad news?'

Sugar steered the Whaler through the first markers into South Creek. A big dive boat heading out at full power, its decks crowded with tourists, sent a wake curling up behind it, a five-foot tsunami of dark green water with nowhere to go in that narrow mangrove-lined channel. Sugar took the shortest direction through it, plowing head-on, slamming up and over the wave. Kirk pitched hard to the side and had to grab the console rail to keep from going over.

When they were in the quieter water, Sugarman glanced his way.

'Sorry.'

Kirk had taken a good dousing but said it was okay, no problem.

'Thanks for your help.'

'Man, Sugar, I never saw you this worked up.'

'Never been this worked up.'

Sugarman kept the throttle flat, roaring through the channel's hairpin turns, flushing herons and flocks of egrets that had been clutching peacefully to high perches in the mangroves. One great blue heron trumpeted a hoarse bray, disentangled itself from the branches, and with a couple of lazy strokes swam up into the clear sky. Slowest wing beat of any of the wading birds.

Sugarman followed the grayish-blue bird as it caught a current and settled in for a ride. An elegant bird, but like every other creature, it survived from one bloody moment to the next. Gristle and bone, plunge and kill, cut and run.

'Annie's going to be fine,' Vic said from the doorway of her bedroom. 'Now let's you and me have a talk, Thorn.'

Anne was resting, eyes closed, breath coming evenly. Thorn went to the window and cranked the wood blinds tighter.

Out in the hallway Marty had reappeared and was leaning around Vic for a view of the scene. For Messina's benefit, Thorn walked to the bed and touched Anne's cheek with the back of his hand, lingered there for a couple of beats. He might have bent to kiss her on the forehead, but he didn't want to push it, give Marty a reason to be mistrustful.

Maybe it was Thorn's wishful imagination, but when he looked over again Messina seemed to have tightened his frown a notch. Eyes hardening.

Perhaps it was that cruel edge in Marty's face that brought Janey's face swimming into Thorn's head and staggered him for a moment. He had to force down a breath, relax his hands, or else he would have charged the two of them right there. For Janey's sake, he worked up a stiff smile and showed it to Vic.

'Yes,' Thorn said. 'She's doing fine.'

Vic led them to his downstairs study and shut the door and walked over to stand behind his desk. On one wall a double set of French doors looked out at the Atlantic, and the other three were covered with floor-to-ceiling bookcases painted a glossy white. While Vic watched, Thorn wandered the room, scanning the man's library. It was, as far as he could tell, devoted entirely to seafaring novels, from *Treasure Island* to Peter Benchley. Conrad shelved beside Jimmy Buffett. Several volumes dedicated to Blackbeard, Captain Kidd and Gasparilla, Sir Francis Drake, and an entire wall of what looked like swashbuckling paperback romances. Garish colors and giant sabers and deep necklines. Stunted by his mother's infatuation with pirate lore, clearly, Vic Joy had never managed to broaden his interest beyond that training. Some might politely call him a specialist. But Thorn wasn't feeling polite. Junk was junk. A lifetime of drinking rotgut didn't qualify you as a connoisseur of anything.

'Vic's a reader,' Marty said.

Thorn took down a leather-bound copy of *Robinson Crusoe*, strummed the pages, releasing a fine musty powder into the air.

'Show him the site plan, Marty.'

Eyeing Thorn with a complicated smile, Vic stood behind a sweeping oak desk that was littered with folders and documents.

Marty rolled what looked like a room service table

away from the wall. Spread out on its surface was an architectural model of what appeared to be a standard-issue tropical beach. A few miniature coconut palms arched toward the blue plastic sea, a crescent stretch of snowy sand. Filling almost every inch of the property adjacent to the beach was a massive structure, five stories high, a slab of concrete with windows, each with a view of Blackwater Sound. The mixing trucks would be rolling for a year just to lay the foundation.

When Thorn looked up, Vic reached behind him and tugged a sash, and the red drapes that Thorn had mistaken for window coverings pulled aside to reveal a large watercolor of the same beach as the model that sat before him.

Thorn set the book he'd been holding back in its slot on the shelf.

'Van Gogh?' Thorn said.

'You want me to disembowel you right here? Keep being a wiseass.'

Even in the flattering golden light filtering through the fronds outside, the painting looked to Thorn like something Sugarman's daughters would have discarded as a botched attempt. A hideous purple sky. A cliché beach.

'My mother did that. So yeah, it's not going to hang in the Met anytime soon. But the woman had a vision. You got to give her that. She poured her heart and soul into that painting.'

Marty gave Thorn a crafty sideways smile. A

private communiqué that dared Thorn to mock the painting.

'So do you see?' Vic said.

'See what?'

'You see where you fit in? What this is all about.'

'I'm a little slow,' Thorn said. 'Everyone comments on it.'

'Okay, here.' Vic shuffled through the papers on his desk till he located a file folder. He drew out a stack of glossy color shots and fanned them like an oversize deck of cards. Thorn touched the edge of one and pulled it free of the pile. Then he drew out another and looked at it. 'Now do you see?'

'You took these from the parasail.'

'Hadn't been for you fucking my sister, Thorn, I would've never seen your land firsthand. Hell, until then, I'd overlooked it altogether from the air. But I took one look that day, and I said, Eureka. I'm going to have that little stretch of coastline.'

'The Island House motel,' Thorn said. 'You bought that and knocked it down so you could build the Great Wall of China?'

Vic ran his finger across the plastic sand of the model.

'Land's scarce, Thorn. That five acres you're sitting on is about the last prime piece around. How it'll work, I join your land with the Island House property and the one in between, which I already own, then I build a resort ten times bigger than anything the Keys has ever seen. And the highlight of the whole place will be that pretty little beach exactly like the one in the painting. A nod to my dear old mom. Hang her painting in the lobby.'

'That's Miami Beach, not the Keys. It's the goddamn Fontainebleau.'

'You've been playing pioneer too long, Thorn. People don't want charm anymore. Some ramshackle cottage with warped floors and a ceiling fan that moves the hot air around. They want comfort. They want a view. The world's changed. And you're still hogging that chunk of land, playing your kid's games, pretending you're some asshole Daniel Boone. Well, that's finished, my friend. You just got your fucking eviction notice.'

'You're nuts,' Thorn said.

'You just figuring that out?' Vic said. 'I guess you *are* a little slow.'

Thorn saw the tick of a blue vein at Vic's temple. Muscles tightening in his jaw and throat, sinews rising.

'You already own a dozen resorts,' Thorn said. 'And you kidnap a little girl so you can own one more?'

'I'm taking your fucking land, Thorn.' Vic aimed his eyes across the room at the rows of books. 'I offered you a fair price and you pissed on my shoe. This is what comes next.'

His eyes were the color of the fake water his model makers had chosen. He let his gaze drift across the shelves of books until almost as if by accident his line of sight intersected with where Thorn happened to be standing. Vic's face had assumed the most casual of expressions. But Thorn sensed the rage was still there, constricting his throat, narrowing his veins. Pressure building just beyond the edges of his blasé face.

'My people have already drawn up the closing papers. Done the title search bullshit and all that, got all the t's crossed.'

'I sign and then Janey Sugarman magically appears.'

'You sign, then you get an item of equal value.'

'How do I know she's still alive?'

'How does a man know anything?' Vic said. 'In this life, you got to take a lot on trust.'

'I want proof,' Thorn said. 'Or I don't sign anything.'

Anne Bonny pushed open the door and stepped into the room.

Her flesh had regained most of its coppery hue. She glanced at Thorn briefly, then back at her brother.

'I'm going, Vic. I need that money.'

'Shopping?'

'Yes,' she said quietly, 'shopping.'

'All right,' he said. A smile for his sister. Stooping to draw open a drawer, pull out a stack of bills, begin counting out a sum.

While he counted, Anne looked at Thorn, and though he might have designed a slightly more provocative display for Marty's consumption, Thorn was happy enough that she raised her right hand and grazed her fingertips across his bare arm. If Thorn had witnessed a similar touch to Alexandra's flesh by any man, his skin would've writhed and he would have barked in protest. So all in all, he didn't feel compelled to do more than just stand there and savor the lingering simmer of that touch.

In the next moment a flush came to his face, and he found himself replaying a rapid sequence of moments from their long hours in his bed, sex that was disconnected from all knowledge of each other, their personalities or their pasts, two anonymous people grappling with each other for hours at a time.

And as Vic handed Anne Bonny the stack of bills, Thorn felt a lurch in his chest, the visceral other half of the recognition he'd just had. That even though he didn't feel for Anne any of the complex, deeply rooted devotion he did for Alexandra Collins, still, this tall, troubled woman who turned to him now and spoke his name and waited for him to resurface from the far place where he'd gone, this woman aroused him in ways that he'd all but forgotten were possible.

'Go get the Cadillac, Marty,' Vic said. 'Annie's going shopping.'

'No,' she said. 'Thorn will take me. Won't you, Thorn?'

Vic smiled at his sister and shook his head.

'At the moment, Annie, Thorn's occupied with a

small real estate matter. Marty can drive you where you need to go.'

'I'll do it, Anne,' Thorn said. 'You ready?'

'I'll get my things,' she said, and walked past Marty out the door.

When she was gone, Vic pushed a sheaf of papers across the desk.

'Forget it. I'm not signing anything without proof she's safe.'

'You sign the papers, you get your proof. That sweet little girl is fine for the moment, but there's no way to know how long she can hold out in her present predicament. You don't want that on your pious conscience, do you, Thorn? The blood and guts of an innocent child?'

Vic took a fountain pen off his desk and uncapped it and was still focused on slipping the cap onto the butt when Thorn made it around the desk.

Not in the script, not even close. But the surge of anger blindsided him and he seized Vic's ears and hammered the man's head back against his mother's silly painting. Once, twice, ripping the canvas, opening a gash halfway across that sandy beach.

Vic managed to twist his head a few degrees to the side and saw the damage and it sent a groaning shudder through his body. He snarled a curse and Thorn felt the fountain pen gouge through his shirt and into his belly and then a second stab, settling deep in the soft tissue lower down.

Thorn slammed a forearm into Vic's left temple

and was drawing back for another when Marty Messina grabbed him by the arm and slung him backward across the room into the shelves of books. All that prison muscle finally paying off. Books tumbled down across Thorn's shoulders.

The pen was only buried a half-inch, but it was a half-inch of solid pain. Thorn pushed himself away from the shelves and gripped the pen and wrenched it free, threw it on the rug. Vic was touching the ragged seam in his painting, muttering to himself while Marty stood in the center of the room in a wrestler's crouch, daring Thorn to make another move.

'You're fucked, Thorn,' Marty said.

'Tell me about it.'

He backed out of the room and onto the landing. One of the female servants was coming through the front door. She halted, stared at the blood drenching the waist of his shorts, and dropped the stack of mail in her hand.

Thorn hauled himself upstairs, leaving splatters and smeared footprints on the white maple steps.

As he made it to the top step, Anne was coming out of her room.

'Christ, Thorn. What the hell is this?'

'Pen's mightier than the sword.'

Anne looped an arm through his and towed him into her room, shut the door, and turned the lock. She laid him on her bed and undid his belt and drew aside his shirt. As she drew open his clothes, her eyes seemed to soften, as though she were drifting along with him back to that other time. The loosening of underclothes, the tugging of elastic bands and silk, the urgency to expose and be exposed.

Anne Bonny went into the bathroom and ran the water and brought back a warm washcloth and dabbed at the first puncture. Then she had to roll down the elastic band of his Jockey shorts to get at the lower one. His penis partly revealed, though some of it still hidden by her guarded handling.

'Bleeding's slowing down,' she said. She kept the washcloth pressed hard to the wound. 'They don't look that bad.'

'I'll take your word for it.'

'What happened?'

'I lost my cool.'

'Easy to do with Vic. He feasts on that, provoke and conquer.'

'Tore a little gash in that painting your mother drew.'

'Oh, God,' she said. 'Anything but that.'

She went back to the medicine cabinet in the bathroom and retrieved a bottle of peroxide and some small Band-Aids. She sat down again on the edge of the bed, cleaned the wounds, and crisscrossed them with bandages.

When she was done, the throb had eased. With her free hand caressing his chest, his senses were scattered, hard to focus on the ache. A warmth rising in him as he looked up into the shadowy heat of her eyes.

'Old times,' he said.

She nodded. Eyes turning inward for a long moment. Then coming back to his, her mouth crinkling into a restrained smile.

'We were good,' she said. 'In a lot of ways.'

'Yeah,' Thorn said. 'The physical part, that was special.'

'Takes more than that for things to work.'

'I know,' he said. 'But we handled that part well.'

'We did. Damn well.'

She used the washcloth to wipe away the smears of blood on his ribs and at the narrowing of his waist and then scrubbed at the bloody tufts of pubic hair.

'Everything's a trade-off, isn't it?' she said. 'No way to have it all in one neat package.'

'Maybe,' he said. 'But some packages are neater than others.'

Thorn closed his eyes and fixed his mind on the receding pain. He was here with her, behind a locked door with Marty Messina fully aware of his presence. He was satisfying Jimmy Lee Webster's assignment better than he would have imagined. No further action required. The appearance of intimacy. Tweaking Marty's suspicions. If Webster's theory was correct, then Thorn had accomplished all he needed to do to bring Daniel Salbone out of hiding. He could simply shut down, lie still, wait for half an hour, and walk away from that house forever, having done all he could do to get Janey back.

So it startled him to see his own hand rising like a draft of smoke to graze her cheek, to cup that fine-boned face, hold it in his palm for several seconds while they searched each other's eyes, and then his hand eased her head down slowly without resistance on her part. Until her eyes closed and an involuntary moan escaped her throat and her lips parted to join his, eager and pliable, that blend of force and gentleness that had marked their kissing from the very start.

As the heat deepened and spread through his chest and the kiss grew more serious and probing, some circuit tripped in his libido and Thorn simply shut down.

With the hand cupping her cheek, he exerted the slightest pressure on her jaw and edged her away.

The question was in her eyes. Thorn drew a deep breath and studied her lips and eyes and the taut coppery skin. An exotic beauty who stirred him still, in fact, even more, now that he understood something of the horrors she'd been struggling to free herself from.

'What is it?' she said.

Thorn considered it for a moment, breathing her breath, her foreign scent that was still so familiar, so richly seasoned with memories.

'I can't,' he said. 'There's other people now.'

'Other people?'

'Yes.'

It was more than he could explain. For it wasn't Alexandra alone, though she was most of it. There was also Lawton and Sugarman and Janey, too. There was even the damn dog.

It had been so long since he'd been a part of a family, he'd forgotten the sensation, the sense of duty and mutual respect – those deeper pleasures than simple self-indulgence.

Anne Bonny drew back and settled herself upright on the bed beside him.

'It's always something.' No bitterness, just a faint trace of regret.

'Yeah,' Thorn said. 'Always something.'

She lay down beside him.

'Is this all right?' she asked as she nudged closer.

Thorn swallowed. Over it now, though the heat of the kiss still lingered.

'Sure,' he said. 'Sure.'

And they huddled close, her head tucked into the hollow of his shoulder, Thorn closing his eyes, willing himself to relax, following his breath in and out until it slowed, until finally he drifted off into a restless, guilty nap.

Maybe it was an hour later, maybe more, when he felt himself rising through the smoky layers of dream, feeling hands fumble at his opened clothes, tug his crotch, careful fingers working to separate his parts.

In that slow, groggy resurfacing, he was aware of the heat and tightening in his penis, and he groaned and reached down to nudge Anne's fingers away and felt instead the sudden cold sting of steel against his scrotum and a strong and hairy hand holding him firm.

He tensed and came instantly awake. And looked down to see Vic Joy perched on the edge of the bed. A hunting knife in one hand, Thorn's balls gripped in the other. The blade of the knife was touching the tender wrinkled skin at the base of the sack.

Anne sat up beside him.

'Vic!'

'Tell him, Annie. Tell him how hard our mother worked on that goddamn painting. What it meant to her. How much of her heart is in those trees and sand and water.'

'Put the knife down, Vic. Put it down.' Annie rose from the bed and raked a strand of hair from her face.

Thorn swallowed and strained to stay still.

Vic said, 'Some men would be squeamish to touch another man's genitals. But not me. When I was a boy I castrated hogs. Tell him, Annie. Tell him about the hogs and that stray dog that kept coming into our yard bothering us. Tell him about the animals from the woods. Tell him, so he'll know.'

'Vic, you can't do this. It's not right.'

'A man comes into my house and mocks me, he tears a gash in my birthright. Tell him about the Woodsons. Tell him about the collection you saw.'

She went slowly around the end of the bed. Quiet footfalls as if to keep from waking a sleeper.

'You're not such a cocky bastard now, are you? Where's the smart mouth, asshole? Come on, say something clever.'

Vic tightened his hold and adjusted the blade so a half-inch thrust would do the job. Thorn closed his eyes, holding back the howl that was storming in his chest. Lights flickered behind his eyes as Vic twisted his grip a half-turn.

'I've held bigger balls,' Vic said. 'And I've cut them loose.'

Anne stood beside him and laid a hand on his shoulder and Vic looked up at her, but his grip did not relax a fraction.

'There's Woodsons who've done less to piss me off than this man has, and those boys are walking around without their sex.'

'I know,' she said. 'Thorn was wrong to do what he did. But listen, Vic: Our mother, she wouldn't want this. She wouldn't want you to cut a man like this, not in her own house, her sanctuary. There was never violence, Vic, not at home.'

Vic's eyes were glassy and vague as he looked up at his sister. Years melting away, his features smoothing.

'Mother's dead and gone. She's not here to speak for herself.'

'Vic,' Anne said. 'Give me the knife. Give it to me.'

'She'd forgive me, no matter what I did. She'd find it in her heart. She always forgave me. That woman was a fucking saint.'

Anne reached down and touched the back of his knife hand, and the contact registered with a keen bite against Thorn's flesh.

'Give it to me, Vic. It's going to be all right. We'll get the painting repaired. Anything can be fixed, Vic. You know that. It can be patched as good as new. Right?'

'I'm going to kill this fucker. It'll never be the way it was. Never.'

'You need him alive, Vic. You need him to sign the papers for his land.'

'I can forge his goddamn signature. I got people working for me that'll take care of it. Fuck him.'

'You need him alive, Vic. Don't you? Think about it.'

Thorn could feel Vic's grip relax by some tiny measure.

'All right,' he said. 'For you. All right.'

Vic was still looking at his sister as she pried the knife from his hand. Then she took it across the room and set it on the dresser. Vic released Thorn's scrotum and stood up and rubbed his palms hard against his pants. His face was a ghastly gray and his mouth quivered like a child about to break into a wail.

'Okay,' he said. 'Now get the fuck out of my sight, the both of you. When you decide you want that little girl to live, then you come back here ready to sign those papers. But believe me, Thorn, the next time I see you, you better be down on your mother-fucking knees.'

20

Drenched in sweat from the two long hikes across the parking lot to his car, Sugarman slammed the back door of his old Ford and turned and trotted back for the third and what he hoped was the final trip to the checkout desk of the Key Largo Library.

But as he approached the desk, just as Jill and he had feared, the head librarian, Ruth Mercer, materialized from her office to see who this man was who was raiding their natural history section.

'It's a project I'm working on,' Sugarman told her as he began to pile the remaining books into his arms.

'We have checkout limits, Mr Sugarman. Didn't Jill tell you?'

'I waived the limits, Ruth,' Jill Johnson said. 'It's a very important case.'

'A detective case, I suppose?'

'That's right,' Sugar said, and added two more to the pile that was propped against his chest and came nearly to his chin.

Ruth Mercer brought her glasses down from her hair and locked them into place against her nose and studied the titles of his books, then shook her head.

Jill came around from behind the desk and said, 'It's about what happened on the yacht. Andrew Markham, the transmigration man.'

'I see,' the librarian said. 'So on that basis you waived our ten-book limit?'

'I'll have them back by the end of the week.'

'Why don't you just back your car up to the front door, Mr Sugarman, bring your wheelbarrow in, and help yourself?'

'Oh, Ruth, really. Some of these books haven't been checked out in years.'

Sugarman settled the final one under his chin and turned and headed for the door. Ruth Mercer shadowed him across the library.

'All right,' she said. 'But never again. Ten is the limit. Is that clear?'

'Clear,' Sugar said.

She sighed and turned and marched back to her forlorn station in the rear of that big quiet room.

Sitting in his car in the Kmart parking lot, Sugar used his cell phone to call Jackson Means. He got lucky and found him home on Saturday afternoon, watching what sounded like a baseball game. Probably tilted back in his lounge chair with a beer and chips. Wife and three kids off somewhere.

Sugar got the preliminaries out of the way in five seconds, explained what he needed to know, and answered Jackson's question with, 'Because you're the only guy I know in telecommunications.'

'Christ, I'm a lineman, Sugar. I climb the poles. If you want to give that a bunch of syllables, okay. But basically I'm an electrician.'

'But you know somebody I can call.'

He thought about it while baseball fans cheered in the background. Not a home run, but more than a single.

'Claudia Shelley.' His voice was strained. 'She's up in Miami, used to be a district manager for BellSouth security operations. Now she's gone private. Try her.'

'Use your name?'

'I don't know,' Jackson said. Then quiet for a long moment. 'We had a thing, but it was a while ago. She might remember. I'd be interested to know if she does.'

From memory Jackson gave him the woman's home number and Sugar thanked him and hung up and called and a woman snapped it up on the second ring with a curt, 'What is it?'

Music in the background. Classical piano.

Sugarman watched a family he knew coming out

of the Kmart with arms full of shopping bags, two young boys. The father nodded at Sugar. Five or six years back the guy had spent six months in jail for blacking both his wife's eyes, knocking out two front teeth. Sugar had put him there. Things looked okay now, but you never knew.

'Claudia Shelley?'

'If this is a sales call, I don't take them at home.'

Tough voice. A woman doing work on the weekend, don't bother.

'My little girl's been kidnapped.' Then in a rush he explained the situation. Video camera, satellite phone. A jungle maybe a thousand miles away. He wanted to do a call trace. How hard was it?

Claudia paused, turned down the piano music, came back, and said, 'Do I know you?'

Sugarman gave her Jackson's name and she was silent.

'Look, this is urgent,' Sugar said. 'I've got to know if this can be done. Technically, I mean. First if it's possible, and if it is, who to call. I thought it'd be quicker to talk to somebody in the private sector than go through cop channels. I used to be in law enforcement and I know things can get bogged down. Even emergencies.'

'Your daughter is kidnapped and you haven't notified the police?'

'It's complicated,' he said.

'Complicated?'

Sugarman was getting impatient, the woman

wanting too much information, but he hit her with it anyway, to get her back on track, show her the seriousness.

'A branch of government might be involved in holding her.'

'Oh, come now. I very much doubt that, Mr Sugarman.'

'Listen, Ms Shelley, I just want some facts, if it can be done. Who to call.'

'This is not what I do, Mr Sugarman. We're a security firm. We wire computer networks, build firewalls, write antivirus code.'

'I guess I was misinformed.'

A man dressed as a clown was standing outside of the Kmart handing out red balloons. Jingling a pot for donations.

Sugarman heard Claudia Shelley sigh. He was half a second from hanging up on her when she said, 'Satellite phone transmissions are actually fairly easy to monitor, compared to wireless. Communications satellites track users' locations by tracing their SIM, their subscriber identity module, every time they turn on their phone.'

'So it can be done, it's easy.'

'Not so fast,' she said. 'No satellite phone company is going to open up its accounts for a private citizen. They'll listen to law enforcement, consider requests, but unless they already have a working relationship with the FBI, they'll probably require a subpoena. So you need to get somebody official involved. And

I can tell you first-hand, any federal help is going to be hard. Oversight on domestic telecom issues is with the FBI, and they have the equipment to triangulate cell phone towers and home in on a particular user.

'But if it's international then it becomes a CIA issue. Their intel people are set up to analyze, cross-reference, or listen to transmissions. They can access Echelon; it's a system nobody wants to talk about it, but it's there. A way of intercepting data or voice, tower to tower, microwave links, phone cables, Internet backbone networks. It's operated by the NSA. Spies, counterintelligence. Tracking drug guys and terrorists. Then they got black box data sifters they use to tap into e-mail, or video chats, like you're describing.'

'Listen, I'm sorry,' Sugarman said. 'I don't really need an education on this, just yes or no, can it be done?'

'Like I said, yeah, it can be done, but only if you can clear the legal hurdles. And if the agency has the budgetary flexibility to work on a domestic abduction case. First you got to make your case, get somebody jazzed enough to take the time. But yeah, they can intercept satellite phone transmissions, pinpoint locations. Put a cruise missile on the goddamn spot if they want to.'

Sugarman was quiet, holding back the sudden swell of anger.

'I'm sorry,' she said. 'That came out wrong.'

'It's okay.'

When she spoke again her voice had softened, but it was still a technical problem for her, not getting emotionally hooked.

'Do you play golf with a US Senator by any chance?'

'Not lately.'

'Then it could take weeks,' she said. 'That's been my experience, just to get in the front door.'

She paused, this time for several seconds. When she spoke again there was an undertone of sadness, but she was trying to hide it by shifting into professional mode.

'Your situation certainly warrants a strong, immediate response from the authorities, Mr Sugarman. The proper action on your part is to call the local FBI and let them respond. But if it were my child, to be absolutely frank, and knowing what I do about the legal difficulties, I'd pursue other avenues. Pay the ransom, hire a private investigator. I could give you the names of people in the field.'

'I am one,' Sugarman said. 'A private investigator.'

'You are?'

He said yes, yes, he was.

'Well, then there's your answer. Given our present geopolitical situation and the huge demands on tracking systems, call tracing on this level would require substantial influence. I doubt they'd pick it up as a priority, move it to the top of the stack.'

'They could do it, but they wouldn't, not for a little guy.'

'They couldn't refuse. You're a citizen; it's a serious crime. They'd put a man on it, maybe two. I'm sorry. That's just my opinion. You should go on, call the FBI field office, prove me wrong.'

One of the balloons had escaped the grasp of a young boy. It bobbled into the sky, then was scooped up by a current of air and sailed off to the west. The boy began to wail.

Sugarman thanked her for her time. She was quiet for a second, then in a different voice, her real one probably, she said, 'Please tell Jackson hello for me. And that I'm sorry. He'll understand.'

One more quick call to Frank Sheffield at home. He came on with a brisk, 'Okay, okay, I'm out the door.'

'Frank? Frank Sheffield?'

Sugar told him who it was, gave him the three-sentence version.

'That thing in Key Largo? The yacht with the con man psychic?'

'Right.'

'I thought everybody went overboard.'

'I've been talking to her, Frank. She's alive.'

Sheffield was quiet for so long, Sugarman was about to ask if he was still there when he said, 'Look, I'm on my way out of town, Sugar. Got two weeks in Alaska with my fiancée and her son, combination cruise and fishing trip. Plane's leaving tonight at eight. We got to run around, do a few things before we go.'

Sugar said okay, he understood.

'You actually talked to her?'

'Video cam. I talked to her, saw her, too.'

'Goddamn.' Frank thought about it a minute, figuring. 'She's going to call back when?'

'Six,' Sugar said. 'That's what we agreed on.'

'Give me your address. I remember the mile marker but not the street.'

Sugarman gave him the address, a couple of landmarks on the highway.

'What about your cruise?'

'I'll be at your place at six, plenty of time to get back to MIA before the plane. Hannah will understand.'

'Maybe you should pass this on to somebody else,' Sugarman said. 'You're in a hurry.'

'I got a kid in my group who's up on all the latest gizmos. I'll give him a call, see if he'll ride along. We'll take a look, see if there's something to do.'

'It's a satellite phone,' Sugar said. 'It could be difficult.'

'Be there at six.' And he hung up.

21

With Vic glaring from the front porch and Marty beside him with his arms crossed over his heavy chest, Anne and Thorn crossed the yard and headed out to the front gate. Thorn half-expected Vic to shoot him in the back or at least for one of them to come running and drag Anne Bonny back. But he was wrong.

The Hell's Conchs seemed to have taken the afternoon off, so Anne and Thorn pushed through the gate and walked briskly to his car and got in. Thorn started it and blew out a breath that he'd been holding for a while.

'Thank you,' he said as he pulled the Beetle onto the overseas highway. 'That was damn close.'

'You're welcome,' she said. 'Did he hurt you?'

'Maybe a nick,' Thorn said. 'And I might have a

little trouble peeing for a while. All the sphincters down there are locked shut.'

'Can we go to your place?'

He looked over.

'Don't worry, Thorn, I won't jump you. I'll sleep in the hammock tonight if you don't kick me out before then. I'm thinking of taking the cash and heading off. But I don't know. I guess I just need to take a deep breath, figure out what I'm doing.'

Her electric eyes were fully charged.

'Yeah,' he said. 'A deep breath sounds good.'

She looked out the windshield at nothing.

'Listen, Thorn. I need to get this in the open.'

'Okay.'

There was a spatter of his blood on the lap of her khaki shorts. She scratched at it with a nail.

'Do you know anything about my recent history?'

'What do you mean?'

She watched the shops of Islamorada crawl by. The island had recently seceded from Monroe County and was turning into a more upscale version of its former self. Same shops, better facades. Same motels, higher prices.

'After you and I split up,' she said, 'I was alone for a long time. I guess I was a little vulnerable, off-balance. Then this man came along.'

Thorn was silent. They were following a gold-and-green motor home from Canada that was towing a color-coordinated SUV. He watched the big vehicle carefully.

324

'And by the way,' she said, 'I'm sorry about how I acted last night. Walking out like that, no explanation.'

'I assumed it had to do with that story you told about your family. We weren't ready for that.'

He could feel her looking at him, but Thorn was concentrating on the motor home, driving carefully, keeping a safe cushion between him and the Canadian, not sure how good his reflexes were at the moment, the twin wounds in his gut throbbing again, a dull ache growing in his testicles.

'It was the story, yeah,' she said. 'But what do you mean, not ready?'

'Too much honesty, too soon.'

'Oh.' Anne went back to her window.

Thorn glanced over and saw a single glistening track on her cheek. He reached out for the hand balled against her tanned thigh and she relaxed the fist and let him hold it for a moment.

'That story I told you,' she said, with her eyes still on the bars and T-shirt shops, tackle stores. 'I lied.'

Thorn tugged his hand away to shift gears, then drove on in silence.

'Most of it was the truth,' she said, facing forward. 'Ninety percent. Just the ending was a lie. I was trying it out on you, I guess. I wanted to see if I could tell the whole story to someone, tell it how it truly happened. You seemed honest and straight. And I'd heard things about you, how you had plenty of your own secrets, and because of that I didn't think my pitiful story would bother you too much.

'But when I got to the end, I just couldn't do it. So, I lied. That's the reason I left that night, why I wouldn't talk to you again. I was ashamed, Thorn. I poisoned everything, between us, and inside of me. Poisoned it with a fucking lie. Made it worse than it already was.'

The motor home pulled off into a gas station and Thorn pushed the ancient VW up to the speed limit and just beyond. He didn't feel the need to speak. She was doing pretty well without him.

'You want to hear the true ending, Thorn? How it really was that night?'

'Okay.'

'I know it's too late,' she said, 'to fix things.'

'Fix what things?'

'I mean telling it straight this late in the game won't do anything. Not really. I don't believe that. Despite what I said to Vic, I think there's some things that won't mend once they're broken. The things that hold people together.'

'I hope you're wrong about that.'

She reset herself in that saggy bucket seat, turning to face him. Her sleeveless blouse was dark blue and printed with yellow *alamanda* blossoms. The top two buttons were undone and the gusts from her open window ballooned the shirt and one dark nipple was briefly exposed.

He directed his eyes back to the road.

'Do you remember that story, Thorn? Is it still clear in your head?'

'Oh, yeah, it's clear,' he said. 'Very clear.'

'All the pirate crap was true, the schooner in the yard, the way my mother was crazy and drove the rest of us crazy. My daddy, small-time drug runner. An ignorant country boy. Everything was accurate, except what happened out on the porch at the end.'

'The shootings.'

'That's right. The shootings.'

She wiped away the damp streak.

'It wasn't Vic who went out the door when the shooting started. It was me. Mother had already shot Sherman, the younger Woodson, and the older brother, Al, had put two bullets into her with his pistol and she was lying there bleeding, still alive, making awful noises. And Dad was there with his hands in the air, trying to bargain with the Woodson boy. His wife dying at his feet and he's telling this redneck that it's all going to work out okay, they'll bury young Sherman and then they'll bury my mother, and no one needed to know the difference. Get right back to business. Saying he was even willing to take a cut in pay to make things right. And then, I guess to seal the deal, he said he knew Al Woodson had his eye on me. Liked the way I was built. And then my daddy said Al had his blessing, anything he wanted to do, take me now, if it suited his fancy.'

'So you shot him. You shot your father.'

'He was a loser. And his stupid petty thievery is what killed my mother, and almost killed the whole lot of us. He was going to give me to that stupid boy like I was some truck stop whore.'

Thorn was silent. Anne looked down at the fists in her lap.

'I blew him through the front window, then shot Al Woodson before he could say a word.'

'And Vic?'

'Cowering inside the whole time. Hiding in our bedroom closet.'

'I see.'

'When I told you the story that night, I gave you the same version Vic and I worked out between us. Making him the hero. Turning him into the one that saved what was left of the family. We drove together all the way to Florida and that's what happened on the trip. I made up that story and I gave it to him. At first he was dazed and blubbering half the time. So I led him through it step-by-step, planted it in his head. He didn't accept it at first. He kept looking over at me and shaking his head, refusing, refusing, but mile after mile I went over it again, very patient, very slow, every second of what happened in my imaginary version, until by the time we drove into Key Largo, that's what he believed. He was a hero.'

'You also convinced him he was a killer.'

'That wasn't my purpose. I wanted to protect him, make him strong. I needed him when we got down here. We were two kids, runaway teenagers. I needed to count on him. I needed him strong.'

'Well, he's crazy now.'

'Yeah. He's out of control.'

'A little crazy goes a long way.'

They passed through Key Largo, then drove beyond the black area of Hibiscus Park, past the Publix, and on toward Pennekamp Park. Not talking for those three miles. The road less strangled with traffic. Most of the winter people already home. Just some weekenders heading home to Miami and Lauderdale.

'That's three shots,' Thorn said.

'What?'

'Your mother fired once and you fired twice. You said it was a shotgun.'

She looked at him for a couple of moments, mouth tight.

'What, you think I'm still lying?'

'Clarification,' he said. 'That's all.'

'Why would I lie? I'm telling you how it was.'

'I didn't say you were lying. I just asked a question.'

She sighed.

'Mossberg AOW, twelve-gauge. It's a three-shot shotgun.'

Thorn kept his eyes forward, but he was seeing that night from her eyes. A teenage girl, her mother dead at her feet, then killing her own father. Trying to imagine how that had forever reshaped the landscape of her heart. How she coped then, how she'd continued to cope over time. Getting a glimpse of the hard woman she'd turned herself into, but still vulnerable. Still parts of her easily wounded.

'You were going to tell me about your recent history. The man you met.'

She looked down the highway, then turned back to him. Her eyes seemed brighter. Relieved of some inner pressure. Finally shattered the flimsy history she'd invented as a child and had been carrying around ever since.

'It's all just a bunch of stories, isn't it?'

'What is?'

'The past,' she said. 'Just one lie overlaid on another. That's what we do; we fiddle with the facts, find a better way to tell it. Dress things up, add, subtract to suit our needs, make what we've done more tolerable. Any way you cut it, memories are just one story after another.'

'Stories maybe,' Thorn said. 'But somewhere inside, everybody knows what's true about their past. Even Vic.'

'You think so? I'm not so sure.'

'It's in there somewhere. It may be down deep, buried under a lot of muck. He's a coward and a fool and he knows it.'

'If he does, it's under a whole lot of muck,' she said. 'A ton of it.'

She drew a breath and let it go.

'I murdered two men,' she said. 'And I gave that

to Vic. I guess I never admitted that part of it. I was trying to make him strong, but without meaning to, I was also handing off the guilt. Turning him into the fucked-up individual he's become.'

'You did it to survive. You were a kid in a terrible situation.'

'Doesn't let me off the hook.'

'At least it helps explain how he is now. The thing with the knife. Vic's got a lot of proving to do. And you seem to be his number-one audience. Though I'm not sure exactly what I've done to piss him off so bad.'

'You're with me, for one thing.'

'The protective older brother. Comes and has a talk with all her boyfriends, lets us know we're swimming in dangerous waters.'

'That's part of it,' she said.

'And what else?'

'He wants what you've got.'

'My land, you mean. Or my nuts?'

'He wants what you have, Thorn. Something he doesn't have and you do. It enrages him that you're like you are. Not impressed, don't give a shit about his money, his possessions. He doesn't run across that very often and it infuriates him when he does. You're not even particularly afraid of him.'

'I wouldn't go that far.'

'You're in his sights now, Thorn. The crosshairs are on your forehead.'

'I realize that.'

'You don't seem too worried.'

'Oh, I'm worried,' he said. 'But at the moment I'm a little more worried about what's happened to a nine-year-old girl.'

'I know Vic took her,' Anne said. 'He admitted as much. But I have no idea what he did with her.'

'Square one,' Thorn said.

He drove in silence for a while. The declining sun put the palms along the highway in sharp relief. Birds on the telephone wires were dark silhouettes surveying the endless flow of traffic. The hot wind coming into the car brought that hazy, festering smell of a full-moon low tide, the sulfurous stink of exposed marl and rot of barnacles and shellfish and decomposing seaweed. A lush and sticky breeze that marked the last quick days of spring giving way to the heavy suffocation of summer.

'Well, as long as I'm confessing,' she said.

He looked over and met her eyes.

'You sure you want to hear this, Thorn? It's another tragic story.'

'Ready if you are.'

She began to describe that day in February at the Lorelei when Thorn and Alex and Lawton and Sugarman and his girls had come to lunch. Right after Anne had served them, she'd met a striking young man out on the sunny deck.

Thorn listened to her as he was slowing for the shrub-veiled entrance to his driveway.

'Aw, shit. Now what?'

A Monroe County Sheriff's car was blocking the mouth of the gravel drive, its blue lights spinning. A couple of deputies were lounging around, which meant, of course, that there were more inside, doing the real work.

Thorn swerved into the cut-through, gunned across the highway, and stamped the brake and the ancient VW bumped onto the shoulder and slewed through the gravel to within a foot of the left front fender of the cop car.

A few minutes later, when the deputies finally let them pass and they pulled up next to his stilt house and parked, he saw Sheriff Taft down by the dock with the others.

Taft ambled up the sloping yard to meet them. There were half a dozen cars scattered across Thorn's yard – a white van, an ambulance, two cop cars, and a navy blue Crown Victoria.

'I been trying to reach you, Thorn.'

'I must've left my beeper at home.'

Uniformed cops and two slender men in white shirts and dark slacks were milling around down at the water's edge. He supposed the white-shirts might be Mormon missionaries, but more than likely they were FBI. Thorn counted seven people in all before Taft stepped into his line of sight.

He looked at the bloody mess on the front of Thorn's shorts.

'What the hell?'

'Hard day at the office.'

Anne stepped up beside him, and Taft paused a moment to take her in. She was a few inches taller than the man, and he tilted his wary eyes up to hers.

'Anne Bonny Joy,' she said. Then a second later, 'Vic Joy's sister.'

Sheriff Taft looked back at Thorn, studying him for an awkward moment.

'Man, oh, man, what kind of shit have you gotten into, Thorn?'

'Goddamn it, Taft, what's going on?'

The sheriff glanced again at Anne, then unbuttoned his shirt pocket and drew out a photograph and handed it to Thorn. A black-and-white police mug shot, taken head-on. It took him a half-second to place the guy. The red-haired mongrel outside Vic Joy's house. Same hooked nose, same sneer.

'We got a match on the fingerprints on that knife in your door. The guy's a local. Marshall Anthony Marshall.'

Thorn handed the photo to Anne and she took a minute with it.

Thorn wasn't sure which way this was spinning. Those men down by the water weren't here because of a mug shot. The ambulance, the white van, the dark Crown Vic. Those were out-of-towners. Probably Jimmy Lee Webster and his gang throwing their Washington weight around. The idea of handing over Marshall Marshall to the authorities didn't faze Thorn, but the consequences did. Getting

Vic entangled with Sheriff Taft, forcing him and Marty Messina to waste time on the legal horseshit that would arise, did nothing to get Janey free any sooner. Not that he could see.

'Don't know him,' Thorn said. 'Looks like a nice young fellow, though.'

'He's not,' Taft said. 'He's got more priors than the pope has beads.'

'I'll be darned. Looks can be deceiving.'

Taft burned him with a look.

'You want to get this thing solved, Thorn, or are you going to keep playing this one-on-one bullshit?'

'Don't know him, Sheriff. Wish I could help.'

Anne shook her head. Didn't know him, either.

'Sorry,' she said.

'Yeah, right.' Taft snapped the photo out of Anne's hand and slid it back in his pocket and buttoned the flap. 'Thanks so much for your assistance. Now there's this other little thing.'

He half-turned so Thorn could view a slice of the activity at the shore.

'I came over here a couple of hours ago to run the photo by you. I knocked, I waited, but you weren't around. I was starting to leave; that's when I saw something in the trees down by the water.'

'In the trees?'

'It wasn't birds,' Taft said. 'Nothing natural.'

Thorn tried to step past him, but Taft put a rough hand on his chest and held him in place.

'Since I couldn't locate you,' the sheriff said, 'I

took the liberty of tracking down your friend at Miami PD. The ID tech lady.'

Thorn drew his eyes from the bustle by the water and looked at Taft.

'Yeah, and what does Alex have to do with this?'

'I thought maybe she could help me track you down.'

'Well, I'm here.'

'Yeah, you are, but she's still coming down from Miami. On her way right now so she can give us a hand with things. Since she's a fellow officer, I thought I might actually get some honest answers from her about what the hell kind of game we're playing here.'

'Great,' Thorn said. 'Perfect.'

'What time was it when you left your house today, Thorn?'

'I don't know. Nine, nine-thirty.'

'And you noticed nothing unusual on the premises when you were leaving?'

'What is it, Taft? Why don't you just tell me?'

'You noticed nothing unusual on the premises this morning?'

Thorn sighed.

'That's right, nothing unusual. Would I have seen this thing? Maybe I walked out and it was there and I didn't notice.'

'Oh, you would've noticed this, Thorn. No two ways about it.'

The sheriff brushed a hand across the front of his

shirt, then tugged on both cuffs. Getting prissy around an attractive woman.

'Miss Joy,' Taft said. 'You might want to stay up here, spare yourself the ugliness.'

She glanced at Thorn.

'Is she free to go?' Thorn said to Taft.

He stepped back and grazed her body with an unnecessarily long look.

'Better if she stayed. Unless she's got some really powerful reason to flee a homicide scene.'

22

Four o'clock, two hours till his next talk with Janey. Sugarman was trying damn hard to keep from imagining the details of her situation, the fright and confusion she must be feeling, the small, hot cell where she was imprisoned. And his own dread was getting in the way as well, clouding his ordered thoughts. Putting a quiver in his handwriting as he scribbled down a list of everything he could remember from their earlier conversation. Smell of the ocean, a blue iridescent butterfly with wings edged in black, those animal sounds coming from nearby, heat and rain. And pulling that together with what he'd picked up from Kirk Graham. A thousand nautical miles. Maybe even eleven or twelve hundred.

He used a razor blade to cut a page from the

musty *Encyclopedia Americana*, a map of North America, then he dug an old metal compass out of a tool drawer in the garage. He calibrated the compass against the map's legend, setting it for eleven hundred miles, then drew a circle with the center point in Islamorada.

The pencil tip traced a path that went as far north as Philadelphia, as deep into the west as Kansas, Texas, and central Mexico, then curved south and east to include all of Central America and turned due east to skim at least a hundred miles inland across northern Venezuela and Colombia before the dark line arced out into the Atlantic and encircled Puerto Rico and the string of small islands of the West Indies, from Martinique and Saint Lucia north to Nevis, Saint Kitts, and Barbuda.

He set the compass down and looked at his circle. Next he might have spent some time doing the math and figuring the square miles of his search area, but he could see no point in that. A number that large would only increase his sense of utter futility.

Janey was somewhere eleven or twelve hundred miles away. Seven or eight hours by air, in a hot, rainy, animal-rich region somewhere near the sea. It sounded like a rain forest, a tropical jungle. Which meant he could rule out Philadelphia and Cleveland and Memphis, in fact, all of the noncoastal US and even most of the coast, which was, for the most part, too densely developed or too temperate to match her description. There might be a few areas along the Louisiana or Mississippi shore that would qualify, swampland where animal life was abundant and the smell of the sea was nearby. Surely he could eliminate a good deal of arid and desert Mexico. Which left him hundreds of thousands of square miles of territory, both the coastal regions rimming the Caribbean Sea and the islands scattered throughout it. A search area so vast, it took his mind out of focus. Sent his spirits spiraling downward.

As he was mulling his next step, studying the map and his enormous circle, the terrible notion came to him that the pilot of that plane might not have flown in a straight line at all – for any of several perfectly ordinary reasons. Dodging thunderstorms perhaps could send him hundreds of miles off course. And then there was Cuba lurking out in the middle of the Caribbean Sea, a huge no-fly zone that would make any flight path heading south or southwest from Islamorada have to add a lot of extra miles.

He needed Kirk Graham for a better idea about how many. But his own quick calculations, using the compass to step off fifty-mile chunks of possible flight paths, showed him that hundreds of miles and as much as an hour or two could be lost by a wide diversion around the island of Cuba.

And then, of course, there was the disturbing possibility that the pilot of the plane had been sufficiently devious or paranoid to intentionally add flight time to the trip to throw off any such computations as Sugarman was now attempting. But because he could not confirm that, his only choice was to go with the zone he'd outlined and hope there was time for him to shrink that enormous circle down to a single dot before Janey's situation got any worse.

The smell of the sea was something. And the blue butterfly. And there'd been a bird she'd mentioned. But now he couldn't recall.

He set the map aside, looked across at the dark screen of the laptop, then began to comb through the volumes he'd borrowed from the Key Largo Library.

'It's called a gibbet cage,' Anne said. 'It's a pirate thing.'

Taft swung around and stared at her.

'A pirate thing?'

'Eighteenth-century pirates, yes. You don't see a lot of them anymore.'

'No shit,' Taft said.

Thorn was sitting nearby on the yellow bench watching the forensics people taking photographs, measuring the site, searching the grass and the muddy shoreline for footprints or any other traces left behind.

Hanging from a heavy limb of the oldest gumbo-limbo in his yard were three men. They hung side by side, a foot or so between each body. A ton of stress on that limb, but it was holding up fine. Each of their naked corpses was locked inside a tightly fitted frame of what looked like reddish iron. A one-inch flat band of metal circling the neck, another around the chest, and two more around the torso. Their legs were banded at knees and ankles like braces on a child with polio. Iron bands ran along the shinbone and joined the ankle and knee braces together and linked them to the rest of the cage. The men's heads were gripped by four iron strips that looked like the inner frame of an ancient diving helmet. Two heavy chains connected the helmet with the hip bands. Apparently it was a device meant to hold a man stable, not necessarily to torture or kill.

Jimmy Lee Webster and Zashie and a man Thorn didn't know were hanging there. Throats slit, then hoisted up to the tree branch. From the swaths of blood on their white chests it appeared they'd been caged and hung from the branch with their hearts still beating.

The two white-shirted investigators nudged close to Anne and were listening to her recitation. She seemed eerily casual about the scene, while Thorn noticed that even the cops were taking care not to lift their eyes to the three bodies in the tree.

'After pirates were executed, they were hung inside these devices so their relatives couldn't cut them down and bury them. Public humiliation. Before the condemned man was killed, he was measured for his suit of iron, and pirates were supposedly more terrified of this than of their coming execution.'

'How do you know all this?' one of the white-shirts asked.

Anne looked up at the bodies swaying in a hard breeze.

'Unfortunately, it's my area of expertise.' Her voice was vague and far removed from the moment, and Thorn realized then that it wasn't casualness he detected but a numbed state somewhere between bewilderment and panic.

Anne said, 'Originally the contraptions were forged by blacksmiths. Each one custom-fitted so the bones of the dead man would stay in place for a long time after the flesh rotted away.'

She glanced again at the pennant fixed to the old flagpole at the end of Thorn's dock. He'd noticed it himself a few minutes earlier. No flag had flown on that pole for years. This particular pennant was intended to be secured to the mast of a ship. It was triangular and across its black field printed in gold script were the words the *Black Swan*.

Neither Taft nor the other men had mentioned the pennant. No reason they should notice it, really. The three men in the tree were occupying their full attention. While the investigators worked, Thorn sat on Lawton's yellow bench and looked out at the water and tried to draw a few even breaths. His own personal iron band was tightening invisibly around his chest.

As a pontoon boat motored by out on the sound, a sunset party with drinks and finger food, Thorn heard the noises he'd been anticipating: the crunch of gravel in his drive, the throaty purr of Alexandra's Accord.

Anne took that moment to draw away from the investigators and walk over to Thorn's bench and sit down close beside him.

'They said I could take a break.'

Thorn inched away slightly. Like that would do any good.

'You doing okay?'

'No,' she said. 'Not at all.'

'That pennant? You recognize it?'

She swallowed hard and watched Alex and Lawton climb out of the Honda.

'It's part of that long story I was getting to. That flag is from the boat he was on the day I met him. The guy at the Lorelei.'

'Daniel Salbone.'

She stiffened, then turned her head slightly so she was using the extreme edge of her peripheral vision to see him. As if to look at him head-on might push her beyond her limits.

'How did you know that? Vic told you, didn't he?'

'No, not Vic. One of those guys in the tree told me.'

'What guy?'

'The little one on the end. He was chasing Salbone.'

'He was?'

'Former Secretary of the Navy, Jimmy Lee Webster.'

'When was this, that he told you about Daniel?'

'Last night.'

'So what does that mean? You're working with them? Trying to capture Daniel?'

'I couldn't care less about Salbone. I'm trying to recover Janey. That's all.'

She swiveled slightly and peered at him for several seconds, her mind working at the tangle until after a moment she seemed to grow weary of the effort and turned her gaze back toward the dock and that flapping pennant.

'I knew it,' she said. 'Down in my gut I knew he was still alive. Now he's come back to get me. He told me he would, and now he's here. Daniel's here.'

'Maybe,' Thorn said. 'It's damn strange, though, murdering three men, then leaving behind your calling card.'

'He's not a violent man. Something bad must have happened.'

Thorn watched Alexandra and Lawton having a conversation beside the car, Alex probably warning him to behave himself.

Thorn said, 'With people like Jimmy Lee Webster chasing him, trying to kill him or put him away, it might've brought out a different side of the man. A side you don't know.'

'Why here?' she said. 'Why didn't he try to find me at Vic's?'

'I've been wondering the same thing.'

Thorn watched Alex stride across the yard. She was wearing faded blue jeans and a white collarless blouse, weekend clothes. She had on a blue Miami PD baseball cap and her long jet-black hair was tucked up inside it.

Because of her dark sunglasses, Thorn couldn't tell if she looked his way or not. She kept her head erect, appeared full of no-nonsense gravity. Strictly business. She marched over to the base of the gumbo-limbo where Taft stood talking to two of the white-shirts. She glanced up at the bodies in the tree, then shook hands with the investigators. Lawton peeled off from behind her and headed over to the bench. The puppy galloped along at his heels.

'That goddamn bus come yet?'

'No, Lawton. Not yet.'

The puppy lifted his leg on the side of the bench and made it his own.

'Hell, I've decided I don't like Miami anymore. Too many goddamn Cubans jibber-jabbering everywhere you go. I like it better down here, more like America. Why'd we have to leave anyway? You kick us out because of something I said? Did I insult somebody?'

'No, Lawton, you were fine.'

'Well, why then? Why'd we get our walking papers?'

'You don't have to leave,' Thorn said. 'You and Alex are welcome to stay as long as you want.'

346

'Oh, yeah? Well, that's not what Miss Bossy High-and-Mighty says. She says we're not living in the Keys anymore.'

'She said that?'

Anne stood up.

'Hey, you're not going to introduce me?' Lawton said. 'Juicy young thing and I don't even get to know her name. I'm available, you know. A highly eligible bachelor. Got a good monthly stipend, plus Social Security. Got my own teeth, and my prostate is tough as a little acorn.'

'You'll have to pardon Lawton,' Thorn said.

But Anne wasn't listening. She was staring at the gibbet cages.

Lawton picked up his puppy and held him in his arms. The dog seemed to be doubling in size every twenty-four hours. A gloss to his coat, his ribs no longer showing.

'"Death isn't the greatest loss in life,"' Lawton said to Anne. '"The greatest loss is what dies inside us while we live."' Lawton set the puppy down. 'That's my Zen wisdom for the day. Ignore it at your peril.'

Anne glanced around and seemed to notice Lawton for the first time. He gave her an old goat's lusty smile.

'So what's with the tree ornaments?' Lawton said. 'Is it goddamn Christmas again already?'

Alexandra shook hands with Sheriff Taft and turned and headed over to the bench.

Thorn stood up. 'Let's go, Dad. They don't need us here anymore.'

Alexandra tucked a business card into the pocket of her jeans and motioned for Lawton. The puppy pawed at Alex's leg trying to get the top dog's attention, but she was ignoring it.

'Thorn said we could stay. No hard feelings. Stay as long as we like.'

Alex kept her gaze fixed on the old man.

'We've got to get back. Thorn's got some problems he needs to attend to. He doesn't need us around.'

'That's not true,' Thorn said. 'I do need you. I need you very much.'

She half-turned, reached up, and removed her glasses. Staring at him with eyes that had changed since morning. Grown neutral and remote. Looking at him with almost scientific distance, as though she were examining a victim lying before her, choosing the best camera angle. No hint of anger, no sign of love.

'I'd say three dead men hanging from the branches of your tree constitutes a fairly serious problem, Thorn. I don't believe you'll be having much time for distractions anytime soon.' Although Anne stood less than a foot away from Thorn, Alex didn't look at her. She put the sunglasses back in place and waved at Lawton again. 'Now come on, Dad. We've got to go.'

'Please don't leave, Alex. I need to explain a few things.'

'No need,' she said, still looking at Lawton. 'I think I've got the picture. Dad, come on.' And this time she used her police voice, do-it-by-God-or-else, and Lawton shrugged at Thorn and followed her back to the car.

23

It was five after five, an hour before their next scheduled conversation, when Janey called out, 'Daddy, Daddy,' while across the room Sugarman was paging methodically through the slick pages of a guide to tropical wildlife.

He swung off the bed and rushed to the computer.

'I'm here,' he said. 'What happened? Something wrong?'

'I know it's early, but I couldn't wait,' she said. 'So much is going on.'

'What? Where?'

'In the jungle,' she said. 'So many birds and things. I had to tell you before I forget them all.'

Sugarman leaned back in his chair. He smoothed a hand across his forehead, the muscles clamped tight.

'Did the police trace the phone line? Do you know where I am yet?'

'No, sweetie. That isn't going to work. We're going to have to do it ourselves, the old-fashioned way.'

'Oh.' She looked away and wiped sweat from her face. 'Well, I saw a flock of toucans, Daddy. Four or five.'

'Toucans,' he said. 'You're sure?'

She was excited again. A kid who'd seen some exotic birds.

'With big bills, lots of colors. Yellow faces and throats, black bodies. Their bills are like candy corn. Red, yellow, green, a lime color. They flap their wings a few times, then glide. I saw them twice while I was looking out. And a giant green iguana and a great blue heron and a cormorant.'

'Go slow, Janey. I'm writing this down.'

'The battery is lower. It's below half. And I ate a whole sandwich but only drank one Coke. I'm not that thirsty.'

'Good, good.'

'What about that butterfly, Daddy? Did you look it up?'

'I looked it up, yes. I'm afraid it's no help.'

Trying to find a neutral tone between the gloomy truth and false hope.

'Why not?'

'It's a blue morpho butterfly,' Sugar said. 'It's called 'the emperor.' It's all over Central and South America, out in the Caribbean, Trinidad, Tobago. All over the place. So it doesn't tell us anything real specific.'

'Oh,' she said, her voice falling away into a sigh.

'It's okay, honey. Don't worry. We're going to do this. I promise. Now there was a bird you mentioned before. What was it? One you saw right at first.'

'No, wait,' she said. 'I forgot this other thing. An animal. It was very cool. Like a squirrel with long legs and fat and no tail.'

'What color?' Sugarman said. 'Hold on, I have a book.'

He swung from the chair, hurried to the bed, and pawed through the volumes littering the guest bed until he found the *Rain Forest Mammal Guide*.

'Reddish brown,' Janey said. 'It was walking down the path that runs along the edge of the jungle. I thought it was a rat at first, a giant rat, but then I got the binoculars and it looks more like a squirrel with long legs. And fat.'

Sugarman paged through the mammal book until he found the plates. Drawings of squirrels, pages and pages of rats, porcupines and armadillos, rabbits. And then a page of creatures he didn't recognize.

'No tail?' he said.

'Yeah, and pointy face like a squirrel.'

He held the page up to the Web camera. Pointed at one.

'Like this?'

She paused, peering into the screen.

'The one above it.'

'This one? You're sure?'

'I think so. Is it reddish?'

'Yes, reddish, no tail, like a giant squirrel. Only with long legs.'

Sugarman checked the numbered print against the descriptors on the opposite page.

'An agouti,' he said.

'Agouti?'

'Yeah, I guess that's how you say it. Agouti. Hold on, I'm checking its geographical range.'

Sugarman used the index, tracked down the page. Read the paragraph.

'What's it say, Daddy?'

He read aloud.

'"Chiapas and Campeche, Mexico, southeast through all countries of Central America. Northwest Venezuela, north and west Colombia, and Ecuador west of the Andes."'

'Wow,' she said. 'I'm really far away, huh?'

'Yeah,' said Sugar. 'Really far.'

'Does that help, Daddy?'

'It helps, yeah. You're not on an island. I think we can rule that out. Mexico, Central America, northern South America. You're on the coastal mainland somewhere. That's an important step.'

'But the toucans, they were so neat. Like a zoo.' She paused for a second. 'Daddy? What're you doing?'

'Looking for the toucan, sweetie.'

She was humming a song. Something he vaguely

recognized from the radio, the pop stations she and Jackie preferred. His nine-year-old daughter was singing in a jungle somewhere a thousand miles away while Sugar paged through the heavy bird guide, past the owls and cuckoos and nightjars, the humming-birds, trogons, and jacamars, birds he'd never seen, never imagined. Finding at last the toucans, which shared the page with the woodpeckers, motmots, and kingfishers.

'What did its bill look like, Janey?'

'I told you, Daddy. Like candy corn. Yellow with a pink or orange tip. Blue on the bottom beak.'

'Keel-billed,' he said. He held it up for her to see.

She squinted for a moment, then said yes, that was it.

'Listen, Janey, can you see the horizon out your window?'

'The horizon?'

'Where the sky meets the land, can you see it, or are there trees in the way?'

She got up and walked around the room. The Web cam caught her at one window, peering between the slats. In half a minute she was back.

'Yeah, out two windows I can see it.'

'Okay, good.'

'Why, Daddy?'

'It's something we can do tonight. Something I remembered from when I was in Scouts. Listen. Do you remember which direction the sun came up this morning?'

'In the east, Daddy, where it always comes up. I'm not a little kid.'

She stepped back from the camera and held up an arm and pointed toward one wall and recited, 'North, south, east, west.'

'Good, Janey. So can you see the eastern horizon?'

She looked behind her, then back at the Web camera.

She said yeah, that was where the marina was.

'So the sun came up over the water this morning?'

'Uh-huh.'

'Great,' Sugarman said. 'Then tonight, just as it gets dark, we'll try something that should help tell us where you are. It's still a full moon. It should work.'

'Really?'

'Really.'

'Oh, I remember,' she said. 'It was a kingfisher, Daddy. That other bird. The one I saw before. It looked like a kingfisher, but it was different. Smaller.'

'Can you describe it?'

She was silent for a moment, looking to her left, grimacing.

'What's wrong, Janey?'

He saw her rise from her seat, then bend down to the screen, mouth twisted out of shape, gritting her teeth.

'I need to go to the potty.'

'All right.'

'My stomach's not feeling so good all of a sudden.'

'Oh, sweetheart. I'm sorry.'

'I maybe ate my sandwich too fast. I was so hungry I couldn't help it, so I kind of wolfed it. Or it was the water. I don't know. But I gotta go, Daddy. I'll sign off and call you back in a few minutes. Okay?'

'Okay, sweetie. Go on. Sign off. I'll be here waiting.'

And she disappeared.

Sugarman sat still for a moment staring at the screen, blinking away the fog in his eyes.

It only took him a minute to find the correct page for the detailed description and a moment more to discover that the keel-billed toucan, despite its exotic coloration, its enormous quirky bill, was a bird quite at home in a lot of places in the Caribbean lowlands from tropical Mexico all the way to South America, the same territory as the agouti. Telling him nothing he didn't already know.

His circle had shrunk to just a quarter of its previous size, but it was still one hell of a giant slice of pie.

The interrogation took place in Thorn's living room. A solid breeze dancing in the old lace curtains. One of the white-shirts handled the questioning while his two partners talked quietly a few feet away on the upstairs porch.

Thorn planted himself in the upholstered chair,

an overstuffed softie that angled beside the window with a western view. He glanced out, watching the ID techs finish their work and some other men from the ME's office balanced atop two tall stepladders taking down the bodies from the tree.

Anne accounted for Thorn's whereabouts from about ten that morning until that very moment. He'd been at Vic Joy's estate in Islamorada all morning and through the afternoon.

'Those bodies weren't here when I left,' Thorn said. 'So they were strung up between ten and whenever the sheriff arrived.'

'We'll handle the math, thanks,' the white-shirt said.

The man wore black-rimmed glasses that looked like they'd been hastily plucked off the rack at a drugstore checkout counter. He was Thorn's height and roughly his build. Lean but wide-shouldered. Black trousers and black shoes. Maybe not a Mormon missionary, but a zealot nonetheless. Probably with his own share of rehearsed speeches at the ready.

He informed them that his name was Ralph Fox. Special Agent Fox, head of a joint task force made up of agents from both the CIA and the FBI and a couple of other federal agencies. He paused to see if Thorn registered the magnitude of his position.

Thorn considered saying, 'Wow,' but restrained himself.

'And you say you met with Mr Webster and Mr Rasmussen last night?'.

'I was shanghaied into a meeting,' Thorn said. 'And Zashie is the name the big guy used.'

'What was the nature of that meeting?'

'I was recruited to help with their investigation.'

'Recruited?' Taft said, and chuckled. 'You, working with these guys? Come on, Thorn. Give us something credible here.'

Agent Fox stared across at Taft for a long moment, a little jerk on the chain of command. The sheriff scowled but shut his mouth and took a seat on one of the stools a few feet farther from the action.

'And what were you being recruited to do?'

'If you're this big task force czar, how come you don't already know?'

'What were you recruited to do, Mr Thorn?'

Fox tugged on an earlobe, looking off at the far wall.

'I'm not at liberty to say.'

Taft shook his head and glared at Thorn.

Unperturbed, Agent Fox did a slow tour of Thorn's living room, giving the place a cold analysis. Though Fox was probably in his late forties, his face was nearly unlined, as though he'd held his expressions in check since childhood, no grins or grimaces allowed, an eternal poker face.

Anne Bonny's eyes kept drifting to the far window, as if at any moment her pirate hero would appear and whisk her away from all this turmoil.

'Who's the other guy in the tree?' Thorn said. 'He

the one telling lies to Sugarman last night? Or was that you?'

'How do you make your living, Mr Thorn?' Fox was examining the bookshelves, Thorn's paltry library, mainly hardback novels he'd picked up for pennies at the flea market. Adventure yarns, his share of sea stories, a couple of literary novels he'd been trying to wade through for years.

'I tie fishing flies,' he said. 'Bonefish lures. You know that fish?'

'And you can earn a living doing that?'

'It keeps gas in the Rolls.'

'Thorn, don't be a prick,' Taft said. 'This isn't a game show.'

'Hey, if the suggestion here is that I've been supplementing my income with a little maritime piracy, I'd like to dispel that idea right now. I tie lures. It doesn't bring in much, but I don't need much.'

'Nobody's said anything about maritime piracy, Mr Thorn.'

With his back to the others, Agent Fox took a book from the shelf, riffled its pages, then put it back. He walked over to Thorn's chair and reached into his shirt pocket and handed Thorn the mug shot of Marshall Marshall. Thorn took it and looked it over. The mongrel hadn't gotten any prettier.

'The sheriff says you failed to identify this man earlier. Is that correct?'

Thorn said nothing.

'You see, Mr Thorn, your defiant attitude isn't helping your situation. We know Mr Marshall sometimes works as front gate security at Vic Joy's estate. We know you had an encounter with the man this morning because it was observed by our surveillance team. So you see, Thorn, we know you've already provided false testimony to us once. What I don't understand is why you would lie if you have nothing to hide.'

'He's a jerk,' Taft said. 'That's why. It's his frigging nature.'

'Sheriff,' Agent Fox said.

'Okay, yeah,' Thorn said. 'So I had a brief encounter with Marshall. Fine, you nailed me, congratulations on the sharp police work.'

'What other facts have you misrepresented to us?'

'Ask me some more questions, I'll see what I can do.'

'Why would a federal investigator recruit such a man as you, Thorn? Can you help us with that? What do you bring to the table?'

'You'd have to ask Webster.'

'Jesus Christ, Thorn. Give it up, man.' Taft stood up and stalked to the door. 'He's not going to tell you shit. You're wasting your time, Fox.'

Taft let the screen door slam behind him.

Special Agent Fox took off his glasses and reached into his back pocket for a handkerchief. While he rubbed at the lenses, he turned his pale eyes on Thorn.

'I understand you don't trust me, Thorn. You don't believe I have your best interests at heart, so you're going to be as perverse as possible.'

'That about covers it,' Thorn said.

Fox put his glasses back on and tucked the handkerchief away. He came close to Thorn's chair and squatted down in an Indian crouch, bringing his face to within inches of Thorn's.

'I assume this mistrust springs from negative experiences with law enforcement in the past.'

'Nicely put,' Thorn said.

Agent Fox reached out and laid a hand on the back of Thorn's bare arm. It was a weird gesture – neither friendly nor overtly intimidating. But not an innocent touch, either. His hand lay heavy against Thorn's flesh, warm and somehow exploratory, as if he were a human polygraph and could read Thorn's errant pulse.

'Would you mind, Miss Joy?'

'What?'

She'd been staring out at the dock, paying no attention.

'Could you give us a moment of privacy?'

Fox smiled over his shoulder at her, and Anne looked at Thorn.

'It's okay,' Thorn said. 'If he tries anything funny, I'll shriek.'

Anne went outside and the other men gave her room at the rail. Everyone watching silently as the last of the bodies was cut down from the limb.

'I'm going to take you at your word, Mr Thorn.' The agent's hand still lay on his forearm.

Thorn could have moved his arm aside, but this felt like some kind of alpha dog contest, a tactile staring match, and though it struck Thorn as a silly game, he couldn't seem to back down, either.

'I'm going to assume that James Lee Webster did, in fact, enlist you into some aspect of his operation. You mentioned maritime piracy, so I presume that Webster also informed you to some degree of the nature of his enterprise.'

'He put on a slide show,' Thorn said. 'The Wide, Wide World of Pirates.'

'And for some reason you agreed to cooperate with him.'

'He was more persuasive than you are. He shared a little.'

Fox nodded.

'A few minutes ago you asked me a question. You wondered who the other man was hanging beside Webster and Rasmussen.'

With Fox cozied up so close beside him, touching his flesh in that intimate way, Thorn had the feeling that this was something of a religious ceremony for the agent. A baptism into some secret order.

'To lose Secretary Webster is distressing enough,' Fox said, 'but losing that other gentleman, Mr Thorn, I don't mind telling you, it's a colossal setback. For us personally and for the welfare of our country.'

'Let me guess,' Thorn said. 'This was the guy who'd penetrated one of the pirate gangs.'

Agent Fox blinked, then notched up an eyebrow.

'Obviously Secretary Webster had a high level of confidence in you.'

'I think he was just desperate.'

'It's a breach of FBI policy to involve civilians in bureau investigations.'

'I'm not crazy about the idea myself,' Thorn said.

'But in this case,' Fox said, peering into Thorn's eyes, 'we're at a critical juncture and we need all the assets we can find.'

'I already know more about this bullshit than I want to,' Thorn said. 'Why don't you keep it to yourself, Fox?'

The agent appraised him for a long moment, then shook his head.

'And you're certainly not my idea of a helpful assistant, either. But at the moment you're all I have.'

Fox glanced toward the window, then turned back to Thorn.

'Things have ratcheted up in the last week, a real spike of activity. And now we're blind. We've lost our eyes and ears. Sammy Ching was the third man in the tree. As you suggest, Ching had penetrated a very active, very well-disciplined gang of maritime thieves based in Singapore. While he had not yet gained access to the highest levels of the organization, he was moving that way quickly. Now this, finding him so far from his base of operations, executed and hung up for display. These are the kind of people we're dealing with, Mr Thorn. This is why extraordinary measures are called for.'

Agent Fox gave Thorn's arm a solid thump and rose from his squat.

Baptism complete. Now he was one of them, deputized, Citizen Thorn. And it was his turn to come clean. A cute technique, all so earnest and heartfelt, how could Thorn not reciprocate?

In fact, Daniel Salbone's name was itching on Thorn's tongue. It would damn well be comforting to have a contingent of federal agents hiding in the bushes when the jealous Mr Salbone appeared to reclaim his lover.

But Thorn couldn't shake the feeling that getting any more entangled with these people would mean more delay in Janey's release.

'So I'm sure you can appreciate, Mr Thorn, how devastating it is for us to lose Sammy Ching. And how totally incomprehensible.'

'I can see that, yes.'

'Do you have any idea why his killer might have chosen this location to hang these men?'

'Not a clue.'

'All right,' Agent Fox said, letting go of a breath, ready to close the deal. 'Why don't you tell me something I don't know?'

'There's a little girl missing.'

'We're aware of that, but at the moment that's beyond our bailiwick.'

'Beyond your what?'

'My mission is very focused and precise, Mr Thorn. We are attempting to disrupt the final coalescing of several large criminal enterprises.'

'The confederacy of pirates,' Thorn said.

He felt Agent Fox staring at him, but Thorn's gaze was fixed on that final body being handed down to the men on the ground. Jimmy Lee Webster, his days of strutting finished.

Thorn looked down at his bloody shorts. Feeling the lingering burn of Vic's blade in his crotch and the twin aches of the stab wounds in his gut.

He looked up and met the agent's stare.

'Look, Fox. Webster claimed his people, which I assume would also be *your* people, had Janey Sugarman under their safe control. Was he lying?'

Fox meandered through the room, taking a moment to compose his answer.

'We're aware of the disappearance of Dr Markham's yacht, as well as the loss of life of his passengers. However, we can't know for certain that a kidnapping has actually occurred. At the moment the operating theory is that the child you're referring to was lost at sea and her body has not yet been recovered.'

'There was a goddamn ransom note. You have the mug shot of the guy who knifed it to my door.'

'Marshall is no more than an opportunist, Mr Thorn. Trying to extort money from a grief-stricken family. Such scam artists surface frequently in high-profile cases. Preying on the vulnerable.'

'So that's the cover story, is it? That's keeping the press away.'

Fox cleared his throat and straightened his shoulders. Going to dig in, make a last push with this idiot civilian.

'Because of certain partitioning that exists between investigative agencies, one faction of agents is not always fully apprised of the missions and strategies of other factions, even within a single task force. And to complicate matters further, Secretary Webster was fond of operating in a somewhat autonomous manner. The end result is that our team was not always up to speed on the direction Webster's inquiries were taking. Now that he's gone, it's crucial for us to know everything we can about the progress of his investigation. So I'm asking you one more time, Mr Thorn, to enlighten me about what exactly Secretary Webster recruited you to do.'

Thorn took one more look at the grim work unfolding in his yard, then he stood up and walked across the room and stood close to Fox.

'Was Webster lying to me? Do you have any fucking idea where the girl is? Is she under your control?'

Fox considered the question for a moment, his gaze drifting toward the far wall.

'I'm sure Secretary Webster had very good reasons for presenting the situation in the manner he did.'

'Meaning he had a good reason to lie.'

'Secretary Webster's methods were not always ones we sanctioned.'

'You fucking people.'

'It's important that you keep in mind, Thorn, that there's a great deal more at stake here than the welfare of one little girl. Although we take her disappearance seriously, as I noted, we're also under serious time pressure on other fronts. In his final transmission a few days ago Ching was clear that a large gathering was about to take place. A sit-down of the top men of several of these organizations. We don't know where or when, but there are indications that this meeting is imminent.'

'A pirate bash.'

'The implications are enormous, Mr Thorn, the scale of this merger of criminal elements is beyond anything we've—'

Thorn cut him off, waving his hands a few inches in front of the agent's face as if to wake him from his bullshit trance.

'Yeah, yeah, I heard that speech already. The future of Western civilization hangs in the balance.'

'You can sneer, but it's true. The stakes are huge.'

'Maybe *your* Western civilization is hanging in the balance,' Thorn said. 'But not mine. It just so happens that my bailiwick includes only one thing at the moment, and that's getting Janey Sugarman home safe. So unless you're going to arrest me or lock me up in a gibbet cage, you can just get the hell out of here. I'm not cooperating with you people. Go on, do your job and stop those gangs of pirates from coalescing. That's not my concern.'

Fox was silent, looking through his black-framed glasses into Thorn's eyes with something close to disinterest. Already plotting his next move and the one after that.

'All right, Thorn. If you're unwilling to assist, fine, that's your right as a citizen. But let's be very clear about this. Whatever your relationship was with James Lee Webster, it's finished. You're no longer involved in any aspect of this case. And I'm giving you fair warning, Thorn. Stay clear. Don't stick your face into this again, and if you don't listen to me and you get in trouble, don't come to us begging for help. It won't be there. You're on your own.'

'Yeah,' he said. 'The way I like it.'

24

Sheffield arrived at Sugarman's at quarter to six. Alone. Telling Sugar his high-tech assistant had the day off and was visiting in-laws in north Florida.

Frank was wearing khakis and a white shirt with epaulets, new boat shoes. A lot dressier than his normal look. Airplane clothes, off on a fishing safari. Sandy hair still cut scruffy. Looking as lean and suntanned as he had when he'd worked alongside Sugarman on a murder-for-hire case ten years back. Sugar acting as liaison between the county cops and the feds. They'd hit it off. Frank was a slightly straighter version of Thorn. Neater, more orderly, held a job. But with a heavy dose of devil-may-care. Quicker with a 'fuck it' than any cop Sugar'd ever met.

'She's gotten sick to her stomach,' Sugarman said. 'She called a while ago and said she was going to call back in a bit.'

'I can wait,' Frank said. 'A while anyway.'

Sugarman sat down in the chair and stared at the blank computer screen.

'Computer visitation,' Frank said. 'You're not allowed to see her in person?'

'Twice a month I see her and her sister. The computer thing's a bonus.'

'No postmarital fighting going on?'

'It's not that, Frank. Jeannie and I are fine.'

'Had to ask.'

Frank was pacing the room, touching things lightly, moving on.

'What's eating you, Sheffield?'

'I called around on this. Sounded so weird.'

'And?'

'I gather this is part of something larger,' Frank said. 'I can't tell exactly what. But the word I got was that this whole deal was already in the pipeline.'

'What? Finding Janey? Somebody's working on it?'

Frank stopped circling the room and sat down on the edge of the daybed. Hunched over, elbows on his thighs, with a sour look like a ballplayer sent to the bench for screwing up an easy play.

'Couldn't get a straight answer, Sugar. Spent the hour drive down here on my cell talking to one guy after another. Inference I'm drawing is that there's some territorial thing going on, some squabble about who's running the show, top dog shit. You know how it is. Who gets to piss on which tree. It happens with these interagency task force things. A lot of big people running around looking for the biggest tree.'

'Jesus Christ.'

'You saw her? You talked to her? On the computer, satellite hookup?'

'Yeah, Frank. I wasn't hallucinating.'

'These heavyweights,' Sheffield said. 'That could be a good thing, it could be bad. But how it looks, Sugar, they got people swarming all over this thing.'

'So what're you telling me? Whatever can be done *is* being done?'

Frank looked at Sugar, then shifted his eyes to the tree branches out the window. Took a long time with that like he was framing his reply.

'If Hannah wouldn't kill me for missing this goddamn trip she's planned for six months, I'd stay and see what I could stir up. Even though I've been assured your case is already in good hands.'

'And is it? What's your gut tell you?'

He brought his gaze back to Sugar.

'I'd like to say yes. I been with this outfit going on twenty-eight years, but I don't know, Sugar. I can't honestly say what the fuck's going on, what kind of hands you're in. I just know there's a lot of people in town who don't usually get this far south. Some seriously hot and bothered types.'

Sugarman nodded.

Frank said, 'Janey can call you, but you can't call her?'

'I'm logged on to the video chat room. All I can do is wait for her to show up, but she has to come in from her side.'

Frank dusted his hands across his white shirt.

Sugarman said, 'These heavyweights? They know she's been kidnapped, they know I'm talking to her?'

'Can't say for sure.' Frank took a long look at the silent computer screen. 'But I'll be making some phone calls, see if I can light a fire under anybody. I'll write this up on the flight out to Alaska. Soon as I'm on the ground, I'll fax it up and down the chain of command. Make sure Andy Meeker gives you a call, too. He's the kid, the hightech guru. He'll get with you and if a call trace can be done, he'll do it.'

'Memos,' Sugarman said. 'Always memos.'

'Good or bad, that's how we do it.'

Sugarman looked at the blank screen.

'Thanks, Frank.'

'Shit, I'm sorry, Sugar. I'm really sorry. I'll do what I can.'

Sheffield waited another half hour, but Janey didn't log back on and finally Frank had to leave.

The afternoon sun was disappearing behind a thick bank of clouds out over the Florida Bay. The squirrels in Sugarman's backyard had retreated to their hiding places before the big nocturnal birds arrived for the night's hunting. Janey still hadn't dialed back in.

For the hour since Sheffield had left, Sugarman tried to occupy himself with lists of questions to ask, the observations he wanted her to make. He'd had a hopeful half hour as he jotted down the step-by-step procedure he recalled from his Boy Scout days, a trick to narrow the search zone dramatically, then as the minutes passed and the video screen stayed dark, that hope turned to worry and now that worry was taking a fast plunge into gloom.

He occupied himself by paging through guides to birds and mammals. He found pages and pages of giant green iguanas but learned they were all abundant throughout the region, that band of rain forest and jungle that ran for over a thousand miles along the rim of the Gulf and the Caribbean Sea from Mexico to Venezuela.

He closed the *Rain Forest Mammal Guide*. He held it for a moment, then cocked his arm and flung it at the far wall. He walked over and picked the book up and slammed it into the wall again. He looked at it lying on the rug. Its cover dented, its spine chafed. He stared up at the ceiling and squeezed his eyes closed and roared until his lungs ached and his throat was raw.

When he'd gotten his breathing back under control, he picked up the guidebook and gathered together all the other volumes that exclusively featured wildlife in the islands, ruled out by the agouti, and stacked them carefully by the front door.

He sat down in his TV chair and flicked through the local channels. Evening news on all four. On Channel 10 he caught the tail end of a press conference Jeannie had given earlier in the afternoon. With the beach in the background and Jackie at her side, she told the Channel 10 reporter that she wasn't angry or upset that the search-and-rescue mission had been called off. It was her strong faith in reincarnation that was getting her through this difficult period. With the dark, restless surf crashing behind her, Jeannie blinked back tears and spoke into the camera, saying she was absolutely certain her daughter Janey was now living happily in a better place and time.

Beside her, Jackie chewed gum and stared out at the waves.

Sugarman switched off the set and went back to the desk and sat for several moments staring into the blank screen. When he finally roused himself, he began to flip through the books until he located one with several pages of kingfishers. But then he couldn't seem to concentrate on the images, much less the tiny print, the careful, scientific descriptions of habitat, behavior, the sounds of calls, the distinctive patterns of markings.

He set the book aside and stared into the dark computer screen, willing it to come alive.

At seven-thirty, as the light in the branches of his oak tree was failing, Sugarman once again looked over his sheet of scribbles but saw nothing there he hadn't seen before. Cormorant, blue heron, king-fisher, agouti, blue morpho butterfly, green iguana, smell of the sea.

'What now, Thorn?'

He'd been asking the same question himself and had no answer.

The investigators were gone. The bodies carted off. Photos taken, measurements made. Yellow crime scene tape staked out in a large square around the base of the gumbo-limbo tree.

At the end of his dock, Anne Bonny Joy and Thorn stood below the black pennant, watching a ribbon of fire simmer along the horizon.

'You ever seen the green flash?'

She gave him a sidelong look.

'What're you talking about?'

'Green flash, it's supposed to come just after sunset. You ever seen it?'

She shook her head. Thorn touched the flagpole, staring out at the silver sheen spreading across Blackwater Sound.

'People claim they see it, but I've lived here all my life and watched thousands of sunsets and never seen one green flash. So either they're lying or else I keep blinking at the wrong second.'

Anne was silent, waiting for him to get to the point.

'Then again, maybe they're not lying. Maybe I'm just one of those idiots that can't be hypnotized.

Won't let myself surrender. Too skeptical, too locked up in my own head. Sometimes I wish I were the other kind, the one that can see the green flash. They see it because they really want to see it. I admire that, people who can suspend their disbelief, throw themselves headlong into something far-fetched and weird. Believe in the unbelievable.'

'Like Vic,' Anne said. 'Or my mother. You admire that?'

'Hell, with Vic, it could've been stock cars or coin collecting.'

'What?'

'The pirate bullshit, that's an accident of fate, just what happened to come along, so he latched onto it. Uses it to distract himself, or try to. Vic strikes me as a guy hungry for something he can't find. A guy who could gobble everything in sight from now till the end of time and not satisfy his hunger.'

'Because he's hollow,' Anne said. 'A bottomless pit.'

'Greedy people are like that sometimes. Need to have ten things going on at once to keep themselves from feeling the vacuum in their chests.'

'I think that about nails him.'

'What about women?'

'Vic and women?'

'Yeah.'

'I don't know for sure,' she said. 'From the gossip I've heard, apparently there've been a few who threw themselves at him over the years, but he pushes them away, like he's too busy or maybe too drained from fucking over his business competition.'

'Maybe he's not interested in women. I mean, the way he was holding my balls.'

She sighed.

'I think it's probably something else.' She tilted her chin up, closing her eyes, and said, 'There *was* one woman when we first got to the Keys. We were kids, teenagers sharing an apartment down in Matecumbe. Vic took up with her, Francis Colmes, our landlady. Couple of weeks after we got there, he moved all his stuff upstairs and started sharing her bed. He was eighteen, she was in her fifties. It lasted a few months, then one day she threw us both out. Threatened to call the cops. Vic never talked about it, but I could hear them up there sometimes. Francis bossing him around. Giving him chores, scolding him for not doing things right, humiliating him. It was sickening. I couldn't stand to listen to it. His shriveled voice. Whining.'

'Mommy's little boy.'

Anne's mouth was tight for a moment as if she were fighting back the urge to scream.

She turned her eyes toward the last scarlet tatters of the sunset.

'After Francis Colmes, Vic didn't seem interested. At the restaurant I'd hear about these women now and then who tried to tempt him. Went to his place, threw themselves at him. But far as I know none of them ever succeeded. He's cold. Asexual, maybe. I don't know.'

'Maybe he's just waiting for you to be available. It could explain him scaring off all your boyfriends. Like they were competition.'

'I've thought about that,' she said.

They were silent for a moment. A squadron of ibis coasted high above the sound, heading toward that last seam of light in the west.

'About the green flash,' he said. 'My point was that I respect you, Anne.'

'You what?'

'I respect you for letting go the way you did, running off with Salbone. It was crazy, reckless. But hell, without some of that, what's the point? Play safe? Lie low? What the hell kind of life is that? Better to crash and burn out in some wild place than live happily ever after in your foxhole.'

'You're working yourself up to something.'

'I'm going back to Vic's,' he said.

'Sign away your land?'

'If I thought I could beat it out of him, I'd try that.'

'Don't be an idiot, Thorn, you can't bargain with the devil. He'll scoop out your heart and walk away laughing.'

'There some other choice? If I saw one, I'd take it. I'm going to give him what he wants, see if he can deliver Janey.'

'And if he's bullshitting you and doesn't have the girl?'

'Then it's crash and burn time. Adventure hour. I'll have to get creative.'

'Well, I know one thing,' she said. 'You shouldn't be here when Daniel shows up. Even though nothing's happened between you and me, he can be a very jealous man.'

'This is my house, Anne. I'll go when I'm damn well ready.'

She stepped away from him, gripping the flagpole.

'You're angry. Well, you should be. I dragged you into this.'

She looked out at the bay. He was angry all right. But Anne wasn't at the top of that list.

'You're not afraid?' he said. 'Going back to that life. It doesn't scare the shit out of you?'

'A little bit, sure. I'd be crazy if it didn't.'

'And you still don't believe he killed Webster and the other two?'

'I don't know,' she said. 'But if he did, it was unavoidable.'

'Yeah,' Thorn said. 'Unavoidable.'

'Look, I'm sorry, Thorn. I'm sorry about the little girl. I'm really sorry. You've got every right to be pissed at me.'

'It's everybody's fault,' he said. 'Yours, mine, Webster's, Vic's, everybody's. There's a lot to go around.'

'I'm sorry,' she repeated.

'Just do me one favor, Anne.'

'Of course.'

'Don't be here when I get back.'

25

'I think it's the flu, Daddy. I'm hot and I hurt all over. Inside my bones.'

'Aw, sweetie. I'm so sorry.'

It was almost dark outside his windows, a radio blasting from his neighbor's house, Mrs Selwyn, a deaf widow, listening to her bigband station.

'I was so worried something happened to you, Janey.'

Her face seemed on the verge of collapse. He could see her eyes glisten.

'Janey, listen. I know the flu is terrible. But you're going to be strong, okay? We need to keep working at this. You need to help me find where you are. We've made good progress, but there's other things we have to do.'

'I just want to lie down, Daddy. My bones hurt. I threw up all my sandwich. I really, really hurt.'

'You need to drink a Coke, Janey. Fluids, you need fluids.'

'I am.'

She held the bottle up to the camera.

'It's still light there, isn't it? I can see you, but you're dimmer than before.'

'The sun's going down. It's going to be dark soon.'

'So we know you're a good deal west of here. That's good. Now we need to figure out just how far.'

'I feel terrible.' Then she groaned.

'Can you do this one thing for me, sweetie?'

She looked woozy, her face pinched and drained, the light fading around her.

'The animals are very loud. I think there's a monkey out there, or something. It's screaming.'

'Look out your window, Janey. Look east, okay?'

There was a knock on his front door. Sugarman leaned back in his chair, but he couldn't make out a face in the small eye-level window.

'Hold on, Janey. There's someone at the door.'

He trotted into the living room, pressed his eye to the window, and flipped on the porch light. He unlocked the door and opened it.

'Hi,' Alexandra said. Lawton was standing beside her. 'We came to see how you're doing.'

He nudged past them and ran out to the edge of his yard. He stepped out into the middle of his quiet street and looked east down toward Largo Sound.

The moon was halfway over the horizon. Full and golden. He waited there until the last edge of it came into view. He tilted his watch toward the streetlight and read the time.

Then he sprinted back to the house, waving Alex and Lawton inside.

'I'm in the back bedroom,' he said, and trotted to the laptop.

'Alex and Lawton are here, Janey. Look.'

Alexandra came into the room, leaned close to the screen.

'My God,' she said. 'Where is she? What's going on?'

'In a minute.'

Lawton said, 'I know that little girl. Look, she's a television star.'

'Janey,' Sugar said. 'Listen, go to your east window, okay? Turn your computer around so I can see you.'

'Daddy, I got goose bumps on my arms. I'm cold. I'm starting to shiver.'

'You've got a fever, darling. It comes with the flu. Be strong, you need to be strong. After we do this you can lie down and rest. But we have to do this now. Right now. We can't wait.'

She swiveled the laptop around and walked to the window, hugging herself tightly.

She walked out of view.

Her voice was distant, barely audible, saying, 'All right.'

'Do you see the moon coming up, any part of it?'

'I think so,' she called out. 'A little bit.'

They were losing the illumination, Janey being absorbed into the darkness. He heard a faint screech, one of the animals from her jungle.

'Tell me the exact second when it comes over the horizon, okay? The second you can see every bit of it rise out of the water.'

'All right,' she said. Her voice growing weaker.

He could see the dimming of the light in her tiny room. A minute passed, and then another.

'It's almost there,' she said.

'The whole thing,' Sugarman called. 'The whole big ball.'

'Right now, Daddy. It's above the horizon.'

Sugarman looked at his watch and wrote down the number on the pad by his laptop. Did a quick computation. Subtracting his moonrise time from hers, then some multiplication. Got the total.

'Okay, good. Good work, Janey.'

She had moved back into the camera's range.

'I can still see you Daddy. Can you see me?'

'Just barely, Janey. You're pretty dark.'

'There aren't any lights here. The only light is from the screen. Your face is lighting up my room, but only just a little.'

'Yeah.'

He looked up at Alexandra. Her eyes were fixed on Janey's shadowy image. Alex didn't seem to be breathing.

'What's your battery signal say?'

'I don't know, Daddy. It's lower than before. It's running down.'

'What about that sign? Is it still hidden?'

'Yeah. Behind a palm frond.'

Sugarman pawed through the books on his desk until he found the atlas. He paged quickly to the largest map he could find of the Caribbean Sea and checked the longitude.

'This is good, Janey. You did great. I've got your longitude now, or something close to it. You're at eighty-four degrees west. That's somewhere along the coast of northern Central America. Do you understand me, Janey?'

'I sure as hell don't,' Lawton said. 'What're you talking about?'

Alexandra shushed him.

'I don't feel good, Daddy. I'm hot now. Really hot.'

'Is there still ice in your cooler?'

'No.'

'Is there a sheet or a towel?'

'There's a sheet, yeah, on the bed.'

'Soak a corner of it in the water in the cooler and press it on your forehead, Janey, and hold it there. That's what your mother and I used to do when you had a fever.'

'Does Mommy know where I am?'

'I haven't talked to her yet. I will. As soon as I have something definite. I'll call her.'

'And tell Jackie hello, too. Okay? I love them. I miss them.'

'I'll tell them, I will.' Sugar closed his eyes briefly and opened them again. 'But we need to turn your computer off now. I need to think some more, figure out what to do next. But you can log back on anytime. I'll be here. Right here waiting.'

'Okay, Daddy.' Her voice was growing feeble and he could no longer see the outline of her face in the darkness.

'Wait a minute, Janey.'

'What?'

'That bird you saw. It was a kingfisher? Can you describe it?'

'Yeah, I think so. But it was little and green. Like that car we had when you and Mommy were still married. A weird green.'

'The Chevy,' he said. 'Metallic green?'

'Yeah,' she said, 'with a brown breast, and its throat was lighter brown.'

'Tufted like the kingfishers in Florida?'

'No, it had a smooth head, I think. But it had a kingfisher beak, long and narrow. But I don't know. It might've been something else. Not a kingfisher at all.'

'I'll look it up, sweetie. I'll tell you next time we talk.'

'Okay.'

'So we should go now, I guess.' Sugarman glanced up at Alexandra. She'd closed her eyes and bowed her head and was shaking it slightly.

'Okay, I'm turning it off now, Daddy. I'll call you when I feel better. Bye.'

'I love you, sweetie,' he said. 'I love you.'

But she didn't answer. The screen dark, the connection broken.

'My God, Sugar. My God in heaven.' Alexandra leaned down and hugged him around the shoulders, pressed her cheek to his. 'I'm so sorry.'

He patted her other cheek and she straightened.

'I been holding it in, staying hard,' Sugarman said, feeling the tears starting to build. 'I got to stay focused, goddamn it. I can't let it take over.'

He wiped his eyes harder than he needed to.

'You're right, you're right,' Alex said. She touched him on the shoulder.

Sugarman said, 'She's alive, that's what's important, Janey's hanging in there, and we're making progress. Shrinking the search area.'

'What was all that about the moon?'

'Yeah,' Lawton said. 'You confused the diddly-shit out of me.'

'Boy Scouts,' he said. 'No big secret. One revolution of the Earth is three hundred and sixty degrees, right? The moon goes around the Earth in twenty-four hours. So you do a little long division and it works out the moon moves fifteen degrees every hour, or three degrees every twelve minutes. That's longitude, the east-west measurement.'

'I'm still lost,' Lawton said.

Alex said, 'If her moonrise is twelve minutes later than ours, she's three degrees west.'

'Right, and that's exactly what it was, twelve minutes, twenty-five seconds, roughly three degrees.' Sugar moved the atlas to the edge of the desk. 'In the Keys, we're at eighty-one west longitude, so you add three; that puts it here, on a line along the coast of Honduras, Nicaragua, and a narrow slice into Costa Rica. She's a long way south of here, but not that far west. It's all rough-and-ready figuring. I mean, I could be off by some fraction. The line could be a little farther west, but it couldn't be much farther, because she can smell the ocean, and it can't be too much farther east, because that's the Caribbean Sea. So it's got to be along this patch.'

He ran his finger along a two- or three-hundred-mile curve of Central America. Honduras, Nicaragua, the northern tip of Costa Rica. Still a huge area, but so much smaller than before.

'She's on a satellite phone?'

'Yeah, it belonged to Markham. Built into the computer.'

'So maybe it can be traced,' Alex said.

'I looked into that. Didn't look promising.'

'You want me to give it a shot? Use my police clout?'

'Sure, if you think it's worth a try.'

'Okay, I'll go outside, use my cell.'

Lawton leaned down close to Sugarman's face.

'A painting of a rice cake doesn't satisfy hunger,' he said.

Sugarman nodded at the old man.

'Good point,' Sugar said.

'I may be old and slow and dumb about longitude, but I know a few things.'

'You do, Lawton. You're a fountain of wisdom. Indispensable.'

The old man gave a rumpled smile, not buying the flattery but happy enough to have it. Alexandra headed out to the porch to make her call.

Sugarman picked up the volume of *Birds of the Tropics* to see if he could locate that undersized kingfisher. The big book fell open in his lap to a page of vultures and large black raptors. Giant birds, dark and iridescent, with short, powerful beaks and humped backs. Killers, predators, scavengers.

Lawton leaned over his shoulder and said, 'Jesus, those are some badass birds. Not a good omen. Not good at all.'

26

Nobody was manning the front gate at Vic Joy's estate, at least nobody Thorn could see. In the VW he crawled past and parked fifty yards down the road, then walked back to Vic's compound in the shadows. The gate was shut. Twenty feet high.

He scanned the area toward the highway, the only place where a surveillance crew would have a line of sight to the front gate. No one out there. No cars parked, no vans. No men skulking in the shadows. Nothing he could see. Even if they were there, he didn't care. He was beyond that. No longer in their service. No longer in anyone's.

Plan A was to sign the real estate papers. Plan B was to drive to Miami, go to Alexandra's house, explain everything, try to make amends, bring her into it. The police route.

Thorn hitched himself into the lower limbs of a mahogany and climbed ten feet into the tree, then reached out and scaled the last four feet of the wall. Perched on the top, he surveyed the compound. Floodlights illuminated the squat brick Harlan house, and a half-dozen other bright lamps shined out into the restless ocean. The main house was dark and he could see the floatplane was gone.

He could've jumped down the other side and prowled the estate, but the place look so deserted, he doubted it was worth the effort. Guard dogs were a possibility or maybe an armed sentry or two lurking in the shadows. He was angry and fired up, but he wasn't feeling suicidal. Not yet anyway.

A few feet away along the top of the wall he saw a fist-sized chunk of concrete, a leftover from sloppy construction work. On his knees he crawled to it and hefted it and found a comfortable fit in his throwing hand.

The French doors on the back of Vic's office were less than fifty feet away, just at the edge of Thorn's pitching range. He ran his eyes around the inside perimeter of the wall and saw no easy access back up and over, so he reset his butt, used his other hand for leverage, and hurled the chunk of cement at the glass doors.

He was short by a yard, but the fragment bounced off the wood porch and took a lucky hop and smashed into the lower panes. The alarm was triggered instantly. It was as loud as an air-raid siren, and a full complement of floodlights snapped on. Thorn flattened himself against the narrow rim of the wall and waited, but no one showed themselves, no one fired. No armed militia, not even a uniformed servant.

All of which told him a little: Vic and his entourage had flown the coop. Beyond that, he couldn't say.

Plan B was calling.

After another moment, Thorn climbed down through the mahogany branches and went back to the VW and pulled out onto the narrow asphalt road that paralleled the Overseas Highway. As he slammed through the gears and hauled ass out to the main thoroughfare he heard a shrill siren in the distance, and as he was passing through the village of Islamorada he had to pull onto the shoulder to avoid two speeding patrol cars heading toward him and then on past with their blue lights whirling.

Anne waited on the end of Thorn's dock, below the pennant. It was drooping now, the night air still, an occasional mosquito whirring at her ear. She stared out at the black water that rippled with faint moonlight, and the wild racket she'd been hearing inside her head finally calmed and the tension ache in her jaw muscles was starting to ease.

She'd never believed in destiny. Everyone had

choices. Once she'd escaped from Harlan, she'd constructed her world brick by careful brick, built the solid fortress she'd inhabited for almost two decades, a secure, unvarying routine. She believed she'd successfully gone beyond the reach of her mother's madness, purified herself of that polluted air, the stench and desolation of that place. Until Daniel Salbone stormed her castle, revealed it for the flimsy construction it was, and carried her away. Damn her mother, damn her bones.

It all seemed so inevitable now. Named for a pirate, Anne became one. And those years of the waitressing work her mother had so disdained, the quiet evenings on her skiff, the string of meaningless men she'd taken to her bed, that was gone forever now. No possible return to those simple duties, those easy, uncomplicated days. That afternoon at Golden Beach she'd stepped across a permanent divide. Her Blackbeard, her Captain Kidd, her Errol Flynn had whisked her off to a place she'd never allowed herself to imagine. But it was all real to her now. The shipboard life, the rowdy men who fell in line at Daniel's brusque commands. The endless movement, the wind, the long nights of heat and sweat and the brackish taste of his flesh.

She'd worked so goddamn hard to thwart her destiny but finally had only managed to stall it for a while.

Anne Bonny Joy followed the running lights of every vessel that passed across the sound. It was nearly midnight and the boat traffic had all but ceased. Once or twice she felt the air shudder overhead, a bat or nighthawk, doing its silent work.

She leaned her shoulder against the flagpole and strained to see across that empty prairie of moonlight. And when she saw the green and red bow lights heading directly toward shore, she knew it was him. Idling slow across the silver sheen, coming back to retrieve her as he had promised.

With her heart thumping madly, she unknotted the thin rope on the flagpole and ran down the pennant. She unclipped it from the line and held it in her hand and watched the shimmer of the boat's wake spread across the sound. The craft was long and narrow, and even when it was still fifty yards away she made out its glossy black hull and the low burble of its V-8 engine.

The bow lights switched off as the boat eased into the shallows near the dock, making a sweeping right turn to come alongside where she stood. Then inching close in the careful, precise way that Daniel had with boats.

Anne stood watching, silent, tense. Not wanting to shout out his name. Determined to be as cool and strong and confident as Daniel, repress the giddy schoolgirl exhilaration she felt. If only to keep from embarrassing him in front of his crew with some sappy display.

She held out her hand to receive the dock line and make it fast. A good sailor, a competent partner.

But no dock line came, and as the boat drifted close and bumped one of the forward pilings, she could make out three men in the small cockpit. One tall and two smaller, chunkier men.

And then with a heavy thump, one of them jumped onto the dock with the bowline in his hand. He bent down to secure it to the forward cleat.

'Daniel?' She reached out and grabbed hold of the gunwale and leaned her weight backward to tug the heavy craft closer to the piling, holding the boat in place.

The big engine shut down.

And the man who'd been fastening the line straightened up.

He snapped a lighter and cupped his hand around the flame as he lit his cigarette. In the wavering light she recognized him, but it took another moment to place the man. Someone from another frame of reference. Light-years across the universe. The man from the mug shot Sheriff Taft had shown her, the man at her brother's front gate.

When he had his cigarette lit, he extended his arm, bringing Anne Bonny into the halo of his flame. He limped closer to her.

'My, my, look who we got here,' he said. 'If it isn't the bitch who shot me in the fucking foot.'

Anne Bonny felt a strangled gasp escape her.

'What?'

'You don't remember?' Marshall said. 'The *Rainmaker*, blasting me in the fucking foot before

394

you jumped overboard? Shit, there's seventeen steel pins in there now; that goddamn foot isn't ever going to be right again.'

Marshall Marshall stepped close, his heavy plaster cast thumping on the dock, the scrawny long-haired man drawing back his open hand to take a vengeful swipe at her.

'Leave her alone, brain death,' Vic Joy said. 'That's my sister. She's precious cargo.'

Anne felt the sky spinning fast and dark above her.

'You killed him, you son of a bitch. That was you, Vic. You killed Daniel.'

'What a loser. Jesus, you'll thank me someday,' Vic said. 'So hey, Annie. Where's your boyfriend, that fucker Thorn? He around here or what?'

Anne heard the scream a moment before realizing it was her own, a shriek full of fire and acid and despair torn loose from the twisted depths of her bowels.

Thorn had enough sense to park along the highway and sneak down his own drive. He had no intention of stumbling into the middle of a reunion of pirates. He was hoping they'd come and gone, Anne safely on her way back into the arms of Daniel Salbone. Thorn was headed to Miami to drop in on Alex and Lawton and had only stopped to be sure that Anne was no longer there. If somehow he succeeded in convincing Alex to return with him, he sure as hell didn't want Anne Bonny Joy camped out in his bedroom when he got back.

He was halfway down the drive, staying on the soft earth that was matted with pine needles, listening for any sign that the gathering might still be in session, when he heard her scream.

It didn't sound like Anne. It didn't sound human. Some jungle cry from high in the canopy. He fought back his instinct to rush toward the noise and halted near the slick trunk of a gumbo-limbo.

He saw figures down near the dock. Two men, maybe three, scrambling around, then heading up the sloping yard and disappearing behind the cover of the trees. For the next few seconds he caught small darting movements, men sprinting from tree to tree. The moon was no help and his eyes were still dazzled by the half-hour drive into the stream of headlights. But they seemed to be searching the grounds, running tricky, unpredictable patterns like men dodging machine-gun fire.

Thorn heard no voices and lost the three men, or two, or four. He held his position, waiting for something definite, some sense of what game was unfolding out on his darkened lawn.

He should've had the upper hand in this skirmish. Lived here virtually all his life, tracked across every inch of his five acres a thousand thousand times, but what he was seeing made no sense. A helter-skelter game of hide-and-seek. He heard someone crash into a limb and curse, and when he ducked his head out to see, another curse came from less than twenty feet to his left.

He flattened his back against the tree, waited till the huffing man moved a few feet out of range, then in a crouch he headed for the house. A year ago, he'd tossed his only handgun into the Florida Bay, an act of contrition and a vow to reverse the violent course his life had taken until that moment. No pistol now, but inside the house there were other weapons. A baseball bat from his high school days, a few knives. Reason told him to retreat back to the car and get the hell away. But reason had never driven his choices.

He stayed low and moved from tree to bush. Getting up the stairs without being seen would be a challenge, but if he made it that far, he imagined he could do that final dash in time to seize the bat that stood behind the front door and at least crush a few bones, go down swinging.

His eyes were working now. He saw through the darkness a third boat at his dock, black and shiny. He was thirty feet, maybe forty from the house, sizing up the last open stretch of yard, hearing the men prowling nearby, the snap of a stick, the crunch of gravel, a wheeze. He was picking his moment, lowering himself into a crouch to make that run to the steps, when he smelled the dizzy fumes of gasoline and heard the unmistakable slosh of fluid.

He came out from behind the oak tree, saw the

shadowy outline of a heavyset man moving around the frame for Lawton's new room. He carried a ten-gallon can in his hand, and another man was on the stairs splashing gasoline onto that old hardwood Thorn had salvaged from the Miami landfill. As if they were the assessment team, here to test his long-held belief that those oily hardwoods from the center of the ancient Brazilian rain forest were impervious to all things. Organic steel.

He charged the closest man, hit him in the back with a flying tackle, and the big guy belly-flopped, the air exploding from his lungs. Thorn was on his feet before the man had regrouped. He grunted and tried to rise as Thorn drew back his leg and kicked the man flush in the temple.

The kick sent the big man sprawling to his left and Thorn would have followed and delivered another blow, except he knew the noise of the struggle must have gotten the attention of the others. He grabbed the plastic gas can and slung it into the dark. Thorn's heart was bulging inside his chest, working triple-time to keep up with the needs of its human host.

Then he felt the spurt and surge of blood he knew from a dozen other moments in his past, a wild boost of energy, a blinding resolve to go forward, driven by some secret long-ago animal nodule in his brain screaming its message down the ages, that reptilian part of him, the morsel of primeval taffy buried deep beneath the layers of culture and manners and good sense and a thousand lessons in comportment and restraint exploding like a nucleus of napalm jelly, bits of liquid fire, the scattering shrapnel of his id.

He made it halfway up the stairs as the tall, rangy man was hustling down. Thorn lowered his shoulder and blew the guy backward against the railing. All bones and tendons and gristly muscle, the man bounced off the rail and tumbled sideways onto the hard angles of the steps. His plastic canister came loose from his grip and bounced down the stairway spraying gasoline.

Thorn got a flash of his whipping silver mane, Vic Joy's hair. Not that it mattered, not that he could fine-tune his rage at this point, adjust the bestial rush that was running the show. With a grip on Vic's T-shirt, he hauled him upright and levered his body straight, jamming the small of his back into the rail, then rocking him backward. Ten steps up, twelve, thirteen. It didn't matter. The fall was high enough to do more damage than Thorn could manage with his fists. Vic kneed him, but Thorn felt it coming and blocked it with his thigh, and with a groan he bulled Vic Joy up the extra few inches and hitched him onto the rail, seesawing him for a moment while Vic tried to brace himself, fighting for balance, clawing for a hold on Thorn's shirt, scratching at his eyes. But Thorn had the superior angle and gave a last shove and Vic Joy tipped over in a backward swan dive onto the hard-packed earth below.

'Hey, wiseass. Got a light?'

Thorn looked down at the smallish man at the foot of the stairs. He was scratching the wheel of his lighter in small, ineffectual increments.

'Don't do it,' Thorn said.

'Yeah, and why not?'

Thorn made a half-turn so he was facing the man full on. Inching forward, curling his toes against the edge of the stairs, preparing to attempt his own swan dive.

'Told you I'd see you again, and sure as shit, here we are.'

Marty Messina limped into view behind the little man. A glint in his hand, the flash of chrome. Aiming the pistol up at Thorn. Vic groaned from a few yards away.

'Don't light him up,' Marty said. 'Vic wants him along for the ride.'

'What the fuck for?' The short man, Marshall Marshall, scratched his flint again, but no spark showed.

'Vic's sister,' Marty said. 'To get the code out of her.'

'What? We get to torture him?' Marshall grinned.

'He's mine,' Vic said, rising from the ground. 'Don't touch him.'

'Come on, Thorn,' Marty said. 'Time's a-wasting. We got to move.'

'What code?' Marshall looked back at Marty, scratching his lighter idly, and this time the flame sputtered and caught and the heavy fumes ignited

400

in a blue-white *whoosh*, the air turning to a super-heated solid that battered Thorn in the chest and pitched him up and over the rail. He backstroked through the blazing wind, tried to right himself but failed, and smacked on his rump a yard from Vic, then slumped back into the grass.

His hair was singed, head fogged, and eyes nearly sightless from the blast of light. A numb heat flowed up his spine. Flat on his back, he groaned and pried his head a few inches off the ground, and as his hazy vision cleared he watched the green-and-orange flames crawl along the stairway and snap at the walls and then there was a secondary flash and rupture of fire along the pilings that supported the house.

All around him the air was sucked from the night. A howling vacuum that shot sparks into the sky, twisting upward on the powerful drafts, a stream of embers lifting off like spirits returning to the heavens, ten thousand specks of wood flickering and dancing, serving their last purpose on earth before they winked out against the stars.

27

'This is it,' Sugarman said. 'Green-and-rufous king-fisher.' Lawton bent to look at the shiny color plate, the little green kingfisher perched there amid rows of candy-bright exotics, the motmots and half-dozen different woodpeckers, toucans.

Sugarman squinted at the small print on the adjacent page.

'This is the bird she saw. I'm sure of it. "Dark metallic green. Rufous underparts."'

'I knew a Rufus once,' Lawton said. 'Rufus Slotsky. But I never saw his underparts.'

Sugarman looked up at the old man and felt a smile rise to his lips.

Alex was still out on the front porch, pacing back and forth in front of the screen door, the cell phone at her ear, using her free hand to swat at the moths and gnats swarming around her head. Earlier, when she began making her calls, Sugarman hadn't been able to hear her, but as the evening wore on she'd started talking louder, more emphatically, annoyance creeping in, flashes of anger. Same thing over and over, talking to someone she knew at Miami PD or Metro, getting the number for someone higher up, a referral to Washington, local FBI, then speaking to people she didn't know. Waking them from sleep, apologizing, saying it was an emergency. Over and over explaining the situation, a nine-year-old girl kidnapped off her soon-to-be-stepfather's yacht, five people murdered, yeah, yeah, that one, the one off the Florida Keys, big boat, the psychic guy. Yeah, yeah, but the point is, now the girl has contacted her father via satellite phone, and she's being held hostage in the jungle somewhere in Central America, trying to keep it simple and clean, four sentences, five. They needed a trace; how hard was that? Then listening to the response, sometimes two or three clipped questions from Alex, the pleading tone coming into her voice, or more exasperation, then hanging up and calling the next one. Everybody passing her on to somebody else. This was out of their area of specialty. Was a known terrorist holding the girl? Well, it required a subpoena, get in line, put your name on the list. Three hours of that, approaching four.

A while ago Sugar had gone out to the porch

when she was between calls and told her she could stop. It was obvious no one was going to help, but Alex shook her head.

'So much for my clout,' she said. 'How about the *Herald*? One of those pit bulls looking to make a name. That'd light a fire under my so-called friends in law enforcement.'

'Circus time,' Sugar said, shaking his head. 'TV trucks would be camped on the front yard by morning. It'd all blow up. Vic would find out about it, know Janey's talking to me, and he'd pull the plug. Or worse.'

She looked out at the empty street, the quiet working-class neighborhood. Plumber, fishing guide, grocery store manager, druggist.

'That bird thing doesn't seem to be working, Sugar.'

'Oh, yeah, I think it is. I'm getting it narrowed down. We're almost there.'

'Almost? Looks to me like you're down to Honduras, Nicaragua, and Costa Rica, three fairly large countries last time I checked.'

'Closer than that.'

'Even if you had her exact location, then what? Charter a private jet, fly down there, guns blazing?'

Sugarman hadn't considered the 'Then what?'

'Maybe I will,' he said.

Alexandra frowned at her phone.

'I'm going back to the phones,' she said, and she was still at it. Not once mentioning Thorn.

Green-and-rufous kingfishers preferred forest swamps, less often small forest streams, keeping to deep shade, which made them difficult to see. They plunged from low twigs or vines for small fishes, aquatic insects. Solitary or in pairs. A song of *week* . . . or *wick wick wick wick* with high, thin notes. But the part that mattered, the part that had his heart thumping hard, was its range: southeast Nicaragua to western Ecuador. A large area, but if he'd figured the longitude correctly, the only portion of that area that overlapped with eighty-four degrees west was a small section of the southern coast of Nicaragua and maybe a tiny slice of northern Costa Rica.

Not a dot yet, but a tiny crumb of that former pie.

It was nearly one o'clock and Lawton was prowling Sugarman's guest bedroom, snooping in drawers and under the bed. Some of his old homicide detective brain cells sputtering to life. Out on the highway a string of sirens raced past, sounded like a multiple-car pileup or a serious fire. Down the hallway and through the screen door, he could see Alexandra with her phone in her hand. She'd closed it up and was just standing there, the moths dancing over her head like some outlandish halo.

Sugarman was staring at the computer screen. It was still dark, but he thought he'd heard something. He used the touch pad to raise the volume bar to the very top.

'Janey?'

'Shhhh,' she said. 'Shhhh.'

'What's wrong?'

Alexandra came into the room and stood behind Sugarman.

'There're people.'

'People?'

'Shhhh. Turn your lights off, you're glowing. They'll see.'

Sugarman motioned to Alexandra and she flicked off the overhead lights.

'Who is it, honey? Who's there?'

'Men,' she whispered. 'Some women, too. Some of them naked.'

'What?'

'Naked?' Lawton said. 'That any way to act around a child?'

Alexandra put her arm around Lawton's shoulder and held a finger to her lips.

'They're drunk and they're shooting guns.'

'Guns?'

Sugar leaned close to the screen to try to pick up her outline. But saw nothing except the black sizzle of electrons.

'Machine guns,' Janey said. 'Listen.'

He could barely make it out. A string of pops answered by several short bursts.

'What's happening, Janey?'

'They're not shooting at each other. They're aiming at the sky. They're having a party, a big party, I think.' Her voice dropped to a near whisper again.

'Three men came to my cabin and looked inside, but I was hiding down in the corner on the floor and they didn't see me. They tried to pull the boards off the window, but they got tired and left. They've started a big fire out by the lagoon.'

Sugarman heard more machine-gun fire in the background. And voices, screams, cheers, or cries of pleasure, it was hard to tell.

'The naked woman,' Janey said. 'They're in a circle around her.'

'Oh, God,' Sugar said quietly.

'I saw the sign, Daddy.'

'The sign?'

'Out front, the sign.'

'You did?'

'Yeah, I was looking with my binoculars at two men fighting and one of them fell against it and knocked the sign crooked. So I can see it now.'

'What's it say, Janey? What's on the sign?'

'Shhhh. They're coming. Shhhh.'

Then the dark computer screen grew darker and the machine-gun fire abruptly ceased.

28

The gashes in his belly were aching again. Sitting in the tight airplane seat, Thorn felt the warm trickle of blood running beneath his belt. Reopened from the five or six body blows Vic had administered while Marty held Thorn from behind.

And the wallop Thorn had taken on his rump was starting to spread fiery tendrils around his tailbone, coiling upward like a vine strangling a sapling. His neck was stiff and his hands were swollen and the heavy vibration and grim roar of the airplane were drumming deep inside his joints. Plucked strings throbbed up the backs of his legs. Whatever limberness he'd felt earlier in the day was gone. His sack of skin had been emptied and refilled with dried-out cartilage and brittle tendons and bits of broken glass.

After rendezvousing with his seaplane out beyond Shell Key, Vic and Marty and Marshall Marshall dragged Thorn and Anne Bonny out of the boat and strapped them into a couple of rear seats. Vic cranked up the engines and took off toward the west, then when they were airborne, he swung the bulky float-plane back toward Key Largo and took a heading south of Thorn's property, coming in just above the treetops.

As they passed overhead, Vic tipped the wing so they could view the flames consuming Thorn's house. He had been dead wrong about the fire-resistant nature of that wood. The blaze was vigorous as hell and looked to be spreading into the tangle of vines and trees on the south edge of the property.

A pump truck had arrived and several pickups from the volunteer force; men were scrambling about, but the only rush of water Thorn saw was aimed at the surrounding foliage. They were containing it. The house was a lost cause.

Once before his house had been destroyed by explosives, and another time the floor had been riddled by bullets fired by a cowardly killer who tried to murder Thorn without actually confronting him. Now his home was gone again.

All it contained of value was a few trinkets that had survived the previous destruction. Photographs of his adoptive parents, a handful of mementos, and the possessions he'd accumulated since. Only a few of those he truly valued. Mostly the tools of his trade, the custom vice grip, the fine, precise scissors, a couple of first-class fly rods, and an assortment of fur and feathers that seemed to have some supernatural power to lure fish.

Aside from some odds and ends he kept aboard the Chris-Craft, most of what he owned had been inside those four walls, but as the plane banked away into the dark heavens, his immediate sensation was a sense of release. No longer burdened by belongings. Truly now there was nothing he couldn't do. He was free to drift up the highway, leave Key Largo for good. A rucksack, a good pair of shoes. Start over somewhere else, build each night's nest in a tree, then move the next morning. A hobo, a drifter, an aimless vagabond. See the places he'd only heard about. Settle in a city, make peace with concrete, accustom himself to horns and late-night sirens and exhaust fumes instead of air. Maybe Vic Joy had done him an inadvertent favor, freeing him from that belief he'd been clinging to, that somehow he belonged to this island, belonged anywhere. Lately as it had become nearly unbearable for Thorn to watch the slow unraveling of the fabric of the Keys, the crystal waters filling with sludge, sea bottom and reefs bleached to a sterile white, more and more it seemed time to go. Past time.

Maybe climb aboard the *Heart Pounder*, his old cabin cruiser, fill it with gas, and motor as far as the tank allowed, find a job, work for the next tankful. Small increments up the coast or across the Gulf

Stream to the islands or over to Mexico. An expatriate with no identifying numbers, no destination, wandering from port to port. Why not? What did he have to keep him? Alexandra gone, the loyalty and frankness that bound them shattered by his childish deceit, his willingness to play Jimmy Lee Webster's fool.

Even Thorn's oldest friendship seemed to be finished. Sugarman was rightfully enraged that in some fashion Thorn had been the cause of Janey's abduction. There was no one left. No friends, no lovers, no reason to remain.

The swell of grief rose in his throat like a gluey bubble. The bitter tang of self-pity. Sugarman had been right. Everything Thorn loved eventually got torched. He had nothing, and nothing was all he deserved; hell, nothing was more than he could manage. The life of a vagabond might even be too great a challenge. For if he succeeded in leaving the island, surely wherever he went, he'd be towing along that same black thundercloud, daggers of lightning regularly striking down anyone in his proximity and destroying everything he cared for. 'Beware, all ye who encounter Thorn. For grave consequences shall follow this sinner to every corner of the earth, and surely if you so much as touch this man, you shall perish and all that you once loved will turn to ash.'

'Don't you just love a good fire?' Marty grinned at him from across the narrow aisle. 'Hell of a lot cheaper than a bulldozer. All finished in one night, right down to the dirt.'

'You're a riot, Marty.'

Marty rubbed at the lump Thorn had delivered to his temple.

'Vic's pissed, man. He's going to slice your balls off. And I'm going to be there, front row.'

Vic was at the controls and Marshall sat in the copilot seat. Charlie, the other biker from Vic's front gate, was tucked in the seat just behind Thorn, and Anne Bonny was wedged in beside him. All the men wore the same uniform: green camouflage fatigues and black T-shirts, heavy black boots. A pirate special forces team. With their pistols in black webbed holsters on their hips.

Anne had been silent since they had abandoned the *Black Swan* and climbed aboard the floatplane. Stunned, lost, broken. The resurrection of her lover had been a cruel hoax, the pennant on Thorn's flag-pole probably nothing more than Vic's ploy to keep Anne in one place waiting hopefully while he made his final preparations.

Thorn turned in his seat and peered back at her, and the collapse he saw in her eyes, the doomed acceptance of her fate, gave Thorn a harsh slap. She was even more forlorn than he. And seeing her hopeless eyes, recognizing the sagging surren-der in her face, sent the blood flooding back into his veins.

Maybe he had no future, maybe he had lost

everyone and everything he cherished. But he still had the one thing that had carried him through every struggle since his childhood. Thorn's personal curse. A blind pigheaded urge to push on, one step after another, and in this case, to do whatever he could to wreck the plans of these sadistic assholes. And if somehow at the end of this plane ride Janey Sugarman was still alive, he might even have a last shot to make that right as well.

He sat still for a moment reclaiming himself, letting the blood cleanse away the stink of defeat, until he felt himself rising out of the gloom. He drew a long breath and blew it out.

A moment later he leaned out into the narrow aisle, closer to Marty.

'So let me get this straight.'

'What's that, lover boy?'

'You sold out Salbone, gave him up to Vic?'

'One way to look at it.'

'There's another way?'

'Cut myself a better situation,' Marty said. 'Traded up.'

'And now what? We're heading off to that pirate shindig I been hearing so much about?'

Marty gave Thorn a steady look. Maybe Thorn had been underestimating him. What he'd thought was stupidity was actually disdain, a simple contempt for anyone not willing to backstab those who blocked his path to greater fortune. A perfect sidekick for Vic Joy.

'What do you bring to this, Messina? Muscle, is that all?'

'What do you care, Thorn?'

'Hey, I'm dead meat, what difference does it make if you satisfy my curiosity?'

'Fuck you. I'm not telling you shit.'

'Because see, what I think is, Vic is using you like he's using his biker dudes. You're maybe a half a point smarter than Marshall and Charlie, but basically you're just a big boulder Vic can hide behind when the guns go off. That's what I see going on here.'

'I got something he wants, shit-for-brains. I got leverage.'

'Yeah? Maybe you did when you were Salbone's lackey. But I don't see you bringing anything to the table now but about ten pounds of body hair.'

'You're wrong, asshole, as usual.'

'Anne knows the code, but you don't know it. Salbone didn't share it with you.'

'Salbone was paranoid. He was the only one who knew all the pieces.'

'And what piece did you know? How to drive the boat?'

'The contacts,' Marty said. 'I did the contacts.'

'Contacts?'

'See, you don't even know how the fuck it works.'

Thorn leaned back in his seat. Not interested anymore. Dozing off. It took almost a minute, but Marty couldn't leave it alone.

414

'Without the contacts, you got shit,' he said. 'Who you going to call to unload five thousand Honda motorcycles or generators or ten thousand gallons of olive oil, for chrissakes? Well, I know who to call. That's what I did. I got the contacts. Names, numbers, all of it.'

'And Vic needs you for that.'

'Damn right he does,' Marty said. 'Vic knows how to storm a fucking boat. He knows movie bullshit, and history. Sir Francis Fucking Drake and the *Golden Hind*, Harry Morgan, all those guys. But his connections are in real estate and marinas and business shit. Vic can steal all the product in the world, but he doesn't know squat about moving it. If you can't move it, you're fucked. Damn right he needs me. The man wants to expand to the big time, I'm indispensable.'

'Wow,' Thorn said. 'Indispensable.'

'Fucking-A I am.'

'What's with these code bullshit?' Thorn said. Eyes closed, head resting against the seat, like he could give a damn. Marty off-balance now, determined to prove Thorn the useless know-nothing he was.

'The code gets you into the shipping Web site.'

'Sounds boring,' Thorn said. 'I thought the pirate life was all thrills.'

'It's a business,' Marty said.

'Like I said, boring.'

'Hey, every fucking ship in the world of any size

415

is on that site. You got the code, then you know where they are every minute of every day, where they're going, what they're carrying. You can get their maintenance records, names of the crew, any fucking thing you want. Without the code, you're out there blind, sailing around looking for whatever the fuck comes along by chance. Or trying to follow ships out of port, tag along without being noticed. Or you gotta have a spy onboard, using a cell phone to send the GPS coordinates. But all that's bullshit. There's a hundred different ways it can fuck up. Having the code changes everything. Makes it efficient, makes it work.'

Thorn opened his eyes and looked at the big man. That little curl of hair was holding firm across the front of his black flattop, glistening like it was held in place by a glop of lard. Marty scowled back at Thorn, eyes pinched, chin hard; one more little shove and the swinging would start.

Marty Messina would've probably turned out okay if he hadn't been busted so young. Probably still be sitting on his stool at Tarpon's, married, with kids in junior high. Drinking too much, shooting off his mouth, rubbing shoulders with tourists and business hotshots around Key Largo. He could've pulled that off. Had enough raw smarts to supervise dishwashers and waitresses and bartenders. Getting his macho kicks bullying suppliers, using a little muscle to wrangle better prices on yellowtail and grouper and shrimp and lobster. But Marty didn't strike him as a guy fated to be a killer. Just a poor slob who got unlucky in his formative years and went to jail and took the crash course in dog-eat-dog one-upmanship that was required inside. When he got out, he was just as dim-witted as before, but now he was full of cocky swagger. Muscles pumped, brain dazed, whatever half-assed morals he'd had long gone. And then Salbone threw him a simple job. Essential to his operation, but no great challenge. Making phone deals, talking to guys around the globe who handled warehouses and trucks and drivers. Thorn didn't know for sure, but he suspected those guys were close relatives of guys he'd met who handled legitimate warehouses and trucks and drivers. Not talking neuroscience.

'So what's the pirate party about? Vic's coronation? He gets his crown, takes charge of the world?'

'You'll see soon enough.'

'And that's his entrée with these people, huh? The code.'

'Something like that.'

'Sounds like your run-of-the-mill hacker could figure that out. What's the big deal?'

'Don't be so sure,' Marty said. 'Salbone's computer guy was a freaking genius.'

'Whiz kids are a dime a dozen, Marty, haven't you heard? These days every ten-year-old is hacking the Defense Department.'

'Maybe,' he said. 'But nobody's thought of this. Salbone was the only one doing it. All those other disorganized fucks are out there cruising around without a clue, wasting fuel; half the time they hit a ship it's empty, deadheading back to port. They need the code and they damn well know it.'

'Any of these clowns actually met Vic? They know what they're getting into?'

'What's that supposed to mean?'

'The guy's a fuckup, Marty. You haven't noticed?'

Marty stared at him for a moment but said nothing. Then he busied himself with brushing lint off the chest of his black T-shirt and fixed his eyes on the seat back in front of him. Thinking about it, registering it, maybe for the first time – that he was going into battle with a full-fledged gonzo at the helm.

Thorn swiveled in his seat and peered back at Anne. She was hunched forward, eyes tight and wet, her body shaking, her sobs lost in the furious clamor of rushing wind and engine noise.

Thorn turned back to Marty, leaning into the aisle to be heard.

'Was it you who slit Jimmy Lee Webster's throat?'

'Yeah, like I'm going to talk about that shit with you.'

'I see you as more of a small-arms kind of guy. Bullet in the back of the head when no one's looking. Like those sad old folks on Markham's yacht the other night. But throat slitting, I don't know, that's too in-your-face for Marty Messina. Sounds more like a Vic Joy specialty.'

Marty looked up the aisle at the cockpit, check-ing Vic, seeing if he was eavesdropping through all that motor noise and vibration. He wasn't. Then Marty turned back to Thorn with a sour smile.

'You're pretty smart for a fucking dead man.'

'And those cages,' Thorn said. 'Got to hand it to you guys, that was a nice touch. A little historical flashback.'

'Marshall's a welder,' Marty said. 'He goes into Vic's workshop; half hour later, he's whipped one of those together. That little shit can fly.'

'Webster told me that he and Vic made some kind of deal. Vic copped a plea or something. What was that about?'

Marty considered it for a moment.

'You didn't know about that, Marty? He leave you in the dark?'

'I'm a full partner, asshole. I know every phase of the operation.'

'Is that right? So you knew about Webster? Or maybe that was one phase he left you out of, one of Vic's side deals?'

'Vic conned him,' Marty said. 'He was scamming him, that's all. Same as he does everybody. Webster was freelancing, trying to pick up some spare change. Hitting on Vic for payoffs, and Vic was leading him on.'

'Dirty? No way. Webster was a true believer.'

'Wouldn't call it dirty,' Marty said. 'More like the guy had aspirations.'

'What? To be a pirate? To join in?'

'Him and Vic were birds of a feather. Talking all that pirate shit. You should've heard those two dumb-shits go at it. Webster might've even known more than Vic. Buccaneers, privateers, brigands. Man, I get nosebleed listening to that crap. Like sitting in school.'

'He was Secretary of the Navy.'He's not going to flip for Vic Joy.'

'Webster fucked up somehow,' Marty said. 'A while back, I forget when. He ordered some ship to be sunk but got the wrong one. People died. Some damn thing like that. It was a big deal in the news-papers. They dragged his ass in front of a Senate hearing. It pissed him off and he never got over it. He was going to get his reputation back by bringing down Salbone, but deep down I guess he was still pissed at the navy and government types, so Vic got to him. Found his soft spot: pirates and money.'

'Found his soft spot, then whacked him.'

'Hell, Vic didn't do that,' Marty said. 'Him and me were off in the jungle when those guys got hit. Way I heard it, Webster and his friends kissed you good night and that was their last official act on earth. Old Marshall's pretty proud of himself. Him and Charlie taking down three big-time spies.'

Thorn remembered it then. The Cadillac pulling up to Webster's room, the two men getting out.

Marty said, 'What really turned Vic against the guy was how Webster kept going on about Salbone. Salbone this. Salbone that. This great big ex-Mafia guy, like he's some kind of rock star. Vic hated that. Hated hearing it all the time. Vic's offed Salbone, wiped out his crew, taken over his business, and he has to hear from Webster how great the guy is, how all the pirate hunters in the whole world are after him. I mean that was part of Vic's plan, make the law think Danny was still out there roaming around somewhere. Make them spend time looking for him while Vic went about his business. But he just got tired hearing that shit. Salbone, Salbone, Salbone. Pissed him off in a major way.'

'No respect,' Thorn said. 'Feeling slighted.'

'Vic's big on respect. Like guys I knew in the joint. Worst thing you could do was forget to salute when they came in the room.'

'If it was all a con, why'd Webster put on that big show for me? He had about a thousand slides, this big speech. Doesn't make sense.'

'You're not listening to me, man. Webster thought Salbone was still out there. He was working his ass off to nail him. Playing footsie with Vic on the side. That's all. It was just a matter of timing. He wound you up, sent you off, then he turned around and Marshall's there slitting his throat.'

'Well, it isn't going to work, Marty. Sooner or later, they'll put it together, realize Salbone's dead, follow the bread crumbs back to Vic.'

'Whatever you say, hotshot.'

'The feds aren't stupid. They're going to put it together.'

'He's got that covered, too. Vic's thought it all out. That's what you're for, Thorn, to take over after they finally put two and two together.'

Marty looked away.

'What're you saying?'

Marty laughed to himself.

'You don't get it, do you? Smart guy like you, missed the whole thing.'

Thorn was silent, eyes open now.

'They're going to put it on you, asshole.'

'What?'

'Put it on you. Make you the fall guy. You're sniffing after Anne, hanging with Vic, then when it's over, you're holding the shitcan. Vic wants your land, wants to do that bit of business with you, but it's not his way to do just one thing at a time. He's got this two birds, one stone philosophy. He takes your land, then hands you the shitcan and walks away. You're still alive, or you're dead, it doesn't matter.'

'How the hell could I be a fall guy?'

'Cops love guys like you, Thorn. You got no standing. What're you going to tell them, "Hey, wait, don't put me in jail, this guy, the Secretary of the fucking Navy, deputized me"? Yeah? Who the fuck's going to believe that?'

'Stupid, Marty. Never work.'

'Whatever you say, Thorn. You're the smart guy. Except you haven't been acting real smart lately. You swallowed the whole thing, just like Vic said you would, came charging into his place, acting all cool. Mr James Bond, secret agent, putting on a show for me. Man, it was all I could do to keep from laughing in your face. A fucking puppet on a string, Thorn. You and your buddy Sugarman, you guys were perfect, running around, making a big fuss. Getting the sheriff involved. Couldn't ask for more. So when Vic gives you up, everybody's all primed and ready to haul your ass off to the dungeon.'

'For what? I kidnapped my friend's daughter? I killed those people on the yacht? I killed Webster?'

'Could be,' Marty said. 'You got any alibis?'

'What garbage. Where's my motivation? Why'd I do it?'

'Ask Vic, it's his story line. He's working out some movie idea. He's the star, and you're the sucker. I'm sure Vic's got a line of bullshit ready. Do you, Thorn? You got a story anybody's going to believe?'

'Fuck that,' Thorn said. 'Nobody's going to believe I killed those guys, hung them up in cages in my own backyard.'

'Maybe, maybe not. I guess we'll have to see. Best story wins.'

'Sheriff may not be a fan of mine, but he won't buy that.'

'You heard Vic talk. Can you match that?' Marty chuckled. 'And look at it from the cops' angle. Is it easier for them to pin something on a hothead with a long history for fucking up or against Vic Joy? Owns half the Keys, two hundred lawyers on twenty-four-hour standby. My money's on you, bud. You're going down. One way or the other.'

Thorn stared at the bulkhead. It sounded crazy. Implausible as hell. But as he ran back through the last couple of days, he could recall an uncomfortable list of moments that would be hard to explain. Things he'd done that could be misconstrued, twisted around, made to appear suspicious. Wrong place, wrong time, giving Taft a ration of shit; Fox, too. Even Alexandra had doubted him enough to leave. Sugarman had stormed off.

He turned back to Marty. The big man was smiling at him.

'You realize, Marty, you've got some other feds sniffing your trail, too? Guy named Fox talked to me this afternoon. He seemed to have a bead on you and Vic. Been watching your place. Wouldn't surprise me if they're tagging along right now. Out there in the clouds behind us somewhere.'

Marty sneered.

'We got that covered, too. A diversionary movement.'

'Yeah? Hoodwinked the CIA, huh? You sure about that?'

Marty said, 'Three Cadillac limos go racing out of his place this afternoon. One right after another. Whole fleet of cars with the staff riding inside. Dark windows so nobody can tell what the fuck's going on. You're standing outside watching the front gate, what would you do?'

'Follow the Caddies,' Thorn said. 'If I'm stupid.'

'They are,' Marty said. 'Don't get your hopes up. The Caddies are still driving up I-95, headed to fucking Georgia with a convoy on their tail. Nobody's going to save your ass. You're done, you've made your last wisecrack, Lone Ranger.'

Thorn looked out his window for a few moments. Then turned slowly back to Marty.

'And what if Anne doesn't come across with the code? My bet is your new pirate friends are going to be a little disappointed. Might get messy.'

Marty worked up a grin.

'She'll come across.'

'You think she gives two shits what happens to me?'

'I saw the way you two were going at it; even if it was an act, you were turning each other on.'

Thorn watched a fly sail past Marty's head toward the small window next to him. It butted against the plastic, circled back, and butted again.

'Anne's in love with a dead man, Marty. A man you assholes killed. Why's she going to help you out?'

'Cause she's like you, Thorn. Cut from the same cloth.'

'Which cloth is that?'

'Guys like you, man, I've seen it over and over. You fuckers can't help yourselves.'

'So, tell me. I need to know. How do guys like me work?'

'You got your Dudley Do-Right rule book stashed in your mattress. Every night you get it out, memorize how to act tomorrow.'

'I wish,' Thorn said.

'Stand up and salute, recite the pledge. That's who you are.'

'My mattress burned up back there, Marty. The rule book's in ashes.'

'You fuckers always got a cute answer. Well, this time you don't, Thorn. This time it's me and Vic with the cute answer.'

'Anne won't give you the code,' he said. 'She doesn't care about me.'

'You better hope she cares.'

'Between you and me, Marty, I can't see her helping out with anything her brother wants to do. Ever again.'

'A couple more hours, I guess we'll see about that.'

'Yeah,' Thorn said. 'I guess we will.'

29

'The sign, Daddy.'

'What? Huh?'

Sugarman had dozed off, head down on his folded arms lying atop the little antique desk. Alexandra waked him with a thump on the back. Janey was whispering again; in the background the machine-gun fire had ceased. Sugar rubbed the focus back into his eyes.

'The sign, I saw the sign.'

'You did? Good. Good.'

'Two men were fighting and they bumped into it and knocked it crooked and now I can see it. Part of it.'

'What's it say?'

'*G-r-a-y-g-h,*' she said, spelling it out. 'That's all

I could see. Two words. Gray something.'

'Okay, Janey, that's terrific. We can use that. It'll help, I'm sure it will.'

'I feel terrible, Daddy. I'm hot and I'm shivering and I've been throwing up. My stomach really hurts.'

'Have you been drinking the Cokes, sweetheart?'

'No.'

'Do it, darling. Drink a Coke. You need fluids.'

'They're Chinese, I think.' She was whispering again.

'Chinese?'

'The men outside. Some of them are Chinese. They killed an agouti, Daddy. They shot it and cut its fur off right outside my cabin. It was gross. And some other kind of people are out there, too, not just Chinese. Weird talking.'

'How many people have you seen?'

'I don't know.'

'More than ten?'

'Yeah, more than that.'

'Twenty?'

'I don't know, Daddy. A lot. A lot of people. Mostly men. But some women, too. And some of them have those things you used to use in the backyard to cut down the agave plant. A big blade.'

'Machete?'

'Yeah, a machete. Some of the men are waving those around.'

Sugarman sat straight in the chair. The air hardening in his lungs.

'Listen, Janey, listen to me, okay?'

'Okay.'

'We're coming to get you.'

'You are? When?'

'As soon as we can figure out this last thing. But soon.'

'Tonight?'

'Soon,' Sugarman said. 'But we need to know where you are, which cabin. What the arrangement looks like.'

'Arrangement?'

'The way things are spread out. How many buildings there are? How they're spaced? Are you on one end of the area or the other?'

'I'm south, Daddy. I'm on the south. There's, I don't know, five or six buildings I can see. All of them look alike, except for one big one that has a screen porch. Mine is next to a little pond.'

'Okay, that's super. You're doing a fantastic job. Now, Janey, you need to go into the bathroom and shut the door and lock it.'

'The battery thing is blinking, Daddy. The computer is making a beep.'

'Okay, okay. Listen, go into the bathroom right now, Janey, and lock the door and stay there until—'

But his screen had gone flat again, the hiss of static silent.

'Oh, God. Jesus Christ.'

Alexandra laid a hand on his shoulder. Telling

him in a soothing voice that it was going to be all right. They'd figure it out. They would.

'I don't know,' he said. 'Jesus God, help me.'

'You have a dictionary, Sugar?'

He turned and looked up at her.

'Dictionary?'

She waited.

'On the shelf in the living room by the TV.'

She patted him on the shoulder, but Sugarman hardly registered it. He was staring at his crappy computer. His daughter's image vanished. He tried to picture it – the way that fragile beam of electrons had fired out of the Central American rain forest and launched into the atmosphere, where it bounced off some passing satellite, then ricocheted back to Earth and found its way through a thousand miles of cables to his machine, carrying her voice, her face. The magic of that. The horror of it. The aching emptiness he felt now that the machine was silent.

Sugarman's shoulders were draped with a lead shawl. His breath was dead in his lungs, chest cavity gutted.

He heard Lawton snoring on the daybed and Alexandra in the next room paging through the dictionary. The puppy had awakened and was chewing at a flea on his tail. More sirens screamed on the highway. But he wasn't there. He was locked in a small, foul-smelling bathroom. He was huddled on the floor gripping a pair of eleven-hundred-dollar binoculars to his chest. He was sipping on a Coke and shivering and trying not to cry. Hot and cold and aching in every joint. He was a thousand nautical miles away, surrounded by strange foreign men with automatic weapons and God only knew what else. He was alone. More alone than he'd ever been before. The screams of the jungle, the heat and stench and darkness.

Alexandra dragged a chair up beside him.

'I know,' she said. 'This is hard. You're overcome.'

'That's not the half of it.'

She touched his cheek, took hold of his chin, and guided it around so he was facing her.

'But we need to shake this off. We have to go online for a few minutes.'

'What?'

'Gray *g-h*,' she said. 'We need to do a search.'

He was groggy now. Sleepless for two days, hardly any food. Pulse falling from its frantic high to some bottomless place. A beat, then a pause while the globe spun a complete rotation before another beat came. He was finished. It was over.

'*G-h*.' Alexandra flopped the dictionary open on the desk beside him. 'There's only a few *g-h* words. *Ghastly, ghetto, ghibil, ghost, ghoul*. Only a few, and only one that really fits with *gray*.'

He wasn't following her. He was huddled in that bathroom. The men prowling outside. Men peeking in the window, pulling the boards loose. Drunk, crazed men.

'Sugarman? Are you listening to me?'

'Yeah,' he said. 'Trying to.'

'Gray Ghost,' she said. 'It's the only one that makes sense.'

'Bonefish,' Sugar said. 'Gray ghost. That's its nick-name.'

'Okay,' she said. 'That's good. Now we need to go on-line. We've got to search this. We know it's a region on the Central American coast and we know something there is called Gray Ghost.'

'Yeah,' Sugarman said. But he was still riding that shaft of light, a laser that rose from the jungle floor and pierced the sky and came rocketing back to Earth with his daughter's voice riding along, Janey's face and her thrill over toucans and her fright and pain.

Alexandra swiveled the computer to the side and tapped the touch pad a few times, and he heard the modem's chirp and squall as it connected to the server. She tapped more keys and then a few moments later she spoke quietly: 'Okay, okay, good.'

'What is it?' Sugarman said.

'Twenty-two hits,' she said. She swiveled the computer so he could see, then scrolled down the list. 'Most of it is John Mosby, a Civil War soldier. Also known as "the Gray Ghost."'

'Civil War?' Sugar's mind was stuttering, two steps out of sync.

Alex worked down the list, brought up each Web page that seemed likely, scanned it, and quickly moved on. In three or four minutes she was done.

'We could try another search engine, but this is usually the best. Google.'

'How do you know this stuff?'

'It's very basic, Sugar, I use it at work. Now "Gray *Ghost, Central America*." Is there another thing to try, another word?'

'*Nicaragua*,' he said.

She tapped it in, got over sixteen hundred hits. They scanned the list together, Sugarman starting to come out of it, head clearing, feeling this had to work. The last resort.

'Too many,' he said. 'Try *gray ghost, kingfisher*, and *Central America*.'

Alex killed the first search and tapped in the fresh parameters.

A few seconds later, she said, 'Nothing, no documents.'

'All right, try *gray ghost* and *Costa Rica*.'

'I thought you said "Nicaragua."'

Sugarman reached out and grabbed the pages of notes he'd made, pawed through them quickly, found the map he'd cut out of the encyclopedia.

'This longitude, eighty-four degrees west, it skims into the northeastern edge of Costa Rica. The kingfisher overlaps with that, too.'

She put it in. *Gray ghost* and *Costa Rica*. A half-second later the hits came up.

'Here,' she said. 'Right there.' She touched a finger to the screen, the third item down. 'Gray Ghost Lodge. A fishing camp. Ten cabins, on the coast of

Costa Rica in the Barra de Colorado, Limón Province. Bingo.'

'Double bingo.'

He was fully awake now, staring at the computer as Alex brought up the Web page for the Gray Ghost Lodge. The page taking forever to load.

The three small pictures finally unspooled, showing a clearing in the jungle. Wood cabins, walkways, a marina, small airstrip. Five hundred dollars a day to fish for tarpon and bonefish or take guided ecotours into the rain forest. 'A vast array of exotic wildlife,' the ad copy said. 'Toucans, three-toed sloths. The lodge offers a rare combination of quality service, comfort, and unspoiled wilderness. The complete isolation provides an atmosphere of absolute relaxation.'

'You have any idea where this is, Sugar?'

'I don't,' he said. Feeling a flood of heat in his face and chest. 'But we're about to find out.'

'It's four-thirty in the morning, for chrissakes,' Kirk Graham said on the phone. 'I got a trip tomorrow, Rio and back with a one-day turnaround.'

Lawton was inside the house sleeping while Alex stood next to Sugar out on the front porch. He was using his cell to keep from waking the old man.

'Hey, Kirk, I'm desperate. You're my last chance.'

'Man, I got to fly tomorrow. Didn't you hear me?'

'It's about Janey, my daughter. She's been

434

kidnapped and she's being held in the jungle in Costa Rica.'

'Christ, call the police.'

'Kirk, listen to me. I need an amphibian. A plane like the one we saw at Vic Joy's. Steal it, rent it, borrow it, whatever it takes. But we need it, and we need it now.'

Kirk laughed.

'You don't want much.'

'Can you do it, Kirk?'

'And I guess you want me to fly it, too, over to Costa Rica?'

'I guess I do, yeah.'

'Man, Sugar. Man, oh, man.'

'Do you know where we can get a plane like that?'

Kirk was silent for a moment. Alex was staring up at the stars, a clear night, the heavens peeled open to reveal all their secrets.

'There is this one guy I know,' Kirk said.

'Great,' Sugarman said.

'But I don't know about the range. It's a beauty of a plane, a big single-engine Cessna Caravan. But hell, a thousand nautical miles, I don't know, that might be a hundred or so beyond what this baby can do on a single tank.'

'So we'll stop somewhere and fill up again.'

'Out in the middle of the Gulf of Mexico? Right.'

'And there'll be two others along. Adults.'

'Two others? Jesus. That's cutting it damn close, Sugar.'

'They're coming, Kirk. No way I can leave them behind.'

'Well, we'll have to stay low, avoid the head-winds. That would offset some of it. Maybe clip Cuba a little.'

'Where do we meet you, Kirk? Give me a location.'

Alexandra brought her eyes down from the heavens. She smiled at Sugar and balled her hand into a fist and held it shoulder-high. Yeah!

With his blue duffel full of handguns sitting by the front door and Alex and Lawton waiting on the porch, Sugarman went back into the guest bedroom, sat down at the desk, and reconnected to Markham's server and clicked his way to the video chat room. The screen was blank. Outside his back window, the sun was beginning to waken the mockingbirds and blue jays. On a low branch a fat squirrel twitched its tail at a neighbor's cat and jeered.

He waited for a minute in the empty room.

Alexandra came to the bedroom door and stood there for a few seconds watching him.

'We'd better get going, Sugar. It's six, seven hours. We'll be lucky to get there by noon.'

'I know. I know.'

Alex dug into the pocket of her jeans and came out with a business card and held it up.

'I got to call this guy,' she said. 'Before we go, I have to call him.'

'Who?' Sugarman stared at the empty screen.

'Agent Fox, the guy I told you about at Thorn's. You understand that, don't you? It's my duty.'

'I understand.'

Sugarman was still staring at the empty screen.

'I don't want to do it,' Alex said. 'I know how those SWAT types can be. When he hears about this, he'll come with everything they've got. All those thugs gathered in one spot. I mean, I could try to wheedle a promise out of him. Rescuing Janey would be his top priority or I refuse to give him the details.'

'You can't do that,' Sugar said.

'It's what Thorn would do. He'd finagle something. He wouldn't play by their rules.'

'You're not Thorn. You've got obligations.'

'I don't know, Sugar. But with all those men in that camp, the place swarming with them, I just don't know. It's such a volatile situation, no way to know how it'll break if the feds hit them head-on.'

'We can't control their strategy,' Sugar said.

'You sure? It's your call.'

'It's the right thing to do,' he said. 'They're the proper authorities.'

'Are you all right? You sound like you've given up.'

'No,' he said. 'I'm all right. You'll call Fox, because it's what's right and proper. But just don't do it till the last second before we take off. That way the chances are we'll get there first. If the layout looks right, we take a shot, just you and me. We know where Janey is. We make a run at it before the cavalry arrives.'

'I can live with that,' she said.

Sugarman pushed back his chair and was reaching for the touch pad to disconnect when there was a tiny pop and Janey's ghostly face materialized on the screen.

'Holy shit.' Sugarman sat up straight. 'Janey?'

'I've been trying,' she said. 'The battery's beeping, it might go out. But I had to try.'

'What is it, sweetie? We're about to leave. We know where you are now, we're on our way.'

'Thorn's here,' she said.

'What?'

'He's in a cage, hanging from a tree, Daddy. It's Thorn. I looked at him in the binoculars. He's hanging from a limb. I don't know if he's still alive.'

And she was gone.

Sugar was getting into Alex's car when he heard his phone ringing. He sprinted back, got the door open, made it to the phone, ripped it up. Dead.

He punched in the star code to callback and got a young man's voice.

'Who is this?'

'Who is *this*?' the young man said.

'This is Sugarman. You just called me.'

'Oh, yeah, hello. This is Special Agent Meeker. I was told by Agent Sheffield that you needed a call trace on a satellite phone.'

'Already did it,' Sugar said. 'The old-fashioned way.'

And hung up and sprinted to the car.

30

Anne Bonny Joy was lying on the mattress she and Daniel had shared for so short a time. His scent was gone from the pillow. Replaced now by a musty scent and the tang of wood smoke from the dying bonfires. Only the last wisps still rose from the embers.

Outside, men were sprawled in the shade on blankets and in bedrolls; the ones she supposed had more status were crammed into a few of the cabins. She'd seen a couple of women, too, as she and Vic and Thorn and the others had tramped up from the marina a while ago. Prostitutes, from the look of them, small half-naked Mayan women curled close beside the sleeping men. The gagging stench of sweat and putrid food filled the camp.

Whiskey bottles littered the grounds; automatic weapons and handguns lay close beside the sleepers; machetes had been stuck deep into several trees. Everywhere she looked there were scraps of bread and tortillas, chicken bones, and the charred remains of greasy meat hanging from spits. There were even some fast-food Styrofoam containers scattered about, as if some of the men had made a quick stop in San José or Puerto Limón to pick up food along with the women before finishing the last short leg to the jungle.

Two small planes were parked on the short asphalt runway. Several boats and a small trawler were tied up at the marina. Anchored a half-mile offshore she'd seen three heavily chromed sportfishing yachts. Boats that cost millions, though more than likely their current owners had not paid a cent for them.

She'd counted maybe thirty men as she picked her way to the cabin and found it empty. Reserved for Vic and his entourage.

Now she was alone, lying flat on her back, staring up at the naked rafters, listening to the rain forest. That at least had gone unchanged, the clamor of the jungle, the songs of insects, the hiss and shriek and cawing of dozens of hidden creatures, flittering and darting just beyond the range of sight. Listening to it. As she listened to the bright noise, the screams of ecstasy and terror, her head gradually cleared. The dense mist parted. And without warning, all her senses seemed to clear. She saw and smelled and heard everything, absolutely everything. No thoughts, no worries, no grief, no confusion.

Just this! This place in the wild. The reek of the moment. Only those noises and the perfume of wood smoke. No Anne Bonny. No Antoinette and Jack Joy. No Harlan. Nothing but the sag of the mattress beneath her weight, the rising light, the voices waking outside, men stirring.

It felt religious. Like incense in a cathedral, and sunlight fractured through stained glass, and organ music swelling in the enormous sanctuary. The holiness. A vast opening inside her, filling with light, filling with sacred oxygen. Like nothing mattered. Like she didn't matter. For the first time. For the first time since before she could remember being alive. Way, way, way back before anything. Before galleons, before the dreary, ridiculous pirate novels, before breath itself.

Just this. Just this place, this mattress and this cabin and this body.

Drunk, stoned, ecstatic, swimming beyond herself, rising through an airless grave to break through to the oxygen, the holy air. It didn't matter. It truly didn't. None of it. Loving, hating. Living, dying. Every touch, every word and gesture. It was just flux. Simply the endless ticker tape of trivia.

Anne stood up. She walked without knowing where she was headed. To the heavy oak dresser that stood against the west wall. Looking at it for a moment, then reaching out and opening the third drawer. In a swoon, a dreamy wakefulness, she pulled out the empty drawer. Turned it over. Carried it back to the cot.

Peeled off the adhesive. Held the cool weight, the mechanical beauty of blued steel. Fit her hand to it. No need to check the magazine. She knew it was loaded, she'd watched Daniel do it, watched him tape it there so many ages ago. The Beretta .25-caliber. Perfect for the purse. Perfect for her hand that curled around it and hefted it like some hallowed stone, some bright precious gem full of luxurious light, richly bright, terrible and mighty and utterly without meaning. That's where everything had led. To this wild place. This Eden where everything had started, where everything was about to end.

Just this!

Okay, so maybe Thorn was still alive, maybe he wasn't. At that second, he didn't know. All he knew was that his brain was busy with a vision of a few hours earlier when he'd first arrived at Vic Joy's compound and Vic had examined his body so carefully. Like a slave trader at auction. And now Thorn knew what that was all about. Measuring him for his new suit, all this thought out in advance. Giving himself plenty of time to construct this metal cage that Marshall and the other biker had hauled out of the rear of the floatplane, clanking and rattling, then lugged it up the hill to the campground.

When he'd seen what was coming, Thorn had chosen that precise moment to move. Swiveling on Marty, he'd popped him once in the point of his jaw and sent him reeling backward into the two bikers. But Vic's silent rage at Thorn had given him hair-trigger reflexes.

Vic clipped him hard on the skull, and as Thorn wavered, watching a flock of toucans fluttering into the sky, Vic cracked him a second time and sent him down into the splintered darkness.

When he woke, he was suited in the armor, suspended ten feet off the ground. Still alive, maybe, but it was taking a while to be absolutely sure. The sensation bleeding back inch by inch, fingertips, toes, joint by joint, lips and tongue, the soft tissue parts of him.

A good view of the grounds from up there. Ten cabins, a dining hall. Men gathering around the tree branch to horse around and punch one another in excitement and celebration. A giant party favor hung out for their amusement. Thorn, the piñata.

Either he was alive or else in the first few minutes of death some lagging senses still operated and allowed the freshly departed one final glimpse of the world's harsh beauty.

Thorn scanned his body. Felt the throbbing crack in his skull, worked lower through his neck and chest and torso, where the twin wounds from Vic's fountain pen had begun to fester, then went guardedly down to his crotch to see if there was deadness

444

there or the warm flow of blood, or any sign that Vic had completed his castration. But he felt nothing, and with a heave of relief, he sent his mind down each leg. Both of them were numb but with growing twinges of awareness, the creak and swell and bruised tenderness of kneecaps and shinbone and the other dozen parts that apparently had been well scuffed as he was locked inside that custom-fitted cage.

Flexing his parts, he was surprised to discover there was give in the metal. Softer than steel. Tin perhaps. He could twist his foot to the side, wriggle it a half-inch against the bite of the bands, and feel some elastic movement. He tried his wrists, up and back, bringing sudden blood to his arm and waking a hundred needles that poked in unison into his flesh.

Some of the men below him had started dinking pebbles at him. Bits of food. A rabble collecting, other men waking their brethren from slumber, gabbling at them and pointing up at Thorn. Oh, what fun. A man hanging from a tree in a metal suit. Still half-dark, a cloudy twilight, a hot storm building in the western sky. Pebbles struck his belly and his arms and one sharp stone drew a trickle of blood from his cheek. A couple of tall Hispanic men stood aloof at the back of the mob, watching carefully with the cold disdain of professionals.

Small dark women joined the fray, flinging whatever they could grab in wild pitches that mostly missed. The high, wailing jibber of another continent, another race. Thorn was feeling oddly detached. Working his wrist against the supple restraints. Feeling the pressure on the arches of his feet and his crotch, a pinching at both his armpits. Tailored a bit too tight across the chest. That suit would need some letting out if he was going to wear it in polite gatherings. Which this gang assembling below him most definitely was not.

He'd spotted a cabin off to one end of the encampment. Boards nailed across its windows and a couple across the door. A prison cell. And though he had no more than that to go on, it seemed ample evidence to assume that this was where Janey Sugarman had been stashed.

Which gave new energy to his rocking movements, done in full view of the crowd below but no doubt mistaken for the flinching of panic. Thorn could feel the metal at his right wrist already on the verge of parting, so he began to work on a fresh band at the other wrist. Back and forth, trying to duplicate the motion exactly, making a crease and working it till the soft tin began to split.

Changing his focus, Thorn peered at the two strips of metal that were only inches from his eyes and detected the silver puddles where the separate bands had been fused. The end of one band overlapping the end of another, the joints held together by a simple dot of solder, not welding at all. Like those plastic straps used to seal cardboard boxes. Impossible to break with a tug, but pry a fingernail under the juncture, they popped easily apart.

What it looked like was that all Thorn had to do was work his hands free, then reach up and peel apart each and every seam. The soldering would have been sufficient if the frame held a corpse, but for a live man, a man brimming with fury, the gibbet wouldn't last a day of serious testing. If he had a day. If he had an hour. He wasn't sure. Hadn't heard that part of the plan.

Beyond that, the physics of his situation were sketchy. He was having trouble feeling how his weight was distributed, some on his lower parts, some on his crotch. It would seem like the helmet should be taking most of the stress, except that's not how it felt. There were chains connecting the helmet directly to his lower parts, and when he jiggled the few inches he could manage, shifting slightly off-center, he felt the pressure mostly on his feet. Which was excellent. He sure as hell didn't want to peel out of the suit only to find that he'd suddenly shifted his entire mass to the band around his throat.

On the flight he'd had Marty on the run, milking him for the facts, but he hadn't thought to question him about how they planned to extort the code from Anne. They'd hinted torture, but Thorn had been imagining a gun at his temple, and in his scenario Anne had immediately wilted. Without consciously realizing he was doing it, Thorn had pictured that moment as his best chance for escape.

The split second when the gang of pirates turned to the computer and tried out the code and showed it off to the others, he'd make his break.

But he hadn't pictured the gibbet cage. Had under-estimated Vic Joy's devotion to the outrageous. Thorn's mistake. He wouldn't do it again. If there was an again. If there was an hour. Or ten minutes.

He worked his wrists against the pliant tin and ducked and cringed as the hail of pebbles continued.

The cigar was for show. Vic didn't like the taste, but it gave him a certain gravity, which he felt he needed in this situation, so he lit up and took a puff or two, but after five minutes he dropped the stinking thing on the plank floor of the screened-in dining hall and stubbed it out with the heel of his boot. They'd only been at this for minutes, barely gotten past the howdy-dos, and already things had tightened up. Language barrier for starters, not to mention the culture gap.

In all there were four of them, the leaders of the rabble hooting outside. Three Chinese guys who between them controlled hundreds of ships in the Far East. Two of the Chinese guys were so indistin-guishable to Vic, it would've taken him a week with a microscope and color chart to tell them apart. The fourth man was a tall, slender, bearded Latino who resembled the ancient news photos of a young Fidel coming down from the hills in triumph. That was

Ramon Bella, a Venezuelan who'd been buying most of the yachts and sailboats Vic had commandered in the last few years. His phone pal till today.

Ramon was businesslike, razor smart, and though this was the first time Vic had met the man in the flesh, he felt the beginnings of rapport. But the Chinese fucks were another story. Snippy little men who twittered incessantly to one another, then shook their heads at once like three toy monkeys on a stick.

Side by side they sat in stiff-backed wooden chairs. One medium height, while the twins were barely five feet. Those two short ones wore dark pajama pants and white blousy shirts, and the third guy, the bigger one who spoke a few words of English, had on a dark blue jumpsuit like a paramedic.

Ad lib time hadn't gone well. Nobody talking. Vic doing all the adding and libbing, floundering around, trying to warm them up, get them to laugh, anything. Without planning it, he'd started telling them about the movie he was planning. A full-length feature film. Lots of action, derring-do, pirates as heroes, get the facts right for once. But they'd looked at him blankly, not saying a word, so he decided, fuck it, it was time to deliver the pitch.

Vic stepped in front of them and looked at each up close – the Chinese guys stared back at him as coldly as three slit-eyed copperheads.

He started his spiel with a little history, talking about Sir Francis Drake. A guy empowered by the queen of England herself to attack the Spanish Main.

Vic reminding the Chinese guys how Drake had taken the *Cacafuego* near Cape San Francisco just north of the equator, not all that far from where they stood right now. A ship laden with gold and silver bars, silver coins, tons of bullion. The greatest pirate haul of all time. Drake went on to sack cities, plunder cathedrals, pillage and more pillage. Even got knighted for his efforts, retired to the English countryside. Maybe, just maybe, they'd get that lucky themselves, find a country that valued their hard work, rewarded them with that nation's highest honor. He knew it was a little extreme, but it had happened once; why not again?

The Chinese guys looked puzzled or bored, so he brought the speech to a close, saying that all Sir Francis Drake had done was nothing compared to what they were going to accomplish, with their concerted efforts, their joined forces, their synergy. And of course with Vic Joy's leadership.

When he was done, the Chinese guys talked among themselves for a few seconds, then the whole bunch of them snickered. Looking at Vic and tittering like twelve-year-olds. Like Vic had just told a long and idiotic joke. Like they'd never heard of Drake or Sir Henry Morgan or William Dampier. Doing what they were doing without any historical perspective, without a sense of the tradition or dignity of their profession. Bunch of savages.

Vic waved his hand like he was washing away a bad smell.

'Marty, talk to these friends of yours. They're starting to piss me off.'

'They're not my friends, Vic. I talk to them on the phone is all.'

'You must've been talking to their goddamn translator then, 'cause we don't seem to be getting through to these guys.'

'They got more English than they're letting on, Vic.'

'Ask 'em why they came all this way if they don't want to deal.'

'You ask them. It's your goddamn party.'

Vic turned back to them again. Toughest audience he'd ever had. He looked around the big dining room, gathering himself. Eyes falling on a small brown thing up high in the far corner. He stepped that way, peered up. Thing was hugging the wood, some kind of brown furry creature.

'It's a bat, Vic. They're all over the place.' Marty pointed around the room. And Vic saw them, counted a dozen, and stopped.

'Jesus Christ.'

'It's the jungle, man. That's the way it is.'

Vic had just been looking at the Chinese guys and hadn't been tuned in to anything else, but now as he glanced around he noticed on the front windowsill the long green shape of an iguana. Sunning itself there. Big saw-toothed hump running down its back. Eyes closed, dreaming of fruit. Twice as big as any he'd seen before in the Keys. Last time he'd been here to drop the girl off, seal up her cabin, and split. He'd taken only the quickest look and liked the lay of the land.

'Fucking place is infested,' Vic said.

'They live here,' Marty said. 'We're just passing through.'

Vic looked back at the Chinese men. Six eyes staring at him uneasily like they thought Vic was about to crack. He cleared his throat, rubbed his hands together, got back to it.

'All right, gentlemen. So come on, what's the fucking point here? If you don't want to join forces, why come all this way? You writing this off on your taxes? A little expense-paid holiday?'

One of the Chinamen chattered something back at Vic.

'They want the code,' Ramon Bella said. 'That's why we're here, to get the code.'

'You understand that gobbledygook, Ramon?'

Ramon made no gesture, just looked deep into Vic's eyes. Bella's fatigues were scruffier than Vic's and Marty's. Hard-used. Just one more reason that Vic now felt the sudden sting of silliness, like he'd overdressed, overprepared, overdone the whole goddamn gathering, like he was an impostor, a clown, a boy among men. And these guys were the real thing. No bullshit slingers, just ruthless brutes full of contempt for this gaudy American.

The same sensation had come in waves all his fucking life. From the Harlan playground right on

452

till today. Kids mocking him, making fun of his gift of gab, his talk talk talk. And Vic fighting back the only way he knew, with more words and more. Heaping them on, talking till his antagonists were dizzy and exhausted and walked away. Later on he beat back the sensation by listing to himself all his successes. The zeros on his bank account. The yachts he'd taken, the lives he'd snuffed. He didn't need to impress a bunch of Chinese fucks. Who the hell were those little twits? Paint some whiskers on their upper lips, they'd look like mole rats.

Then why the hell was he feeling that rube-from-the-hills thing? That squirmy, holding-back-a-fart feeling that he was being ridiculed, playing the fool. Heat flushing his cheeks. That queasy sense that everything in Vic Joy's world was founded on a lie, teetering near collapse. Why the hell was that, when all the facts said otherwise?

'You want the code, do you?'

The Chinaman in the jumpsuit said, 'We don't need history lesson. We know plenty of history already. What we need is the code.'

'So you'll get the code. But you'll damn well pay for it.'

'Of course,' the Chinaman said. 'We prepare for that.'

Ramon Bella rose and sighed with exasperation.

'I've set up my laptop, Vic, over here on the big table. Satellite relay. We need a demonstration, then we negotiate the numbers.'

'And then what? Go our separate ways?' Vic said. 'Miss this golden opportunity to merge our skills, blend our organizations?'

'We're independents, Vic. None of us are looking for a leader. We *are* leaders.'

'Apparently there was a misunderstanding then.' Vic swung around and stared at Marty. 'Or was there?'

Marty gave him back the look.

'You pulling a Salbone on me, Marty? That what it is? Somebody make you a better offer?'

'Fuck, no. They wanted the code, you wanted a meeting. I made both things happen.'

'You sure, Marty? You positive about that?'

'I may have fudged a little about them wanting to work with you. But that's all. I didn't think you'd mind. That's how you operate, right? A little exaggeration now and then. It's a simple deal. You give them the code, make some money, everybody's happy. What do you care? They're over on one side of the world doing their thing, we're over here doing ours.'

Vic rubbed the bristles on his cheek and looked at the gathered men, then back at Marty.

'It's okay when I fudge, Marty. But you don't get the same privileges.'

Ramon walked over to the head table and fiddled with his laptop.

'Okay,' said Ramon. 'We will see it before we buy it. And I pray that no one has exaggerated what this process can do. We have all put ourselves in an awkward position by coming here, Vic, and I know I speak for my friends when I say that if this is some kind of hoax, we're going to be gravely disappointed.'

'Go get Anne, Marty.'

'Anne?' Ramon asked.

'My sister. She's the expert in the code.'

'You don't know how to operate it yourself, Vic?'

'Anne's the expert.'

Ramon gave the Chinamen a darting look.

'All right then,' he said. 'Someone should go get Anne. The expert.'

Vic was about to say something more, give him assurances, soothe the guy, when he saw the bright green lump on the floor in front of him. A frog looking up at him with red bulging eyes. A frog had hopped out of nowhere during Vic's speech. A goddamn frog mocking him, too.

'Am I seeing things, Marty? Does that fucking frog have red eyes?'

'It's a frog, man. What's wrong with you?'

'I know it's a frog. But look at it. Jesus Christ, you didn't tell me there were all these fucking outer space things here.'

Ramon cleared his throat.

'Yeah, yeah, okay.' Vic motioned at Marty. 'Go get Anne. Time for the demonstration. On your way back point out Thorn. Let her know what's at stake here.'

As Marty was turning to leave, outside on the

plaza a woman shrieked and a man barked an order and another man laughed raucously. Vic leaned to the side and peered out a window. Thorn was still swaying in his gibbet cage, but the pack of idiots was no longer tossing rocks at him. They'd moved several yards away and had circled something he couldn't see. Vic walked out to the porch for a better view.

'Marty! Get out here.'

Messina trotted to the porch.

'Some of those coolie dumbshits pulled the boards down and carried that little girl out of her cabin and now they're messing with her. Go get Annie and hurry up. We got to get this done before it all turns to shit.'

'What about the kid?'

'Kid's irrelevant. Thorn'll sign whatever I put in front of him. I'll fucking cut off little pieces of him till he signs. We don't need the girl.'

'Just going to let those wolves have her?'

'Do what I said, go get Anne. She shows these guys the code, we get our money and we get the hell out of this stinking jungle.'

'You wanted a pirate hideaway, Vic. I thought you liked this place.'

'Too creepy for me, man, way too many weird creatures.'

31

Kirk Graham had been staring at the fuel gauge for the last hour. Glancing now and then at the rest of his instruments, keeping them on course, but mainly watching that needle fall. When they sighted the first dark silhouette of land, he seemed to start breathing again.

'It's a miracle we made it.'

'We haven't yet,' Sugarman said.

Alexandra leaned forward from the first row.

'Hey, whose plane is this anyway?'

'Guy I play tennis with,' Kirk said. 'Judge Carney, Seventeenth Circuit. Has a weekend place down in Tavernier.'

'Oh, great,' Sugar said. 'A judge.'

'It's all right,' Kirk said. 'Bobby's cool. Did some

crazy stuff himself back in the bad old days. If we make up a good-enough story, embellish it a little, he'll love that he was part of something colorful.'

'Embellish it?' Alex said. 'Let's hope we have to.'

Lawton shouted from the last row.

'You heard this one?'

'What, Dad?'

'"A good explanation never explains anything."'

'That's good,' Sugarman said. 'Keep that one in the routine, Lawton.'

Kirk skimmed north along the coastline, jungle, jungle, and more jungle. No clearings. No sign of civilization of any kind. Some rivers, estuaries, lagoons. But Sugarman saw nothing resembling the Gray Ghost Lodge.

'You sure about the coordinates, Kirk?'

'We're close. You said you didn't want me to fly right into the place.'

'Right,' Sugar said. 'Yeah, that's good.'

'Another mile or two, if the gas holds out. I'll put it down just short and you can use the inflatable.'

'Keep Lawton amused, would you? While we're gone.'

Sugarman turned and looked back at the old man and Alexandra sitting quietly in the rear. The puppy was curled up asleep in the aisle.

'And how do I do that, keep him amused?'

'Ask him about Ohio, where he grew up. He loves to talk about that.'

Kirk swallowed and looked back at Sugarman.

'I was a fighter pilot in Nam,' he said. 'Went through basic, fired an M-16 on the range like everybody else, but I never was much of a shot. I flinch.'

'It's okay, Kirk. We can handle this. You stay with the plane. Wait for us. If someone doesn't get back to you in a couple of hours, then you make your decision. Fly inland, fuel up, go home. We'll understand. This isn't your fight.'

Kirk kept them skimming low, a mile offshore, the jungle still solid.

'You got the right coordinates?'

'I *can* read a map, Sugar. It's up ahead. Right around that point, look.'

And yes, he saw the clearing in the distance. Not much. Might've missed it if he'd blinked. A thumbprint carved out of the dense green landscape. Small cabins, a tiny marina. Three good-sized yachts anchored offshore.

A good distance short of the camp, Kirk swung the plane out to sea.

'I'll put it down back near that cove. It's maybe half a mile, south. That be all right?'

'I owe you, Kirk. I owe you a big one.'

'We got here,' he said. 'But I don't know if we have fuel to go anywhere else.'

'We'll be okay,' Sugar said. 'Don't worry. I got a good feeling about this.'

* * *

459

All those years Anne had kept herself shut down. Stopped the feelings. Now here they came. A volcanic spew. Like she was going insane. Or no, maybe what it was, she'd always been crazy, driven that way by her childhood, her tainted blood, by the killings she'd carried out as a kid. Always been crazy, from the very start, and now she was going sane.

Yeah, yeah, that's what was happening to her, going sane. Seeing everything clearly for the first time, everything with a bright, stenciled outline. A sharp focus. The world as it was. The world made simple and clear.

They wanted the code. Whether she gave it to them or not, Vic would go on being Vic. And the world would muddle ahead being the world. It didn't matter if she did or didn't. None of it mattered. But as she considered the code itself, the idea hit her. Another lava flow of thoughts, another revelation. All those ones and zeros, that binary stuff. Computers were built on that. Everything was built on that. The whole world could be captured that way; photographs, music, every sense could be caught. If not now, then eventually, just a matter of time before they found a way. Everything was binary. One, zero. Plus, minus. On, off. It was the code, the way it was written. The way her own brain worked. The way her synapses received and passed on data, opening and shutting, yes no yes no. Her heart, too. Pump, relax. Pump, relax. The slow drumbeat. The Morse code of reality.

She'd been off and now she was on. She'd been cold and now she was hot. She'd been dead, now she was alive. Black white. Up down. Yes no. Everything held together by that simple truth, the positive and the negative charge binding into one unit. The yin and yang, the glue of the world. North meant nothing without south. East needed west. Everything was that. She'd been bad, and now she was good. She'd been dead, now she was alive.

Out her window she saw Marty crossing the plaza. Love and hate. There was another one. You couldn't know one unless you knew the other. Hills and valleys. Heaven and earth. Good and evil. It was the universal glue. Push, pull. Watching Marty march toward her cabin. Marty Messina, whom Daniel had trusted. Marty, who had taken over all those contacts Daniel had established from years of careful grooming. And in no time Marty had appropriated them, made them his own. And on one of those phone calls that he was always making, he had spoken secretly to Vic Joy. Offered him a deal. Angry at playing second fiddle to Anne. Wanting a bigger slice. He'd told Vic about the *Rainmaker*, times, dates, locations. And that night aboard the ship when they'd been ambushed, Anne had seen Daniel die. Not believing it at the time, creating an illusionary memory instead, that Daniel had rolled out of range and escaped. Holding to that version, over the weeks that followed she'd given it the heft and solidity of fact. But he was dead. She'd seen him die. In the shadows. Her own brother striking down the only man she'd ever loved.

Daniel and Marty were Jesus and Judas. You needed both. No heaven without hell. No grace without sin. Hot cold, life death, good evil, mind heart, truth lies. All of it just an endless balancing of opposites.

Anne Bonny Joy had never let herself think and now she was thinking. She'd never let herself loose and now she was flying. Seeing how it worked. A universal plan. So simple. Plus and minus. Stimulus, response. The gun in her hand, the bullet in the gun. Even a bullet had its opposite. But as Marty came onto the porch, she couldn't think what it was. Bullet and what?

He stepped into the room and looked at her standing by the front window. He hadn't seen the gun, wasn't afraid. He was talking to her. Telling her it was time to perform. Time to show the others what she could do.

Bullet and what? Bullet and what?

Thorn's right hand was loose and he was hard at work peeling open the metal joints. Working on the first band across his face, very first one, he sliced his thumb good and deep. But going on. Stripping it back, popping the joint loose. That band and the one below it and the one around his throat. His head was loose now. Stretching it out of the open face of the helmet, flexing his neck.

While the men and a few women whooped and heckled Janey Sugarman. Reaching out to touch her blond hair, to pinch and poke her snowy flesh, stroke her rumpled party dress. One man tore the binoculars from her grip and pressed them to his eyes and another man ripped them away from him. A scuffle broke out between them. The attention on Janey shifted to the two men who were swatting at each other. The dark clouds massing over the jungle trees sent out a freshening breeze ahead of them.

Working loose a band across his chest, Thorn sliced the other thumb, and blood ran down both wrists, making the work slippery and nearly impossible till he wiped the stickiness onto his belly, then dug his fingernail under the next seam and pried it apart. Two bands across his chest, another across his belly.

Popping open the junction at his navel sent him jolting down, driving all his weight against his feet. He pitched forward, had to struggle a moment to right himself.

The bands around his hips and legs remained, and he had to free the chains that held the contraption to the tree branch. The chains were locked to the thigh bands by stainless-steel fasteners. Sailor's clips. Those Thorn would save for last. Simple enough to open, but hanging in his position, they might be the most difficult trick of all.

Thirty feet away one fighter wrestled the other to the ground and found a headlock and butted the man's skull into a rock, which won an ovation from the crowd. Janey looked up at Thorn and watched him scrabbling at the band around his hips. A stronger joint than any of the others. It took both bloody thumbs to work it loose and then he was hanging precariously by just the chains that went from the branch to an outer clip on the bands around each thigh. As if he were balanced on a swing set, only instead of the flat wooden seat holding him up, the chains of the swing were hooked to the tops of a pair of hip boots. Clumsy and off-kilter.

Thorn scanned the ground below him. Rocks and patches of weeds. Nowhere particularly inviting to land. The fine mist was turning into a shower.

It was impossible to predict what would happen when he worked one of the clips open. Wrenched to one side? Spun upside down?

No time to figure it out. He rocked himself from side to side and got some slack in the right chain and unsnapped the clip and it came away. And he lurched hard to the right, tore free, and was dumped straight down into the rocky soil, where he smacked hard on his right shoulder. Lost his breath but kept his eyes open this time.

The rain was heavier now, but the fighters were still thrashing about, though some of the audience had begun to drift toward the shelters. Janey was headed his way. Behind her one of the Latin men who'd been standing at the back of the crowd was gliding around the edge of the wrestling match, drawing a pistol from the shoulder holster he wore outside his shirt.

Thorn peeled the last few bands off his legs and pushed himself to his hands and knees and tried to stand, but his legs were weak as a newborn's and they buckled and he came back down to a crouch. They'd left him in his fishing shorts, bloody and sagging now with the weight of rain. He was on his knees, working one leg up to make another attempt at standing. Janey was a few yards away, calling his name, hurrying through the downpour.

When the gun blast sounded from a distant cabin, the slender Latino halted and spun around. The fighters continued to scuffle, but the crowd went silent as they watched Marty Messina appear on the porch of the cabin at the end of the row. With delicate steps he came down into the rain, smiling at the assembly, picking his way carefully around the puddles and the piles of trash like a drunk coming home late, determined not to cause a stir.

He ambled down the slope and the crowd parted for him, and Marty continued his stroll, that smile coming into better view as Thorn rose from his crouch. Not a smile at all, but a grim contortion. Gritting his teeth like a man shouldering an impossible burden while he marched mechanically toward the water's edge.

'Marty?' Thorn said as he passed close.

But Messina didn't register the sound and continued to advance toward the lagoon. As he approached,

Thorn missed the entry wound, probably because it was hidden by the thick dark hair, but as Marty moved by, he saw the ragged breach behind his left ear, the blood washing across his neck, diluted to pink by the rain.

Janey came alongside Thorn and gripped his hand. Her hair was drenched and hung in matted tangles. The Latino turned and loped off toward one of the buildings, probably to relay these latest events to his boss.

'I thought you were dead,' Janey said. 'You were hanging from a tree. I told Daddy you were dead.'

Thorn reached down and picked her up and hugged her and cradled her in his arms. Her wet clothes were sour and her eyes had aged in the days since he'd seen her last.

'Your daddy? Sugar's here?'

'He's coming. He's on the way.'

'I hope he's bringing an army.'

Marty hobbled across the narrow beach, leaving deep prints in the sand, and staggered into the water to his ankles, then his knees. Then halted and tottered for several moments, gazing out at the sea beyond, then he fell forward, splashing onto his face, and seconds later his body rose up to float with hands outspread on the rain-spattered surface like a snorkeler peering down at some colorful spectacle.

'Come on, asshole, you're not going anywhere.' The barrel scraped his ribs. 'Go ahead, try something, Kewpie doll, give me reason.'

It was Marshall Marshall with Charlie as backup. In the rain Marshall's crinkly red hair had broken into dozens of lank tendrils. It made his face seem larger and his crone's nose even uglier.

'Can I set the girl down?'

'Go ahead, but do it slow.'

Thorn eased Janey to the ground, took her hand again, then straightened.

'Things are falling apart,' Thorn said. 'Sure you want to stay with this, Marshall? Might be a good time for a strategic retreat to the floatplane.'

'Yeah, right. Run off and do what? Tie flies the rest of my fucking life?'

Charlie chuckled.

Janey tightened her grip on Thorn's hand.

'Up that way, to the big building. Come on, cute guy, you got a special part in the show. It's torture time. The left nut first, then the right one.'

Thorn started up the slope, Janey holding firmly.

'What happened to your buddy Marty?'

'Looks like he bought it,' Charlie said. 'That or he sure is good at holding his breath.'

They moved past the gang of men. The wrestlers were finished now, bloody but smiling as they shared a bottle of gin. The rest of the pack watched them pass, but no one made a move or spoke a word.

'Sorry about the gibbet cage, Marshall. Hated wrecking your artwork.'

'You never turn off the comedy shit, do you, Tinkerbell?'

'I was born to entertain,' Thorn said.

Marshall poked him in the spine all the way to level ground and then up the stairs into the dining hall.

Anne was there, sitting behind a laptop computer. A few feet away to her right were three Chinese men, a tall bearded man in faded fatigues, and Vic Joy.

Anne had a pistol in her right hand, a compact automatic. The handgun was aimed in the general direction of her brother, but it was a twitch away from hitting any of them. And they seemed quite aware of that fact.

Thorn caught a look passing between Marshall and Vic. Should he shoot her in the back? And Vic giving back a firm negative.

'I miss anything?' Thorn said.

'I shot Marty,' Anne said, without looking at him. 'Bullet and brain.'

Her voice sounded drifty and unfamiliar.

'They want the code, Thorn. The binary code. Ones and zeros. It's why they're here. So they can be more efficient in their thievery.'

'Yeah, I got a pretty good idea of the story.'

'Love, hate,' she said. 'Truth, lies.'

'Hey, Annie, listen.' Vic took a half-step toward her and Anne lifted the pistol and he froze. 'I'm in a fix here. I'm counting on you to help me out. You just need to show these gentlemen how it works and we'll all be on our way.'

'A fix.' She smiled, eyes unlocking, playing with a memory, then a few seconds later returning. 'Just like old times. Little sister gets you out of a fix.'

Thorn caught a peripheral glimpse of the slim Latino who'd been stalking him outside. He moved into the room and took a position to their right flank. Thorn didn't turn to see if he had his gun unholstered. Pretty sure it was.

'Why'd you do it, Vic?' Anne waggled the pistol in her hand. 'Why'd you kill Daniel?'

'Hey,' he said. 'We're trying to do some business here, Annie.'

'It was because of me, wasn't it? One way or the other, it was about me. The little sister thing. Protecting me, or else proving you were for real. Tough and mean. That's it, isn't it, Vic? To make up for what you didn't do when you were a kid.'

'I'm sorry, Ramon.' Vic shrugged at the bearded man. 'She's a little spaced out.'

'I'm just a stand-in,' she said. 'I'm Mother and I'm Dad, too. You look at me, Vic, you see ghosts. You need to prove yourself, show them you can do now what you couldn't do then. Right? Do I have it right, Vic?'

'Miss Joy, my name is Ramon Bella.' The man beside Vic bowed in her direction. 'We all can see that you're upset about some personal matter. None of that concerns me, however, nor does it concern my colleagues.' He nodded at the Chinese men. 'We're simply gathered here to see for ourselves that this system we've been told about actually performs in the manner described. When we see that, our business is concluded and we'll be on our way and then you are welcome to sort out whatever problems you might be having with your brother.'

'You're very polite,' Anne said. 'Nice manners. But I'm sorry, I won't be helping you. I won't be getting anyone out of any more fixes. Just this.' She smiled back at Thorn and said again, 'Just this.'

She raised the pistol and pressed it to her temple and fired. Her body slumped off the chair and fell to the floor at her brother's feet.

In the next second, Thorn shot out his right arm and backhanded Marshall in the nose, and while the man's eyes were blurred, Thorn tore the pistol from his hand. But the quiet Latino must have anticipated Thorn's move, because his own pistol thumped immediately into the middle of Thorn's back.

'Raise it into the air. Do it now, my friend.'

Thorn lifted the pistol and the man snatched it and tossed it to his colleague who had joined the festivities.

'All right then,' Ramon Bella said, stepping around Anne's body. 'Am I correct in assuming that there is no one else who can demonstrate the code?'

Vic was staring down at his sister. His mouth was slack and the years had drained away and changed him into a boy, full of wonder and horror and raw panic.

'You know, Vic,' Ramon Bella said, coming close

to him, extending a long slender finger and touching it to the underside of Vic's chin, lifting it, so he could stare into Vic's eyes, 'I am told by people who should know that at any given moment the average man has four pounds of shit working its way through him.'

Vic squinted into Ramon's eyes.

'But in your case,' Bella said, 'I think we could safely assume the number to be at least ten times that.'

'We can fix this,' Vic said. 'Here's the deal. I'm going to give you a bigger cut of the boats I take. That's it. We'll double your profit. That'll help, right? Compensate for your inconvenience, this trouble and misunderstanding. Right? That'll work, won't it? Double?'

Ramon dropped Vic's chin and stepped away. The pistol against Thorn's spine stayed tight. At his side Janey whimpered. She let go of his hand and squatted on the floor and covered her face and shook with silent heaves.

'No, Vic,' Ramon said. 'The only possible way we might fix this situation is for you to demonstrate a process you apparently don't know. So what will you do, invent something for us right now, make white pigeons appear from your scarf? How will we fix this, Vic? Tell us, please.'

'Triple, Ramon. Triple the profit on every boat I take from this point on. A slice of my other action, too, casino boat, restaurants, marinas, across the board. We can work that number out. But a healthy slice. Make this all go away. I can see you're angry. But I'll make it right, just give me a chance.'

Ramon sent another look to the Chinese men, and the largest of them stepped swiftly behind Vic and seized his hands and wrenched his arms in some way that made Vic Joy yelp and hold perfectly still.

Janey looked up with tears streaming, then buried her face in her palms again. Thorn touched the top of her head with his fingertips.

Vic opened his mouth to speak, to protest, to talk his way out of this one. But the Chinese man reached around Vic and raised a blade to his throat.

'Hey!' Marshall yelled, and started forward, but Ramon Bella's other thug barked for him to stay put and leveled his pistol. Marshall halted.

Vic grunted once and dipped to the side and ripped free of the Chinese man's grasp and ducked below the swinging blade. He was across the room, halfway to the door, when the Latino behind Thorn raised his pistol and aimed.

'No!' Ramon Bella yelled. 'Let him go. He's no use to anyone.'

Vic tore through the door and swung to the right and sprinted into the dense foliage behind the dining room.

'Angel,' Bella said. 'Go disable his floatplane; blow it up, burn it, whatever's easiest. Vic Joy won't last a day in this place by himself. In a week the vultures will be cleaning his bones.'

The heavy Latino replied in Spanish and marched from the room.

'All right, that's done.' Ramon Bella looked over at the man guarding Thorn. 'Benito, we're leaving now. I want you to take care of the Americans. Tidy up, *me entiendes*? Be gentle with them. Show them the courtesy you would an honored guest.'

'Certainly,' Benito said. 'It will be my pleasure.'

32

Alex took the Glock from Sugar, jacked the slide, and that's when he knew they were going to be okay. With Sugarman leading, they sloshed along the shoreline holding pistols in each hand, no words passing between them. He hadn't even looked into her eyes to check if there was a blip of worry. Pretty sure there wasn't but didn't want to see it if there was.

By the time the vegetation had begun to thin and some daylight showed up ahead, Sugar was drenched from rain and sweat. Fourth or fifth time he'd soaked through that particular shirt since he'd put it on three days ago. He smelled like a camel, and his breath tasted foul.

He stopped behind a thick tree and peered through a notch in the brush. There were birds in the canopy, squawks and screams and whistles and *pish pish* noises, things whooshing up there, unsettled. On the beach and in the marina, boats were roaring to life and heading out. Inflatables full of men, some random gunfire. Automatics firing in irregular bursts – the sputter and pop of celebration or farewell salutes.

'They're leaving,' Alex whispered. 'Party's break-ing up.'

'We're not too late,' he said. 'We can't be.'

She touched him on the shoulder.

Sugar said, 'She's in the cabin on this end, south side. A pond, she mentioned a pond.'

'Stay together or separate?'

'You stay on this line, keep working north. I'll hook into the brush, come at it from the west.'

She nodded. The woman was an ID tech. Good with a camera. Brushing for fingerprints, vials of Luminol, carrying her science kit full of fine-tooth combs. But she looked very comfortable with the gun in her hand. Maybe *comfortable* was wrong. But experienced. Okay with it.

'How do we tell friend from foe?' she said.

'If you don't know their middle name, they're foes.'

'Maybe we should wait a second, let more of them leave,' Alex said. 'I don't know if we got ammo for this many.'

'I'm after Janey,' Sugarman said. 'If Thorn's here, him, too. Shooting is a last resort.'

'Spoken like a cop.'

475

He said, 'I'll get to the cabin in two, three minutes. You might be quicker, so wait at the edge, find some cover. Better if we're coordinated. Go in together.'

'Take it away.'

Sugar groped through the vines and half-light. The shower had let up a few minutes earlier and now steam rose from the forest floor. He held a course just twenty or thirty feet off the shore, digging through the branches and undergrowth, sweat stinging his eyes.

Then up ahead he heard a voice, someone speaking in English but with a tinge of salsa. Not Cuban; he knew that accent very well. This voice was dignified, almost British. Couldn't make out the words, but the tone was snake-charmer calm.

Maybe it was because he was tuned to her pitch, a father's extrasensory awareness, for among all that raucous jungle music and gunfire he heard a cry, a soft whimper, and knew it was Janey. Knew it down to the root of his spine.

He changed his angle toward her voice, a line closer to the beach, still trying to keep from rustling the leaves, snapping a stick, but moving faster now, in a crouch. Using the barrels of the pistols to tug aside the web of brush. The voice speaking again in English with that soft and careful enunciation of old Spain. Calm, respectful, well-bred. Sugar's skin was prickling and his head was empty. His future didn't matter anymore. Throw himself on a grenade, whatever was required.

Sugar ducked through the matted branches, fumbled forward through the thick weave of twigs and vines, till shit, he was almost on top of them. Four people on their knees, their backs to Sugar. Two steps away. Thorn, Janey, and two other guys with long, scraggly hair. From his position Sugar couldn't tell if the Latino was alone or if there were a dozen others standing close by.

As he craned to the side for a better view, the Latino speaking in that soothing voice said he wanted them to stay exactly like they were, frozen in that position, while one of them counted slowly out loud to a hundred and he and his friends had time to get safely away. The man suggested that Thorn should do the counting. Then the man asked if they fully understood the instructions, nothing short of a hundred. And when they mumbled their agreement, he told Thorn that he could begin with the counting.

Thorn hesitated for a moment, head bowed forward, but Sugarman could see he was straining to see behind him, then he said, 'One,' while the Latino stepped in close behind the red-haired guy in a black T-shirt and camouflage fatigues and aimed into the back of his head and fired. Snake-quick the Latino pointed at the next kneeling man.

But in that fraction of a second the scene blew apart. Thorn swiveled and rolled his body over Janey's and slung a handful of mud and leaves at the Latino's face, then hooked a leg around the shooter's ankle and dragged him down, the man tumbling onto his back but recovering instantly and sighting his pistol into Thorn's chest, and Sugarman stepped forward and fired twice and hit the man with both shots in his stomach, and a half-second later Alexandra hurtled out of the bushes ten feet to the east and fired four or five shots into the head and shoulders of another Latino Sugarman had failed to see, a man who when he fell was taking aim at the center of Sugar's forehead.

Thorn lay atop Janey till the gunfire was done.

And then as he lifted up and looked across at Sugar and Alex, his face torn and bleeding but with a lopsided smile, overhead black helicopters filled the sky.

Sugarman whisked Janey into his arms. Thorn looked up at the choppers, four, five, a couple more arriving from the west. Then he looked at Alex. She was gripping a pistol in each hand, but she lifted her arms and held them open and Thorn walked into the embrace. She turned her head to the side and laid it on Thorn's shoulder and he breathed in the scent of her hair and the heady tartness of her sweat.

She held him tightly and he felt the poke of the pistols in his back, and then that sensation and every other one dissolved as she clenched him harder and he gripped her with equal force.

'You son of a bitch,' she whispered into his ear. 'You worthless bastard.'

'Yeah,' he mumbled back. 'I love you, too.'

The pirates in the boats and the others still on land had opened fire on the helicopters, and the men in the choppers were returning it. An amplified voice rumbled from the sky, giving orders to the fleeing men, but the voice was garbled in all that noise and fury and gunfire.

Alex eased out of the embrace. A step away, Sugarman was cradling Janey, both of them weeping. The other biker was long gone.

'That's Fox,' Alexandra said. 'And America's finest.'

'How the hell did you find this place?'

'Birds,' she said. 'Birds and butterflies and moonrises. You got a great friend, Thorn. A real great friend.'

'More than one, I hope.'

'We'll see about that,' she said. 'We'll have to see.'

Ten feet behind them a spray of machine-gun fire tore into the cabin, slugs ripping open the shingled roof, then more lead kicked up a patch of dirt near one of the fallen Latinos.

'Hey!' Thorn stepped out into the open ground and motioned up to the descending chopper. Dark-clothed men hung from the open bay and sighted on their group. Thorn held up his hands. 'Hey!'

Marshall Marshall's body jumped as the automatic weapon fire riddled his remains and more gunfire danced around them, spurting in the dirt.

'Never a dull moment,' the old man shouted. Lawton stumbled out of the snarl of vines, his puppy

479

trailing him. Behind them Kirk Graham rushed into the clearing.

'He got away from me. I'm sorry, I'm sorry.'

Thorn was waving his arms at the helicopter. The loudspeaker roared some command, a man speaking in English, but his words were again lost in the racket.

'They think we're the bad guys,' Sugarman said. 'Let's go.'

Lawton ducked down and seized a handgun lying next to the Latino and raised it and fired three quick shots at the chopper before Thorn could grab him and spin him around and haul him into the dense foliage.

All about them bullets ripped the leaves and splintered branches. Chunks of the damp ground erupted at their feet. Janey screamed and they fled into deeper cover. Branches snatched and lashed at them, vines tripped them. Sugar leading the way with Janey in his arms. Thorn and Alex gripped Lawton's arms, dragging him along. The puppy barked in a frenzy and trotted beside them and took nips at Thorn's ankles.

The voice in the sky rumbled again, but the blare of engines drowned it out. Thirty, forty yards in, the jungle grew more dense, but in every direction slugs continued to shred the brush.

A few feet ahead of Thorn, Kirk Graham bellowed and went down, and Thorn got to him first. A tear had opened across the meat of his right thigh.

'I'm all right,' he said. 'I'm all right. I'm all right.'

Thorn looped Kirk's arm across his shoulder and hauled him forward through the maze of green. His eyes blinded by the bite of twigs and stung by nettles. The chopper swung away and was gone for a moment, then circled back, hovering close and letting loose another barrage.

'Hold it!' Sugar shouted.

The group halted, then gathered around him.

'They can't see us from here, but they'll be putting people on the ground. They may be on the ground already. We need to wait.'

'And then?' Thorn said.

Kirk groaned and sagged heavily against him.

'Then we pick our moment and make a dash for the plane.'

'These are our guys. We didn't do anything wrong,' Kirk said.

'Yeah, we did,' Sugar said. 'We got in their way.'

At the edge of the jungle, they waited within sight of the inflatable. The chopper came and went; no doubt the men up there had binoculars and were scanning for breaks in the canopy.

'Forget the boat,' Thorn said. 'Too big a target; we'll never make it. We're going to have to swim.'

'Swim?' Lawton said. 'I could use a swim. It's hot as hell in this place.'

The puppy yelped and slumped hard against Thorn's leg and when he looked down he saw that a slug had sheared off a few inches of the dog's tail.

'Goddamn it,' the old man said. 'Lawton's wounded.'

Alex tore the sleeve from her shirt and wrapped the puppy's tail.

While she made the knot tight, Janey came over to the injured dog and sank down beside him and stroked his head, and the pup calmed and washed his tongue over her bare leg.

The chopper had been gone for several minutes when they heard quiet voices in the jungle behind them, the muffled grunts of men following the same path they'd traveled minutes earlier.

'All right,' Sugar said. 'Buddy up and let's do it.'

'These are our own frigging guys,' Kirk said. 'What're we doing?'

Thorn took Kirk. Alex took Lawton.

They followed Sugarman as he sprinted out of the shadows of the thicket with Janey in his arms. He trotted along the edge of a mucky beach, the jungle a few feet to their right, the glittering blue water stretching off on the other side.

A half-mile out at sea several helicopters hovered above three white yachts. Thorn could see the wake boiling up behind the big boats and the bright yellow flashes of ordnance coming from the decks and answered from the sky.

Kirk was gimping along fairly quickly given the ugliness of the wound, his right arm still slung over Thorn's shoulder. Sugarman waded out into the water and let Janey go and they started breast-stroking side by side, Sugar giving her words of encouragement.

The floatplane was a hundred yards away, but it might as well have been ten miles. Out on that open water there was no hiding. But the helicopters appeared to be engaged with the yachts and this was their moment.

They swam. Kirk struggling, thrashing his arms hard. Lawton did a graceful crawl, head held high and steady, like something he'd learned at the YMCA a hundred years ago and not forgotten a bit of. Beside him the dog kept pace. Alex slid along in a sidestroke beside him, looking across at Thorn, sending him eye messages. Despite the embrace, the words of love, there was sadness there, and he knew forgiveness was not going to come easily.

Ahead of him, Sugar paused midstroke and took a backward glance at the beach and frowned. Thorn followed his gaze and there, thirty, forty yards away, standing knee-deep in the water, was Vic Joy. He was naked, with what looked like a large hunting knife clamped in his mouth.

Thorn swung around and headed back to shore, but Alex lurched out and grabbed him by the shoulder and Thorn halted. A foot or two apart the two of them treaded water while the others swam on.

'What're you doing!'

'I've got to get him.'

'Get him?'

'Kill him,' Thorn said. 'The fucker kidnapped Janey. He burned down my house.'

'Your house!'

The others were only forty yards from the plane. Sugarman was calling back to them to hurry up, come on, come on.

'That man's going to keep coming after me, Alex. I got to take care of this now, or I'll be looking over my shoulder the rest of my life.'

'Goddamn it, Thorn. Leave it alone. You're putting us all in danger. We've got to go now. Right now. No time for this. Let the feds have him.'

She gripped Thorn's shoulder and tugged him toward the plane. He resisted for a moment, then put himself in motion and began to swim again close beside her.

The slices on Thorn's hands were stinging and seeping blood, and he was leaving a filmy trail through the crystal sea. A shark attractor, though sharks were hardly high on his list of concerns. He took another quick glance back to the beach, but Vic had disappeared. Thorn swung back into his stroke and caught up with Alex.

They were halfway to the boat and the water around them was so blue and clear that when he opened his eyes as he swam he could see the conch shells and rays scooting along the bright white sand fifteen feet below. A small cluster of orange elkhorn coral twisted up from the sand, bright fish weaving through the spiny branches.

Ahead, the floatplane was tucked into a cove just this side of a jut of land. Half a football field away, an easy jog if they'd been on land, but his arms were already weighted with weariness and the silky water seemed to be making him even more sluggish. Loss of blood, lack of sleep, the deep plummet of his body's chemistry that came after the last surge of adrenaline burned away. He looked ahead at the other swimmers. His friends, his lover. The inner circle of his heart.

Alex drove forward with a strong, even stroke and a hard-bubbling flutter kick and she caught up to her father and Thorn brought up the rear, swimming freestyle, an easy stroke he'd mastered as a child, swimming alone in the shallow waters of the Keys.

Of course Alexandra was right about going back for Vic. It was pure selfishness, a mad impulse that risked the lives of these people he cherished. Another bad instinct formed by a lifetime of isolation. A man living alone could do as he pleased, follow his codes, develop his eccentric routines, his peculiar addictions. He could lash out at those who threatened him without fear of endangering others. But in this new circumstance, he was bound by a different set of rules. To live within a group required a limberness of spirit, an absolute need to compromise and adjust. Subordinating his maverick urges to the needs of the common good. By God, it ran contrary to every inclination Thorn had acquired over the years, but as he knifed through the water, he found himself, for no reason at all, trying to mirror Alex's stroke, swimming in unison for once. Adjusting his natural willfulness to the needs and wisdom of the group.

Sugarman and Janey were only seconds from reaching the floatplane when the black chopper swung around the nearby point of land, roaring twenty feet above the water.

The two men leaning out of the open bay were close enough for him to read their name tags. Janey screamed as a spray of bullets dimpled the sea all around them. Sugarman stopping short, sheltering his daughter with one arm, sculling with the other. The chopper hovered close as if the marksmen were choosing the best angle, and the water kicked into foamy chop while the shooters fixed their sights.

They would've all been dead in seconds, chewed to pulp by those streams of lead, if it weren't for a shipment of military arms that had been stolen months earlier by pirates in the South China Sea, a cargo that James Lee Webster had described to Thorn, serious, heavy-duty weaponry, a payload that must have included at least a few heat-seeking missiles, because that's what flashed off the nearest yacht, one after the other. Shoulder-fired, streaks of wind and scorching light.

A half-mile away, hanging over the open sea, one of the choppers exploded, and the helicopter that was hovering over their own group held still for a moment, then tilted hard to the right and set off to give aid to their fellow warriors.

Sugarman and Janey raced the last short distance to the plane and Thorn saw his friend clutch the base of the ladder mounted on one of the wing floats. He reached down and hauled Janey out of the water and then put out his hand for Kirk Graham.

As Thorn swam on, watching the others board the plane, he felt a flutter against his thighs and belly. Like the *whoosh* of some startled sea creature flushed from its hole by splashing swimmers. He ducked his head and peered into the transparent blue.

Just beneath him, a little more than a body's length away, he saw the billowing trail of gray hair passing below him, like a silver cape undulating through heavy current.

And then the naked white body of Vic Joy frog-kicking through the water. At that moment Vic turned his head, looking above him, and his eyes met Thorn's, holding still for a half-second in that silent column of water between them. A cloud of bright bubbles exploded from Vic's lips, and then with a hard scissor-kick he shot toward Thorn, the blade in his right hand.

Thorn sucked down a breath and plunged his head into the water, thrashing his feet and digging his arms.

Driven upward by the buoyancy and his savage kick, Vic rocketed past him to the surface. He took a deep gulp of air and swiveled and smashed the knife into the water, a bright arc flashing by the spot where Thorn's face had been only a second before. Thorn snatched at Vic's wrist but got only a handful of foam.

For a moment Vic floated on his belly, pressing his face below the surface, tracking Thorn's movements. Thorn backstroked out of range and surfaced ten feet away. The others were climbing aboard the plane. Only Alex had stayed behind and was treading water five yards away.

'Go on, Alex! Go to the plane. I'll be there. Go!'

With a wild swing Vic lunged toward Thorn, but his knife hand splashed a yard away. He sputtered and choked and surged up from the water and slashed at Thorn again, plunging the blade into the water closer this time, but still a foot or two out of range.

Thorn could keep this up indefinitely, floundering backward, wearing Vic out. He chanced a quick look past Vic at the battle in the distance. Hard to tell who was winning, but three helicopters were still scattered above the yachts and he could hear the faint retorts of gunfire.

'You worthless prick.' Vic inched closer through the calm sea. Knife out of sight. 'I'm taking your balls and putting them in a jar.'

'Come on, Vic. Enough talk.'

'You're destroyed, Thorn. You and your fucking friends. This is the end.'

Vic treaded water, closing the gap between them.

'Some pirate you are, Vic. Cowering in your room the night your parents bought it. I bet you're still in there, aren't you? Dark, claustrophobic. How about it, buccaneer? You still in there, sucking on your thumb?'

Vic lunged, and Thorn wallowed backward beyond

his reach, but this time Vic didn't swipe his knife. The thrust was a ruse, for in the next second he splashed to his left toward Alexandra and was suddenly stretched out and swimming hard and fast, catching her unawares.

She pivoted and fell forward into an efficient stroke, getting her feet moving, headed toward the plane, but not fast enough. By then Vic was almost on her, slicing through the water at an awesome clip. Thorn took the shortest angle and in four strokes Vic's feet were slapping inches from his face.

But Alexandra must have sensed Vic closing in, because she halted and turned on him. Thorn lifted his head from the water in time to see Vic slash the blade at her throat. Her hand shot up to block it.

In their quiet months together, Thorn had forgotten her skills in martial arts, years of karate training. Forgotten her hair-trigger reflexes, how calm she was, how focused. She met Vic's strike with a vicious chop to his wrist and the knife popped loose and splashed a few feet to his right. Alex aimed a backhanded punch at his chin but clipped him only lightly as Vic flopped backward away from her, then disappeared below the surface.

Thorn heaved forward and swiped at the man's right ankle but was a second late. Vic was thrashing toward the knife that lay in the sand a few feet from the patch of elkhorn coral.

'Don't, Thorn!' Alexandra shouted. 'There's no time. Now, come on.'

'It has to be done, Alex. No choice.'

Thorn drew a breath and tucked into the water.

Fifteen feet below, Vic fumbled with the knife and lost it in the sand, kicking his feet wildly against the buoyancy.

Thorn came from overhead, grabbed a handful of Vic's hair, and wrenched him to the side. Seizing one of the razory stalks of elkhorn coral near its thick base, Thorn levered Vic a half-foot out of the range of the knife. But he twisted and lurched, scrabbling in the sand, then he flailed his arm backward, the glint of the blade flashing inches from Thorn's face.

Thorn's hand was shredding against the spiny coral, blood clouding the water. But he held on and rattled Vic's head from side to side. A stream of bubbles broke from Vic's mouth, and he twisted hard against Thorn's hold and swiped the blade at his arm, missed, but gouged his chest instead, leaving a burning track through the bands of muscle and flesh. A single plume of blood floated upward in a filmy spiral. The impact of the blade against Thorn's chest knocked the knife loose. Tumbling from Vic's hand, it disappeared into a swirl of sand.

Thorn's left arm was deadened, but he kept his fingers knotted to Vic's hair and the other hand clutching to the trunk of coral. A sudden drowsy warmth seem to permeate the water as the airless compression of the sea tightened around Thorn's chest. He'd been holding his breath for half a minute and now every tick dimmed the light in his head and pumped his chest full of burning pressure.

Vic Joy thrashed against Thorn's grip. But couldn't break free. Thorn's hand was locked deep into the heavy snarls of hair. The equation forming in his head crowded out all doubt, all rational thought; even the growing throb in his chest eased. He was calmer than he'd been in years. Clear-sighted. Certain.

This wasn't about justice or right and wrong. The sharp tang of revenge played no part in it, either. It was simpler than any of that. This man was a danger to every person Thorn loved, and if it took Thorn's own death to cancel out Vic Joy, then it was a fair exchange. Some small karmic payback for the suffering Thorn had caused over the years in his own selfish pursuits.

He held on beyond endurance. All about him a crimson mist was suspended in the still sea. His vision darkened and black spots danced inside his eyes. The oxygen in his lungs was failing, but he couldn't let go. In a groggy moment he considered inhaling seawater and staying behind with Vic, the two of them knotted forever on the sandy floor. A fitting conclusion to Thorn's wayward, fucked-up journey.

At that moment he tilted his head and looked upward at the spangled surface of the sea. Thousands of light-years away, Alexandra Collins was floating facedown, watching him, waving her arm in ghostly slow motion, urging to him to come on, come on.

Vic's struggling slowed and finally ceased. Thorn yanked Vic's head backward and watched his face as a string of small bubbles escaped Vic's lips like words too small to capture meaning. His body went slack and his kicking died away.

Up on the surface Alexandra watched Thorn hold on for a few seconds more, then release the corpse. He let the water lift him, and with his last flicker of resolve he held his breath those dozen feet until he broke through to the air.

When Thorn opened his eyes, Kirk Graham was behind the controls. The plane was taxiing across the blue shallows, then lifting up. Overloaded and clumsy until it was free of the drag of earth and began to soar. A mile or so to the east, the sea battle continued, one yacht on fire, another listing hard to its starboard, going down. The choppers winning. Air supremacy.

Lawton rode in the copilot seat. In the first row Sugarman and Janey were huddled together. Alex sat beside Thorn and pressed a wad of cloth hard to the rip in his chest. In the seconds before he fainted again, he watched the puppy trot down the aisle, oblivious to his injury, wagging his tail, spraying them all with flecks of his innocent blood.

33

'Thorn has been sleeping in that little tent?'

'Sometimes in his boat,' Sugarman said. 'Sometimes in the tent.'

The pup tent Thorn had been using was so small, he couldn't roll over without knocking it down.

'Why'd they burn his house down?' Janey asked.

'I don't know why,' Sugarman said. 'Whys are hard.'

They worked for half an hour driving the pegs into the hard ground. The four-man safari tent had cost Sugarman six hundred dollars at Sears. Money he didn't have, but what the hell? Mosquito netting across the door. Room inside for a cot, a camp table, a cooler. Sugar had bought a Coleman lantern, too, so Thorn could read after the sun set. See his way around at night if he couldn't sleep.

'Those Zeiss binoculars were nice,' Janey said. 'But I like the one you gave me better.'

Jackie was out on the dock, hurling rocks at the water. Chanting along with the rap music in her earphones.

'Sorry they're not nitrogen-purged.' Sugar hammered another peg into the stony soil.

'Oh, they fog up a little, but that's okay,' said Janey. 'I like them. I saw a palm warbler a little while ago.'

'Wagging its tail in the dirt,' Sugar said.

'Yeah,' Janey said. She whacked a stake with the rubber mallet. Five whacks and it was in deep. A strong little girl. Damn strong. Amazingly strong. Stronger than he deserved.

'Where'd Thorn go?'

'He took a trip up north,' Sugar said.

'The North Pole?'

'Not that far, no.'

'He'll be surprised by the tent, huh?'

'Yeah,' Sugarman said. 'He'll be surprised. He'll love it.'

'Thorn's pretty cool.' She whacked another peg into the earth.

'Yeah, he is,' Sugar said. 'He's a pretty cool guy.'

'He sure gets in a lot of trouble, though.'

'Yeah,' said Sugar. 'But we should try not to hold that against him.'

'I like him. I think he's funny. Someday I want to marry him.' She sank another peg into the ground.

Sugarman watched her work. His little girl. His flesh and blood. My God, she was strong.

'No, it's okay, we don't mind, please come in.'

Lawton had a folding spade in his hand. A green trenching tool from his army days. Alexandra and Thorn stood on the porch of the white clapboard house at 215 Oak Street in Columbus, Ohio.

The couple who owned the house were named Prevost. Retired high school teachers, they said. Mrs Prevost explained that she had a mother who, like Lawton, needed a little looking after. They understood, understood completely.

'The dog okay?' Thorn said. 'We can leave it in the rental car.'

'The dog's fine,' Mr Prevost said. 'We love dogs.'

'Well, come in, come in,' Mrs Prevost added.

The Prevosts stood aside and without a word Lawton marched through the house and out the back door. The dog trotting behind.

'Some coffee?' Mrs Prevost said. 'While we watch the excavation.'

'Sure,' Alexandra said. 'Thank you.'

They sat in a sunny breakfast room with a bay window that looked out at the small backyard. Lawton was standing beneath a maple tree that was full of fresh leaves. He turned around and pressed his back to the trunk and took three paces toward the back of the lot.

'We'll clean up any mess he makes,' Alex said. 'He'll lose interest in a few minutes anyway, I'm sure.'

'What happened to you?' Mrs Prevost motioned at the sling on Thorn's left arm. Immobilized for weeks while the throbbing sinews rejoined.

'Swimming accident,' Thorn said.

'Sharks?' Mr Prevost said.

'A lower life-form than that,' Thorn said.

Mrs Prevost was smiling out the bay window. She had gray hair that she wore loose and long. She looked a little like Thorn's high school math teacher. Clearly a nice woman married to a nice man.

'We knew the Morgans,' Mr Prevost said. 'We bought the house from them. But we didn't know the owners before them.'

'My father's parents built this house,' Alexandra said.

'It's a nice house,' said Thorn.

'Well, we've been very happy here,' Mrs Prevost said. 'Twenty years of marital bliss.' She smiled at her husband. She'd probably been a wonderful teacher.

Lawton was digging now and the puppy caught on quickly and worked at the edge of the same hole, spitting dirt out between his hind legs. His tail was three or four inches shorter than it had been, but it didn't seem to bother the dog. Just allowed him to wag it faster.

'When I was a kid I buried a time capsule myself,' Mr Prevost said. 'But it was so long ago, I can't remember where. I remember the house, but I'd never be able to find the spot again.'

'I don't think Dad remembers, either. But he's been talking about it so much. We thought it was worth the trip.'

'You're from Florida?'

'The Keys,' Thorn said. Then looked at Alex. 'And Miami.'

'Since we retired, we go to Disney World once a year,' Mrs Prevost said. 'I'm a sucker for all that stuff.'

Lawton was coming toward the house. He was holding a glass jar.

'I don't believe it,' Thorn said.

Lawton came into the kitchen and sat down at the table.

'Too tough for me,' Lawton said, and handed the jar to Thorn.

With his good hand, Thorn unscrewed the lid and handed it back.

Lawton dumped the contents on the kitchen table. A skeleton key. A few coins. A red-and-green lanyard. And a photograph that had gone almost white. A picture of two boys, each holding long cane fishing poles. Both of them had blond hair cut in bangs, and the older boy was holding up what probably was a fish, although that part of the photograph had turned white.

'That's Charlie and me,' Lawton said. 'Our first catch. Charlie's dead. Died of cancer. Isn't that right, Alex? Cancer?'

'That's right.'

'He died when he was young. But I just keep living on and on.'

'We're glad of that,' Alex said.

'Charlie and I did everything together,' said Lawton. 'Hell, we'd scrap like a couple of pit bulls sometimes, but look at us there. You'd never know we were anything but best buddies.'

'You were cute,' Mrs Prevost said. 'Both of you.'

'What kind of fish was that?' Mr Prevost asked.

'A marlin,' Lawton said. 'Caught it in a pond that used to be right back there behind our yard.'

'A marlin, Dad?'

'Well, okay. It wasn't a marlin. Some other fish, crappie probably. But it's gone now. We ate it, me and Charlie. Fried it up for supper. First fish I ever caught.'

'We'll try to make sure it's not the last,' Thorn said.

Alexandra stood up from the table and thanked the two retired teachers.

'You've been very kind,' she said. 'We'll go fill in the hole.'

'No, no,' Mr Prevost said. He was beaming. 'I know what we should do, Millie, we should bury one of those things ourselves. Something for our old age.'

'Yes,' she said, smiling at her husband. 'What a lovely idea.'